RESCUING CARMEN

Guardian Hostage Rescue Specialists

BRAVO Team
Book 3

ELLIE MASTERS

JEM Publishing

Dedication

This book is dedicated to my one and only—my amazing and wonderful husband.

Without your care and support, my writing would not have made it this far.

You pushed me when I needed to be pushed.

You supported me when I felt discouraged.

You believed in me when I didn't believe in myself.

If it weren't for you, this book never would have come to life.

Also by Ellie Masters

The LIGHTER SIDE

Ellie Masters is the lighter side of the Jet & Ellie Masters writing duo! You will find Contemporary Romance, Military Romance, Romantic Suspense, Billionaire Romance, and Rock Star Romance in Ellie's Works.

YOU CAN FIND ELLIE'S BOOKS HERE:

ELLIEMASTERS.COM/BOOKS

Military Romance

Guardian Hostage Rescue Specialists

Rescuing Melissa

(Get a FREE copy of Rescuing Melissa

when you join Ellie's Newsletter)

Alpha Team

Rescuing Zoe

Rescuing Moira

Rescuing Eve

Rescuing Lily

Rescuing Jinx

Rescuing Maria

Bravo Team

Rescuing Angie

Rescuing Isabelle

Rescuing Carmen

Rescuing Rosalie

Hearts The Last Beat (book 7)

Contemporary Romance

Firestorm

(KRISTY BROMBERG'S EVERYDAY HEROES WORLD)

Billionaire Romance

Billionaire Boys Club

Hawke

Richard

Brody

Contemporary Romance

Cocky Captain

(VI KEELAND & PENELOPE WARD'S COCKY HERO WORLD)

Romantic Suspense

EACH BOOK IS A STANDALONE NOVEL.

The Starling

~AND~

Science Fiction

Ellie Masters writing as L.A. Warren

Vendel Rising: a Science Fiction Serialized Novel

To My Readers

This book is a work of fiction. It does not exist in the real world and should not be construed as reality. As in most romantic fiction, I've taken liberties. I've compressed the romance into a sliver of time. I've allowed these characters to develop strong bonds of trust over a matter of days.

This does not happen in real life where you, my amazing readers, live. Take more time in your romance and learn who you're giving a piece of your heart to. I urge you to move with caution. Always protect yourself.

ONE

Carmen

____

My roommates, and best friends, Kaye and Barbi, dance around me in their cap and gowns, excited to finally graduate from UCSF. They're ready to cut loose and have a night out on the town, excited for their futures.

I wish I was as excited as them, but my future isn't mine to control.

"We did it!" Kaye lifts her arms overhead, overjoyed and triumphant.

"Yes, we did!" Barbi hugs Kaye, then grabs hold of my arm, bringing me in for a group hug.

It's a beautiful afternoon in San Francisco. The sun beat back the morning fog from the Bay, leaving clear, blue sky overhead. That sun shines, warming our faces and chasing away the lingering chill in the air. The aroma from scores of champagne bottles popping open at the same time swirls around us in a festive fizz, infusing the air with its sweet scent. It's the perfect day to celebrate the end of a long four years at UCSF.

A group of co-graduates stands off to the side, shaking more bottles of champagne before opening them. The fizzy foam shoots into the air as they guzzle down what's left in the bottle. They laugh.

They smile. They egg each other on. Graduation gowns twirl and lift as they jump in the air and spin around. It's hard not to let a smile creep across my face. I should be happy, like them.

Kaye grabs my hands, trying to get me to join in the dancing, but my attention snags on the motorcade parked next to the curb. The jubilant bounce in my step dies and that joyous feeling falters.

"What's wrong?" Barbi props her hands on her hips. "You look like someone killed your puppy. Come on… We gotta celebrate." She grabs me and spins me around. "Dance with me."

Knowing Father's security personnel watch from inside those vehicles, I let Barbi spin me around once, then pull away and act the way a woman of my station, and breeding, is supposed to act.

Undeterred, Barbi cups her hands over her mouth and shouts into the air. "Watch out San Francisco! We're going to own the town tonight. *Whoop! Whoop! Whoop!*" She punches the air and bounces up and down.

Beneath our graduation gowns, we're dressed for a night on the town. The plan is dinner, then dancing. The form-fitting red silk of my skimpy dress pairs phenomenally with expensive four-inch heels. They make my tanned legs look fantastic.

Kaye joins in with Barbi, shouting at the top of her lungs. Our fellow graduates hoot and holler with my friends as they spill out onto the street and head to their celebrations.

Their exhilaration is palpable. Overwhelming. They're excited.

Everyone, but me.

It never crossed my mind Father would send his men to collect me on the day of graduation. I figured I had at least the night to say goodbye to my friends.

I wish I could join Kaye and Barbi. We had the best night planned, but the Bentley, with its motorcade, makes that impossible.

With lead and tail SUVs full of security personnel, any joy that comes from graduating UCSF summa cum laude disappears between one beat of my heart and the next.

"Ladies, I have to bow out." The words tumble from my lips before I hide my disappointment.

"Bow out of graduation night?" Kaye, with her pert lips and

perfect pout, looks at me through fake lashes and far too much makeup. She layers it on, both in makeup and personality. "But we've been planning this night for months. You can't bow out." Her lower lip pushes out in a pout.

"I've been summoned home." I gesture toward the motorcade.

"No way." Kaye turns with Barbi toward the street. Her jaw drops. "You really are a big wig."

They know my father's the Minister of the Interior for Nicaragua, but it's clear they have no idea what that means or dismiss its importance because Nicaragua is a small country compared to the United States of America.

Kaye hits the nail on the head, however, but misses one small detail. I'm not the big wig. That distinctive honor belongs to my father, Maximus Angelo. The only man more powerful than my father is the president of Nicaragua, although some might argue my father holds more power than the president.

"Why is there a motorcade and a Bentley waiting for you?" Barbi's eyes practically pop out of her head. Like Kaye, her lower lip pushes out. They're disappointed by the change in plans. This was supposed to be *our* night, a time to celebrate.

"That's Father flexing his paternal muscles." It's his way of telling me play time's over. He's indulged me long enough, and it's time to come home. In typical, overbearing fashion, Father delivers the message with no room to misinterpret his intent.

"Down with the patriarchy!" Kaye and Barbi shout the feminist slogan at the cars, getting those milling about to join in.

The crowd around us echoes the words, not understanding the context, while I lift my shoulders to my ears and try to disappear.

I get their enthusiasm, but they don't understand how very different our two worlds are or how precious their freedom is. Not to mention, there's no way I want to be associated with anything remotely connected to taking down the patriarchy.

My father is the embodiment of everything the patriarchy encompasses, and my survival depends on supporting him. Support, in this context, means ensuring I marry into a family with the wealth and political power to further his aspirations for power.

In America, young women have the freedom to determine their path in life. In Nicaragua, that's not how the world works. Daughters submit to the will of their fathers. Wives submit to the demands of their husbands. Widows submit to the decisions their sons make as head of the household. There is no freedom for a woman to pick and choose. Women who try find themselves quickly silenced.

This is something I know far too well. It's the story of my life, but times are changing.

I hope.

"Ladies, I wish I could stay, but I can't ignore this summons."

"Don't spoil tonight." Kaye takes my hands in hers. "We've been planning this for ages."

Barbi's brows bunch as she scans the motorcade. "He couldn't give you one night?" More than Kaye, Barbi reads the situation. She understands the message.

"Doesn't look like it." My shrug is as defeated as I feel. Ruining our graduation celebration, especially after spending so much time planning it, turns my stomach. "I'm so sorry."

"Don't let him steal your dreams or extinguish your light. You're meant for more than marriage and babies." Barbi folds me in a hug.

Yeah, Barbi gets it.

Kaye? Not so much.

"Just don't go." Kaye hugs me next. "We'll make a run for it."

"In four-inch heels?" I laugh as we hug for what is likely the last time. My time in the United States is measured in hours.

My role may be that of a docile and obedient daughter, but these past four years, I armed myself with knowledge. Knowledge and something far more powerful.

If I can pull it off.

If I don't get caught.

A man I know well climbs out of the Bentley and stands beside it. Juan Sanchez's brooding gaze scans the crowd of festive graduates. The moment he sees me, those dark eyes latch on and hold tight.

There's no escape.

For a moment, I watch those around me. Former classmates,

many of whom I don't know, eagerly race out of graduation to celebrate their grand accomplishment with friends and family. They laugh. They hug. They call out to one another, confirming plans for tonight.

I'm happy for them and wish I could be like them.

"Ladies…" I grab each of their hands and pull us in for a group hug. "Promise you'll tell me everything you get up to tonight."

"I promise." Kaye wipes away a tear.

"Promise you'll call?" Barbi squeezes my hand. "I don't want to lose touch."

"I promise." This might be the first lie I tell my best friends, but the truth is too difficult to bear. This part of my life is over. "We won't."

"I'll keep you to that promise." Barbi pulls me in for a hug ten times tighter than the one before.

Envy shoots through me, followed by frustration and defeat, but I tamp down the useless emotions and grit my teeth. Fixing a smile on my face, I angle toward the motorcade, gliding across the sidewalk like a princess going to a ball.

As if it's my choice.

No one ignores the summons of Nicaragua's Minister of the Interior, not even his only child.

Juan steps away from the car with a flourish and a smile as false as the one I plaster on my face. "Congratulations, Señorita Carmen." He speaks in the melodious Spanish of home. "Your father asked me to express how exceptionally proud he is of your accomplishment."

"Is he?" Chin level. Shoulders back. There's a quiver in my jaw I refuse to acknowledge. "I take it he couldn't spare a day for his daughter?"

A rhetorical question. I expect nothing but the canned response received over a lifetime of similar disappointments.

"Affairs of State keep him."

"Of course. They always do." That last bit comes beneath a mumbled growl of frustration and disappointment.

There's no use expressing my feelings. All that does is chip away at whatever's left of my heart. Best to bury that stuff deep where it will never see the light of day. After twenty-one years, there's little remaining of that useless organ. What's left is bitter and cold; nothing but a shriveled husk left behind.

I swallow whatever joy graduation brought me, however fleeting it was. Gathering strength, it's time to erect the protective walls I created over a lifetime to shield myself from the bitter sting of disappointment and the resentment that follows.

I bite back words that never do any good. Nobody cares, least of all the sperm donor who gave me life.

"He is eager to see you, *Señorita*." At least Juan tries. He believes the lies spilling from his lips.

"No doubt he is." That false smile tips down.

There was never a chance my father would fly all the way to California to see his daughter graduate.

That was my dream.

Not his.

My dreams are worthless indulgences.

My worth, whatever that is, comes only from the political alliances Father can secure using me to his advantage.

Juan shifts foot to foot and scrubs his hands, betraying unease. It's telling and frightening.

Chipped out of cold-hard stone, Juan isn't known for expressing emotion. Except for the extreme loyalty he extends to my father. The man's a zealot. His adoration of, and devotion to, my father burns as bright as the sun.

"*Señorita* Carmen, our flight leaves in three hours. Traffic's heavy and we need to get to the terminal to check in."

"The terminal?" That sparks outrage. Bile churns in my gut, pouring fuel on the simmering rage within me. "I take it Affairs of State prohibited him from sending the plane?"

"Yes, *Señorita*. Now, if you don't mind…" Juan opens the door and gestures inside.

Flying commercial is my father's way of punishing me for the past four years.

"I'm sorry, but that won't do. I haven't packed…"

I need to get back to the townhome I share with Kaye and Barbi. There's no way I'm leaving my things behind, especially my last doll. Given to me by my governess, Lucinda, on the day of my *Quinceañera*, that doll means the world to me.

"Your father's instructions are to leave it all behind." Juan's words catch me by surprise.

"Behind?" Eyes widening, I take a step back as a shiver ripples down my spine. "I can't."

"He says you need none of it."

"But my…"

"His instructions are clear."

"I don't care what his instructions are, or aren't. I need my things." The sharpness of my tongue generally makes the strongest men cringe, but Juan doesn't fear my anger, my sharp tongue, or anything about me. He fears something far worse and returns an expressionless mask.

To think, moments ago, the dreams that were spinning in my head as I took part in UCSF's commencement ceremony have been wiped off the face of the earth by the imperious command of my father.

"You don't understand—I need to pack my things."

It's a short drive from the commencement ceremony to the townhome I share with my best friends. That townhome has been my refuge, but my father's orders come with a stark reminder to remember my place.

"There's no time." Juan stands firm.

I hate you, Papa.

There will be no negotiation, not when Juan parrots words fed to him by my father. I dislike Juan, but I absolutely detest my father.

Juan pivots a quarter turn and opens the back passenger door. With movements as rigid and precise as a robot, he holds the door, knowing full well I'll obey. The serene smile on his face isn't for me. It's adoration for fulfilling my father's orders.

This is how my father expresses himself. He sends mindless henchmen to do his bidding.

Playtime is over.

I've been recalled. Not with a phone call, voice, or video call. Not even with the perfunctory precision of text messaging or the simplicity of email.

Not me.

The summons I receive comes at the end of an indulgence, which has run its course, and a graduation he never planned to attend.

Despite all the above, if anything, I'm a dutiful daughter. So I fix a smile on my face and slide into the back seat. Juan shuts me in, sealing me safely inside the vehicle. With my palm gliding over the buttery smooth leather seat, my gut twists as my heart breaks.

There are no tears.

I learned long ago not to waste time leaking useless emotion. Tears are for the weak, and I'm stronger than steel. What doesn't break is my faith in myself.

Four years.

Summa cum laude.

Two degrees.

One in political science.

The other in environmental conservation.

I armed myself with powerful weapons to use against my father.

On the way to the airport, I pull off my cap and gown. Smoothing the wrinkles in my dress, I stare out the window while my fingers twist and that fire in my belly burns.

Instead of spending the night partying with Kaye and Barbi, I process through expedited airport security in a body-hugging, red silk dress and four-inch heels.

Juan and four security men join me in first class luxury for the seven-hour flight from San Francisco to Managua, Nicaragua, while I drown my sorrows in glass after glass of complimentary champagne.

TWO

Rafe

"Rafe?" Piper's perpetually positive and perky voice calls out to the small waiting room. No need to announce my presence. I'm the only bloody person in the waiting room. "How's the leg?" She greets me with her chipper smile and eyes that sparkle with enthusiasm.

Her question is exactly the same since rehabilitation began.

I hate it.

"Gone and missing." My snide response is the same as it's been for a year.

"And the phantom pain?"

Hard to believe so much time's passed. When an explosion in a Cancun shipyard ripped off my lower leg, I thought my job with the Guardian Hostage Rescue Specialists was over.

"Still there." The phantom pains in my lost leg suck, but I'd much rather have those than the alternative. I'll take breathing any day over being dead.

The only reason I survived that explosion is because Brady yanked me out of the way. Bravo One took the brunt of the blast, which left him with burns over half of his body and half of his face. Those scars are his for life.

Hayes and Alec each lost two fingers a piece. Zeb was peppered with shrapnel that almost cost him the use of his lower legs. One of those shards nestled right alongside his spinal cord, and it was touch and go for a bit.

In many ways, I lucked out.

I just lost half my leg.

Just? As if that makes the loss more palatable.

"I see you're chipper today." Piper's smile is as obnoxious as her perky attitude. "Any problems with the socket?"

A mold of what remains of my amputated limb, the *socket* is what fits over the stump that's left of my lower leg. Many would say I'm lucky. As a below-the-knee amputee, there are plenty of options as far as prosthetics go.

"No."

"That's great news." Her smile beams bright. "You know what today is?"

Yes. How could I forget?

"No." I'm not interested in celebrating this particular milestone.

"We've officially passed the one-year mark." Her chipper attitude grates on my nerves.

"So?" My shoulders lift and drop with as much *un*-enthusiasm as I can muster.

"It's an important date for amputees." She props her tiny fists on her hips and gives me a stern look.

"Whatever."

"Don't '*whatever*' me. It's a big day, and you're not going to be a sour puss and ruin it. You're doing so well."

For amputees, the first year sees a lot of *stabilization* of what's left of the amputated limb. After the initial healing phase, Piper, and her team, used temporary prostheses as my body healed, reformed, and remolded itself. She doesn't handle the prosthetic per se, but physical therapy is an integral part of adjusting to my new leg. With Guardian HRS, I've got access to the best of the best, which means I get her.

"I'm good." Short and to the point, I keep my answers brief. There's nothing *well* about me.

"Now that you've had a chance to adjust to the latest iteration, how are you finding the fit and function?" Piper plows through my surly disposition, not letting the sourness of my mood stick to her.

The *latest iteration* she refers to are the microprocessors built into the joint of the prosthetic. Those tiny sensors constantly adjust to my changing gait, allowing me to walk naturally, run without difficulty, and travel uneven terrain like a pro. With long pants, it's almost impossible for anyone to tell I'm an amputee. Those microprocessors also adjust to various surfaces, providing enhanced stability when climbing stairs, walking on pavement, rugs, and even sand. That little bit blew my mind.

At least I've got that going for me.

"Good." I blow out a breath, feeling defeated. The microprocessors are fantastic, futuristic, and fabulous. What they aren't is my old leg.

"Just good?" She cocks her head to the side. "You know that won't do. These one-word answers of yours are only going to keep you here longer."

"We wouldn't want that." My snide remark is met with a soft smile.

"You love my perky nature. Admit it." Piper's perpetual positivity never fails to draw me into conversations I'm not interested in pursuing.

"I'll never admit it." There's a grin on my face that says otherwise.

Piper's a really cool chick and she takes none of my crap. The days I wanted to quit, she forced me to give her just a little bit more —then a little more.

She kept pushing; her and her perky positivity forced me to get through what I think of as the dark days when I wanted to quit. Not only did Piper convince me recovery was possible, she proved it despite my moaning and groaning and general defeatist attitude. She proved me wrong when I took the first step of my new life without any assistance from her.

Piper literally taught me how to walk again. She helped me

build up the strength in my arms, my last leg, and my cardiovascular system. She taught me how to run again.

As a former Navy SEAL, and now a Guardian, I thought I was in peak physical condition before I lost my leg.

I couldn't have been more wrong.

With one leg, my body works harder now to compensate. I push harder than ever before, determined to never give up. I'll never admit it to Piper, but the prosthetic is *almost* better than my other leg.

Almost.

I take no credit for the success of my rehabilitation. Piper did that. Because of her, I walked on my own for the very first time after the explosion that severed my leg below the knee.

I have a love/hate relationship with my physical therapist.

I believed my life was over. She pushed and proved me wrong. I owe Piper more than I can ever repay.

My job as a Guardian is only the tiniest bit of what I owe my persistently perky, and forever positive, physical therapist. I owe her for removing the word *can't* from my vocabulary. She got me through the worst of this past year, and I paid her back with a piss-poor attitude and grumpy disposition.

"Now, is it really *just good*?" Her brow arches and she writes something down on the tablet cradled in her arm.

"Barely know it's not my leg." Muttered under my breath, it's not my intent for her to hear, but Piper's got fantastic hearing. Not to mention, her entire job focuses on watching, assessing, and adapting to her patients' needs.

"I see you brought your piss-poor attitude today." She gives me a once over, dragging her gaze up and down my body—judging, assessing, measuring, and documenting all of it on that damn tablet.

"What can I say? It's a good day. Not great. Not shitty. What more do you want?"

"I want nothing other than for you to reach maximum physical proficiency." Her reply comes quick, a rapid-fire barrage. "I'll accept nothing less than your best."

Piper takes everything I've got, then squeezes out more. She demands nothing less than total commitment from her patients to get better. In return, she gives nothing but her absolute best.

I hang my head and run my fingers through my hair. It's getting long. Longer than I kept it during my Navy days. As a SEAL, I didn't have to conform to the regulation haircut, but I did because I'm a rule follower. As a Guardian, I love letting my hair hang past my eyes and curl over my ears. The chicks seem to dig it.

Or did.

The whole amputee thing puts a major damper on my sex life—or lack thereof.

Chicks dig the hair but pull *waaaaay* back when they see the leg—or don't see the leg. If we get to the getting naked part of having sex, the stump sends them running.

"Any pain or discomfort?" Piper cradles that tablet in her arm.

"Not really."

"Is that a yes, or a no? Meet me halfway, Rafe. I don't have time for grown-assed men acting like children."

"Fine. I did ten miles on it this morning with the guys. Fit feels good. Stump feels great. The sensors smoothed things out. It feels bloody fabulous."

"Now, was that so hard?" She glances down at the tablet and scribbles some notes. Piper never fails to get me to open up. "Come on back. Let's take a look at your leg." Piper waves me through the doorway. "We're going to see how good it is. Today's a fit check and stump eval."

"Ugh!"

"Don't 'ugh' me. You know the routine. Today is fit and finish day."

Don't I know it.

"Ladies first." I gesture for her to go ahead of me.

No need to show me the way. I've been coming to physical therapy three times a week for over a year, ever since the blasted explosion turned the lower half of my leg into hamburger meat.

"No. I insist." She winks. "I want to assess your gait from behind."

"You just want to check out my ass." The teasing comes naturally.

Three times a week, sometimes more, we've spent a lot of time getting to know each other over the past year. I got the better part of that deal in that transaction as Piper is fun to be around. Unfortunately, she got my mopey, can't-do attitude and the wild mood swings that plague my recovery.

"Bent will have me draped over his knee if he catches me checking out your ass."

Bent is Piper's husband. He's also the bass guitarist for the mega rock band Angel Fire. She lives with her husband, and the rest of the band, at Angel Fire's retreat, *Insanity*, perched over the rocky cliffs of California's coastline not too far from Guardian HRS headquarters. If she wasn't taken, I may have made a play for her, but she is, and I didn't. I'm not the kind of guy to poach another man's wife, but I will flirt a little. As much as I hate to admit it, her banter and perky positivity brought me through the darkest parts of my recovery.

"How are you going to assess my gait without checking out my ass?"

"Because, this is work, and part of the job requires me to stare at that mighty fine ass of yours, but it's not like I'm checking you out."

"You're literally doing exactly that." I point to the tablet. "Checking the boxes on that screen of yours."

"Move on out, frogman, and show me how that mighty fine ass of yours moves." Her lilting laughter brings a smile to my face.

"You're impossible. You know that, don't you?"

"I strive to be the best. Now, do as you're told."

"Yes, ma'am."

Because she's watching, an acute sense of self-consciousness overcomes me as I stride down the long hall. My steps feel stilted, awkward, and unnatural as bloody hell. I feel the leg and hate it.

Most days, I'm able to forget I'm less than I was before.

Almost.

The prosthetic Guardian HRS fitted me with after the explosion is better than my good leg. Better in that my run times are faster. My endurance is greater, mostly because I'm faster now with the new leg.

In many ways, the prosthetic is like having a superpower, but there are downsides. It's definitely not a chick magnet. More like chick repellant. It's a major cockblocker, to be honest.

"Stop thinking about your gait," Piper calls out from behind. She lets me get a few feet ahead of her before following me down the hall.

"How can I not think about my gait when I know you're watching my ass?"

"Just don't."

"That's not helpful." A sly grin twists my lips.

Nowadays, the only time I slip up is when I think about the prosthetic. Most of the time, I barely notice my lower leg's missing. Knowing she's watching, assessing my progress, and gauging how to adjust my therapy or whether it's time for the next iteration of my prosthetic, all I can think about is my leg.

I make it down the hall and pivot on my good foot. My only foot. The other one is a polycarbonate modified spring shoved into my boot.

"What now?" My hand rests on the doorknob leading into Piper's therapy gym.

"Go ahead and go inside. We'll put you on the treadmill and try a few things out."

"I thought we were checking the fit?"

The first few prostheses irritated the stump left behind, leaving ulcers that took too long to heal.

That's my fault.

Stubborn by nature, in my mind, the only way to recover was to push past the pain. Piper said exactly the opposite and chastised me like I was a child.

The stump needs to heal and develop a thick enough callous.

You need to take things slow.

One step at a time.

Turns out, she was right. Since then, I've been the perfect patient. It's the rule follower in me. As a result, that stump is the picture of health; fully healed, thick callous, great blood flow, and more.

"We'll check the fit after you run five miles." She sets the tablet down and moves to the treadmill to adjust the settings. "I'm putting you on an incline to start."

"Five?" My head tips back and a groan escapes me. "I wish I'd known that sooner. I wouldn't have gone running with the guys."

Since Booker's gal, Izzy, got snatched by a Nicaraguan cartel, Brady's been doing everything under the sun to keep Booker busy, his mind off his girl, and him out of trouble. It's an impossible task, but we're doing what we can to support our teammate while the technical team tracks Izzy down. Which means we practice as a team from sun up to sun down, keeping Booker too busy, and too worn out, to go crazy over Izzy's kidnapping.

Technically, Izzy got re-snatched, rather than kidnapped.

The cartel that took her the first time, the *Coralos* cartel, isn't the one that came after her when she flew home. It was the *Laguta* cartel. They tracked Izzy to her hometown in Laredo, Texas, where she, her four brothers, and her mother engaged in an old-fashioned shootout with the cartel.

It was bloody impressive. Unfortunately, we were literally minutes too slow. Booker watched as his woman's kidnapper flew her away.

The whole thing is a colossal mess.

She's been missing going on a week, and Booker is going out of his bloody mind. Brady's attempt to physically exhaust Booker only goes so far.

As far as mounting a rescue attempt to get Izzy back, that's in the hands of Mitzy and her genius technical team.

I feel for Booker, but I trust Mitzy's team. They're beyond compare, and they'll figure out a way to track Izzy down. Once they do, it's Game On. Bravo team will rain holy hellfire down on the cretins who dared to take one of our own.

Until then, we do what we can to help Booker.

"Stop whining and get on the treadmill." Piper moves around me and ignores my grumbling to set up the video cameras used to record my gait from every angle. "Five miles is like a walk in the park for you."

"Can we at least play something cool?" Five miles may be a walk in the park, but I get bored running on a stationary treadmill.

"Sure." Perky and positive, Piper nods. "What are you in the mood for?"

"Something with a beat."

Any song by Angel Fire will do, but I say nothing. Secretly, I'm a major fan of the mega rock band, but I don't want to look like a dork in front of Piper.

"I can make that happen."

A few taps on her tablet and Metallica blares through the speakers. Piper drifts back and gestures for me to begin.

Early in the morning, Bravo team went on a ten-mile team-building run. We ran with rucks the way we trained as SEALs, back in the day. I always look forward to running as a team. If not for the Guardians, I would miss the Navy and the grueling physical conditioning required of a SEAL.

After five boring miles, I'm more than happy to get off the treadmill, but Piper's waiting for me.

"Let's take a look. Jump up on the table." Piper pulls up a stool.

On the therapy table, when she sits in front of me, she's at eye level with my crotch. Normally, I'd make use of such a thing, crack a few snide remarks, but it's Piper. After the year we've had, she's family.

Annoying little sister comes to mind.

If that isn't deterrent enough, her husband, Bent, is a big, burly, bear of a man who won't think twice about going toe to toe with me. I can take the guy out. He's just a rock star, but the fallout would be *ginormous*. Not to mention, Piper is professional as shit. The woman's interested in only one thing; heal me.

"Pull up your sweats." Piper props her hands on her hips and angles her head to look up at me. "Why the hell are you wearing sweats anyway?"

"'Cause."

"'Cause?" She gives a dismissive snort. "You don't have to hide it. Especially from me."

"Not hiding it."

"You sure about that?"

"Just do your thing, so I can get out of here."

A text comes through my phone.

Brady wants the team to join him and Booker on the range. We're supposed to go to Brady's for a beer after work, but I have a feeling the trip to the range is on account of Booker needing his brothers around him.

Piper pushes my sweats past my knee.

I grasp the fabric and hold it mid-thigh, beyond the prosthetic, and out of the way.

"Don't tickle my toes." I fake-jump when she grabs my boot and places it on her thigh.

"A comedian, I see."

"Just keeping it real."

"Tell me, how does the fit feel?"

Normally, I don't like other people messing with my prosthetic, but with Piper, it's different. She doesn't make me feel like less of a man and only sees my potential, rather than what I lost.

Without her encouragement over the past year, I wouldn't be where I am now. As of a month, or so, I'm back on active status after a year of rehabilitation. If not for Piper's persistence, her perky positivity, and overall positive outlook on life, who knows where I'd be? Six feet under comes to mind.

How many times did the thought of quitting the Guardians cross my mind? How many times did I think they'd sack me and kick me out?

In addition to physical therapy, there are other therapists involved in my recovery; mental health professionals who walk me through the stages of grief following the loss of my leg.

I'm supposedly *in mourning* over the loss of my leg. Not sure if I agree with the shrinks, I do as I'm told and keep the therapy sessions, both mental and physical.

It was Piper, however, who pointed out how my run speeds

increased after the prosthetic. Not enough that I'd chop off my other leg for a matched set—I'm not stupid—but she's the reason I'm still here.

Still on Bravo team.

Still in the best physical condition of my life—if not better.

There are mental issues; psychiatric things associated with not feeling whole. I'm not comfortable in my own skin, but I'm confident that will all sort itself out somehow.

"The fit feels fantastic, but your fingers are ice cold," I complain as her ice-cold fingers on my stump make me jump.

"Sorry." Her fingers move quickly, releasing the straps that hold everything in place, pulling down the fabric sleeve that covers my stump. She calls it a sock for my nub, but a *nub sock* simply isn't funny.

Today, she says nothing about my nub sock.

For the next few minutes, Piper exposes my stump to the air. She examines the skin and callous formation. Tests for sensation and overall health of what's left of my leg.

"Since we fitted you with this new prosthetic, your leg is looking really good. I think we found the right fit. How's it working for you?"

The new prosthetic is a couple of weeks old. It's my tenth prosthetic and there will be more as the leg and the stump mature.

"Barely notice it's not the real thing."

"That's good." She leans back and her brows knit together. "You're not being snarky with me, are you?"

"No. I'm being quite honest. I run well on it. Went to the climbing wall and it worked just fine."

"Good. I'm concerned about things like that, but I'm curious about functionality in all situations. How about swimming? Have you been to the pool?"

"I don't like the pool."

"Why?" Piper slants her gaze upward. Concern lines her features, but there's something else there as well. Sadness.

Do I tell the truth?

Honestly, most people have no idea my lower leg is fake. With shoes, or boots, as long as I wear pants, I look like any other dude. Needless to say, I don't bother with shorts, let alone swim trunks. Don't care how damn hot it is. I just don't.

"Not interested."

"Don't blow smoke up my ass. You're a frogman. You love the water." She taps her lips, thinking. "At least that's what I'm told."

"Just not interested."

"That's not good enough, and we both know it's a copout. You know how I feel about copouts." Her attention returns to my stump, and she continues providing encouragement I don't want, but sorely need. "People will see beyond what you no longer have. You lost your leg. There's no going back. Suck it up and move on. With the technology we have available in composites and microprocessors, your new leg is an asset. Not a disability. Year after year, prosthetic technology evolves. The sensors are just the tip of the iceberg. We haven't talked about osseointegration surgery…"

"I don't want metal drilled into my leg."

"It improves sensory feedback, increases your range of motion."

"And makes me a bloody robot."

"We'll settle on not quite ready for the best of the best. We'll save that for next week." She leans back to stare.

"How about never?"

"That's not good enough." She points to her temple. "You know it up here, but you don't feel it in here." Her finger points to her heart. "Stop worrying about what others think about you. You're a frogman. SEALs love water, and you have to be as confident in the water as out. I don't need to tell you how important that is."

"You sound like Doc Summers."

"I should. Our job is to get you back into fighting shape. You're doing the runs, the weights. You're trying out the walls. Skye cleared you for duty and you have one successful mission with Bravo under your belt. It's time to shuck the pants and hit the water. We need to know how it works when it gets wet."

One of the few times she calls my prosthetic an *it*, the message isn't lost on me. *It* isn't a part of me. No matter how technologically advanced the leg is. At the end of the day, it's not me.

It never will be.

"I don't mind the new leg…" Total lie. "I'm just not interested in sharing the fact I have one with the rest of the world." My answer is punctuated with a shrug. "People look at me differently when they realize I'm disabled."

"But you're not disabled." If she were standing, Piper would stomp her foot on the floor. "You're fully functional, better than most able-bodied men. You've got a bionic leg. Use that as your pickup line and see how it goes with the ladies."

Bionic leg?

"You're not serious?"

"Chicks dig scars. They love heroes even more. The more damaged the better."

"That's all well and good until this thing comes off."

"Is that where this is stemming from?"

"What do you mean?"

"Your insecurity."

"Not insecure."

"Whatever…" She flaps her hand, dismissing my comment. Then Piper leans forward and lowers her voice to a whisper. "Whoever said you had to remove your prosthetic while having sex?"

"What?" Okay, she wins this round. I'm speechless. My eyes must bug out because Piper laughs.

"Cat got your tongue?"

"We're supposed to focus on my leg, not my sex life."

Or lack thereof.

"Rafe, do you need me to give you permission to have sex with your prosthetic on?" Her left brow quirks up, mocking me. "Dude, if it bothers you, you don't have to do it in bed. You're a strong man in the prime of your life. Pick her up. Slam her against the wall. Use those hips to…"

"Stop right there." I hold up a hand, praying she'll stop. Damn, if Piper doesn't make me blush.

She's pretty frank when talking about sex.

The real shame is she's one hundred percent correct. If I take the bed out of the equation, and shimmy my pants down over my hips, there's no reason my pants ever need to come off. No reason to send chicks screaming when they see the leg.

It's been too long since I've had a woman; a year too long. After hitting the range with the guys, I'm going out. Brady and Booker won't go. Brady's got Angie and Booker's all torn up about Izzy.

Zeb, Alec, and Hayes will hit the bars, happy to take me. They ask all the time. The few times I've gone with them, however, the only one who went home alone was me.

Time for that to change.

THREE

Carmen

___

For many, homecoming is a blessing. Mine? Not so much.

This is because Juan doesn't take me home after we land in Managua.

"Where are we going?" I look to Juan, demanding an answer.

"Your father asked that we stop at Señor Gonzales's residence first."

"First?"

"Yes, *Señorita.*"

"Why?"

"That is not for me to say."

"Not for you to say, but you know."

The bastard knows but is too chickenshit to tell me, or he's under orders from Father to say nothing.

Figures.

The way Juan presses his lips together is my answer. He's commanded to silence.

When the driver pulls up to an opulent estate, paid for by the sweat of impoverished peasants and the blood of innocents, I cross my arms and refuse to budge.

Juan exits the vehicle and comes around to help me out. The door of the black SUV opens.

"*Señorita, Señor* Gonzales and his mother are waiting." Hand extended, he's confused when I don't take it.

"His mother?" Acid burns in the back of my throat.

Father's not wasting time. I expected something like this, but this soon? With great difficulty, I tamp down the anger rising within me.

"Yes." Juan tugs at the collar of his shirt.

There's only one reason Artemus Gonzales, a filthy rich, forty-five-year-old political powermonger would have his mother in attendance for a visit from me. He wants what Father can provide, and my father needs Artemus's wealth to secure the capital for what he wants.

"No." I bite my tongue and swallow a long line of curse words trying to rip their way free from my throat. "I'm not getting out."

"You must." Juan shifts back and forth. Perspiration beads his brow.

That dark suit of his is not well suited to the oppressive heat of Nicaragua. The air smells sweet from tropical plants that grow like weeds, but there's no escape from the humidity or Juan's stench.

"No." I refuse to step a single foot out of this car. "Take me home."

While Juan sweats, the front door of the house slowly opens. Artemus's mother, a shrunken woman, pushing her late eighties, creeps out of the house. Behind her, Artemus pulls the front door closed, then steps beside his mother, offering his arm. Her bony fingers dig into his flesh and the two of them shuffle down the long walkway.

He gently covers her hand with his, a doting son taking care of his mother. Her bony fingers cling to the crook of his arm, stabilizing her teetering frame.

All that money Artemus commands? It comes from that tottering woman. She's a prominent force within Nicaragua's political climate; a woman who manages to sway the minds of the men she touches, and she rules the men in her family with an iron fist. In the US, she'd be called an old battle axe, matriarch of a powerful family. Here, she's a silent threat to my happiness.

I find her beyond intimidating, and before this moment, I've never been the subject of her attention.

"*Señorita*, I must insist you exit the car." Juan's unease escalates. His tone sharpens.

"I'm not doing it." Pouting like a schoolgirl, this is an argument I won't win, but I do it anyway. I need to allow myself this bit of defiance.

"You must."

"For the love of G…" No matter how upset I am, I won't take the Lord's name in vain. I swallow what I was going to say and restate, "For all that's holy, you would really force me out of this car?"

"Your father's wishes are clear." Juan will never answer such a question with a *yes*,' but there's no need.

"And what are those wishes?" I gesture toward the ponderous procession headed toward me.

"Please." Juan clasps his hands and semi-bows at me. "Your father…" Those hands shake and his fingers tremble with fear.

Failure to do as Father commands comes with significant repercussions. Not that Father will kill Juan for failing to deliver me to my presumed new fiancé, but it will not go well for Juan if he fails. Maximus Angelo doesn't tolerate failure, and as much as I despise Juan, his death isn't something I'll have weighing on my conscience.

I take Juan's hand and exit the vehicle under protest. To my surprise, he stands by my side rather than abandon me to my fate.

But how to get out of this?

Nothing like facing a problem head-on.

Father lured me into a trap—the kind that comes with a life sentence—but I will find a way out.

How?

How do I escape this? Good question.

Father's condemned me to a life without parole attached to Artemus Gonzales. My jailor is a man twice my age, known not only for his philandering ways but his inability to keep his previous two wives alive and kicking. My warden is none other than his mother.

Artemus draws close. Releasing his mother's hand, he spreads his arms out wide.

"Carmen, it is such a pleasure to see you. Congratulations on your graduation."

Empty words; his tone is far too informal. *Señorita* Angelo is how I should be addressed, but he already slips to the informality of family, even though we're not married.

Not yet.

I plan to make this as painful as possible without making him lose face.

"*Señor* Gonzales, it is nice to see you." There's no way to avoid the hug or the kisses to both my cheeks, but in addressing him formally, I send a clear message.

Hands off!

As the younger woman, I approach his mother and kiss her on both cheeks. "*Señora* Gonzales, you are looking well." Brief. Perfunctory. I check all the boxes.

She looks to her son, then back at me. A puzzled expression deepens the crags of her weathered face.

Her rise to power came after a childhood spent in the fields and her youth spreading her legs for whichever man furthered her dreams. Deep wrinkles and sun-damaged skin testify to chronic sun exposure when she was young. Those deep, craggy crevices line her face, turn her expression into a powerful mask of displeasure.

It speaks to her roots and her lineage. That lineage extends to her son. He may be wealthy, but he's nothing more than a peasant. Artemus and his mother can only aspire to be within striking distance of my social standing. While their wealth bridges that gap, it doesn't close it completely.

"I apologize for the visit. I was not aware…"

"Artemus?" *Señora* Gonzales silences me. She looks to her son for guidance when she is really the one in charge. "Are we not…" Her words are cut off when Artemus pats her arm.

"Don't worry, Mama. It's been arranged." Artemus turns toward me. "Won't you come inside?"

Arranged?

No way in hell is this arranged.

I cross my arms over my chest, acutely aware of the form-fitting dress I wear.

It was intended for a night on the town, not a seven-hour flight and whatever this is. My actions draw Artemus's eye as I had intended to draw the attention of random men at the club.

I should be with Kaye and Barbi, tearing up the town.

"I'm sorry, *Señor*, but I must decline. It's been some time since I've seen my father, and I'm eager to get home." None of what I say is true. "This meeting is premature." Not to mention inappropriate. I should never be the one to call upon a man. He should come to me. Is this another message sent by my father?

As far as Artemus is concerned, this is a point I need to be exceptionally clear about. I am not here to accept his hand in marriage. I would rather die than suffer the degradation that brings.

"But we have much to discuss." Unfazed, Artemus continues as if my opinion means nothing.

Unfortunately, that's my future if I agree to this union.

His hungry gaze rakes over my body, sending a ripple of disgust slithering down my spine. The man is fat. His skin is lumpy. His fingers are nothing but grotesque stumps—greedy, ugly things. Oily, black hair and bushy brows bring bile rising in the back of my throat.

I will not give myself to this man.

"No doubt you and my father discussed…" I make a vague gesture and inject as much spite as I dare into my words. "But I am not in a position to accept. Especially since my education is, as of yet, unfinished." A smile fills my face and covers the lie I say next. "I'm excited to continue my studies in environmental conservation."

That makes him suck in a breath. Their family's wealth comes from stripping the land. Raping is a better word, but too vulgar to say in mixed company. This is a critical moment; one I must successfully navigate if I have any hope of saving my country from greedy men.

The culmination of a lifetime of sacrifice, I've waited too many years to be where I am now—within striking distance of the man I hate the most.

"Carmen…" Artemus takes a step toward me. His fat fingers rub against one another. "Perhaps, you do not understand what your father and I discussed?"

Discussed? The two of them sat down at a table and bartered away my freedom, trading me for political favors in return.

How could Father do this to me?

The rumors surrounding the deaths of Artemus's previous two wives are rarely spoken out loud, but they're out there—circulating in the darkest corners for whoever is brave enough to listen. The bunching in his muscles, and the menace in his eyes, tell me there's far too much truth in the rumors whispered in the dark.

Is this the future my father wants for his daughter? To be victimized by my husband? Beaten into submission by day and raped through the night?

How the hell am I getting out of this?

"This meeting is premature." I place a hand over my belly.

Shoulders back. Chin level. I meet his stare with fierceness in my gaze, but I let that gaze drop and land on his mother.

She'll understand.

His mother's jaw drops. Impossible, but she reads me like an open book. Or rather, a book full of lies. This is one lie I'm going to have to breathe into life. It's the only way.

Artemus remains oblivious to the silent conversation exchanged between his mother and me. Fury darkens his gaze. Anger bunches in his muscles. His expression darkens and his tone turns ominous and threatening.

"Your father promised." This is a man used to getting his way. His family's climb out of poverty gives him an exaggerated sense of self-worth. "It's been arranged."

"My apologies, but Father isn't aware of…" I draw out the

pause, ensuring his mother believes the lie. "I need to speak to my father before this proceeds any further."

"Artemus…" His mother tugs on his sleeve. "Let *Señorita* Carmen discuss the matter with her father. He will explain what's been discussed. Our meeting is premature."

Holy father, did that really work?

How will I explain this to my father? And what will I do when Artemus's mother learns about the lie? My hand hovers over my belly. Her gaze zeroes in on my hand and her mouth twists in disgust.

Really? It's a bit much. Although, I may be able to use this to my advantage.

I will be her son's third wife. Does it matter if I'm a virgin? Does it matter if she assumes I'm pregnant? I never spoke the words. The woman is shrewd and jumps to conclusions too quickly. Normally, I would be mortified by such an assumption. Now, I'm furiously figuring out how to use it to my advantage.

The pinching of her brows and the disgust filling her face says it matters. Looks like I solved one problem only to create another.

Not that I care.

I refuse to be traded to a monster as a means to further my father's political aspirations. Neither my father, nor Artemus, respect the holy sacrament of marriage.

But I do.

Fidelity means everything to me, and if I'm completely honest with myself, I believe God intends for love to be the glue that binds a couple together. Not agreements or business transactions between power-hungry men. As for the virginity Artemus's mother holds sacrosanct. It buys me a few months.

Nothing more.

Perhaps the time I spent in the US makes me wish for the same freedoms Kaye and Barbi enjoy? There's no question whether they'll marry for love. There's no doubt their families will be precisely planned. I want that freedom—the ability to choose my destiny. What I don't want is an agreement made between monsters without my consent.

My relationship with God may be shaky at times, but at the end of the day, I go to my knees and bow my head in prayer. I believe God is good. He will not force me into a loveless marriage. If I marry Artemus, my only escape will be through death. Unfortunately, divorce or suicide aren't viable options.

"I'm sorry for the misunderstanding." I look to his mother, sealing my lie with a penitent bowing of my head. With a precise pivot, I dismiss Artemus. My attention shifts to Juan. With a glare, I issue an order. "Take me home."

"*Señorita…*" Juan shifts uncomfortably on his feet, gaze shifting quickly between me and Artemus's mother.

"*Señora* Gonzalez, I am sorry for the confusion. May God bless you this day." I bow toward Artemus's mother.

"And you." Her forehead wrinkles and her brows practically touch as she looks to her son. "Take me back inside." Her voice snaps, acidic and unforgiving.

At least I succeeded in this. As for the rest, I'm at a loss. Juan forced me to leave all my belongings behind. Father thinks to separate me from that life, but that isn't happening. I've waited too long and sacrificed too much.

Artemus curls his fingers. Those massive hands of his form into fists. He takes a step back, following the commands of his mother. He knows better than to lay hands on me. I'm not his to touch. Not yet.

But that doesn't keep him from wanting me. If anything, he wants me more than before.

Not yet, Artemus, you fat bastard.

There is still time.

Leaving them gaping, I spin about and gracefully take my seat back inside the air-conditioned interior of the SUV. The pulse in my neck bounces with the racing of my heart. My hands shake and my breaths turn rapid and shallow, but I'm in the clear—for now.

It takes Juan a moment, but he joins me. Once we're back inside the vehicle, he breathes out a long sigh. "Your father… He will be furious. What am I to tell him?"

Juan is right to be confused. As a man, the subtleties of the brief non-verbal exchange between me and Artemus's mother went right over his head. Word will get back to my father, but there's still time to escape.

In doing so, I'll give up any hope of protecting my country from those who wish to rape the land to feed their pockets, leaving hundreds of thousands scraping to stay alive.

"I will deal with my father."

All I can do is stall the inevitable. We're a Catholic nation, which means certain things are prohibited. Divorce is one of them. Abortion is another. Both are unforgivable sins. I convinced Artemus's mother I was soiled and unworthy, but she knows, as do I, that time will tell. Once finalized, the engagement will be short. I'll find myself walking down the aisle before I know it. If that happens, my life is forfeit.

But how?

How do I get out of this mess?

On the drive to my father's private residence, desperation drives me to find another way. Once word reaches his ear that I may be pregnant, Father will demand proof.

What will I do then?

He'll force me to see a physician, confirm I'm pregnant, or not, then press forward with the marriage. My time is counted not in weeks or months, but in days.

It's hopeless.

It takes an hour to drive out of the city limits of Managua; another to reach our family's home. The expansive villa lies past the outskirts of the county's capital, where small farms dot the countryside surrounded by dense jungle.

The walled estate never felt like a home. It was always a prison. Beyond the walls of the estate, farms lead off to the west, while the dense canopy of the rainforest encroaches every day from the east. Too high to scale, those walls keep everyone outside from coming in, and those inside from escaping the privileges wealth brings.

As we pull up the long drive, I brace for what's to come. There's nothing to do but face things head-on. Tension mounts within me as I exit the car and head inside. Mid-afternoon, it's hard to imagine, just this morning, I celebrated graduation with my two best friends. Literally a world away, those are memories that will die with time.

Exiting the vehicle, Juan is on my heels. Perhaps, he thinks to escort me, but with one look, I send him scrambling. This may be a prison, but it's my home. Everything within these walls is mine—mostly mine. The point being that he no longer needs to provide escort. His duties as a guard end the moment I enter my home.

My heels click over travertine floors as I make my way through the extravagant estate. I pass by a courtyard I used to play in as a child when my mother was alive. Wrought iron cages stand empty where once beautiful birds used to sing sweet melodies to me. It took years before I understood how captivity ruined their lives. Father raged at me when I opened the cage doors, freeing them, and my tears hardened his heart. They've stood empty ever since.

My steps hurry past memories too painful to face. The empty cages mock me. As a child, I thought I was free. Not once did I realize these walls were the same to me as the bars of those cages were to the birds trapped inside.

At a crossing of two corridors, Matias, Father's right-hand man, drags a raven-headed beauty down the hall.

There was a time running into Matias would draw me up short. The man terrifies me. He once believed Father would give my hand in marriage to him—as if I was a great reward for the service he gave my father. Fortunately, Father's been exceptionally clear that will never happen.

Matias offers no advantage to Father's aspirations. Which means, I'm too important to waste on rewarding loyalty. Since I'm in a foul mood after dealing with Artemus and his mother, I call out to Matias, looking to let loose some of my anger on another man I hate.

"Matias..." I wait for him to stop and turn my attention to the woman he drags through the halls. "Did my father give you another plaything?"

The woman turns terrified eyes on me. She's stunning. Her raven hair is as dark as mine, but it hasn't been brushed in days. Her clothes are rumpled, dirty, and sweat-stained. I dismiss her, too tired to care.

I can't save her. Therefore, I won't acknowledge her silent pleas for help.

After years of seeing such things, I no longer engage in such futility. Some may think that makes me a bad person—as if I'm cold and unfeeling—but this is a fight I can't win.

The woman pleads with me with her terrified gaze, perhaps wondering who I am and why I don't care about her plight. If Father did give this woman to Matias, I don't envy the poor thing.

Matias pulls up short. Immediately, there's a change in his demeanor; probably the result of the skin-tight dress I wear and the heels I love so much. I know exactly what he sees and let him know that none of this will ever be his. As for the dress, I'm ready to get out of it. After spending four hours at the airport, another seven hours flying through the night, two hours driving here, stopping in for that visit with Artemus, and I've been in this dress for far too long. Unlike the woman, however, my appearance shows none of the wear and tear she shows.

"I didn't know you were coming home, *Señorita* Carmen." Matias's hungry gaze devours my body. The man longs for what he can't have.

Is he the only person who doesn't know I was called home? Did Father not tell him to expect me? From the surprise on his face, maybe Matias has been otherwise occupied.

By this woman?

My attention shifts to the terrified female.

Call me callous and unfeeling, but there is only so much I can do. Saving her life isn't on that list. God forgive me, but her fate is in her hands and hers alone. Although, I will pray for her plight to improve, or that she's graced with a swift death.

As for Matias, he lacks the abject adoration of Juan because he's smarter than Juan, which makes him incredibly dangerous. Some-days, I wonder if Father understands how much power he gives his second in command.

Matias is tied to the Angelo family by nothing more than loyalty.

In an unstable country, with shifting power bases, Matias is a destabilizing force. Does my father not see the threat? Or does he keep Matias close because he does?

"Father sent Juan to meet me at graduation and brought me home."

"Is that so?" Never one to hide his desire, his gaze rakes me from head to toe. Father would feed Matias his balls if he was here to see the way Matias looks at me, but he's not here to witness Matias's bold stare.

"He brought you straight here?" Matias's brow bounces, revealing much.

"There was a slight detour." Matias is no idiot. He knows Father is arranging a marriage contract with Artemus.

"I see." Matias says nothing as he processes what I don't say.

Curious about the woman who's maybe a few years older than me, I turn my attention to her. Matias notices the direction of my gaze and yanks on the woman's arm.

"She is nothing." A growl escapes the back of his throat as he steps in front of her.

Knowing Matias's proclivities, I swallow the bile rising in my throat and proffer the response perfected over a lifetime of witnessing such evil. If anything, I excel when it comes to survival.

"A plaything then?" My tone sharpens, snapping Matias's spine rigid. He dislikes my derisive tone.

My heart goes out to this woman, and I pray her ordeal doesn't drag on for too long. Matias is not a gentle man and is well known for taking his time destroying his toys.

"For your father." He growls out the words, betraying his irritation.

Father?

Well, this is interesting.

"Please…" The last thing my father needs is another plaything. My concern for the woman intensifies. Matias is bad enough, but I know what my father does to his toys. "I'm surprised he would bother, considering…"

About to mention my father's stable of women, I decide not to finish that thought. It's best if this poor woman knows nothing about what's coming. With a flick of my lashes, I dismiss Matias—and his hapless victim.

It goes against everything I believe in, but there are things I can change and things I can't. My efforts are best focused on changing what I can. Somehow, I need to figure out a way to reestablish communication with my contact in the CIA—if that route is still available to me. My hasty departure likely set off a slew of alarm bells. They may determine I'm too great of a risk to contact now.

"If you're a good boy..." Injecting as much disdain as I can into my tone, I fall into the role of callous and disinterested daughter; a survival mechanism that serves me well when trapped within these walls. "Maybe he will reward you, and let you have his toy once he's through with her."

The woman's lids draw back, revealing fear and revulsion toward me. Years ago, that may have hurt. I know what goes on in my father's domain, but there's little I can do to stop it.

"How was your visit with Artemus?" Matias fires back with a snarl. "I don't see a ring around your finger. Your father will not be pleased."

Evidently, Matias is aware of my homecoming. I remind myself how dangerous it is to underestimate the monster standing in front of me.

He wishes that ring was his. His ultimate desire is to take over what my father built. Only a son, or a son-in-law, can do that. He's been pushed out of what he considers his rightful place.

"That was premature. Something Father and I will discuss later."

It's a lie. All I can do is stall and hope to find a way out of that grotesque union.

"Is that what you think?" Matias tips his head back and laughs. The bastard's feeling pretty safe in his position as Father's right-hand man.

"I have better things to do with my time than waste breath on you." This conversation's gone on too long. Already, I tire of it.

Malevolence swirls in his eyes. Matias takes out his anger on the woman, making her cry out as his grip tightens.

"*Tsk. Tsk. Tsk.* Be careful, or you'll damage his toy." I lift a forefinger, shaking it in front of his face.

What does Father want with her? She's pretty. Or will be once she's cleaned up, but what value does he see in the pretty, but bedraggled, American?

Curious, I close the distance. Some of what I do sickens me, but I put on a show for Matias's and my father's benefit. Cocking my head, I place a finger under the woman's chin.

"What game is my father playing with you? I almost feel sorry for you." My attention shifts to Matias, looking for a reaction I can make sense of later.

For Matias's benefit, my words are cold and cruel. With my guts tied up in knots for that woman's fate, I press my lips together and step back. With a prayer lifted to the Almighty, I do what little I can. Her fate is in God's hands now. Eager to get away from Matias, I blow him a kiss.

"Goodbye, Matias." It's flippant and designed to strike a nerve.

Matias's chest swells as his anger erupts. I breeze past the two of them, headed to the suite of rooms which make up my escape from this place. The red-eye flight, combined with the stop at Artemus's home, leaves me exhausted and disgusted with myself, but things could be worse.

I could be the woman Matias drags through the estate.

FOUR

Rafe

"Damn, you're on fire." I remove my safety glasses and glance at Booker. Our targets bow backward as the cables rush the black silhouettes toward us.

"I missed one." Booker's mouth twists. He scratches the back of his neck and shifts foot-to-foot.

Can't help but feel for the guy. Here he is, shooting on the range, doing bloody nothing while Izzy is who-the-bloody-hell-knows-where. I'd be crawling out of my skin if I was in his shoes.

Since I'm not, I support him as I can.

"Going for the head shots, I see." My attention shifts to his target.

The silhouette head is Swiss cheese, punctured by 99 bullets out of the hundred we shot. Booker didn't technically miss. That one bullet would've taken a chunk out of an ear if the silhouette was a real human.

"What's taking Mitzy and her team so damn long?" Booker scrubs his face and pulls on his chin. "With all their brains, a super-computer to boot, and they still can't find her? I'm going to kill the fucker who took her." His frustrated growl shakes the air.

We're all past ready to get going and do what we do best; rescue those who've been taken, but we count on the tech team to do their job and build out a battle plan.

I remove my hearing protection and check out my handiwork.

That blast from a year ago may have taken out my leg, but it left my eagle eyes and steady hands intact. I'm still the best shot among Bravo team.

Trained as a sniper, I'm equally precise with a handgun as I am with my rifle. My silhouette has two holes the size of dimes. Just two. Fifty bullets to the head; dead center. Fifty to the trunk; smack dab over the heart. All I did was punch through the same damn hole over and over again.

Hayes wanders over and takes a look at our targets. "I missed two at the end. Getting sloppy." He unclips his target and gives it a good look before crumpling it and tossing it in the trash.

Our explosives expert, Hayes, is great when it comes to putting bullets exactly where they belong. Although, he'd rather blow up his targets. Deadly with practically any weapon, he's equally lethal with axes and knives. The man is scary good with an axe, and that's minus two fingers.

Alec saunters over. "Hey, what do you say we put the sidearms away and move to sparring? I could use the practice." Alec's been looking to improve his hand-to-hand combat after the loss of two fingers on his dominant hand. Yet another casualty of the blast that took my leg and left Brady with disfiguring scars.

"Knives?" Zeb glances at his target. He missed none of the hundred rounds we shot. As our alternate sniper, he's nearly as good as me, but he really shines when it comes to tech support.

"How about we call it quits and grab a drink?" Brady, Bravo team's leader, glances at Booker. His eye also catches the head shots on Booker's target.

Given a chance, Booker is taking Matias out.

We know the name of the man who kidnapped Booker's woman. We believe Matias took Izzy to Nicaragua. What we don't know is where, or who, he's taking her to. Mitzy and her technical team are working that angle. Until they have something actionable, Bravo team waits in the wings and Booker stews.

Brady tries to keep him in a good headspace.

The rest of us gather around our brother in arms, supporting him as only we can.

"Only if I get to pick the place," Booker speaks first and gives me the eye. "Not Chinese." That comment's specifically for me.

"You don't know what you're missing at Mr. Wu's." My love for all things Chinese—especially a good buffet—is well known, but I think the guys are getting tired of me always picking Chinese.

"I'm in the mood for steak," Brady chimes in.

A groan escapes me, but I'm not about to argue the point. This is all about supporting Booker, not getting what I want.

After putting everything away, we split into two cars. Alec, Zeb, and I take one vehicle while Brady, Booker, and Hayes climb in the other. We make it half a mile past the outer security fence of Guardian HQ when Booker calls us. Zeb puts his phone on speaker.

"Yo! What's up?" Zeb's deep voice resonates in the enclosed cab of the car.

"We're turning around." Excitement fills Booker's voice.

"Why?" Zeb's brows bunch as he listens.

"Because we're going to Nicaragua." Booker sounds triumphant

"About damn time." Zeb turns us around.

"Izzy?" My heart leaps in my throat.

This is huge. Like a bloody-big-deal huge. When Zeb nods, I pump my fist in the air as Alec turns the car around.

"About damn time." The grimace on Alec's face is one promising retribution. That fucker took Izzy, and she's one of us. That means the bastard's going to pay.

Not too long ago, we rescued both Izzy and Angie from the *Coralos* cartel. At the time, Izzy and Angie worked for the medical relief agency, Doctors Without Borders. Their entire medical team was taken by the *Coralos* cartel and interrogated regarding shipping weapons to their rivals, the *Laguta* cartel.

We discovered weapons had nothing to do with the kidnappings. Jerald, a man Brady killed when rescuing Angie, used Angie and Izzy as unknowing mules to ferry diamonds across *Coralos* controlled territory for the *Laguta* cartel.

We think.

Some of that is still fuzzy.

What we know is the cartel went after Izzy to get the diamonds back. For some reason, they took her and the diamonds. Which is why Booker's barely holding his shit together.

We rush back to Guardian HQ and enter the Guardian briefing room as a team. Sam, who's head of Guardian HRS, CJ, who's lead of the Guardians and Protectors, and Mitzy, lead for Guardian's top-notch technical team, are all in attendance along with the big brass.

"Damn, Forest Summers is here." Alec elbows me in the ribs and keeps his voice low. "This is serious shit."

I don't disagree.

The founder of Guardian HRS, Forest Summers, looks up at our entrance. His brooding expression matches the storm clouds raging in his eyes.

As Guardians, we're all big men, over six feet, and in peak physical shape. Yet when standing next to Forest, we look small.

It's enough to pull me up short each and every time our founder shares the same room with me. Then there's his icy gaze and shock-white hair. The man looks like Thor, God of Thunder, come to life. Some say he's a Norse god, reborn in the flesh. Regardless of what others say, Forest Summers is bloody formidable, even when it looks like he hasn't slept a wink in days. The man looks ragged.

"Take a seat." Sam invites us to sit around the conference room. "Mitzy, go ahead."

Mitzy's briefing is longer than it needs to be. She can't help but show off what she and her technical team accomplished. Bravo team is used to it, so we settle in for her briefing, but our silence doesn't last long.

"What the hell?" Booker slams his palms on the table. "You're telling me the fucking Minister of the Interior kidnapped my girl?"

Our objective is the private estate of a man named Maximus Angelo, Nicaragua's Minister of the Interior.

"Looks that way." Mitzy's normally high-pitched voice is subdued.

The briefing continues with a spiel about Maximus Angelo. In his late fifties, he carries authority well, but there is more to this man beneath the surface. I can tell by his eyes; they're that of a predator, not a politician.

Brady clears his throat. "You want us to infiltrate the private residence of one of Nicaragua's senior-most governmental figures and retrieve Izzy?"

"That's the objective." A bit of Mitzy's snark is back. "By the time you land, I'll have schematics and security info ready."

All I care about is they found Izzy. My teammates echo that sentiment. We're past ready to rescue Booker's woman.

Once the tech briefing is done, it will be Bravo team's turn to get to work. The tech team deals with strategic and operational planning behind our missions. We plan tactics and execution on the ground.

A loud thud sounds as Forest practically slumps into a seat. The massive man looks paler than I remember. More haggard, as if exhaustion pulls at him.

Maybe he's sleep deprived? Knowing our founder, he's been shoulder to shoulder with Mitzy over the past several days trying to find Izzy. I seriously doubt either of them have slept a wink. Nobody says anything as he runs his hands over his face and pinches the bridge of his nose, but we all watch closely.

We scramble over the next hour to grab our go-bags and pack our gear. Mitzy's new fleet of AI robotic dogs will join us, enhancing perimeter defense as Bravo team breaches the interior of Nicaragua's Minister of the Interior's estate to extract Izzy.

The Robotic Ultra Functional Utility Specialists, aka robotic dogs called Rufus I, II, and III, are powered by artificial intelligence. This isn't their first time out in the field. Rufus I assisted Brett, Guardian HRS's first Protector, during his first assignment. However, this will be the first time the robots go out in the field armed. Those armaments will be operated remotely by Mitzy's team. The robots aren't ready for fully autonomous operations with functioning weapons.

It's a seven-hour flight to Nicaragua. Another few hours pass on the ground as Forest Summer's CIA contacts meet up with us in a tiny house in a small village less than two miles from Angelo's private residence. Nearly an entire day has passed. Late in the evening, the sun dips toward the horizon, making our job a little easier as it means we're operating in the dark.

In addition to Bravo team, Sam, CJ, and Mitzy, who brought a small team of her tech junkies, we're joined by Forest Summers, Doc Summers—his foster sister—and two CIA operatives.

"Listen up." Sam stands in the cramped quarters and clears his throat to get our attention. "All eyes up here. Diego Espinoza and Luis Sanchez are our local CIA experts. They're going to brief us on what they know about Maximus Angelo. After that, once Mitzy's team is ready, we'll go over schematics of the residence, then decide on infil and exfil. Time to get your thinking caps on." Sam yields the floor to a man with dark hair, bronzed skin, and coffee-brown eyes.

"Good evening. I'm Diego Espinoza." He takes a moment to scan the room. "I've been on assignment in Nicaragua for over a decade. Much of my information comes from contacts I've developed over the years dealing with the *Laguta* cartel and its kidnapping and ransom operations. We have reason to believe Maximus Angelo runs human trafficking through his estate but have never had a chance to take a look. Luis Sanchez…" He gestures to the other man, "is involved in monitoring the movement of guns, munitions, and the exchange of currency through criminal elements."

Luis lifts a hand in greeting and steps forward. He takes in a deep breath and takes over. "The Angelo family is a prestigious family with ties to virtually every industry and criminal element within Nicaragua. Over the past several decades, they've increased their political presence and solidified their power base. Maximus Angelo, the family patriarch, has strong industrial ties and fingers in nearly every criminal organization, including both the *Laguta* and *Coralos* cartels."

The briefing continues until we're ready to deploy. Despite the difficulties of what we plan, a sense of calmness settles over me and my teammates. This is what we love and we're damn good at our job.

I love the beginning of a mission. All contingencies are taken into account, alternate extractions considered. It's when my excitement becomes a palpable presence.

Blood races through my body, preparing for the action to come. As a devout Catholic, I begin each mission with a silent prayer.

For many, God is forgiving, but I know Him as a vengeful force of justice. I'm merely His worldly instrument; His vessel, as it were, to enact His vengeance.

In addition to praying for forgiveness for the lives I may take, I pray for the surety of my shots and the protection of my teammates. I pray for any innocents we may encounter, hoping they remain safe from harm. Then I pray for salvation and place my future in God's hands.

I do that now—silently—as the last details of the mission are set in motion.

Before I know it, we're out of that tiny house moving in on Angelo's residence with three robotic dogs walking in near silence beside us.

The robots are silent as death and cloaked in one of Mitzy's new stealth technologies. It's a shield that makes them practically invisible to the naked eye. It's freaky the way my vision slips past them.

I'm glad they're on my side. They're bloody ferocious. That comes from personal experience as we train with the robots, participating in their research and development through field trials. At least, it feels normal having them walking beside us.

"One bit about this mission bugs me." I activate the team-only channel as we move through the fields at the outskirts of the village.

"What's that?" Brady responds quickly.

"Why is Angelo not to be harmed?" That order came from Doc Summers herself.

"Fuck if I know," Booker responds with an aggravated snort. "The fucker takes Isabelle and I'm supposed to tranq him and his men? Makes no fucking sense." He continues to grumble as we hit a hedgerow and work around it.

"I know you want a conversation with Matias, but we're only allowed to shoot to wound, not to kill." Brady clarifies what needs no clarification. Our marching orders are crystal clear on that front.

"Shit. I know that. Just not happy about it." Booker falls silent for a minute as we cross the next field.

Talk about being hamstringed. Not that I'll say it out loud, but I'm not making any promises I can't keep. If I need to shoot to kill to save my ass, my team, Izzy, or a noncombatant, I'm taking the shot. I'm pretty damn sure Booker will do the same.

One of the robots ambles up beside me and stops. Absently, I place my hand on its back, like I would a real dog.

All around us, the night is eerily still but far from quiet. Millions of insects buzz and chirp. The distant hoots of monkeys calling to their troop mates punctuates the night. Heat and humidity cling tenaciously to the air and smother the land. Sweat covers me from head to toe.

Mosquitoes are out in force. Their high-pitched whine isn't loud, but it's nonstop and particularly irritating. Bloody pests look for blood to feast upon, and we're warm flesh bags full of it, but they won't get shit from me. Covered head to toe in black tactical gear, not an inch of my skin is exposed.

Despite the droning noise of millions of insects, there's no breeze disturbing the foliage or rustling the grasses. The night is eerily calm, the quiet before the storm.

I stand with my brothers and wait for Brady's signal to proceed. While I check my helmet's integrated Heads-Up Display, sweat saturates my clothes. We operate in the infrared part of the spectrum, which means the darkness comes alive in shades of black, white, and gray.

Mitzy guides us forward, using her fleet of tiny drones to make sure the way ahead is clear. In addition to the three Rufuses—Rufi? —hell if I know how to make that plural, Mitzy's drone fleet operates overhead. Her drones range in size from that of a deck of cards —her dragonflies—to *Smaug*, a strategic drone the size of a small plane, which flies far overhead. I've seen drones smaller than the dragonflies. Tiny things the size of horseflies being tested by the tech team. Bloody awesome what Guardian HRS can achieve.

"A hundred yards out," Brady calls us to a halt.

Tall walls completely encircle the residence. I glance at Booker and find the grim set of his lips. His entire body vibrates with barely concealed rage.

There's a bit of back and forth between Brady, Mitzy, and Booker. Her dragonfly drones are busy gathering the information we need to advance on the residence. Things such as the number of guards inside and out, the weapons they carry, and if they patrol in a circuit, or stand guard in one place.

Brady waves us all in to discuss our options. In the background, Mitzy calls out that she's taking control of the cameras to create a video loop she'll feed back to security inside. That loop will cover our approach to the wall.

Two of the Rufuses—Rufi?—peel off from our group to patrol the exterior and take out any guards that may be outside the walls. One of the robots stays with us.

"Bravo team…" CJ's voice comes over the comms. "You'll be dropping into a courtyard on the other side…"

"Copy that." Brady acknowledges the communication.

There's another pause while Mitzy's drones comb the interior of the residence looking for Izzy. Once that's done, we should be good to go. My trigger finger is getting itchy.

Then the word finally comes in.

"Bingo!" Mitzy calls out. "Target located…"

I hate hearing Izzy reduced to a target, but it is what it is. When I see the grim set of Booker's lips, I exchange a look with Alec. Our buddy is out for blood.

"You ready?" Brady clasps Booker's shoulder.

"Past ready." Booker's attention focuses forward.

"Rafe and Zeb, you're over the wall first," Brady calls out the sequence we'll use to get over the tall walls. "Hayes and Alec guard the rear."

"Copy that." Hayes answers for himself and Alec. Meanwhile, Zeb and I move out.

"Let's get your girl." I knock the top of Booker's helmet as I move in toward the northern wall.

Ahead of us, one of the Rufuses charges forward. At the wall, it rears up on its hind legs, placing its two front legs against the wall. This creates a series of steps Zeb and I take at a run. I'm up and over, first inside. Zeb is right behind me. Brady and Booker follow on our heels, then Alec and Hayes join us.

Armed to the teeth, I put away my weapon. It feels all kinds of wrong.

After a nod from Brady, I draw forth the tranquilizer gun we were issued for this mission. As lead sniper, I go first. Zeb follows behind. The two of us will take out every man in our way as Bravo team advances slowly toward our goal.

Booker's woman is here, and we're going to get her out, no matter the cost.

FIVE

Carmen

I EXCHANGE THE SHORT COCKTAIL DRESS FOR A LONGER VERSION IN deep crimson with a daring slit up the side for dinner. A few minutes early, I wander through the house visiting the rooms I grew up in.

Memories of my mother linger everywhere. They always have, but when I try to remember specific details, like the lightness of her laughter, the joy on her face when she saw me, or the lingering scent of her favorite perfume, memory fails me.

Most of all, I try to remember how it felt when she wrapped me in her arms.

Mother's memories are faint, too distant to recall, as I was very young when she died. All I have is an emptiness in my chest and a hole in my heart—wounds inflicted upon me by my father.

My steps falter and bring me to what used to be my favorite courtyard; the one with the wrought iron cage. As it has for years, the door to the bird cage stands open and the cage remains empty. That cage holds many memories and one important lesson.

My hand drifts of its own account; fingers grip the cold iron and profound sadness presses down on me. My eyes close and a deep breath fills my lungs. The distant memory of rustling feathers and the nervous chirps of the birds once caged inside flood my mind.

When I turned five, Father bought the cage as a birthday gift, then filled it with the most fanciful birds. With their beautiful plumage and entrancing birdsong, I stared at them day after day, completely fascinated by the birds.

I loved those birds and sat outside their cage, listening to their birdsong. While doing my schoolwork, I fed them through the thick wrought iron bars of their prison until the day I finally understood they'd been taken from the wild and caged for my enjoyment.

I was seven at the time.

It made me sick knowing they lost their freedom because of me. My heart broke, and all I could think about was how awful I felt and how cruel it was to take away their freedom.

The day I let them go, joy filled me from the inside out. The birds didn't fly away at once. They didn't trust the open door with its promise of freedom. Instead, they cowered in the corner as I stepped inside to usher them to freedom.

Much later, I would understand why they didn't trust the freedom I offered.

Eventually, after much coaxing by me, those birds spread their wings and flew away. To this day, I imagine they're out in the jungle, flying free.

That day, I vowed to never again cage one of God's creatures. Little did I know, those birds weren't the only things being kept in a cage inside my home.

That came many years later.

My head bows until my forehead presses against the rusty metal. Shame rushes through me with the weight of the years; time while I stood by, doing nothing, while others suffered tragically in the darkness beneath my feet.

Soft footsteps to my left snap my head around. Across the courtyard, Rosalie, one of the maids, and my dearest friend, pulls up short. Her eyes round with surprise and her face fills with joy before being quickly suppressed.

"*Señorita* Carmen." Rosalie furtively glances around. She's excited, but cautious. "I didn't know you were coming home. Forgive me for not refreshing your room."

"My homecoming is as much a surprise to me as it is to you. No forgiveness needed."

"You are very kind." Rosalie is my best friend, but she's a servant of this house first and foremost. "Is there anything I can get for you?"

We're the same age, only months apart. A young girl from the local village, my governess, Lucinda, brought her to work as one of the maids. At first, Father refused, but my governess insisted, stating I needed a companion who was the same age as me. Eventually, Father relented. Rosalie found safety and comfort beneath our roof, while I found a friend and someone I could trust.

"Thank you, but no. I had a few minutes before dinner and thought to wander."

"It's good to see you again." Rosalie knows exactly what this courtyard means to me. Her gaze shifts to the cage.

"It feels good to be home." I continue as if pausing for a moment to admire the courtyard.

We've known each other since we were twelve. She started as a servant, offered food and shelter, but nothing more, to keep me company and clean my rooms. What she became is my dearest friend and the sister I never had.

If I never see this place again, I won't miss it, and she knows it. She's the one who told me what goes on in the basement beneath us. If I had things my way, the whole structure, including the basement with its cages, would be razed to the ground and scraped off the face of this earth.

With a gesture, I tell her we're alone. Father's guards are elsewhere and know to give me space.

Rushing toward me, Rosalie dips to a curtsey, as expected of a maid in this house. There may be no guards watching, but Rosalie takes no chances. She waits for me to acknowledge her and extend my arms first to embrace her.

"How have you been?" I pull her in and hug her tight. With her close, and certain no one can overhear, I whisper a much less formal greeting into her ear. "I've missed you so much." Overjoyed, a tear slips from my eye.

"I am well, *Señorita.*" Rosalie pulls back. "Thank you for asking."

We're exceptionally careful to maintain the distance required of our respective stations within this household.

"Are you well?" I reach out and take her hands in mine. "Is Father…" I clear my throat and start over. "Is he treating you well?" Each time I leave this place, my fear for Rosalie grows more intense.

"Yes, *Señorita,*" Rosalie lowers her voice. "As well as can be expected—considering." Her furtive gaze flits around the courtyard, looking for anyone who shouldn't be listening in.

Those words nearly stop my heart.

"Has Matias…?"

"No." Quick to respond, her response is louder than safe. Rosalie presses her lips together and releases my hands. "I only meant things are as good as can be expected considering the untimely death of your cousin, Miguel, not too long ago." She gives another squeeze, trying to tell me something important.

"Of course. Such a loss to the family."

Miguel is a distant cousin and a criminal. Former leader of the *Coralos* cartel, he met justice as he lived life—suddenly and in violence. He found himself on the wrong side of a bullet. An order, I assume, issued by my father.

The *Coralos* cartel controls territory to the south, where the richest deposits of natural resources are located within Nicaragua. Father wants access to those resources and the riches that follow after extracting them from the land, destroying millions of acres of rainforest in the process.

Miguel's death means little to me, but out of everyone, he's the one I thought might help me. Sadly, Father took care of the barrier Miguel's continued existence presented to his aspirations of power.

"So, Matias hasn't…?" I need to know he hasn't touched my friend.

"His tongue is as sharp as always, and he doesn't make things easy, but he abides by your father's wishes." More formal than expected, Rosalie is trying to tell me something.

As far as Matias goes, he has eyes for my dear friend. His intentions are not only less than honorable, they're downright cruel. He wants Rosalie. He has since the first day she came to work for us so many years ago. He wants her because hurting her hurts me. The man is vicious and depraved.

Father protects Rosalie, forcing Matias to keep his hands off my friend, but not because he cares about what happens to her. She's nothing more than a distraction that makes his daughter happy. Not to mention, having a companion, like my governess promised, keeps me out of my father's hair and out from underfoot. It allows him to run his businesses and pursue his never-ending quest for power, uninterrupted from the distraction a daughter creates.

However, there will come a time when Rosalie is no longer safe.

"Congratulations on your graduation." Rosalie beams with pride. "*Summa cum laude*, not that it should be a surprise. You've always excelled in your studies."

The same can be said of Rosalie. One of the benefits of being my companion is Rosalie joined me in my studies with my governess. Lucinda felt competition sharpened young minds. It's an education Rosalie otherwise would've never received. As for Rosalie, she's a gifted student; a talent wasted in service as a maid.

It's a shame she couldn't join me in California, but Father refused, saying I didn't need a maid in college. He knows we're close —too close for his comfort—but he likes to make me happy, which means Rosalie isn't mistreated when I'm gone, and none of the guards touch her—including Matias.

It's the one thing I'm thankful for when it comes to my father. He dotes on his daughter, but that will end the day he hands me to another man. A chill slithers down my spine. Rosalie takes note of the sudden change in my mood.

"I thought you were hoping to go to graduate school?" Her fingers tighten on mine, showing concern.

"Father summoned me home."

"Why?" Her eyes round with concern.

"He intends for me to marry Artemus Gonzales."

A shadow darkens my friend's face.

When I leave my family's home, Father's promises regarding

Rosalie end. Even if she comes with me, Father will no longer control what happens to her. That would be up to my husband.

If Matias is bad, Artemus is ten times worse.

One day, I hope to free Rosalie from all of this, but that day is not today.

The tower bell rings, alerting all to the changing of the hour.

"I have to go." With great reluctance, I release Rosalie's hands. Dinner service begins promptly at eight, and tardiness is not allowed.

"Be careful, Carmen." Rosalie wrings her hands. "Something is wrong in this house." She closes her eyes and presses her lips together.

She's aware of my desire to end all of this, but there are some things I do that can't be shared with anyone, especially Rosalie. To apprise her only puts her in danger, but she's not dumb.

"I've done nothing except refuse Artemus." It's a lie, not one I tell Rosalie. It's for whoever might be listening to our conversation. "Why?"

Rosalie steps close and grips my upper arms. It's familiar, but not out of the ordinary for the two of us. She leans in and whispers very low. "I overheard Matias telling your father they are close to figuring out who the traitor is in their ranks. I fear for you."

Her words make my heart skip a beat, but I show no outward reaction to Rosalie's words.

I can't.

It's too dangerous.

SIX

Rafe

We move as silent as death through the grand villa that belongs to Nicaragua's Minister of the Interior. Zeb and I take out every man we come across with the tranquilizer darts. Bullets would be better, but tranqs have their uses.

They're whisper quiet and nonlethal.

People think silencers on weapons makes them silent. It's one of the biggest lies out there. Those things are most definitely not quiet, and their distinctive sound sends, or brings, men running.

Men, in this case, being armed guards responsible for keeping Maximus Angelo safe within his own residence. Other people, not guards, run from that sound.

But the darts… These things are wicked cool. The noisiest thing about them is the tiniest pop as I squeeze the trigger. Their flight through the air is imperceptible. When they strike our targets, there's maybe a slap if the guy thinks an insect bit him.

After that?

The men take half a step before falling to the floor. Can't do shit about the thud, but otherwise—silent as a sleeping newborn babe.

Point being, tranqs don't attract attention, and they don't give their targets time to raise an alarm. That's what I worried about when we were told this was a nonlethal operation.

Once the men are down, we tie them up and tuck them out of the way.

Humidity clings to the night's air, thickening it, and holds in the floral abundance of this tropical climate. The sweet, but thick, air muffles our boot steps and silences the movement of the enemy.

But that's not a problem.

We know where they are.

Mitzy's scores of tiny drones are everywhere—mapping out the structure, following the movements of the men, and searching for hidden passages.

Using nothing but hand signals, Bravo team moves down long hallways and across impressive courtyards without being seen.

Mitzy guides us using our HUDs. Her tiny dragonfly drones alert us to guards in our path. We move around them if we can or duck out of sight if we can't. If we can't avoid them, Zeb and I put them to sleep with the tranqs.

It takes some time, but we move to our final position. The dining room is just ahead.

A low wall separates the corridor we're in from the dining room on the other side. Heated voices argue back and forth, switching wildly between English and Spanish.

"Hold for the waitstaff to clear the room." CJ's voice crackles through our headsets.

The plan is for Brady and Booker to enter first. The rest of us rearrange our two-man teams, placing a sniper in each one. Hayes joins me while Zeb moves with Alec to guard our rear.

It won't be long.

While we wait, I go over the next phase of the mission in my head, playing it out and looking for holes.

Exfil will be on foot. Two miles through farmers' fields, over hedgerows, and through dense undergrowth of the encroaching rainforest. With the number of guards stationed here, I'm not a fan of our current plan. Using my tongue to activate my mic, I get ready to voice my concerns, but Booker beats me to it.

"Thoughts on exfil?" Booker's subvocalization crackles in my HUD.

"Challenging," Brady responds. "We're going to make noise."

"Agree." Booker pulls out a flashbang. "If we're going to make noise, let's start off with a bang."

Brady taps the side of his helmet and tells Command and Control we're shifting to the back-up exfil plan. It's riskier, places us in an exposed position, but it's much faster than running through fields with Izzy in tow.

Brady counts down while Booker gets ready to toss the flashbang into the dining room. Nonlethal, it's not without significant physical effects. In addition to temporary blindness, it can rupture the eardrums of anyone who's too close. That blast is known to cause concussive injury, knocking a person out, but it's nonlethal, and that's what we need.

When Brady calls it, Booker throws the flashbang. We turn away from the blinding flash and our helmets cut out the noise, protecting our hearing. The moment the flashbang goes off, Brady and Booker rush the room. Hayes and I follow on their heels.

I check for guards while Hayes tosses a second flashbang behind a door leading into the kitchen. Less than a breath later, the second flashbang goes off.

Maximus Angelo is down, curled into a fetal position. As our medic, Booker checks the man's pulse. He lifts Izzy into his arms, but not until she rips her rabbit's foot necklace from around Maximus Angelo's neck.

There's another person in the room. A woman cups her ears and rocks back and forth on the floor where she fell out of her chair.

Who is she?

Mitzy would know. As for me, the woman is unimportant. For a moment, I consider shooting her with one of the tranquilizer darts, but she's no threat. Not in that dress and definitely not in those heels.

Maximus Angelo is out like a light. The woman watches us and shoots me a defiant glare when she notices me looking at her.

I expect fear. In black tactical gear, I'm bloody scary as shit.

What I don't expect is the fire in her eyes and the challenge they send.

For the briefest of moments, I consider yanking her up and hauling her out of here. We know Maximus Angelo traffics women through this place, but I doubt he invites them to dinner.

Booker carries Izzy out of the room. Brady's right on his heels. Done with the dining room, it's time to make it to our extraction point. I leave the woman and race out of the room with my team.

SEVEN

Carmen

WITH MY HEART LODGED IN MY THROAT, I APPROACH THE SITTING room adjacent to the dining room. Two voices converse in harsh tones. One belongs to Father, the other a woman.

Rounding the corner, I come to a sudden stop.

It's the woman Matias dragged through the halls earlier. Only she's no longer filthy and disheveled. She wears one of my older dresses—my dress!—looking fabulous with flourishes of Rosalie's signature hair and makeup touches.

Who is this woman? And how dare she?

When she was with Matias earlier, I assumed she was one of the cretin's newest acquisitions. Papa likes to reward Matias by throwing him a bone from time to time. Unfortunately, Matias is destructive of his pets, and he was very clear this woman belonged to Papa, not him.

If I could, I'd sweep through this house like a vengeful angel, smiting the evil that lives inside these walls. Papa may be a prominent political figure, second only to the president, but he's rotten to the core.

There will come a time when I no longer have to stand by and do nothing, but that day is not today. Which means I must be callous and cruel to this woman.

Papa expects it.

He stands with his arm wrapped around the woman's waist. From her rigid posture and how she keeps space between her body and his, she's not here of her own free will.

Bringing her to dinner is a test, but who is Papa testing?

Me? Or the woman?

After four years abroad, my loyalty needs to be checked. Something like this is expected, but what about the woman?

What threat keeps her obedient and docile?

The fury swirling in those incredible blue eyes says she operates under severe duress.

But what? What does my father hold over her head?

She's going to need to learn fast if she intends to survive.

As for me, my life is made up of a nonstop string of tests. Her test will be far worse than mine.

What are the chances this random woman is joining us for dinner on the same night I return home? In my world, there's no such thing as coincidence. This is a test for us both. Obedience for her and loyalty for me?

That feels like something my father would enjoy.

It's amazing how much the woman and I look alike. Wearing similar silk gowns, the fabric of her dress clings to her natural curves and pools at her ankles. Unlike me, however, the woman wears no heels. Surprised Father would allow such a thing, I take note.

As I do, he follows my assessment of the woman closely. My eye catches at the missing heels, while he waits to see what I make of his dinner companion.

Her flowing, waist-long hair is the same length as mine. Unlike the deep brown of my hair, hers is true raven black, complete with bluish-black highlights. We're the same height. The same build. She's only a few years older than me. Unlike my chocolate-colored eyes, however, hers are a startling cornflower blue. In those eyes, there is nothing but fear and seething hatred.

I return a different but similar emotion.

Disgust.

People often comment on how I favor my mother. Except for my eyes. They're the same dark chocolate as Father's. Mother, however, had a light cornflower-blue gaze.

My attention shifts to my father. He arches a brow but says nothing. Perhaps waiting to see what I will say first? This entire evening is going to be one test after another, and I'll pass each one.

As for this woman, she could be my mother's twin. Bad luck for her because that's going to get her killed. Not a quick death, but one that comes at the end of a very painful lesson.

I see why Father decided to keep her for himself. He could never give such a woman to Matias; at least not until he breaks her first.

It's her anger that draws him. It swirls in her eyes and cries out in challenge.

He likes when women fight back, and this woman is ready to claw out his eyes and spit in his face. Given a different place, a different world, there's a possibility we could be friends.

I like her attitude and fighting spirit but refuse to allow her to ruin my plans. They've been in the making since I was a kid. Therefore, I ignore the tension spiking the air and focus on my needs.

"Papa…" I lift my arms in greeting and wait for my father to release the strange woman.

"Carmen, you are as beautiful as ever." He welcomes me with a perfunctory kiss to both my cheeks. "But you should not be here. You were to spend the week with Artemus and his mother planning your wedding."

Here it comes. The second test of the evening.

Allowing me to get my BTA degree—Been to America—and graduate from UCSF carries great risk. He's right to be concerned about the influence my American friends have when it comes to how I look at my life now.

Refusing Artemus places that concern front and center. Father won't allow the affront against Artemus and his mother to stand. It's a problem, and depending on how desperate I become, carries a most elegant solution.

American women enjoy freedoms that don't exist in my country.

They focus on individual rights over others, whereas respect for my elders, knowing my rightful place, and faithfulness to God defines mine.

This may be one test I fail to pass, but I knew that going in. These next few weeks will be rocky as I adjust to home and remember how a daughter obeys her father without question. For now, however, I'm due the tiniest bit of insolence.

"Artemus is a dog. I'm not marrying him." Papa expects impertinence. I give it to him in spades.

"Carmen…" Anger bunches in his brows and coils in his muscles. His eyes narrow dangerously as his muscles flex beneath his expensive suit. "You had better not…"

"Papa, don't you want your only daughter to be happy?" I play darling daughter to ease the sting of my words.

"Happiness has nothing to do with it."

"But I don't favor him." I want to discuss this further, but not in front of the strange woman.

Until I know what she means to my father, she doesn't need to know anything about me. I shift gears, taking control of the conversation away from my father. There's no way he's going to scold me in front of this woman.

"And who is this?" I extricate myself from my father's embrace and inject as much derision into my tone as possible.

Father draws the woman close.

"I introduce to you Miss Isabelle LaCroix. Isabelle, this is my daughter, Carmen Angelo, my pride and joy, if not troublesome daughter."

"Papa, you are so funny." Keeping my voice light and my thoughts shallow, this is how I survive.

"Um, it's nice to meet you."

The woman dares address me? I give her an irate look, then shift my attention to my father.

"What brings her here?" I dismiss the woman—exactly as my father expects. "Another of your toys?"

"Isabelle is one of the doctors Cousin Miguel took for ransom. She returned my property."

Property? What property? I hate working in the blind.

"I see." In this place, property means many things. Since I don't know if he's talking about women, guns, drugs, diamonds, or information, I limit my response.

What my father's involved in isn't a secret. The details, however, are highly confidential.

I assess the woman from head to toe, then dismiss her as beneath notice with a flick of my lashes.

"My father loves beautiful women, Miss LaCroix, but tires of them quickly. Best not to get too attached. He will abandon you, but not before using you first."

"Carmen." Father's voice cracks like a whip. "Show a little respect for my guest."

"That's what I'm doing, Papa. Showing little respect." With that, I execute a perfect pirouette and glide into the dining room in my four-inch heels.

Father's only a step behind, dragging the woman behind him. She doesn't withdraw from my father's touch like most of his women do at the beginning. Is it possible he's had this woman long enough to reach the docile stage? Or is the threat he holds over her head that powerful?

What's missing in her demeanor is acceptance of her fate. Which makes me think she's a recently acquired indulgence. I don't like it when things don't make sense. Odd how she withdraws from me, but not my father. Interesting how he calls out how she's one of the doctors Cousin Miguel took for ransom. That's the kidnapping that resulted in Miguel's death.

Too coincidental.

Who are you? And why are you important to my father?

"One of the doctors Miguel kidnapped?" I pretend ignorance and tap my lacquered fingernails on the table, but Father will get too suspicious if I don't show my claws. "Was that before, or after, you issued a kill order on Miguel?"

Miss LaCroix gasps and I pivot to address her. "The man who died was my cousin; second to me, first to Papa. Shot in the back of the head. Killed like a dog because he dared to disagree with my father. Take that lesson to heart. Bad things happen to those who don't do as my father says."

"I had nothing to do with Miguel's murder." Father struggles to control his anger. "You tread on thin ice—daughter."

I strike a nerve. How curious?

"The men who rescued Isabelle murdered Miguel," my father says. "Not me. They will pay for that affront."

A ripple of fear rushes through the woman. It begins at the crown of her head and wiggles down her spine. Her reaction interests me because it may be something I can use later.

"I highly doubt that. You've been after Miguel for years about mining rights on his land."

If someone doesn't stand up to my father, he will rape Nicaragua. It'll be cloaked in lies; touted as the path of progress, but the people of Nicaragua will reap none of those rewards. Their living conditions will not change and likely worsen.

He'll get richer as the people scrape out an existence from one day to the next, barely holding on until they become nothing more than slaves.

The servants clear our dinner plates in complete silence, then retreat, leaving us alone.

"My father is not the man you think he is." I have no idea what this woman thinks about my father, and I don't care.

This show is one I put on for my father's benefit. I tread a narrow path, with danger on both sides if I falter.

I must be loyal and obedient to my father, yet independent enough not to draw suspicion. Papa has no son, and Miguel, despite his loyalty, was not educated enough to take over the family business. That leaves Matias, who my father will never put in that position, and Artemus, who is my father's last chance for a male heir. That son, if ever conceived, will be raised and corrupted by my father. I'll have nothing to do with his upbringing, and that is something I cannot allow.

Handicapped at birth by the unfortunate inconvenience of inheriting the wrong set of chromosomes, my father won't be leaving his legacy to me. He will skip me and wait for the grandson he craves. As for Artemus, he's business savvy. His mother may have worked in the fields, but Artemus is a shark when it comes to managing companies and making money. He's eager to climb the social ladder, trading political favors for wealth. He and my father are a match made in heaven. My worth is in the grandson I'll one day produce. For that, my father will pay handsomely.

As I can't lash out at my father, my anger finds another victim. I turn toward Isabelle LaCroix and let venom drip from my words.

"Be very careful jumping into his bed, although it's probably too late for that. Fair warning, it will be the last decision you make. Women in this household are not free to make their own decisions."

Not free.

That's what I need Father to hear. However, there's a difference between not being free and manipulating my father to get what I want.

"Another word and…" Father slams his fist on the table.

"And, what?" I gesture at the dress Isabelle LaCroix wears. "You'll give her away like you did me?" More tapping of my polished fingernails on the table conveys my anger. "She's a pretty thing, but dressing her in my discarded clothing does not make her…"

"Don't you dare finish that sentence."

A thrill runs through me with the anger lacing Father's words.

"I did not give you away." His voice rises, filling the room.

"You arranged a loveless marriage to a man twice my age, without my consent and against my wishes. That's the very definition of giving me away."

I want to go to grad school, obtain my master's degree in environmental sciences and ecological preservation. It's a vital tool in my arsenal to combat Father's plans to rape our country.

Since I was a little girl, I watched him manipulate people into giving him what he wanted. A strategist, my father's brilliant at chess. He knows what pieces he needs to take and when to take them to ensure his bid for power goes uncontested.

The thing is—my father taught me how to play. In an uncharacteristic bout of camaraderie, he taught me a secret code he developed that uses the movement of chess pieces, and his particular form of shorthand, to spell out words. That's a secret very few people know, but it's been years since he and I played a game. As a result, I learned how he thinks, how he baits his adversaries, and how he turns weakness into a win.

He miscalculated when he taught me how to play chess. As a result, I'm exceptionally skilled at playing the long game as well. Heck, I've been playing it since I was ten.

One of those moves happens right now.

A strategic sacrifice.

"What did Artemus do to secure my hand in marriage?"

"Mind your tone with me, girl. You're dangerously close to crossing a line you don't want to cross." Papa launches a warning shot, demanding obedience.

"I'm not marrying him." Leaning back, I fold my arms over my chest.

"You will."

"You promised me to a man nearly twice my age, consigning me to a holy union that can't be broken, and for what? What does my hand in marriage do to further the great Maximus Angelo's agenda? I have a right to know my worth."

Fury sweeps through my father at my impertinence. To my knowledge, no woman's ever talked back to him the way I do now. His face turns beet red and his eyes rage with thunderous anger.

"You will learn your place, Daughter."

"I know my place, Papa. You never let me forget it."

Our conversation devolves into a shouting match. He says I will marry Artemus. I stand firm, saying I will not. I demand a stay of execution, stating I will attend graduate school first. He tells me my education is complete. There's no reason to waste more time on an education I'll never use.

Our conversation turns heated. We switch back and forth between English and Spanish while his dinner guest's eyes practically bug out of her head. She pushes back from the table, uncomfortable, but the moment she moves, Father points at her.

"Don't you dare move."

I keep up the argument, yelling at my father about how Artemus is fat, old, and stupid.

"His mother is a peasant, Father. A peasant!" My words slip to Spanish as I argue for my life. "You would have me marry beneath my station? When there are other men, better positioned than Artemus, to give you what you want."

"What do you know about what I want?"

"Don't insult me. I've watched you move your little chess pieces across the board since my *Quinceañera*. I'm not a little girl anymore, Papa. I know what you want, and you won't get it with Artemus. I can be of use to you. Let me put what I've learned to good use."

Father wants to grab mineral and mining rights in southern Nicaragua. That will give him enough power, wealth, and financial backing to take control of Nicaragua for good.

Isabelle LaCroix leaves us to our screaming match, growing more and more uncomfortable as the argument escalates. She glances toward the door and my attention shifts with hers.

Something shiny and fist-sized sails in an arc over her head. It drops to the floor behind my father with a clunk. Next I know, a blinding flash and concussive blast knock me out of my seat.

EIGHT

Carmen

The explosion leaves me screaming as pain rips through my ears. The blinding light blows out my vision.

I swallow acrid smoke and breathe in caustic fumes. My father, who was closest to the blast, falls out of his chair. He cups his ears. Curls in on himself. Then his entire body goes limp.

Dead or unconscious?

Is it bad I prefer one over the other?

Vision returns slowly, proceeded by flickering afterimages and spots dancing in my eyes. Then, in the thick smoke, dark shapes swarm in, moving like wraiths all around me.

One of them comes for Isabelle LaCroix.

She reaches for the man with familiarity, as if she knows him. He scoops her into his arms, holding her with incredible tenderness. She clings to his broad shoulders as he checks for a pulse in my father's neck. Suddenly, she leans forward and rips something from around my father's neck, holding it close as if it's some great treasure.

This woman...she's not a random acquisition. Is this why my father took her? To flush out her rescuers? It sounds like something my father would do. He does nothing without reason and always plays the long game. Ninety-nine percent of the time, it's not what someone might think. A seemingly unimportant movement of a pawn hides a greater strategy.

What game are you playing, Father?

This woman is a pawn, and this rescue serves a purpose. He's confirming what he already knows. Or what he thinks he knows. These men—or the outfit they work for—are my father's goal.

None of this comes as a surprise. Maybe the timing of this rescue catches my father off guard, but not his expectation of the outcome.

This woman is important. She means something.

But what?

Whatever that is… Whatever importance my father attaches to these men, I need to know how it impacts my plans.

I'm nothing if not my father's daughter. I, too, play a dangerous game.

In refusing marriage to Artemus, I force my father to question my loyalty. No longer demure and obedient, bending to his wishes, that move plants a seed of doubt in my father's mind.

But I did come back.

I didn't refuse marriage to Artemus. I asked for a few years of reprieve to work on my graduate degree. Not to mention, the engagement caught me by surprise and forced a reckless move.

Time to recover and show my father how devoted I am. How I'll risk my life to save his. If nothing else, he must believe I will do anything for him. My survival depends on it.

One of the men in black opens the door leading into the kitchen. He throws another grenade, or smoke bomb, disabling our servants.

Where are our guards?

They should be swarming the place.

Protecting my father.

Protecting me.

But they're not here.

No response from any of my father's men.

With my ears still ringing, I crawl to my father's side. Spots dance in my vision as it recovers from the blinding flash of light. The dense smoke stings my eyes, forcing tears to blur what little vision I have. The men fade back into the smoke, leaving me and my father alone.

Why would they do that?

From the steady rise and fall of my father's chest, death is not the outcome of this rescue. Papa is not their objective.

They mean to keep him alive.

Me too.

Too many questions swirl in my head, but one thing is certain. Now, more than ever, my father must not question my loyalty, but after Rosalie's hurried whisper, staying here may be far too dangerous.

I disobeyed when I refused Artemus. That puts me at odds with my father. To accomplish my goals, he must trust me implicitly, but I need time to figure out my next move. Only, there's no time to think.

Leaning down, I cup my hand over his ear and raise my voice. If his hearing is anything like mine, and it's got to be, I need to be certain he hears me.

"Papa, I will avenge you." I take his hand in mine. "I'll find them and make them pay." Tears spill from my eyes.

I'd like to say I'm a great actor, but it's the smoke irritating my eyes. Those tears mean nothing.

When I lean over my father, my hand reaches down to grasp his. I restate what I said, yelling louder than before. If he doesn't hear me, the recordings he'll view later will reveal my distress and my vow. I only hope he'll believe what happens next. Lifting the back of his hand to my lips, I place a tender kiss over his knuckles.

"No matter what it takes, I will find out who did this to you."

His lids flutter and he tries to speak. Before he can forbid me, I shift from my knees to my feet, knowing there's no time to spare.

His hand drops to the floor as I kick off my four-inch heels and give my father one last look. In that look, I promise retribution. Turning toward the corner of the room, where the hidden surveillance camera sits, fury and vengeance fill my expression.

In this game, adaptability is the key to survival, and I'll be damned if I'm not the epitome of a survivor.

I leave my father to process my words as he sees fit. All I care about is getting out of this hellhole and reestablishing contact with those who promise to make the nightmare that is my life end for good. With those four-inch heels left behind, I hike up my dress and race behind the men who rescued Isabelle LaCroix.

NINE

Rafe

_____

With the noise we make, the few guards who aren't _tranq'd_ come running. Pops of gunfire sound all around us. Brady and Booker move out with me and Hayes right on their heels. We pass Alec and Zeb, who protect our retreat.

With Booker encumbered by Izzy, Brady stays tight by his side, protecting him. This leaves Hayes and me to race ahead and clear the way.

It's chaos, but this is where years of intensive training come into play. Men rush us from behind and are taken out by Alec and Hayes. Another group assaults from the front. I fill them with tranquilizer darts until that gun empties, then switch to a real weapon.

The only person we've been expressly ordered not to kill is out cold in the dining room. We navigate through the long halls until reaching one of many courtyards. It's the biggest and, unlike the others, this one is empty.

Booker places Izzy on her feet. Brady covers them. The rest of us take care of the last of the guards.

Disorientated from the flashbang, Izzy sways on her feet. She points to her ears when Booker attempts to brief her how we're getting out of here. No surprise, she's temporarily deaf.

Undeterred, Booker pulls nylon straps out of his utility pocket. While we wait for the helicopter, he fashions a harness for Izzy, working efficiently while the rest of us stand guard and wait.

Whomp, whomp, whomp.

Deep vibrations pulse in the air as a helicopter approaches. I fire off a few shots down the hall, taking out two guards, while a thick rope drops out of the sky. Brady grabs the rope and pulls it over to Booker.

Izzy's eyes widen as she takes in the helicopter hovering overhead. While Booker clips into the line, Brady double-checks the carabiner attaching Izzy's makeshift harness to Booker's solid frame. Once he's satisfied, Brady moves down the rope where he attaches himself next in line.

The intense downdraft from the helicopter kicks up grit and sand. Thankful for the helmet, which prevents any of that from getting in my eyes, I focus down the hall, defending my team as they hook into the line.

Alec, Hayes, and Zeb snap in. As the team sniper, I'm last man on the rope. Falling back, I stow my weapon, clipping it to my tactical vest, but only long enough to hook into the line.

Above me, Hayes takes over my role. Assisted by Alec and Zeb above him, they pick off the last of the guards.

The solid snick of the carabiner is felt more than heard. Double-checking the attachment, I hold out my hand, thumbs up, stating I'm set.

The helicopter rises, lifting Bravo team into the air one-by-one, beginning with Booker and Izzy. A blood-curdling shriek from above brings a grin to my face. I don't know Izzy very well, but we all know about her fear of heights.

I glance up the line to where Izzy clings to Booker feeling a little jealous of the intense bond between them. When the rope pulls on me, getting ready to lift me off my feet, I grab hold over my head and brace for the spin that invariably comes next.

Motion in my periphery catches my eye. I turn as a streak of red rushes toward me. Before I can react, the woman from the dining room throws herself at me. Hands loop over my head and clasp around my neck. Legs wrap around my hips, gripping tight.

Acting on instinct, my free hand goes to her back, pulling her toward me. I should yank her off of me and toss her down, but she desperately clings to me as we're lifted up into the air. The helicopter jerks me off my feet and climbs fast. Before I know it, we're ten, twenty, thirty feet in the air. I take my other hand and grab hold of the woman's waist, securing her in my grip.

A fall from this height will kill her if I let her go, and there's no way she's strong enough to hold on by herself. Which means, I've got to keep her from falling. Maybe my initial thought about her is wrong? Maybe she is one of Angelo's victims? It would make sense, and if that's the case, there's no way I'm letting her fall.

My hands move from her waist to her ass. Grabbing tight, all I can think of is: *What the bloody hell?*

My weapon, which should be back in my hands, is clipped off at the D-ring near my shoulder, which leaves me defenseless.

Her too.

Pops of gunfire sprinkle the air. As last man on the rope, my position is to fire back, covering the team above me. With my hands full of the woman, I can't free my weapon.

Her grip tightens and her terrified shriek pierces through the chop of the helicopter and the gunfire below. My teammates take over, peppering the ground with bullets while the muscles in my arms protest the awkward hold I have on the woman.

Her thighs tighten around my hips, pressing the heat of her core against my belly. It's distracting and overwhelming. She's barefoot, ditched the heels, which was smart. Her feet cross behind me as she clings tight. There's a little shifting of our respective grips on the other as the helicopter speeds away from the walled estate. That shifting leads to various parts of our anatomy brushing against each other. I suppress a groan as my dick wakes up to take notice.

Down, boy.

The subtle perfume of lilac and rose floods my nostrils. I take in a deep breath and close my eyes before I realize the scent comes from her. Talk about a fucking aphrodisiac? My mind goes to a million different places, all of them sexual.

My cock rises to the occasion. Starved after a year of zero action, it's ready and able.

Have I mentioned it's been a year?

With the way her legs wrap around me, her pussy rubs against my groin. The friction between us is distracting to say the least.

With the infrared enhancements of my helmet, the world is nothing but shades of black, white, and gray. Her face is a spectral glow. She stares back at me, or rather the visor of my helmet.

Her grip slips and she shrieks.

My grip tightens. She's not going anywhere. No way am I letting her fall.

Her eyes flare and her lids pull back. She twists to look down, which changes my grip. I squeeze her ass—hard—then slowly shake my head as her head whips around to look at me. With a lifting of my helmet, I tell her to look up.

A winch in the helicopter slowly draws up my team. Booker and Izzy are already inside. Brady is next. The moment Brady is up, the line draws up the next man.

Getting this woman safely into the helicopter isn't going to be easy. If I drop her, that's where it'll happen.

The slow twirl on the rope makes the canopy of the rainforest slowly spin beneath our feet. Arms aching, I try to figure out how I'm going to get this woman to safety inside the helicopter.

Another glance upwards reveals Booker and Brady standing on the helicopter skids. They move to the side as Hayes, Zeb, and Alec are winched inside. Looks like they've already given it thought.

The winch draws us up until we dangle a foot below the skids.

We're next.

"Coming down to tie her to you." Brady's voice calls out through my helmet.

The moment Zeb is inside, Brady and Booker lean away from the skids and rappel down until they're even with me. Booker locks himself on the rope, level with me. Brady does the same.

With my arms aching, I hold tight as the two of them weave a modified harness around me and the woman's chest, waist, hips, and legs, tying us together. Once done, Brady gestures asking if I'm good to go. Releasing some of the tension in my muscles, I test the modified harness. It holds, so I nod, letting them know we're good.

The winch slowly draws me and the woman in. Booker and Brody hang below us. If the harness doesn't hold, they're the last defense between the woman and certain death.

There is nothing easy about getting on board the helicopter. If I was alone, it's a matter of maneuvering up and over the skids with a pump of my muscles. By myself, not a problem. It's a simple pull up. Lift my leg over the skid. Place my foot down, then repeat. Finally stand, reach out to the interior, and scramble on board.

I can't do that with a woman tied to me.

Brady and Booker do what they can from below to stabilize the spin on the rope. Alec and Zeb tie off and stand on the skid, ready to assist. Hayes waits inside. As we're lifted to the skids, Alec and Zeb reach down and deadlift us up onto the skid. With the way her legs wrap around my hips, it's not a simple yank upward.

They have to improvise, swinging us out, up, and in. It's awkward as shit.

After a couple of false starts, they hike me up as far as my ass and set me down on the skid. They climb back up inside while Brady and Booker climb their lines and join me on the skid.

With Brady and Booker helping from below, and Alec, Hayes, and Zeb pulling from above, we finally get the woman safely inside the helicopter.

The muscles of my arms burn, nearly cramping. I sit on the floor of the helicopter and do my best not to think about this weirdly intimate embrace, or the way the woman's dress hikes up and around her hips.

Or what she's not wearing underneath.

In addition to my teammates, CJ and Sam are on board. CJ cocks his head. Sam calls in our unexpected passenger back to Command and Control.

"Got yourself a cling-on." Zeb extricates the woman from the straps tying her to me. "She's a looker, too."

"Only Rafe would have a woman jump his bones in the middle of a rescue." Alec gets in a dig, but his eyes cut to my leg. "About damn time."

"Ha ha, good one." I'm blessed in life. God gifted me with a handsome face, and I work hard to match it with a body pushed to achieve peak physical condition. I don't consider myself conceited, but Alec isn't wrong. I'm a chick magnet.

Or, at least, I used to be.

They tried to get me to go out after I recovered from my injury. I did, at first, a few times until I could no longer take the rejection of the women I tried hooking up with, as if the loss of my leg means I'm no longer whole.

Which, I'm not.

The only thing bionic about my leg is the speed with which it sends chicks away, screaming.

Despite Piper's perpetual positivity and her comments about being better than before—I think she calls it bionic—nothing is better than before.

I'm less than what I once was and nothing will change that.

"Yeah, but this is the first time he caught one with the new leg." Booker can't help but join in on teasing me.

"I knew that leg of his came with perks." Hayes chuckles while CJ and Sam try to untangle the mess Brady and Booker made with the straps.

"I've heard of tying a woman to your bed, but Rafe takes it to a whole other level, hooking one with your bionic leg." Zeb's laughter brings a frown to my face.

I don't talk to the guys about my leg. We kind of ignore the whole thing. We put that explosion in Cancun on the shelf of don't touch it, but the truth is—none of us are the same.

Brady's burned. I lost a leg. Hayes lost two fingers. Zeb and Alec were peppered with shrapnel. Sounds like nothing, except that shrapnel almost cost Zeb the use of his lower legs as it nestled right alongside his spinal cord.

Zeb is closest to me, so I haul off and punch him in the arm. He dances away laughing. "Now that he caught one, who wants to bet on how long he keeps her?" Fucker isn't letting it go. "If she's like any other chick, she'll be gone by morning."

CJ and Sam finally get the woman and me separated. I scramble to my feet as CJ guides her to one of the webbed seats, putting her in the middle. He buckles her in while I try to keep the others from noticing my stare. The woman is stunning.

"Y'all are jealous." I feel a need to defend my manhood. "My women come in the morning and keep coming through noon." I grab at my crotch, making a rude gesture.

None of them know how dry my dry spell really is. If they knew it's been over a year, they wouldn't believe me. Out of us all, I'm definitely a bit of a Casanova with no woman being off-limits. As long as she's over eighteen…

Tapping the side of my helmet, I switch from night vision to normal vision. The woman sits rigidly in her seat in a body-hugging, hot as sin, red silk dress. Damn, but she has curves I'd love to get lost in.

She trades stares with Izzy, then looks at me. With a lift of her chin, the woman gives a sniff of disdain. Did she notice my leg?

Well, screw you.

So much for gratitude.

Don't know if it's because I grabbed at my crotch, or something else, but I take offense at the dismissal. Is it because she noticed the difference between my two legs? I'm good enough to cling to, but now that she's safe, I'm beneath her?

Not that I expect thanks, but would it hurt to show a bit of appreciation for saving her life? I try to force her from my thoughts, pretending she's no longer my problem.

But then, she has to go and curl in on herself, wrapping her arms around her shoulders, looking forlorn, lost, and so very afraid. The Guardian within me stumbles. I'm genetically programmed to defend, to save, to shelter, and to protect.

I've never seen such vulnerability.

She looks like she could use a hug. I take half a step toward her, thinking to provide some kind of comfort, but she looks away.

Okay then, I tried.

TEN

Carmen

¡Madre de Dios!

I didn't think this through.

Hands shaking, heart slamming, my breaths saw in and out. I left my stomach and common sense somewhere in the jungle canopy far below. But I survived that dizzying, harrowing ride over the tree-tops with nothing but a stranger keeping me from plummeting to my certain death.

I've heard of people's lives flashing before their eyes. Mine didn't do that. Instead, it played on an endless loop while I cried out in my head.

My work's not done.

My penance remains incomplete.

I vowed to destroy everything my father's built, and I refuse to die until that's done. Instead, I find myself here, with these men, and the force of the helicopter pulsing deep within my chest.

Whomp, whomp, whomp.

One of the men who's not wearing the face-concealing helmet taps me on the shoulder. His mouth moves, but no sound reaches me. Pointing to my ear, I shake my head. He seems to understand because he gestures toward a row of webbed seats. Extending his hand, he helps me to my feet. With his assistance, I separate from the man who held me on the rope with an odd feeling in my chest.

Somehow, I feel—less.

Which makes no sense.

Glancing back, I try to catch his eye, but all I see is my reflection in the visor of his helmet. The man helping me leads me to a seat, and with his assistance, I buckle in. Then he leaves me alone to think about what happens next.

Did my performance convince my father of my unwavering loyalty? Does he believe I'm brave enough to chase after strangers in defense of him? Did he see his fearless and loyal daughter? Or did he see a coward running away?

The answer to those questions will determine my fate. One will bring certain death. The other may very well allow me to live long enough to fulfill my vow and destroy my father for good.

I wish I'd thought things through better. I could've led the men to believe I was a prisoner, like Isabelle LaCroix. They wouldn't have left me behind. There's a chance Father would believe Isabelle LaCroix's rescuers accidentally took me, but they showed no interest in saving me.

The one who looked at me in the dining room turned on his heel and left me behind. I don't know which of the men that was. They all look the same in their black tactical gear and helmets with full face shields.

Having them rescue me would solve the problem I faced staying behind. My father is determined I marry Artemus. I saw it in his eyes. If the men rescued me, I wouldn't be available for a hasty marriage. But they didn't care about me. They left me behind. Which forced a drastic decision that makes little sense now that I have time to think about it.

Will my father believe I care enough to avenge him? Will he believe loyalty forced me to chase after armed men? I've never done anything that brash before, and never anything this dangerous. But he needs to believe I'm on his side—at least until my work is done.

Am I good enough to pull this off? Can I play both sides of a very dangerous game?

My split-second decision leaves me in an unfamiliar place with a military organization I don't know. Do these people work for the CIA? That would help, but it's not something I can ask. Until I reestablish communication with my contact, that's a card I hold close to my chest.

Trust no one. Rely on no one, but yourself. Above all else, tell no one anything about what you plan to do. The words of my contact with the CIA run through my mind. It's a good reminder because I'm desperate enough to want to trust someone—anyone.

The acrid combination of aviation fuel and machine oil flood the air and coat my tongue. I place my palm against the webbing beneath me, needing to feel its substance and know I'm safe. I prefer its solidity to the nothingness of air.

Unrelenting heat beats at me, leaving beads of perspiration coating my skin. The thick, humid air makes it hard to breathe, and my ears throb from that explosive charge. My hearing's slowly coming back, and my vision's no longer blurry.

I take inventory of where I am and the men carrying weapons as if they're extensions of themselves.

Big men.

Scary men.

Eight men plus myself and Isabelle LaCroix sit inside the helicopter; plus, two pilots.

Out of my element and outnumbered, I've never felt so vulnerable.

Or so scared.

But Isabelle LaCroix doesn't fear these men. She sits with one of them. Hands clasped; that's relief on her face. Not fear. The way the man sitting with her curves his body protectively around her conveys a depth of emotion I barely grasp.

I curl inward, and my shoulders hunch. Try as I might, I can't disappear.

All eyes are on me, probably thinking exactly the same thing. They want to know who the crazy woman is who crashed their rescue.

I'd tuck my chin to my chest if I could, but my terrified gaze flits around the open bay of the helicopter, too scared to latch onto any one person, yet too frightened not to take it all in.

I can't believe what I did. What was I thinking?

Escape…

That tiny voice in my head whispers an answer I'm not ready to accept.

The next question—one I really need an answer to—is did I ruin a lifetime of preparation by this impulsive act? Should I have stayed behind and hoped the hasty words Rosalie whispered about a traitor were wrong?

I desperately think about what my next step needs to be.

Do I gather what information I can about who these men are, then return to Father demonstrating my loyalty? Do I attempt to disappear and leave everything behind me? Can I live with that decision? Not likely. I'd never leave Rosalie behind. Not to mention, I lack the resources to disappear. Father will find me. Forgoing that, there's no way I'm running away.

I live with a dirty secret. Evil things happen in my home; despicable acts perpetrated on innocent women and children. I've known about it for years and my inaction makes me complicit in my father's crimes, but who could I tell? Like the clergy, all the police are bought and paid for. He plays rival cartels against one another for fun. The priests belong to him. There's no help there.

I have *no one* to tell. No one to help me bring an end to the injustice occurring within my home.

My greatest dishonor—an unforgivable sin and irreparable fall from grace—is that I've waited this long to do anything. In doing nothing, I'm as morally corrupt and villainous as my father.

Evil runs in my veins.

I hang my head and try to contain the unease fluttering in my gut. I thought I found a way to redeem myself, only to come home and discover my father's intentions effectively ruined years of planning.

Rosalie's words repeat in my head. *"They are close to figuring out who the traitor is in their ranks…"*

I've never been more scared or felt more alone.

Now, I sit with strangers with the power to determine my fate.

Did I improve my circumstance or make things worse? More importantly, will I ever escape my father's reach?

I look at Isabelle LaCroix.

The relief on her face is palpable. She's not one of the nameless victims who fill my dreams with nightmares but could very well have become one of them. What did my father want with her? What value is she to him?

I take a good, long look at Isabelle LaCroix and the way these men protect her, especially the one holding her with an emotion that transcends love.

Envy stirs within me. These men love her. They risked their lives to save hers.

I've never felt more alone and would give anything to have someone care for me with the same ferocious love these men shower upon her. Considering the lies I'm about to tell them, that will never happen.

Not knowing where we're headed, I need a good story to tell these people when we land. I can't let them leave me behind. How do I convince them to take me with them? What can I say without revealing my own plans? The easiest thing would be to pretend to be one of my father's victims, but Isabelle LaCroix knows who I am.

I nibble on the cuticle of my thumb, desperately thinking about what I'm going to say. How do I turn this mess into an advantage?

Another look at the men gives me pause. They stare. No need to hear anything. No need to see their faces to read their expressions. From body language alone, I'm the topic of their conversation, and like me, they're confused as to why I'm here.

The flight gives me a moment to figure out what to do next. These men are part of a specialized military unit sent to rescue Isabelle LaCroix. Why is she important? To them? To my father? I don't understand any of it, but it's clear she's the key.

ELEVEN

Rafe

It takes thirty minutes to fly to the airport where we'll meet up with the rest of our team. I spend every minute of that flight staring at the woman in red, wondering what would compel someone like her to take such a risk.

She's young and pretty—college-aged—slender of build except for some stunning curves. Whipped up by the wind, her dark auburn hair is a tangled mess. That imperfection does nothing to diminish her beauty. In fact, it does exactly the opposite, drawing the eye to her stunning features.

Proud and dignified, her sculpted cheekbones, enchanting eyes, high-arched brows, and long, fluttering lashes make her more than striking. She's bewitching. Add to that honeyed skin that glows from the inside out, and she's easily the most beautiful woman I've ever met.

She turns that stunning gaze on me, making me suck in a breath until I remember she can't see the dazed expression on my face. In a word, she's striking, enchanting, and exquisite.

That may be more than one word, but who the fuck cares? The woman deserves more than a single adjective to describe her beauty.

Given different circumstances, I'd consider myself lucky to have this breathtaking woman choose me. I'd take her to bed, ravish her through the night, and continue on through the day until thoroughly exhausted.

But she didn't choose me.

She latched onto a strange man clothed head to toe in black in an act of desperation.

Why would she do that? Despite her beauty, she's clearly not athletic. That's not a negative, merely an observation. She had to have known there was no way she could hold on all by herself. To place such trust in a complete stranger defies comprehension.

Unless she is desperate?

That makes more sense.

An intriguing mystery, I'm completely captivated; not by her beauty—although, let's face it, she's a looker—but by her inner strength.

What was she running from that forced her to take such a risk? Who was she running from?

I can guess the *who*.

Maximus Angelo is a powerful man and corrupt political figure. The one thing this job's taught me is how powerful men behave when they believe they're untouchable.

"Rafe," CJ calls through the headset. "Until we determine who she is, your cling-on is your problem."

"Gotcha, boss."

My problem? I'll take it. Means I get to keep her close until we figure out what to do about her.

As the helicopter lands, I shift positions with CJ, moving to stand over the woman in red. She looks up at me, then turns away to peer into the darkness toward the lights outlining the airport's runways and taxiways. Down below, a shuttle bus drives to meet us at the helipad.

Brady's out of the helicopter first, followed by Sam and CJ. Next out, Booker and Izzy exit holding hands. She clings to him as he clings to her. The dude's been out of his mind crazy, worried about his woman, but he has her now. I'm thrilled their story comes with a happy ending and hope this is really just the beginning of a very long and loving relationship.

As for my cling-on, CJ may have said she's my problem, but Bravo is a team if we're anything.

I unlatch the familiar buckles of the webbed seating, freeing her from the safety restraints. Extending a hand, it's fifty-fifty whether she'll take it with the defensive body language she's putting out there.

When she places her hand in mine, a jolt of electricity shoots up my arm. She withdraws, as if stung, and rubs her hand against the red silk of her dress.

My action mirrors hers. As I rub my palm against the seam of my trousers, the tingling sensation continues in my fingertips, giving me pause.

It's got to be the metal airframe and the static charge the helicopter carries.

I dismiss the strange sensation until my brain kicks in. That's something that might happen if one of us was grounded and the other one wasn't, but we're both in the helicopter, subjected to the same electromagnetic field. There shouldn't be any electrical shock.

Weird.

I hop out of the helicopter and gesture for her to follow.

She stares at me like I'm a poisonous viper. Instead of letting me help her out of the helicopter, she moves to the edge of the open bay, sits on the metal floor, then dangles her legs over the edge.

Alec shakes his head. I can't see his face, but his body language says it all. Bastard thinks this is funny.

As for the woman, she doesn't appear to respond to my voice, but there's no way she's scooting down from the helicopter on her own without twisting an ankle or falling altogether.

Moving in front of her, I wait for her to jump out. It's farther than it looks, and as I suspect, she misjudges the distance to the ground.

Fully dark, the black tarmac absorbs light and confuses the eye. I catch her halfway down, grabbing her around the waist and pulling her close.

Her hands settle uneasily on my shoulders, and her eyes widen as I lower her gently to the ground. We're close, kissably close, but the moment her toes touch the ground, I take a step back and remove my hands, holding them palms up and out facing toward her. Hopefully, she'll take that as a message I'm not a threat.

She's barefoot, which is a problem. Maybe not as big of an issue as I think. The sun's down. If this was during the day, the pavement would burn the soles of her feet. As it is, the surface is merely warm instead of dangerously hot against bare skin. It's also relatively smooth. So, it shouldn't hurt her feet. Nonetheless, I stand ready to carry her if she needs me to.

She takes a shaky step, grabbing onto my arm for support. Her head whips around as she takes in the shuttle bus, the helicopter, and the whole lot of nothing all around us.

The nearest buildings, aviation hangars, are a few hundred yards away across an active runway. The passenger terminal of the civilian side of the airport is farther still. If she's thinking about escape, there's nowhere for her to go.

"CJ, what do you want me to do with her?" I use my tongue to activate my mic and wait for an answer.

"Bring her with us. We'll sort it out on the way."

On the way to the jet? Or on the way back to California?

His words are unclear, and while we've transported those we've rescued across borders before without passports, it comes with a ton of red tape on the other end.

The moment she's out of the helicopter, Zeb, Hayes, and Alec form a protective ring around me as I escort the woman to the waiting shuttle. By escort, I mean wrap a hand around her upper arm and lead her to the waiting shuttle.

She holds her head high, looking braver than the trembling of her lower lip betrays. One hand presses over her stomach and her fingers flutter over her dress. I've got control of her other arm. She doesn't twist out of my grip, but I find myself growing more and more confused by her actions.

A shiver overcomes her, making her shudder and nearly trip. I slow my stroll, realizing my strides are much longer than her natural step. Not to mention, she's barefoot and walking gingerly across the tarmac.

As for that shiver, it's not cold outside. The ever-present humidity holds in the heat of the day, thickening the air and making everything uncomfortable.

I'm drenched head to toe in sweat and can't wait to rip off my body armor and change clothes for the flight home. All she has is a thin layer of silk. Maybe it's colder than I realize?

"What's your name?" Knowing the effects of the flashbang may still affect her hearing, I raise my voice to a shout.

There's the barest flinch as she steps gingerly over the blacktop. Otherwise, she appears as if she doesn't hear me.

I know otherwise.

Exchanging a glance with Zeb, he inclines his head, telling me he saw it too.

"Do we have any idea who this woman is?" I use the open channel but get no immediate response. "Are we leaving her here? Taking her with us?"

There's no answer as I escort her to the shuttle bus.

Inside the shuttle, Sam and CJ claim the front row of seats for themselves. Booker and Izzy crowd into one of the bench seats on the left, two rows back.

I gesture for the woman to climb onto the bus ahead of me but maintain my grip on her arm. We squeeze past Sam and CJ and move beyond Booker and Izzy. I don't miss the heated look exchanged between Izzy and the woman in red.

I continue all the way to the back of the shuttle, giving Alec, Hayes, and Zeb enough room to commandeer a row each for themselves. At the very last row, I gesture for her to take a seat.

She lowers herself into the middle seat and makes no move to scoot to the side and let me sit beside her. I don't blame her. I wouldn't if our roles were reversed.

She's yet to utter a word. It's one more thing that feels off. If she was a rescued kidnapping victim, shouldn't she be gushing over her saviors? Wouldn't she tell us her name and beg us to call her family? Would she fling her arms around my neck and hold me tight?

Probably no to the last question, but I wouldn't mind it. Inappropriate images follow that train of thought. With great difficulty, I focus on the mission and my professionalism, which is nearly an impossible task. It's in the gutter and going nowhere fast. The woman is drop-dead gorgeous, and my mind fills with filthy fantasies.

Bloody hell, but I need to get laid.

Since she doesn't scoot toward the windows, I remain standing in front of her. The guys take seats in the rows near us as the shuttle driver closes the front door. The vehicle lurches forward, making me sway toward the woman, unintentionally placing my crotch in her face. She rears back as I grab the back of the seat beside me and try to recover. Stabilizing myself as we drive around the airfield, I can't stop the questions flowing through my mind.

A crackle in my headset brings CJ's voice to my ears. "You're never going to guess who your cling-on is…"

TWELVE

Rafe

CLING-ON? IT'S NOT THE BEST NICKNAME TO EARN, BUT THIS ONE seems to be sticking.

The fact CJ uses the comms is telling. We're all together in a small space. He could just say it out loud. Instead, he uses the mic we all have attached to our throat. It allows us to sub-vocalize, speaking in less than a whisper. It's useful during stealth missions but seems a bit out of place here.

"Wait, don't tell us," Zeb calls out. "Are we going to take bets?" He glances around, far too eager and willing to stir shit up.

An odd protectiveness overcomes me knowing my little cling-on is the butt of their jokes.

"I'm up for that." Alec eagerly rubs his palms together.

"I'm going with trophy wife," Hayes jumps in, claiming his guess first.

"Dude, did you pay any attention to the briefing?" Zeb punches Hayes in the arm. "Maximus Angelo isn't married. His wife died over a decade ago."

More like twelve years. I'm a facts and figures kind of man with this weird knack of remembering minutia. Maximus's wife died twelve years ago, leaving a ten-year-old daughter…

Whoa, my head snaps up, and I stare at the woman sitting in front of me. She's about the right age, twenty-one, twenty-two? Could it be?

But that makes no sense. Why is she running from her father?

"He never remarried." Alec shifts in his seat. "Which is sketch."

"Sketch?" I thump the top of his helmet. "Why would that be sketchy?"

"Because the dude is powerful. Second only to *el Presidente.*" Alec gestures with a flick of his hand. "At least in Nicaragua."

"So?"

"Why wouldn't a dude like that get remarried? Doesn't he need a pretty wife dangling on his arm for all those political events?"

It's a good question. Not one I have an answer for. There could be many reasons, but I agree with Alec. It's sketchy. A man with political aspirations the size of Maximus Angelo's needs the positive public image that comes from a wife standing beside him, especially in this deeply religious country.

I pull at the collar of my shirt, hoping for a little relief from the heat.

The thought this woman might be a plaything for that bastard would churn my stomach, but I'm certain she's his daughter.

"I'm thinking we ask her." My attention shifts from my teammates to the woman curled in on herself. Her entire body shakes. It's not a chill. Most likely, it's the aftereffect of too much adrenaline dumping into her system all at once.

On closer inspection, even that is wrong. Palms clasped tight in her lap, she rocks back and forth. Head bowed, her lips barely move, but they do move. It takes a minute before I realize she's praying.

Since we're using our comms channel, she hears none of our conversation. It's the genius of sub-vocalization. Sensors over our larynx enhance the vibrations of our vocal cords to create sound that can be heard through our earpieces.

It feels wrong talking about her when she can't hear us.

Twisting around, I take a good long look at Izzy. She was an equal distance away from the flashbang when it went off. Booker appears to be carrying on a conversation with her just fine. They keep their heads pressed together, but he's not shouting. Turning back around, I take another look at our unexpected guest.

While I wonder whether I'm right, Alec, Hayes, and Zeb argue over which one of them gets to bet she's a mistress, a hooker, or kidnap victim like Izzy.

Betting is a thing we do. You name it. We bet on it. I used to lose a lot of cash until Alpha team's weird betting ritual became general knowledge among the Guardian teams. Instead of cash or coin, Alpha bets with old buttons. It has something to do with Alpha-One, but I'm fuzzy on the details.

Bottom line, it's silly and beyond weird, but the whole button-betting-thing spread throughout the teams. We all do it now.

"You're all wrong," CJ cuts through the chatter. "That is none other than Carmen Angelo."

"Maximus's daughter." I complete the thought, barely registering the words coming out of my mouth. I can't stop staring at Carmen Angelo.

"No fucking way." Brady twists in his seat. "Why the hell would Maximus Angelo's daughter hitch a ride with us?"

Hayes shakes his head and fishes out a raggedy button out of his pants pocket. He hands it to Zeb, who pockets it. When did Zeb guess she was Maximus Angelo's daughter? I shake my head and remind myself distractions can be dangerous.

As far as distractions go, Carmen Angelo is one major distraction.

Her head lifts at Brady's shout, revealing her hearing is coming back.

"I don't know," CJ says, "but we're going to find out."

"Carmen." I like the way her name roles off my tongue. I reach out and press the tip of my finger under her chin. To my surprise, she doesn't flinch and allows me to tilt her head back.

Carmen Angelo regards me with the fiercest stare I've ever seen on a woman. It's almost as if she defies me to—well, to do just about anything. I should pull back, but I can't help myself. For whatever reason, I force her chin up, then force her head to turn left, then right.

I was wrong. She's not gorgeous. The woman is absolutely stunning and royally pissed off.

Her hand darts out. Fingers wrap around my wrist and apply pressure to the nerves on my inner wrist. It's enough to bring a grown man to his knees. My legs buckle, but I stand firm as excruciating pain rips through me. She jerks her chin free and glares at me.

We share a moment, Carmen and I, testing each other's strength. That nerve thing hurts like bloody hell, but I'll be damned if I'll allow her to bring me to my knees. Clenching my teeth, I lock eyes with her and the two of us duke it out like two little kids stuck in a stupid staring contest.

For the record?

She blinks first.

Which means I win.

Carmen releases my wrist and folds her hands primly in her lab. She holds my stare for a second longer before glancing over my shoulder to take in the rest of my team. Fear rims her eyes, but a stony determination holds it in check.

Forgoing sub-vocalization, I clear my throat and speak in my normal register.

"You can hear us, can't you?" When she doesn't answer, I gesture toward Izzy. "She hears just fine, which means you do too." I cross my arms over my chest. "Wanna explain why you're here?"

Carmen leans back and folds her hands in her lap. Red lacquered nails, the same shade as her ruby-red lipstick, tap her arms.

"Not talking?" I cock my head.

I don't tell her we know who she is. Carmen's headed for an interrogation, and I won't hand over any useful intel we have on her. For now, it's best she believes we don't know who she is. That way, we'll know when she's lying.

Her lips press into a firm line and she disengages, turning her attention out the window to the waiting jumbo jet outside. The shuttle slows down, lurching to a stop at the very end. Instead of accidentally shoving my crotch in her face, like I did when we took off, I take a step back to steady myself. My grip on the back of the seats keeps me in place.

As soon as the driver opens the door, everyone piles out of the shuttle. Outside, Sam and CJ take Carmen from me. Sam grabs one arm. CJ takes the other. They corral her between them, manhandling her more than she deserves.

I get it.

Until they understand why she's here, they don't want to give her any chance to escape. Not that she would. The woman risked her life to be here.

But why she did that remains the million-dollar question. Is she escaping her father? Or is she acting as his agent and the whole escape is an elaborate ruse to ferret out who Guardian HRS is?

For what? What would they hope to gain?

We won't know until we question her, and knowing Guardian HRS interrogation techniques, I pray she's ready for what comes next.

As they escort Carmen onto the plane, she turns to look at me. It's almost desperate how she searches for me. Once our gazes connect, the tension in her body eases. Not that it disappears altogether. Her brows scrunch as an unreadable expression ripples across her beautiful face. There's fear, comfort, and something else; a longing of sorts.

Like everything, Guardian HRS doesn't go small with the company jet. The jumbo jet's interior was completely scrapped and remade. Every seat is first class, two on each side. They come with those privacy screens that encase you in your personal bubble, and the seats lay flat, becoming beds.

Not such a big deal, unless you're a guy like me. I've flown first class overseas more times than I care to count, but I'm a big guy. There's nothing worse than settling in for a long, trans-pacific flight in first class, only to find the fucking bed is four inches too short. In this jet, I can lay my seat back, tuck a pillow under my head, stretch overhead, point my toes, and there's still room to spare.

We're lucky to have Forest Summers in charge of approving

jumbo jet modifications. There's no question they took his size into consideration when designing the seats. I don't remember, but he's easily six foot eight. Maybe six ten? The dude isn't seven foot, but he's close. While he couldn't get them to make the ceiling inside the passenger bay over seven feet, he definitely ensured the rest of the plane fit a man like him. Which I find kind of curious.

During my SEAL days, we often flew in C-17s. Those are double-decker planes, handling cargo the size of tanks, deuces, and whatnot with ease. I suppose commercial builds limit what we can do.

As it is, the poor guy still has to duck his head, but I'm happy for the seats. I've slept in them plenty of times. There's room enough to spare, and I'm six foot four. Compared to Forest, I'm short. Compared to the Guardians, I'm simply average in height.

Compared to everyone else, I'm formidable. It's a wonder Carmen doesn't shrink away from my touch. *What I wouldn't give to hold her in my arms.* Hold up. Where did that come from?

It's crazy.

I know it's crazy, but holding her while we flew in the air just felt —*right.*

As if she was made for me and I was made for her.

I don't know if it's my profound dry spell or something else. Maybe the lack of sex is fucking with my brain? But we connected. I know we did. I didn't imagine it. With those thoughts swirling in my head, I move through the plane.

The front of the plane is for the *techies.* Monitors fill every spare inch of the bulkheads. It's their mobile, in-flight workspace. There's also a full-sized conference room toward the back. It's large enough to hold an entire team, along with Sam, CJ, and Mitzy. Mission planning often evolves en route to our destination. The aisle between the seats shifts to the portside of the aircraft to make room for the conference room.

Beyond that are the lavatories. Full-sized bathrooms, complete with showers. Not that we'll be using them during the seven-hour flight home. Beyond the lavatories are the lockers for our gear.

I follow Sam and CJ. When they open the door to the conference room, Carmen glances at me. A hint of fear flickers in her eyes.

I yank off my helmet and run my fingers through my sweat-soaked hair, giving her the first view of my face. Not sure what I expect, she doesn't reach for me. There's a pause, a slight hitching of her breath, but then CJ gives her a little nudge into the conference room. He and Sam follow her inside and shut the door behind them.

Excused from my guard duties, I join the rest of Bravo team in the very rear of the aircraft where our gear lockers sit.

Brady rips off his tactical vest. Like me, he's covered in sweat. I do the same, eager to get some relief from the heat. The moment the helmet's off, I shed my sweat-soaked t-shirt, then tug at my boots.

It's hot here on the ground, but once we're at altitude, it'll cool down substantially. Not to mention, none of us want to spend the next seven hours in sweaty clothes.

"Where are the others?" Booker addresses Brady, who leans against the bulkhead.

"Inbound. Had to stop at the original exfil location to pick up the Rufuses. They're five minutes out." He clamps his hand on Booker's shoulder. "Go ahead and stow your gear. We've got this."

Booker leaves us, hitting up the head, before returning to Izzy's side.

A few minutes later, the rest of our team arrives. Forest Summers boards first, ducking his head and slanting it to the side on account of his height. Something outside the window draws my eyes. I blink and do a double take. All three Rufus robots calmly march themselves up the cargo ramp. No doubt they'll tuck themselves in for the flight.

We stow all our gear, do a quick change, then the guys head to the front of the plane to claim their seats. Nearly everyone's on board. I hang toward the back, content to take a seat in the last row, when the door to the conference room opens.

Sam wanders out, catches my eye, then points inside. "She refuses to talk. See what you can do to change that."

"Yes, sir."

THIRTEEN

Carmen

So far, so good.

It doesn't look like they're going to leave me behind. I can breathe easy.

But where are they taking me?

Two men guide me down the center aisle inside the plane.

I've flown in numerous private planes before, but nothing on the scale of *this.* The insides of this plane are built for comfort. Every seat is first class. This outfit has significant financial backing.

Have I made a fatal mistake?

The men lead me past rows of first-class seats to a door toward the back of the plane. Once there, they deposit me inside what appears to be an airborne command center.

I'd like to look out the windows, see if anyone is racing out to meet us—Police? The clergy? Matias? My father? Artemus?—but there are no windows to look outside. As far as *anyone* goes, there's no way Father's security forces have recovered from the breach tonight. However, I've learned not to depend on such things. A simple phone call from my father brings all of this crashing down.

A long conference table spans the length of the room; twelve chairs sit around it, five on each side and one each at the ends.

Monitors fill the walls, leaving barely a gap between them. There's even a low counter with an ice bucket and several bottled waters waiting to be consumed.

One of the men gestures for me to take a seat. I do so with as much grace as I can muster while minimizing any sign of my unease.

"My name is Sam, and this is CJ." The burlier man speaks first. He pauses for a second while I press my lips together and try to find a comfortable position. "And you appear to be Carmen Angelo, daughter of Maximus Angelo, Minister of the Interior for Nicaragua." He casually inspects his nails. "Care to explain what you're doing here?"

"Not really." I fold my arms in a defensive move.

They deserve answers. This isn't an unexpected question, but I need to be strategic in what I reveal.

Sam glances at CJ. His left brow wings up, surprised by my non-answer.

"We're going to need a little more than that if you want to stay on this plane." Sam mirrors my pose, not to be defensive, but rather to establish authority.

"Are you the one in charge?" I ask.

"I'm the one questioning you." He takes a step back and leans against the wall.

"That's not an answer."

"Correct. Just as yours isn't an answer to the question I asked."

"Do you work for the CIA?"

Life will be much easier if they're CIA operatives. Not that I can divulge anything to them. My contact was very clear on that point. No matter what, that's a secret I'll take to my grave.

The two of them exchange looks, conversing in that silent way of theirs. Beneath my feet, the airplane's decking vibrates with the movement of others getting on board.

"Do you?" Sam unfolds his arms.

"Do I, what?"

"Do you work for the CIA?"

"Why would you ask me that?"

"Why won't you answer my questions?"

This is going to get dodgy. He asks things I can't answer, so I turn the tables on them.

"Your organization came to rescue Isabelle LaCroix, didn't it?"

"Looks that way." The corners of his mouth bounce with amusement. "And you crashed our rescue, *didn't you?*"

"Looks that way." I parrot his words, feeding them back to him. "Why?"

"Why, what?"

"Why did you rescue Isabelle LaCroix?"

"Because your father took something that didn't belong to him. We don't like when that happens."

"I assume it's safe to say Isabelle LaCroix works for you?" The more information I can gather, the better off I'll be.

"You can assume anything you want." He pulls at his chin. "What possessed you to jump Rafe?"

"Rafe?"

"The Guardian who held onto you and saved your life."

"I don't know about *saved*." I use air quotes for emphasis.

"You're saying he didn't?"

"I'm not saying anything."

"Well then," Sam twists toward CJ, "looks like we let her go."

"No!" My shout is more frantic than I mean it to be.

"No?" Sam crosses his arms again. "What are you running from, Miss Angelo? Or, should I rather say *who?*"

"That's none of your business."

"Seeing how you hijacked our mission, I'd say your intentions are very much our business. In a moment, we'll be closing up the airplane, taxiing to the runway, and taking off. We'll be flying out of your country back to ours. You can imagine the difficulties we'll have with the custom's officials when we arrive with a passenger who has no passport."

"I have a feeling your operation does a lot of that. Don't feed me B.S. about not being able to handle that."

"We have a saying around here." He pauses, and I fall right into his trap, too curious to hold my tongue.

"What's that?"

"Never assume, and never jump to conclusions."

"Why not?"

"When you assume, you make an ass out of you and me, and when you jump to conclusions, it's a long swim back. You, young lady, are one massive assumption, and that makes you a major liability. Considering who your father is, bringing you with us could open up a political quagmire no one wants any part of. So, I'm going to ask you again. Why are you here?"

Shoot.

"I want to talk to Isabelle LaCroix."

"Izzy?" CJ, who's said nothing thus far, suddenly pipes up. "Why her?"

"Because I have questions."

"We have questions for you, first." Sam clears his throat. "You're not speaking to Izzy until you answer our questions."

Izzy?

It's a familiar name, which tells me Isabelle LaCroix means something to these men. At first, I figured they were probably hired to rescue her, but it seems there's something else at play. Add to that the interest my father has in Isabelle LaCroix and a million questions swirl around in my head.

"I'll answer all your questions, but only if Isabelle asks them." I have absolutely nothing of value to convince these men to keep me on board. I'll have to throw them a bone that doesn't cost me too much, but what do I tell them? How do I convince them not to kick me out of this airplane?

"We don't negotiate with prisoners." Sam stands firm.

"Am I a prisoner?" I glance around the conference room. "You just said you were going to kick me off the plane. Am I free to go or not?"

"That depends on your answers."

"Fine. I'll tell you whatever you want to know, but only to Isabelle LaCroix and only once we're back on American soil."

"Back?" Sam's brows tug tight together. "You've been to the US?"

"Yes, and I want you to take me home."

"Nicaragua is your home." Sam glances at CJ.

"San Francisco is home."

"Why San Francisco?" CJ softens his tone.

"Because that's where I live."

Technically, that's not a lie. The lease I signed with Kaye and Barbi doesn't end until the new semester begins. It's an annual lease from August to August, which gives me three months to figure out what the hell I'm going to do.

As for my father?

That's a tangled mess I'll have to deal with later. Somehow, I need to convince my father I'm *undercover* learning all I can about these men, while simultaneously working on a way to free myself from him for good.

None of this is going to be easy.

"There's no way Izzy is going to speak with you. You have something to say, you tell us." CJ leans against the only exit from the room. As he does, the plane's engines spin up. The low whine is felt more than heard, but it tells me I'm working on borrowed time.

"I don't know you." I turn to include Sam in that statement. "Either of you, and I'm not telling you anything."

"Then you're getting off this plane." Sam's voice remains firm, but as he speaks, the plane rolls back.

We're moving, and I suddenly realize these men never intended to kick me off the plane. I'm valuable to them. That should be something that reassures me, but I find it disquieting instead.

I decide honesty is the best policy. I need to extend trust to earn some of theirs.

"I know what I did doesn't make sense. It was impulsive, but it was an act of desperation."

"Why did you do it?" CJ's got an accent. It's subtle, but there's the slightest hint of a Texas twang.

I can't help but like him. He's got that all-American-hero-vibe down pat. Sam is something different. The vibe he throws is more that of a secret, undercover agent. I peg him as former CIA or FBI.

Either way, I'm way out of my depth with the two of them.

"The plane's moving." Stating the obvious will force their hand. "You have no intention of letting me go." I lean back and try to run my fingers through my hair. My fingers get caught in snarl upon snarl. The wind from the helicopter turned my hair into a rat's mess, and that ride over the treetops didn't do my dress any favors.

"You're right about that." Sam gestures to CJ. "I suggest you strap in for takeoff." He stoops over the chair closest to him and shows me where the lap belt is tucked up under the chair. "This conversation isn't finished."

"I don't doubt it."

I feel incredibly exposed, and that says something considering I'm generally the one wearing the skimpiest cocktail dress when I go out with my friends.

But that's not why I feel exposed. These men are used to interrogating prisoners. They were soft with me; more of a meet and greet instead of a full interrogation. No doubt that will come later.

My expectations were different, thinking they would demand more and threaten me with eviction, but they don't.

They're as curious about me as I am about them.

With the amount of money invested in this plane, they have the resources to figure everything out about me. From my day of birth to my graduation *summa cum laude* from UCSF, my entire life will be at their fingertips.

But that won't give them the answers they seek. For that, more robust interrogations will begin.

The plane bumps along nicely, proceeding down the taxiway. Sam and CJ stay long enough to ensure I buckle in. Then the two of them disappear.

Knowing there must be cameras recording my every move, I lean back with a sigh. There's no reason to hide my relief. Tomorrow starts a different story. Until then, I'm safe.

The door to the conference room opens and another man enters. I know him. I feel him on a cellular level that makes no sense. I leaped into his arms and he saved my life. The dark and handsome stranger is Rafe.

FOURTEEN

Carmen

Striking enough to steal my breath, I barely manage not to gape. There's a savage beauty about the man staring at me. It vibrates within his powerfully built body and curls on the arrogant smirk on his face.

The energy within the room spikes and heats. With that, warmth fills my cheeks. I glance down, embarrassed by my reaction, which only cranks up the heat burning in my cheeks.

Strikingly handsome and dressed all in black, the helmet with its visor and the bulky body armor is gone revealing hypnotic eyes and a dangerously sinful gaze. Those eyes glint as he moves into the room, making it feel suddenly ten sizes too small. His bearing commands attention, and I give all of mine to him.

A day's growth of stubble shadows his square jaw and draws my attention to full, sculpted lips. Disheveled, raven-black hair spills down his forehead to curl over his eyes, and he casually runs fingers through that hair, pushing the dark strands out of his eyes.

I want to do that; run my fingers through his hair.

Shockingly attractive, my mouth gapes and my breath flutters. The weight of his presence fills the room, making me feel tiny and insignificant.

"You must be Rafe." It's a name I'll never forget.

Captivating beyond compare, my mouth feels as dry as the Sahara. I know this man. I clung to him as if my life depended on it, and he clung right back. I still feel the imprint of his hands on my ass.

"And you're Carmen Angelo." It's not a question. The resonance of his voice catches me off guard. It's too smooth, too deep, too alpha protective to be true.

We stare at each other with an intimacy that shouldn't exist. The very air sizzles between us, sparking with electricity, as the chemistry between us builds.

Without another word, he strides inside the conference room, letting the door behind him slap closed. Dropping into the seat beside me, he leans down to find the straps that will secure him for takeoff and clicks in.

"I'd tell you to make sure your tray table is in its full and upright locked position, but…" He makes a sweeping gesture of the room. "This isn't that kind of plane."

"What kind of plane is it?" I swallow past the lump in my throat, too enraptured by his lethal beauty. Striking and unexpected, my attraction only builds, but I beat back the unwanted emotion. This man is not to be trusted. None of them are, at least not until I settle a few things.

"It's the kind of plane where you and I get to know each other better."

Something about his voice makes my skin heat. It's that crazy electricity sparking in the air.

"You're going to be disappointed." Too sensitive to the currents in the air swirling around us, I draw back and rub my arms. The static charge is normal, or at least that's what I try and convince myself is the truth.

"Why is that?" His hooded gaze rakes over my body, taking me in from head to toe.

"I'm not answering any questions."

"I heard you weren't. Being evasive to those who rescued you doesn't make sense, but hey, I'm not here to interrogate you."

"Not evasive, just cautious."

And I don't believe him. He's here to get answers. All they did was swap out one set of interrogators for another. I've seen my father employing the same tactic, beating someone down, not by physical force, but by relentless questioning.

"That means evasive." Rafe's brow lifts in challenge.

"If you say so." With a dismissive snort, I break eye contact, regretting it instantly. There's something about his smoldering gaze that weakens me, but I crave it as well.

"Look, you're the one who came to us." He holds his hand out, curls powerful fingers, and nonchalantly examines his cuticles. "Whatever game you're playing, this is where it ends." To emphasize his point, he presses the tip of his index finger on top of the table.

"I'm not playing games. I told the men who were in here earlier that I would talk to Isabelle LaCroix. Until then, I have nothing to say."

It's harder than it should be to say nothing. The scrutiny of his gaze makes me want to share. I almost fall for it, but then I realize what he's doing. How he places his body to take up space, intimidating me with his presence, and stealing my breath with his roguish good looks.

"That's a shame." Taunting me, he returns to examining his cuticles. I half expect him to pull out a knife to trim his fingernails, piling on physical intimidation and threat of bodily harm to the rest of it.

The whine of the engines turns to a roar. Thrust pushes me back in my seat as we take to the air and our conversation takes a pause.

Rafe stares at me during takeoff and I return his stare, determined not to say anything I shouldn't.

The thing is, I'm not against talking to these people. A ton of questions spin around in my head. Anything that touches on the things I can't speak about, however, must remain mine alone.

My heart trots happily along as my breath hitches. Did they send him in because that smoldering look of his makes women weak in the knees and dumb in the brain?

He's right about one thing. It's a shame I can't share. Something tells me these people are nothing like my father and the men who serve him.

We say nothing during takeoff. Once the plane levels off, I lay my head against the headrest as an intense wave of fatigue overcomes me. There's also a chill.

The temperature inside the room seems to drop as we climb toward cruising altitude. None of the thick humidity of home remains, exchanged by the aircraft for the thinner, dryer air we fly through. Goose bumps lift on my skin and a shiver overcomes me. The cabin lights flicker and flash.

"We can unbuckle now." Rafe flicks open his seatbelt and leans back.

I'm viscerally aware of this man and acutely conscious of what I'm wearing. The thin silk reveals more than it hides. I run my hands up and down my arms and hunch inward, praying he doesn't see the tight, peaked mounds of my nipples.

It's from the cold. Just the cold.

Please let it be from just the cold.

Shoving down a million questions, I glance around the room, looking for a distraction and finding none. All the monitors are dark, and other than an ice bucket and bottles of water, the room is bare.

"You're cold." Rafe stands. His brows furrow as he approaches me.

I press back in my seat, terrified of what he might do.

"Jumpy?" The corners of his mouth tilt into a grin, but I'm not fooled. Rafe's been assigned as my guard and that's the role he'll play. "Luv, if I wanted to hurt you, don't you think I would've let you fall? I'm not here to hurt you. None of us are."

"Wouldn't you be jumpy? If our circumstances were reversed? I don't know you. I don't know who you work for. Until I know more, I'm entitled to be *a bit* jumpy."

"Instead of jumpy, why aren't you overjoyed for the rescue? You should be gushing with all kinds of information and eager to answer our questions. Instead, you clam up?" He tilts his head to the side. "You can see how that can be concerning, from our point of view."

"I have my reasons." Either it's my imagination or the temperature continues to drop.

"Care to share?" His thick, kissable lips press together as those mesmerizing eyes make another journey up and down my body.

Instead of flinching from his gaze, I lift my chin and dare him to hurt me.

"Not really."

He moves toward me and hitches a hip on the tabletop. Sitting over me, I have no choice, but to look up at him.

"Who are you running from?"

"Who says I'm running?"

"Ah, you got me there. I made an assumption." Those dark eyes of his glint as he leans forward. His voice drops to a whisper. "I won't make the same mistake twice."

I remember what Sam said about making assumptions and determine that's how I'll play this.

"I told them I would talk only to…"

"Izzy." He completes my sentence. "I remember, but I've got to ask—why Izzy?"

"You wouldn't understand."

I learned enough about the woman to know how she reacts under stress and how she uses her inner strength as a shield. It may make no sense, but I trust her to tell me the truth more than Sam, CJ, or even Rafe.

"Try me." He uses his words to prod me, keeping the tone of his voice friendly to encourage me to share.

The thing is, I want to share. I've waited years to get things off my chest, but there's no way I'll throw away a decade of preparation because my interrogator is sexy as hell.

"I asked Sam if you worked for the CIA."

"What did he say?"

"He didn't."

"Ah…" Rafe drags his finger along the table. "I should probably follow his lead."

"Or, you could tell me who you work for."

"I could, but these kinds of things are better when there's a bit of give and take."

"What does that mean?"

"We trade."

"Trade?"

"You answer one of my questions, and I answer one of yours."

"That's a game I'm not playing."

"Consider it a game of twenty questions. It could be fun."

"No."

He pauses, tilting his head to regard me. "How about truth or dare?"

"I'm not interested in playing any games with you."

"That's unfortunate." His voice drops to a heated whisper. "You can do better."

"Better?"

"Yes." He leans back, eyes softening. "Why did you jump me?"

"I'm not answering."

"Fine, you don't have to answer anything, but I've got tons of questions I'm going to ask even if you won't answer.

I shift in my seat, twisting to give him my shoulder, only I forget to release the strap anchoring me to the chair and it turns into an awkward jerk.

"I've been wracking my mind trying to figure out what the hell was going through your mind. You saw the rope. You saw the helicopter, even if you couldn't hear it. It's not hard to put two and two together."

"So?"

"Please don't take offense, because you're stunning. Striking comes to mind, despite…" He makes a vague gesture toward my hair and the state of my dress.

"Flattery will get you nowhere."

"What I was going to say is how in the world did you think

clinging to me would be safe? You had to know you weren't strong enough to hold on all on your own?"

"Consider it a leap of faith." It's a true statement and gives nothing away.

"I saw you praying. Are you religious? Catholic?"

"I am." Again, that answer gives nothing away.

"So…" He leans back again. "A literal *leap of faith?*"

"What about it?"

"Nothing." He taps his chin with his forefinger. "I'm just wondering why a beautiful woman like you is running, in an evening gown like that, toward a man you don't know. What happened that forced you to literally put your life in the hands of a stranger?"

"I'm not answering."

"That's not true."

"I'm not answering your questions." I cross my arms, feeling more chilled by the second.

"Maybe not mine, but you want to talk to Izzy. Why is that?"

"Like I said, I have questions."

I don't trust any of these men. I've seen too many men like them and all they do is follow the orders of whoever commands them from the top of their organization.

That makes them dangerous.

Isabelle LaCroix is a different matter altogether. She'll tell me the truth, which will help me decide what bits and pieces I can share.

"You realize answering our questions will lead to us answering yours?"

Dear Lord, this man is beautiful, especially when he looks at me with those sexy eyes. The energy crackling between us dances up and down my arms, making my skin heat and making me contemplate sinful things.

"It's not that easy."

Rafe folds his arms over his chest, mirroring me. Instead of responding to what I said, he takes a moment to examine me. His gaze begins at my face, moves to the mess of my hair, then wanders down from there. It's a slow, determined assessment, probing in its intensity, flaring every now and then with something dark and hypnotic.

"Please stop that."

"Stop, what?" His gaze flicks back to my face.

"Stop looking at me like that." I rub at my arms, acutely aware of the temperature in the room. It's definitely colder than before. Blowing out a breath, I test a theory. Sure enough, my breath coalesces in the air. "Are you purposefully cranking down the heat? Trying to freeze me out?"

"Excuse me?" He leans back with affront.

"It's really cold in here." I purse my lips and blow out a puff of air. "See?" Pointing at the tiny vapor cloud, I make my point.

"Ah, yes."

"Is it deliberate?"

"No, it's not. Hang on a second." Rafe walks over to the only door leading out of the room. He raps on the door and waits for a second.

The faintest *snick* of a latch disengaging makes me suck in a breath. They locked him in with me. Are they afraid I'll escape? Where would I possibly go?

The door opens a crack. Rafe sticks his head out and the deep rumble of male voices is impossible to make out. I run my fingers through my hair, trying my best to detangle what I can. Without shampoo, and an entire bottle of conditioner, the tangles are going nowhere.

A quick inspection of my dress catches my breath. The long slit ripped without me realizing it. Probably when I wrapped my legs around Rafe, fearing for my life, as we flew over the canopy of the rainforest. The slit goes all the way to my hip, exposing the entirety of my leg, hip, and who knows what else?

Have I been inadvertently flashing him this whole time? Heat kicks in overhead and a deep rushing fills the room with warmth. I glance up as the faintest wave of heated air blows down on my face. My entire body shudders as the heat chases away the cold.

Rafe pulls back from the door.

"How does that feel?"

"Better. Thank you." I appreciate the concession.

"Good enough to answer a few questions?" The smirk on his face says he already knows my answer.

I grab at the ripped fabric of my dress and try to close the gap. The movement snaps his gaze to my exposed skin.

"It's rude to stare." I twist in the seat, giving him my back. I can do that now that I've released the seatbelt.

"Wasn't staring, luv. Just saw it."

"You think I believe that?"

"Hey, I'm not going to lie to you." He holds up his hands, palms out. "Don't know what kind of men you're used to, but I don't ogle women. I know when to avert my eye."

A rush of heat fills my cheeks. That answers the question of whether I inadvertently flashed him. Since I wear nothing under the dress, he got a look at *everything*.

"You look exactly like the kind of man who ogles women."

He looks like the kind of man women trip over themselves to have a piece of. He's a predator; the kind of man who takes what he wants. I bet there are very few, if any, women who've ever told him *No*.

A grin crooks up the corner of his lip.

"It's not funny." I snap at him and lose my grip on the fabric. The long slit falls away, revealing the entire length of my leg exposed all the way up to my hipbone.

Yeah, definitely flashed him that time.

He's well aware I wear absolutely nothing under this dress. My cheeks heat, mortified, but also curious, when he suddenly clears his throat and looks away.

"Since you're not talking, and we have seven hours in the air, how about we do something about that?" He turns back toward me.

"About what?"

"Your state of dress." He clears his throat again. "Or rather —undress."

"Sadly, I forgot to bring something else to wear."

"No problem." He raps on the door. There's that *snick* of a lock again, then he steps through the narrow gap, leaving me inside to stew with my thoughts.

Several minutes go by, but no one returns. I take in a series of deep breaths, trying to center myself and my thoughts. That fluttering sensation in my belly goes away, but the moment I think about Rafe, it returns with a vengeance.

A knock on the door snaps me out of my thoughts. Rafe pokes his head inside.

"You ready?"

"Ready?" My brows pinch. "For what?"

"To get cleaned up and into a set of clothes that don't have a rip halfway up your side."

I grasp the two sides of the slit and bite my lower lip. Did I flash him again?

"How is that going to work?" I gesture around the room. "It's not like I can go shopping."

"No need to shop. We've got several females traveling with us, and they've been gracious enough to put together a kit for you."

"A what?"

"Toiletries." His grin bounces. "Clothes."

"I don't…"

"As you've noticed, this plane isn't like any others. There are two full-sized lavatories on board. Since you're not talking, I figured you could use a minute to take advantage of the facilities, take a shower, and slip into something more comfortable than that dress for the rest of the flight."

"Why are you being nice to me?"

"Because that's the kind of man I am." He pushes the door fully open. "Sometimes, people are exactly what they seem."

"You are a soldier. A killer…"

"Who's inviting you to clean up and enjoy a bit of quiet time alone. No one will bother you. I'll be on the other side of the door, and if you're worried about anyone barging in, don't be. There's a latch on the inside." He folds his arms across his chest. "You look like you could use a moment. Maybe afterward, when you decide we're not all that bad, you'll trust us a little more and share a bit about yourself."

"You already know who I am."

"Which is the biggest mystery." He takes a step back and makes a sweeping motion to join him outside.

I grip the ripped fabric as best I can and join him in the tiny corridor. "Where's Isabelle…"

"You're not talking to Izzy."

"Why not?"

"Because she's not in a place where talking to you makes any sense." He points aft. "Now, off you go. You have your pick of the right or the left. Both are empty."

I turn on bare feet and head to the back of the plane until I come upon two doors facing each other.

"What's that?" I point beyond the lavatories to what looks to be several cabinets.

"Nothing that concerns you." Rafe pushes open the door to the left lavatory.

He said I had my pick, but there's a stack of women's clothing placed on the counter along with soap, shampoo, conditioner, and a brush.

My fingers itch to get in there, but I hold back. "What do I owe them?"

"Nothing. Consider it a gift, and while you're taking that shower, think about how none of us have threatened you, and maybe revisit your willingness to answer our questions."

"How long do I…"

"You can stay in there for the next six hours for all I care. When we land, you need to buckle in. Until then, the only limiting factor is the size of the water tanks and how much they can heat."

"Thank you… I…" With no idea what to say, I slip into the lavatory, confused and surprised. My father would never treat a captive this way.

Although, didn't he do exactly this to Isabelle LaCroix? The woman looked freshly showered. Rosalie's signature touches were evident in Isabelle's hair and makeup. Not to mention, Father gave Isabelle one of my old dresses to wear for dinner.

In fact, the more I think about it, the more I decide this is just another ruse meant to make me feel comfortable and lower my guard. Until I get back to my townhome and retrieve my things, I need to remember my '*WHY*.' Sam's words return to me; *assume nothing and don't jump to conclusions.*

I'd be smart to listen to him.

FIFTEEN

Rafe

It's been two days since the rescue. Bravo team, minus Booker, hangs out in our bullpen, stowing our gear from a practice exercise. Booker took time off to be with Izzy and has been MIA with his woman.

I'm happy for them. Thrilled things worked out the way they did. Any other option would've resulted in World War III as Booker took revenge on those who hurt his *Isabelle*. The rest of us refer to her as Izzy. He's the only one to call her that. Or was. It's still weird the way Carmen only ever refers to Izzy by her full name.

Isabelle LaCroix.

As if it's a title, or a totem against evil? I shrug. Carmen isn't my problem.

As for Izzy, she's a fighter and strong as bloody hell. She's safe in Booker's arms, and the two of them deserve a bit of downtime away from the nonstop operations of Guardian HRS.

Weird to think it's only been two days since Carmen Angelo clung to me while we flew over the rainforest. I haven't stopped thinking about the mysterious brunette with those mesmerizing eyes. Two *looong* frustrating days where my every thought manages to circle back around to Carmen Angelo.

"Any luck with your cling-on?" Zeb yanks off his body armor and hangs it in his gear locker.

Our lockers are six by nine feet, fenced in cages that store all our personal gear and weapons.

"Her name is Carmen." Using my shirt, I wipe at the sweat beading my brow. A quick sniff of my pits and I scrunch up my nose. "Whew, I smell ripe." Calling out over my shoulder, I cup my hand over my mouth. "Y'all better have left some hot water."

"How is *Carmen?*" Alec sits on his bench seat in his gear locker. He, Zeb, and Hayes are headed out, looking to canvas the local bars for fresh meat.

"She had nothing to say when I looked in on her." Bending down, I kick off my boots and take off my trousers.

My lips twist, thinking about our non-interaction. Carmen wouldn't even look at me. Since arriving at Guardian HRS, her lips have been sealed.

"When you say *look in on her…*" Hayes uses air quotes while I roll my eyes. "Are you hoping for a bit of bump and grind? From the way she wrapped those long, sexy legs of hers around you…"

Hayes doesn't get to finish his sentence. I wad up my stinky shirt and throw it at his face. It lands with a heavy *smack*.

"Ewww… That's not ripe…" Hayes tosses my sweaty shirt back at me. "It's foul as shit and should be categorized as a lethal weapon. You need to put it out of its misery and incinerate it."

"My lucky shirt?" I toss the shirt into the laundry hamper. "No way."

After we leave, a cleaning crew will come in to wash our clothes and empty the trash. Maintenance and cleaning of our individual lockers is our responsibility. They're only ever unlocked when we're physically in the bullpen. That way, if anything goes wrong with our gear, we have only ourselves to blame.

It makes sense, considering the million-dollar tech contained within each of our lockers.

"Lucky it didn't kill me with the stench. That thing is so rank, I'm surprised it hasn't grown legs of its own." Hayes grabs his towel and slings it over his shoulder. With a grin, he leaves us as he heads in to shower. "Better hurry up, Rafe, or there won't be any hot water left, although maybe what you need is a nice long, cold shower?"

I cover my groin and turn away. Any thought of Carmen turns my body into that of a teenage boy with raging hormones coursing through me. Fortunately, none of the other guys notice. Either that, or they feel sorry for me.

As for a shower, I reek, and Hayes is right about the hot water. It'll be gone if I don't get a move on. We're odiferous sweat balls after a long day in the heat.

CJ had all four teams out today, conducting joint training with Forest Summers's growing squad of Rufuses. Despite our best efforts to convince Forest to give the robotic dogs individual names, he refuses.

We spent the entire morning out in one of the mocked-up towns we train in. Alpha and Bravo teams paired up against Charlie and Delta. We switched roles as to who was the aggressor and defender. The game of the day was hostage rescue—our specialty.

Our hostages were none other than Jinx and Lily, two incredibly talented women; prior DEA operatives and lethal in their own right, who played the role of damsels in distress perfectly. Neither one of them helped out with their rescue.

Without a cloud in the sky, it was hot, dusty, and miserable. I'm glad we're done and happy to cool off and clean up.

"Are you coming with?" Zeb arches a brow. "Or are you going to check in on your cling-on?"

"Her name is *Carmen*." I suppress the growl rumbling in the back of my throat.

I check in on Carmen in the morning before work and when we get off for the night. It's only been two days, but clearly the guys notice. Not really sure *why* I check in on her, except I feel responsible for the woman, and I want to make sure no one's mistreating her.

"Whatever…" Zeb dismisses my comment. "I hear she's stubborn. I'm surprised you haven't tried to fuck the information out of her yet."

"Don't go there." I ball my hands into fists. Fucking Carmen is the one thing I can't get out of my head, and I don't understand my obsession with a woman I barely know. Correction. I don't understand my obsession with a woman I *don't* know.

Other than her name, and her relationship to Maximus Angelo, I know nothing about her, yet I've never thought about a woman with this level of carnal need coursing through my body.

Sure, I've picked up chicks, imagined fucking them, then went over and closed the deal, but that was the beginning, and end, of the interaction.

With Carmen, I can't keep my mind out of the gutter, and the last two nights have been nothing but one long sex-dream with me playing the five-finger hustle.

"Cool it." Brady saunters out of the shower area, towel slung over his shoulder, nude and completely at ease with the disfiguring scars covering half his body. "Each of you take a chill pill. Rafe, the woman's not yours, stop defending her honor." Brady spins to dress down Zeb. "And you're being an ass because you know it pisses him off when you call her a cling-on."

I don't need Brady stepping in, but I appreciate him cutting things off before Zeb forced me to rip him a new asshole.

Brady's a bloody amazing leader. Outside of a mission, he steps up only when necessary to keep the peace. Otherwise, he's just one of the guys.

The dude had a really bad year, but he's one hell of a fighter. Nothing gets him down for long. Nothing stops him. The man doesn't know the meaning of quit. When we all thought he would die from his injuries, the bastard lived if only to prove us wrong.

It's one of the things that makes him great.

"Rafe's too fucking sensitive. Got his head all wrapped up in that woman. But *Carmen* only wants to speak to Izzy." Zeb refuses to acknowledge the verbal putdown by Bravo-One, but he doesn't say another derogatory word about Carmen.

Glancing down, my eye catches the muted shine of my prosthetic leg. Brady's scars should've been mine. He saved my ass when he yanked me out of the blast radius.

The memories come in a rush. They sneak up on me like that.

We were in Cancun.

At the port.

Trying to rescue a clutch of girls kidnapped and destined for ports unknown.

That tip was a trap.

And I'm the fucker who moved too fast.

I cut the explosive wires set to detonate if anyone tampered with the container.

Brady saw the wires, but it was a second too late.

The whole thing blew up in our faces.

He took the brunt of the explosion, while the lower half of my leg took the rest. Every time I stop to think about what happened, I get sick to my stomach. It feels like getting kicked in the nuts. There's a bit of nausea, plus a whole hell of a lot of visceral discomfort. We barely made it out of there alive.

Booker saved my ass; put a tourniquet on what was left of my leg. Zeb and Hayes carried me out, neglecting the shrapnel wounds they suffered. Booker and Alec stayed behind to take care of Brady's body.

We thought he was dead, but the fucker refused to die. He wears his scars with honor, but like me, he struggles with how his body is different than before.

As for me, my acceptance is slower than his. Piper says I'm a work in progress. I rarely take off the prosthetic in front of the guys. They see it in the shower and when I'm getting dressed, but that's it. Piper would say that's one bit of progress I've yet to make.

Actually, I can't remember a single time I've shown the guys what's left of my leg—the stump. They know I have a fake leg. They were there when it happened and saw the mangled mess.

They've seen many iterations of the prosthetic over the past year while my stump healed and reshaped itself. Piper says it's *mature* now and unlikely to change much from here on out. The guys watched me go through rehabilitation, all the painful stages, but they've never seen the stump.

It is what it is and what it will be for the rest of my life.

Regardless, my *new* leg never comes off in the bullpen. I keep the prosthetic on while I shower and remove it only when it's time for bed.

That's when I massage the sore muscles, check my stump for areas of skin breakdown, and look at its overall health. Heading out with the guys sounds fun, but I already know what I'm going to tell them.

Piper's idea about fucking a chick against the wall has merit, but there's no way to ensure the girl doesn't notice the leg. The last thing I want to worry about while banging some chick is her getting squeamish when she sees the fake leg. Or pity me. That would be far worse.

That right there is enough to put a damper on the whole idea of having sex. Maybe I should become celibate and join the priesthood. My mother would love that. She's never accepted my job requires that I take the lives of others. She'd love it if I forswore killing others and took to the cloth. I'd rather die.

With those rotten thoughts ruining my mood, I snag my towel from where it hangs and wrap it around my waist. I'm not as comfortable as Brady is in his skin and prefer to cover up.

Sure, it's just the six of us, but I'm not the kind of guy who struts around naked. Not to mention, even though chicks aren't technically allowed in Bravo's bullpen, there has been the rare incursion by Mitzy, Doc Summers, and Brady's woman, Angie.

They don't need to see me naked.

Since a night out with the guys is out, that leaves me with what to do with myself for the rest of the evening. Nights are frustrating failures as fantasies of what I want to do to Carmen flood my mind. I've run through every sexual position known to mankind, doing the five-finger shuffle practically nonstop, beating off to all the dirty things I want to do to Carmen Angelo.

Bloody hell, but I can't get her out of my head.

"Why does Carmen want to talk to Izzy?" Zeb looks to me as if I know the answer.

"Dunno." All I can do is shrug.

"That's a good question." Brady runs a hand through his hair.

"Iz doesn't understand why Carmen wants to talk to her. Says they initially ran into each other in one of the halls, then later on at dinner. Carmen was dismissive and derogatory and made a point to be as rude as possible."

Booker may be MIA, but Brady shares a wall with the man in the duplex the two of them renovated. He knows more than the rest of us, but even that isn't much.

"Why don't they put the two of them in a room together and be done with it?" Hayes finishes getting dressed and stows the rest of his gear.

While my day's been physically exhausting, I can't help but wonder about hers. She's been questioned by the best of us. Forest, Sam, and CJ have tried to get her to talk. Doc Summers attempted to get Carmen to open up, thinking a woman's touch might work. So far, Griff, from Alpha team, hasn't been called in, which I'm thankful for. He's an expert interrogator, but his methods aren't suitable for getting a woman to spill her secrets.

"Haven't you tried to get her to talk?" Alec, who's been mostly quiet, speaks up for the first time.

"I tried to get her to explain why she jumped me." No fucking way am I going to use the slur *cling-on* when referring to Carmen.

"And what did she do? Flick those amazing lashes and bat those sultry eyes before telling you to take a hike?" Zeb is pushing me. Fucker's right on the edge. "At least your…"

"Be very careful what comes out of your mouth next." The warning in my voice is more of a primal growl than I'm willing to admit.

"Dude. All I was going to say is Carmen's a ten out of ten." Zeb takes a step back.

I don't believe him, but it's not worth pursuing. He doesn't mean to be an ass. Zeb is a player who only sees what a woman can do for him—or to him."

"Every time, she meets my questions with silence." I pull at my neck, stretching muscles that are tightening up. "Except for her incessant demand to speak to Isabelle LaCroix."

Like the others, I don't get it. It's weird the way Carmen only ever refers to Izzy by her full name—*Isabelle LaCroix*. There's a stiffness to her request, and I can't put my finger on what it is that feels off.

"Izzy's not trained in interrogation tactics. Not to mention, all she wants is to get back to work." Brady leans back and pinches the bridge of his nose.

The door to our bullpen opens. CJ raps on the door. "Briefing at fourteen hundred. Brady, find out where the fuck Booker is and bring Izzy back with you."

"What's going on?" Brady speaks for the team.

"Brass has an update." CJ isn't a talker. A good read of other people, there's something on his mind and he's not happy about it.

"We'll be there." Brady looks at me and Zeb. "Hurry up and get dressed. We'll have lunch in the cafeteria and debrief what happened today."

We did an immediate debrief at the end of the exercise, but Brady always likes to go over things as a team. We're a lot more candid when it's just the team.

I head to the showers and Zeb is on my heels. We lather, rinse, and dry off in record time. When we return to our gear lockers, the rest of the team is waiting. Shrugging into jeans and a comfortable t-shirt, I slip on a pair of sneakers, and follow Zeb and the others on the short walk to one of the many cafeterias located on Guardian HQ proper.

We grab our food and talk about the operation while we eat. Defending with the Rufuses was easy. Trying to extract our hostages when on the opposing side was impossible.

We toss out several ideas about how we can improve against the robotic menaces. To date, none of the operations we've gone up against have had the capital, or technical expertise, to use robots, but the world is constantly changing. The advantage we have today will be gone tomorrow if we don't plan ahead.

"Great ideas, guys." Brady stands and gathers his dishes. "I've got less than an hour to get Booker and Izzy to the briefing."

"Why do you think they want Izzy?" I take another bite of my burger and close my eyes as the heavenly flavors fill my mouth. "She's medical."

"Don't know. Maybe they're going to ask her to talk to Carmen." Brady shrugs.

"Can't see Booker letting that happen." Alec straddles his seat. He finished his food a few minutes ago and is flirting with a table of women sitting a few feet away.

"Either that or Mitzy found something." Brady shrugs.

"Like what?" Zeb wipes his mouth.

"I'm guessing something about the diamonds." Brady gathers his things. "I've gotta go if I'm going to get them back in time. Don't be late to the briefing."

"Where do we have to go?" Hayes makes a gesture, but there is plenty of trouble we can get into while waiting for the meeting, like the chicks Alec flirts with not ten steps away.

"I'm going to look in on Carmen." I glance at Zeb and grimace just knowing he's going to bust my balls.

"Have at it." To my surprise, Zeb says nothing further. "You know those chicks?" He turns his attention to Hayes, ignoring me.

"Naw, just flirting. There's three of them and three of us…" No need for Hayes to finish that sentence, and I don't miss out that he doesn't include me.

Not that I blame him. For the past year, I've declined every invite to go out with them on the town. At some point, they stopped asking, and I no longer care.

The three of them get up and saunter over to the other table. Brady leaves to collect Booker and Izzy, which leaves me free to see how Carmen's day has been.

Fingers crossed she decides to talk to me. Maybe if I bring her a treat she'll open up? Something sweet to show her we're not the bad guys? I'd make it myself. I'm good in the kitchen; better than good, but there's no time for that.

Less than ten minutes later, I find myself in the hallway outside the quarters Carmen's been assigned during her stay. On Guardian HQ proper, there are three sets of dormitories for those who choose to live close and for the occasional specialist who comes for an extended stay.

One of the new Guardian Protectors, Reid, steps out into the hall. He has quarters on this floor. Not because he doesn't have a place off Guardian HQ, but because he's protecting a high-profile client.

"How's it going?" I stop to shake his hand.

The Guardian Protectors are a new branch of Guardian HRS. Personal protection specialists, their specialty is basically what the name implies. Instead of operating on the Guardian teams, rescuing those who need our help, he's assigned to protect one person, and one person alone.

"Pretty good. Heard your team saw some action." His left brow lifts slightly and it's no mistake his gaze shifts to one particular door.

"We did." The operation isn't a secret, but I'm not in a particularly talkative mood. "And I heard things are going well with Lyra?" As big as Guardian HRS is, the gossip chain is healthy and active. Reid's Lyra's Protector. She's some kind of computer savant who challenges what Mitzy and Forest can do. Reid and Lyra appear to be getting along *very* well, which brings a frown to my face.

"They are—and speaking of..." He points to the personal-size cake I carry. "Where did you get that?"

"They have them at the cafeteria." Every time I say cafeteria, I think of the lunchroom at school and the slop they tried to feed us. Like most things, Guardian HRS goes big when it comes to feeding their teams. It's not gourmet, but the food is a cut above, and the pastries are even better. "But you gotta get to them before the lunch rush, or they're gone."

"Good to know. I'll tell Lyra. She's feeling hemmed in and keeps sending me out for pizza."

We chat for a bit more about nothing of consequence, then Reid moves on. Which leaves me standing in the hallway with a personal-sized cake and no fucking idea what I'm going to say to Carmen.

Despite how it seems, she's not a prisoner. There are no guards at her door and no lock on the outside. Forest's been particular about that fact. They're treating her with kid gloves until we have a better idea what threat she presents. Not that she's free to roam the premises. There are cameras in the halls. If she wants to go out for a stroll, she'll be discretely followed from a distance by one of Mitzy's dragonfly drones and maybe a robotic sentry dog.

But Carmen doesn't go out. She never leaves her room.

I knock on the door, knowing she won't answer, then call out.

"Carmen, I hope you're decent. I'm coming in." The last thing I want is to accidentally walk in on her in the middle of getting changed.

There's no answer.

Not that I expect one.

I take in a deep breath, open the door, and brace myself.

SIXTEEN

Carmen

THE KNOCK ON THE DOOR MAKES ME JUMP, BUT NOT AS MUCH AS the reverberations coming from the voice calling out from the other side. That voice does weird things to my insides. My hand drifts up to settle over my stomach, where butterflies flit around and swirl with frenetic energy.

They weren't doing that a few seconds ago.

"Carmen, I hope you're decent."

Rafe.

I can't stop thinking about him. His roguish virility demands attention and his physical perfection fuels my fantasies.

They're positively sinful.

Like the rest of him, Rafe's deep baritone is a force all its own, full of buzzing resonance that makes me squirm with whispers of promises fulfilled only in the darkness between the sheets.

It's the kind of voice infused with power, bursting with virility, and pulsing with sultry tones of seduction. It captivates my senses and sends my thoughts spiraling down dark and dangerous paths. In confusing my senses, it builds anticipation for something more.

Something I shouldn't want.

"Please just go away."

"You know I'm not going to do that." The knob wriggles.

The door's unlocked. He can barge right in, but he won't. Rafe visits me every day, but he never forces his way inside my quarters.

"You don't have to check in on me."

"You know I will." The doorknob rattles.

This strange attraction doesn't make sense. I don't know Rafe. I literally know *nothing* about him. All I can say is he makes me feel something I've never experienced before. The need growing within me is dangerous and threatens a lifetime of preparation. I can't risk letting him get too close.

Maybe it's because I'm weak? Desperate for affection? Starved for love? Craving physical contact?

It could be all three.

So why is that all I can think about when Rafe stops by?

That carnal desire distracts me from what's important. Lucinda told me there would be many times I would be tested along the way. No matter what, giving in to personal *needs*—my governess would never be as crass to call them physical urges—but her message was clear.

Stay focused. Distractions are deadly. Never lose sight of the goal.

After a lifetime of being held at arm's length by a cold and distant father, distractions are inescapable. I crave connection to another. I desire physical intimacy. I want Rafe with every fiber of my being.

Would it be so terrible to *give in?* Even for a tiny taste?

If Lucinda were still alive, she wouldn't hesitate to yank me back on my righteous path. She did what she could to comfort me following my mother's death. She showered affection upon me in the absence of a mother, but it wasn't love.

Lucinda taught me about revenge.

She taught me to wait. To be patient. Above all else, she taught me to bide my time, learn what I needed to learn, and act only when I was absolutely certain of success.

"You better be decent, because I'm coming in." That voice sends a ripple of anticipation zinging down my spine, bringing a whole new meaning to making my body shudder.

I know why I fantasize about the sexy Guardian—Hero worship. He saved me and I turned him into an impossible fantasy, building him up in my mind. My thoughts are untrustworthy. My urges dangerous. I'm fundamentally flawed when it comes to Rafe.

"Go away!" I don't know why I shout; he never goes away.

Morning and night, the man stops by to check on me. Despite my refusal to speak to anyone but Isabelle LaCroix, he's gotten more words out of me than anyone else.

"I bring gifts." His tone lifts, turning from sexier than hell to cordial and uplifting.

Platonic.

I brace for the battle to come. It's too easy to want to *like* Rafe. He's been in my dreams since the night I jumped him and clung to him for dear life. It's too easy to let him get under my skin. It's too easy to relax and lower my guard.

The door squeaks open while I vow to make this visit as painless, and as brief, as possible. My goal is to kick him out as quickly as I can.

"How about the gift of going the hell away?" I make the sign of the cross with my thumb, begging forgiveness for the foul language. "*Amen.*" With a properly penitent bowing of my head, I miss Rafe's entrance but feel him everywhere the moment he steps inside my personal space.

Every cell in my body wakes up and takes notice of his presence. Christ, he's magnificent. A bit rough around the edges, but breath-taking, nonetheless.

"How about a thank you for the visit? You've got to be feeling all kinds of lonely? Scared? Out of your element? Maybe you need someone to talk to?"

His unruly, raven hair curls in front of his eyes. A practiced flip of his head shifts the hair out of his eyes, but it flops right back in place a second later, making him more attractive than before. He flashes a devastating smile and winks.

I respond with an Oscar-worthy eye roll and practiced flutter of my lashes.

Glad he's having fun with this. Everything about him oozes

virility and rugged perfection. He's a force of nature designed to weaken feminine knees and encourage bad decisions.

I'm inadequately prepared to handle him, but it's his smile that devastates me with its power to sweep me away.

"I keep telling you I don't want visitors, and I'm not talking to anyone…"

"Anyone but Izzy. Yeah, that's what I keep hearing." He kicks the door closed with his heel and lifts what he's holding in his hand. "I brought a treat, and if you don't want to talk, that's fine. We can sit and enjoy it together in complete silence."

That's a lie. Every time he comes around, I tell myself I won't speak to anyone but Isabelle, but then I spend time talking to him.

"I'm full." My hand covers my belly because that's a bald-faced lie. I refused breakfast, then lunch, and regret that tremendously.

"Such a shame; it's really good." He lifts the box and makes a show of sniffing the deliciousness that has to be chocolate on chocolate. I inhale the decadent aroma from across the room.

"What is it?" I hate that I cave so easily but dismiss my weakness for valid hunger.

"Cake. I hope you like chocolate?" He opens the lid with an over-the-top flourish and almost makes me giggle like a schoolgirl when he presents what's inside. The giggle gets suppressed, but my smile is real.

"I haven't had lunch. That'll ruin my appetite."

"Who cares?" He checks behind the single plant in the corner. "Nobody's here but us, sweetie." Another dashing wink nearly buckles my knees. "Who's going to tell?" He glances furtively around the small apartment, having fun with his game.

I can't help but laugh, then quickly cover my mouth with my hand. What's it been? Less than a minute and I'm already giggling, ogling, and talking.

Stick a fork in me, I'm done.

There's no defense against a man like him.

Rafe shows me the cake. True to his word, chocolate shavings top decadent chocolate frosting, which top what is most assuredly a very chocolate cake underneath. If the shavings aren't enough, a strawberry dipped in dark chocolate, and drizzled with white chocolate, crowns the delicious masterpiece.

"I brought two forks." He pulls out plastic forks from his back pocket. "But fair warning, we have to eat it quick."

"Quick?" Did I miss something?

"I have a briefing in an hour."

"I don't think it takes an hour to eat cake."

"Probably not, but you look like you could use some company."

"I'm fine."

"Why Izzy?" He cocks his head to the side.

Well, that didn't take long. I shouldn't be surprised. Disappointed, I take a step back and sit on the couch.

"Is that why you're here?" I gesture to the cake. "Bribe me with cake, then ply me for information?"

"You're right. My mistake. It just slipped out. I'm sorry, but we're all curious why you're here."

"And I said I'm not talking to anyone but Isabelle LaCroix." I flick my fingers in his general direction. "Take your stupid cake and leave."

"Leave?"

"You heard me." I deserve a medal for sending that cake away.

"What if I don't want to?"

"You're much bigger than me. All I can do is ask." Disappointed, I turn my nose up at the very delicious looking cake and pray my stomach behaves, but it chooses to announce its displeasure in the silence hanging between us with a gurgling growl. "Sorry."

"When was the last time you ate?" He places the cake on the coffee table. "They're not withholding food, are they?" His tone sounds genuinely concerned. Does he forget he's a part of the collective *they?*

"No, they're not. I just didn't feel like eating."

It hasn't escaped my notice that I'm not being held under lock and key. If I want to, I bet I could walk right on out of this tiny apartment and keep on walking until exhaustion pulls at me, or my father's men find me.

Truth be told, I'm terrified Father will send men out looking for me. How much of what I screamed at him after that explosion actually made it to his ears? It's not a matter of *if*, but rather *when*.

My continued presence here puts all these people in danger, but I don't dare leave. Not until I have a solid plan of action. The problem is I don't know how to reach my CIA contact. We never set anything up for contingencies like this. So far, our conversations have been cursory at best, determining what I could do for them and they for me.

Protection is what I need. Until I'm safe to travel outside this place, I'm staying right where I am. My only hope lies in Isabelle LaCroix and the desperate plea I intend to make.

She's the only one I can trust because she knows what my father's capable of. Which may not make sense. Father had her kidnapped and brought to him, but not to the cells beneath my home. He put her in a guest room, let her get cleaned up, dressed her in one of my gowns, and sat down to dinner with her.

Why?

Why did Isabelle LaCroix warrant treatment with kid gloves from my father?

I know the answer to that, but only because I know how my father's mind works. She has something he wants. That's why I need to speak to her. I need to know the value Father places on Isabelle LaCroix.

"What are you thinking so hard about?" Rafe shoves a plastic fork into the decadent chocolate cake. When he lifts it, my mouth waters. Thankfully, my stomach behaves. There's no more embarrassing growling.

"I wasn't…"

"You furrow your brows when you think too hard, and your eyes shift to the left when you lie."

"They do not."

"If that's what you want to think…" He shrugs, as if it doesn't matter one way or the other, but Rafe gives me valuable advice, intended or not.

I think he's going to eat the bite on his fork, but Rafe takes a knee in front of the couch.

In front of me.

Something dark and woodsy floods my senses. He smells like heaven and chocolate, and offers me the first bite.

"No, thanks." I turn away. It's too easy to forget where I am, who he is, and the danger he represents.

"Please don't tell me I wasted the effort." He pulls back and cocks his head to the side.

"I'm really not hungry."

Rafe sits back on his heels.

"I'm only going to say this once and hope you hear what I'm saying and trust I won't break my word."

"I…"

He holds up a finger and shakes his head.

"It's a single bite of the best chocolate cake you'll ever have. I'm not here to question you, or to get you to spill your secrets, and I'm not going to force you into sharing anything you don't want to share."

"Then why are you here?"

"Because you look like you can use a friend."

"There's no way you and I will ever be friends." I draw in my lower lip, to keep the quivering to a minimum, while static electricity charges the air.

He's too close.

Too sincere.

Too much to take in.

Definitely not friend zone material.

He's in the other zone. The dangerous zone where bad decisions are made and regret follows.

I want to believe him. He's right about me needing a friend.

Only my governess's words come back to me. *You must have patience, luv, and prepare to endure. This requires meticulous planning. Hasty actions are a sure path to ruin. Be careful who you trust. Your father is more powerful than you realize. He has eyes and ears everywhere.*

Those words keep me company when my faith waivers. They did when I was ten, twelve, and on the night of my *Quinceañera*. That was the night I became a woman and was the last time I saw my governess alive.

My father said since I was officially a woman, I no longer needed a governess to look after me. Several years later, I learned the truth of what happened to the woman who held me the night my mother died. The night I watched my father murder my mother.

I prayed. I spent hours on my knees wishing and hoping what I learned about my governess didn't actually happen; that Lucinda merely left our home for another position as a governess to another girl. Unfortunately, wishes and hopes are the folly of children. As a young woman, I knew enough to look at the world from a different angle. From that day on, I accepted the truth.

When I looked into my father's eyes, evil looked back.

"What just happened?" Rafe leans forward. The pad of his finger presses beneath my chin, lifting my face up to meet his.

We're close. Too close. Our faces kissably close. His breath flutters over my skin. If I lean forward our lips will touch, our mouths will part, and he will destroy me. There's no surviving a kiss from this man.

"Nothing." I swipe at the tears threatening to spill down over my cheeks and pull back. I need space, room to breathe, I need…

"When a woman looks like that and tells me nothing happened, I know something important is going on." He rocks back on his heels and wipes an errant tear off my cheek. "You may not want a friend, but you desperately need someone to lean on. I wish you'd open up and let me in."

"Why?"

"So I can shoulder some of your burden for you. Whoever hurt you deserves to suffer in the tenth circle of hell."

"Why would you do that?" It takes a moment for what he said to kick in. I step in to correct him. "You mean the ninth circle of hell."

"No. Tenth. I created a special level for those who hurt those weaker than themselves. The ninth circle of hell is the one for treachery—a frozen wasteland where the greatest traitors go to suffer. The tenth is where those who hurt women and children go to suffer forever, subjected to the same horrors they forced their victims to endure."

"You're familiar with the Nine Circles of Hell?"

"Limbo, Lust, Gluttony, Greed, Anger, Heresy, Violence, Fraud..." He counts each on his fingers. Rafe leans back on his heels. "You don't know me, but in answer to the first part of your question, I'll move heaven and earth to keep you from those who wish you harm. I'll chase them through hell and back."

"Why would you do that for someone you don't know?"

"Because, I do know you."

"My name and who my father is, maybe, but you don't *know* me."

This impressive organization revealed as much. They don't say it out loud, but my father interests them. Isabelle LaCroix interests my father. That mutual interest can't be a coincidence.

"Those are merely facts and figures about your birth." He rises off his heels, lifting up on his knees again until we're at eye level. "You've been hurt by someone you trust—or trusted—betrayed in the worst possible way. You carry that pain in your eyes.

It's a mark on your soul.

You took a leap of faith, trusting in God to take care of you. There are few who carry within them such profound faith. If God put you in my arms, don't you think he might want you to confide in me? It would be my honor to lighten your load."

"I can't... Please don't ask me to..."

"I'm not asking you to tell me anything. In fact, I give you my solemn vow."

"Vow?" I made a vow once. I was ten and it was the worst day of my life.

"To protect you and keep you from harm. If you entrust your secrets to me, I will not repeat them. From this moment onward, I'll not ask, trick, or force you to confide in me. Despite what you said, you can use a friend. If not me, then someone else. You came to us for a reason. Have faith in the path God's placed before you."

"Are you a believer?"

"Catholic." His eyes smolder. "Same as you." He glances at my hand. "I saw you praying in the helicopter."

"Thank you." Overwhelmed doesn't begin to describe my current state. "I hear what you're saying, and I don't mean to diminish or dismiss your vow, but please don't. I can't accept, and I would never put you at odds with your employers."

"What if my employers are not at odds with what you need? We're in the business of helping those who can't help themselves. It's in our motto."

"Some truths are safest when never spoken aloud. If you want to help me, convince your superiors to let me speak to Isabelle LaCroix."

"Truths such as those often come with great danger." He places his hand on my knee. "Have they told you what it is we do?"

"You save those who can't save themselves." I nod. "I've been told."

"Then you know Izzy isn't the first woman your father's taken."

"I know." My chin tucks to my chest. Sadly, that's not my fight.

"What is it about Izzy? You barely know her?"

"I know enough." How do I explain?

"I'll do what I can." He doesn't miss a beat.

It's as if he's determined to help me, even if I won't trust him with my secrets. I would. I'd love to be able to trust Rafe, but in my world, the only people who've ever hurt me are men.

There's no trust to extend.

"Thank you." A lightness fills my chest, as if a heavy burden suddenly lifts.

Rafe's done nothing except convince me there's goodness in the world. Warmth fills me from within, as if the Holy Spirit touches me in this moment. Almost as if I'm exactly where God means for me to be.

Is it possible?

Leaning forward, I wrap my arms around Rafe's powerful shoulders and lean against his chest. I bury my face in the soft hollow of his neck and breathe him in as the first tears fall. His arms wrap around me, holding me tight.

How long we sit there—him on his knees, me on the couch—I don't know. Neither do I know when my tears stop. For the first time in far too many years, I no longer feel achingly alone. Hope stirs within me that my prayers may finally be answered.

His fingers stroke through the tangled strands of my hair. I close my eyes and surrender to the gentle pulling against my scalp. When's the last time I enjoyed the simple affection hidden within a hug?

The night my mother died? The night when I became a woman at my *Quinceañera*? I miss my mother. I miss Lucinda. I miss the healing power of a hug.

Rafe's hand drifts from my hair to wrap around my shoulder. He slowly rocks forward and back, then I'm suddenly up in the air, clinging to him, as he carries me to my bed. Gently, reverently, he lays me down and kisses my brow. It's a tender kiss meant to comfort, but the heat from his lips sears my skin and leaves a mark on my beating heart.

"I'll speak to my superiors and see if they will send Izzy to talk with you. Until then…" The pad of his thumb sweeps the hair from my face. "Until then, sleep. No one will hurt you while you're here. That's one vow you can't keep me from making." He leans forward and those sculpted lips of his press against my forehead for the second time. "I must go, but I'll be back. Until then, try to rest and get some sleep."

When he pulls back, I grab his hand. "Thank you."

Without another word, Rafe leaves me in my room. I don't intend to sleep. Nightmares fill my dreams. Nevertheless, I slip away into the welcome embrace of sleep.

Sometime later, I wake to knocking at my door.

SEVENTEEN

Rafe

Not sure what to make of my interaction with Carmen, I barely make it to the meeting before it starts. Sam and CJ are there, along with most of Bravo team. Brady and Booker have yet to arrive.

"Grab a seat, we're about to get started." CJ gestures to a seat beside him.

"What's going on?"

"Something about the damn diamonds." CJ pulls at his chin and examines the messages on his phone.

The diamonds.

What an interesting turn of events; all of which started when Brady went off on his own to rescue Angie. Newly released from medical hold, he took off for a solo vacation in Costa Rica and wound up rescuing both Angie and Izzy. One of the things they each brought back from that encounter was a matching set of rabbit's feet that just so happened to contain a fortune of diamonds inside.

Doc Summers enters the room with Forest Summers in tow. I trade a look with Alec and Hayes; the Doc and Forest Summers don't usually sit in on these kinds of meetings.

"How's everyone doing?" Sam glances around the table, taking in me, Alec, Zeb, and Hayes. It's a pointed question, directed at Bravo team alone. He glances at CJ. "Where's Izzy?"

"I sent Brady to fetch Booker and Izzy." CJ leans back and folds his arms across his chest.

Alec rocks back in his chair. "What's this about?" He glances at Forest Summers rather than Sam.

Forest says nothing. He looks worn out, like sleep's given up on him.

The door to the conference room bangs open. Brady enters with Izzy and Booker in tow. Both Sam and CJ stand.

"How are you holding up?" Sam gives Izzy a hug, then CJ does the same.

"Why do I feel as if I've done something wrong?" Izzy wrings her hands, looking nervous.

"We've had a bit of a development." Sam presses a button in front of him.

"Hey, boss, what's up?" Mitzy's perky voice fills the room over a hidden speaker.

"Izzy's here."

"About time." Mitzy reminds me a lot of Piper. Or maybe Piper reminds me of Mitzy? Either way, I don't have the energy for either one of them.

"You said something during your debrief that has me wondering." Sam focuses his attention on Izzy.

"What was that?"

"The comment Angelo made about the diamonds."

Izzy was kidnapped because of the diamonds hidden inside the mangy rabbit's foot given to her by Jerald, now dead, who used Izzy and Angie, as unknowing mules, to smuggle the diamonds in Nicaragua.

Actually, there were two kidnappings—separate events. The first, when she and Angie were kidnapped while working for Doctors Without Borders in Nicaragua. Brady executed a solo rescue of the women that kind of went sideways at the end. That was Izzy's first kidnapping. The second one landed Izzy in Maximus Angelo's villa.

"Yes, but I don't know what he meant." From the way Izzy fidgets, she doesn't like being the center of attention.

"Do you remember what he said?" Sam continues to press.

"Sure, it was something about diamonds buy things, but something else buys obedience and loyalty."

"Yes, I've been trying to wrap my head around that and fit it in with what happened to Angie."

"What do you mean? Are you talking about our abduction?" Izzy's brows pinch together. It's clear she wants to be helpful but isn't sure *how*, or *what*, Sam's looking for.

I admit, I'm curious, too.

"We've been discussing it on and off, and something always felt a bit off about it." Sam spreads his hands out on the table in front of him.

The door to the conference room swings open, and Mitzy rushes in with an assistant following behind pushing a cart.

"Hey, Izzy, have you been briefed?" Chipper as always, Mitzy's perky tone brings a smile to my face.

"I don't know why I'm here." Izzy glances around the room, but from the way her shoulders hunch, she's as confused as the rest of us.

"You didn't tell her?" Mitzy's scolding tone goes from light and perky to harsh and cutting. She makes a show of fiddling with the equipment on the cart, speaking under her breath loud enough for us all to hear. "Typical. Just typical. Wasting time like always."

Finished with whatever she's doing, Mitzy turns to Forest, pointing at him. "You know I blame you. It's your job to get your people to do the talking thing. Y'all can't keep expecting me to connect the dots."

"I'm not…" Forest begins, but Mitzy cuts him off.

"It's okay, I'll deal with it." More fiddling, then Mitzy addresses Izzy directly. "They were supposed to brief you, but men never follow directions. You're here because the princess in the dungeon—

Carmen Angelo—says she will only speak to you. I want to know why, and if she can shed any light on our new mystery."

"Does anyone know *why* she wants to speak to me?" Izzy's lids draw back and her brows lift halfway up her forehead.

"Don't know." Mitzy continues fiddling with her gear.

"Mitzy, show her what you found." Sam twists in his seat.

"One sec." Mitzy and her assistant continue doing whatever it is they're doing.

Meanwhile, I lean over to whisper in Brady's ear. "You have any idea why we're here?"

"Mitzy's team found something." His reply is short and to the point but lacks details.

"Like what?"

"I think we're going to find out." He points to the screen as a picture of Izzy's mangled rabbit's foot appears alongside nearly ten million dollars in loose diamonds.

"Your comment about buying loyalty and obedience got me thinking. The diamonds are a distraction for what was really being moved." Mitzy explains her thoughts.

"Since when is ten million in diamonds a distraction?" Hayes leans back with a cocky grin, but he's as confused as the rest of us.

The view on the screen zooms in, not on the diamonds, but rather the raggedy rabbit's foot. Specifically, it zooms in on the metal brad that attaches the rabbit's foot to its chain.

"Keep going." Mitzy gestures to her technician to continue. The view zooms in until metal scoring marks are visible on the brad. "What you're seeing is the brad as viewed by a scanning electron microscope. Are you familiar with those?" Without prompting, Mitzy goes on with a lengthy explanation about microscopes, specifically scanning electron microscopes, and how powerful they are. "When Angelo mentioned buying loyalty and obedience, there's not much worth more than ten million in diamonds except information. I went looking for a message, first on the diamonds. It's common practice to inscribe diamonds. When I found nothing, I noticed the metal brad and hit the motherload. What we have here is another cipher without a key." Mitzy turns to Izzy. "This is where you come in."

"Me?" Izzy points to herself and glances around the table looking for support for what she clearly believes is insane. "I don't understand what you expect to get out of me speaking to Carmen." Izzy protests, but Sam cuts in.

"It's been days and she still insists she'll speak only to you." Sam's a hard man to ignore, and when he starts issuing orders, we fall in line. "We can't keep her here indefinitely. We're running out of time."

Time? I didn't know there was an expiration date on how long we helped Carmen.

Brady and Booker hold a side conversation which sounds a whole lot like a bunch of *fuck yous* and *no fucking ways* tossed back and forth.

"Izzy…" I jump in. "You have to do it."

"I don't know how to interrogate someone." Izzy glances at Booker and nibbles on her bottom lip.

"I've been visiting Carmen morning and night. She's free to move around Guardian HQ but never leaves her apartment. She's scared of something. If you talk to her, we might find out what that is. It could be important."

"You visit her every day?" Booker looks at me with surprise.

"I try to get her to talk. She refuses, but I bet she'll let me listen in." I turn to Izzy. "I get this is hard. You've never done something like this, but it's not an interrogation. We need to know why she's running from her father."

"Or helping him," Booker mumbles under his breath. "She's probably working for him."

"We won't know until the two of them talk it out." Forest jumps into the conversation. His deep bass voice makes the air vibrate. "What we have is something deliberate and high tech. That requires access to very specific types of equipment. Carmen Angelo probably knows nothing about this cipher. We'll let *Jacen* chew on it, but she came to us. I want to know why."

JCN, or *Jacen,* is the name of Guardian HRS's resident super-computer.

"What if she's here to report back to dear old dad?" Booker pulls Izzy to him, holding her tight.

Protective.

Not a fan of using Carmen for anything relating to her father, my fingers curl. A growl builds in the back of my throat, but Brady catches my eye. With a quick jerk of his chin, he tells me to stand down.

"Look…" Mitzy says. "We can make all the assumptions we want, but that gets us nowhere. What we know is Carmen risked her life when she jumped on Rafe. She either saw our rescue of Izzy as an opportunity to escape, or she's fiercely loyal to her father and is working with him to bring Guardian HRS down. When I looked into her, there's nothing suggesting she's a risk taker. She's obedient to a fault, but the girl's no spy."

"Then why send Isabelle in to speak with her?" Booker wraps his arm around Izzy's shoulder. "You're basically saying Carmen is useless."

"That's not what I'm saying at all," Mitzy fires back at Booker. "You need to listen better."

"I'm confused." I raise my hand and look around the room. "Come on, I can't be the only one?"

Hayes, Alec, and Zeb shoot their arms into the air. Brady rocks back on his heels and Booker places a gentle kiss on the top of Izzy's head.

"Sorry, but I agree with the team." Izzy joins us in lifting her hand.

The way she includes herself as part of Bravo team warms my heart. We're a tight-knit group of men. Most of us worked together during our team days; either on the same SEAL team or on the same covert operation. We've never had women join our family until Angie and Izzy came into the picture. It feels all kinds of right. Like we were solid before the girls, but we're stronger now with them being a part of us.

Which is both odd and insanely cool.

Usually, a woman can be a man's greatest weakness, driving him to do things he wouldn't normally do, risking more than he would normally risk. Maybe it's because Angie and Izzy joined not just Bravo team, as a result of their relationships with Brady and Booker, but because they joined the Guardian HRS medical team. They're an integral part of who we are, both as an organization and as a team.

CJ clears his throat. "We're backed up against a wall here." He interlaces his fingers behind his head and leans back in his chair, unfazed by Booker's outburst and our general confusion.

"Well, Isabelle isn't doing it." Booker tries to put down his foot, but he's outgunned by a very feisty Guardian HRS technical lead.

"Last I looked, Izzy has a mind of her own." Mitzy props her fists on her hips and her tone cuts through Booker's BS. "You don't own her, and you sure as shit don't make stupid ass, Neanderthal-like comments about what you *will and won't allow her to do.*" Mitzy's voice deepens at the end and she swings her arms back and forth, pantomiming what I think is supposed to be a gorilla. Instead of looking fierce, it's comical. "Izzy can decide what she wants to do all on her own." Mitzy turns her attention to Izzy, who looks like she'd rather climb under a rock than remain in this room.

"For what it's worth, I think Carmen's hiding," I add in what I think is useful information. "From her father?" CJ unfolds his arms.

"That's my best guess."

"That's your *assumption.*" Mitzy shakes her head in frustration.

"Carmen Angelo is an unknown." Forest clears his throat. "I don't like unknowns...especially when it comes to this man."

"Right, and it makes her dangerous," Booker says. "Putting Isabelle in the same room with her, without backup, makes no sense."

"At least we're getting somewhere." A smug expression fills CJ's face.

"What's that?" Booker places his palms down on the table and glares at CJ.

"You're not against Izzy talking to Carmen."

Booker's brow furrows as he thinks about what he said.

To my left, Zeb and Alec snicker. The two of them have been watching the verbal exchange with tight lips. They think this is hysterical, and I bet they've already placed bets on the outcome.

"Bottom line…" CJ looks toward Sam. "We need Izzy to get Carmen talking." His attention shifts to Booker. "It's not an interrogation. She's the daughter of Nicaragua's Minister of the Interior. Under no circumstances is the woman to be coerced, but that doesn't mean we can't learn what we can while she's with us."

"CJ's correct," Sam says. "Our contacts in Nicaragua say Maximus hasn't elevated Carmen's disappearance through official channels. He's keeping her absence low-key. How long that remains the case is anyone's guess, but Carmen's stay with us is limited."

"If she's trying to get away from her father, we should help her." I can't help but toss that out there.

"If Carmen needs asylum, we'll arrange it, but she has to give us something to work with." Sam isn't happy, but it's clear his hands are tied.

I get it. I totally get it. Carmen's disappearance has the potential to generate official inquiries that hinder Guardian HRS operations.

Pivoting left, I turn to Izzy. "She feels you're the only one she can trust, but I should be there."

"If Isabelle needs backup, I'll do it." Booker accepts Izzy will speak with Carmen, but it's clear he'd feel more comfortable if he was with her when it happened.

"Because, I'm the closest thing Carmen has to a familiar face. You show up, and she's not going to talk."

"Then it's settled." CJ is quick to wrap things up while we're all somewhat on the same page. "Izzy will speak to Carmen. Rafe will back her up." He lifts a finger and turns toward Booker. "I agree with Rafe. It should be him."

"I don't know what to say." Izzy gives a shrug.

"I don't think you need to worry about that," I say.

"Why?" Izzy's still not convinced.

"Because I have a feeling Carmen will lead the conversation." And I'm eager to hear what she has to say.

EIGHTEEN

Rafe

"You ready?" With things decided, I push away from the conference table, eager to get going.

"Now?" Izzy's brows practically climb up her forehead. Unlike me, she's not excited to move this along.

"No time like the present." My response comes in a rush, and when I say rush, I mean a surge of excitement to see Carmen again.

The woman fascinates me. Despite what Mitzy said, Carmen's got grit. She's a risk taker, and I admire people who take risks. Any person able to look fear in the face and act, despite it, is a winner in my books.

Respect.

Carmen needs someone in her corner, and I plan to be there for her. Right now, she's completely alone. No one's got her back. Not to mention, there's a pall of sadness that hangs over her—intense grief and mourning buried beneath the surface.

There's guilt too.

I haven't sorted out what guilt she bears, but it's there. Her stoic nature means her emotions struggle to get out, but every time I show her a little compassion, she lets me in a little bit more.

I like that. Not to mention, she smells amazing. I like that, too. I could stand all day in the same room with her, content to do nothing more than breathe in her sweet essence.

"Okay, if you're sure this is a good time?" Apprehension creates a flutter in Izzy's voice.

"I don't see why not." Glancing around the table, nods of agreement meet my searching gaze.

Doc Summers and Forest lean in close. Lips moving, their private conversation doesn't involve the rest of us. Whatever it is they're talking about, Forest shakes his head. He's not on board with what Doc Summers wants.

The muscles of his jaw bunch and tension fills his powerful frame. It's as if a shadow falls over him, darkening his expression. There's no other way to explain the sudden change. Between one breath and the next, the giant of a man becomes somewhat less than he was moments before. Shadows swirl in his icy gaze, and his shoulders slump as if weighted down by a heavy burden.

Maybe, I'm seeing things that aren't there, but I don't miss the way Doc Summers reaches out to comfort him. The moment her fingers brush against his upper arm, Forest flinches and pulls away as if stung. Skye leans in, murmuring something in his ear. Their heads tip, foreheads touching. It's an intimate moment. A tenderness and a love so profound I don't feel qualified to describe what I'm seeing.

After whatever Doc Summers says, Forest places his hand over hers. He tucks his chin to his chest, looking tired, defeated, and smaller than before. There's the slightest acquiescence at the end of their nonverbal display.

Doc Summers leans back, then shifts her attention to Sam. "We want to move quickly. I'm sorry, Izzy..." Her gaze softens as she turns to take in Izzy. "I know you have concerns, but talking to Carmen is necessary. Rafe should definitely go with you. We need to know what she wants."

Or needs.

The inflection in Doc Summer's voice is hard to miss. *We*, in this case, is not Guardian HRS. It means *them:* Doc Summers and Forest.

"Why?" Izzy accepts her assignment. Like me, she has questions.

"Because he… The man…" Doc Summers's mouth clamps shut and her eyes squeeze tight as if blocking a memory. It's hard to tell, but I think she's choking up. When her eyes open a second later, there's a shimmer that wasn't there before.

And pain.

Terrible pain.

I glance at the brother and sister pair, wishing I knew more about their past. I mean, I know they were abused as foster children. They were raped and worse. Bravo and Charlie teams were there when Forest faced off against his nemesis, John Snowden, as an adult.

We failed him that day.

Forest traded his freedom for Doc Summers's newborn son and fell into the clutches of John Snowden. We lost him for a time; agonizing for weeks while we prepped a rescue mission.

No one forgets the day we watched Forest fall.

Speaking of… Forest's deep, rumbling voice breaks the silence. It reminds me of boulders crashing together; deep, deadly, and powerful.

"Skye and I are no strangers to Maximus Angelo." Forest steps in for Doc Summers. He takes her hand in his. Gives a light squeeze. They trade a ghost of a smile between them. "We know him far too well. If he's sniffing around our organization, we want to know why." He reaches for Doc Summers and takes her hand in his.

"Too well." Doc Summers interlaces her fingers with Forest's.

Mitzy's sharp gaze softens and CJ sucks in a breath.

I shrug when Alec glances my way.

What the fuck? He mouths the words.

I return a *No bloody clue.*

"I suspected as much." Sam shifts, shoulders rolling back, spine straightening. He drums his fingers on top of the table. "You think he's trying to flush you out?"

"Seems like." Forest tucks his chin to his chest and takes in a deep breath.

"This complicates things." Sam covers his mouth, then drags his palm down his chin.

"It does." Doc Summers finds her voice. "Our number one priority is determining what information this rabbit's foot holds." She points to the screen where the electron microscope displays the image of the metal brad with its cipher. "If it's what we think, we're going in…"

"Where he's waiting for you," Sam interjects. "It's a trap."

"And if it isn't?" CJ pushes away from the table and picks at lint on his trousers.

"Um…" I raise my hand. "What do *you* think it is? I thought we were talking about rival cartels, diamonds, and some weird-assed cipher inscribed on the brad of a rabbit's foot. What are *you* referring to?"

One of the things I like about Guardian HRS, compared to my time in the Navy, is we're encouraged to speak freely and voice our concerns. There's a hierarchy within the organization, but the lines of communication flow freely. Which means there's no hesitation asking my question directly to the doc and her foster brother.

Doc Summers and Forest exchange a look, coming to some silent agreement between them. I expect Forest to speak, but Doc Summers answers.

"Maximus Angelo is one of the men who…" Her voice catches. "Sorry. It was a lifetime ago, but the pain is as sharp today as it was then. Whenever I think I've put it behind me, something like this comes up."

"Something like what?" Brady continues my line of questioning. "What *exactly* comes up?"

"Maximus Angelo was one of the men…" She clears her throat. "One of the many who…"

Forest turns their interlaced hands over to lift her hand to his mouth. He places a soft kiss on her knuckles. "He was one of Clark

Preston's regulars—our foster father—who destroyed our childhood. He was a *frequent flier with perks*. Nothing like Snowden, but no better." Our leader uses air quotes to emphasize his point.

"I'm sorry, I…" As the words spill from my lips, Brady sends a signal to shut up. I clamp my mouth shut and wait for Doc Summers and Forest to explain.

"Maximus Angelo is a pedophile with a penchant for preteens and early teens. He preferred Skye over me, but was more of a voyeur…" Forest's gravelly voice grinds to a stop. His nostrils flare as he takes in a breath to continue. "It's been twenty years, but there's no reason to believe he's not still involved in the kidnapping and trafficking of innocent girls."

"We have no proof of anything like that." I turn my attention toward CJ. "Did I miss something in one of our briefings? If there were girls at his residence, how did we leave them behind? How did we not know?" My gut does that twisting thing, making me nauseous. Knowing we were on site, capable of mounting a rescue mission, and didn't, makes my gut churn and bile rise in the back of my throat. "We have to go back."

By the expressions on their faces, Brady, Booker, Alec, Hayes, and Zeb agree. We're on the same page.

"A man like him…" Forest runs his fingers through his hair. "Like a leopard, a man like that doesn't change his spots. What Carmen did and why is a mystery. We need to know if she's involved, or not. If it's what I think, we can turn her…"

"Turn her? To do what exactly?" Heat pricks at the back of my neck, but I bury my initial reaction. There's no room for anger. Not here.

"Help us from within." Doc Summers speaks up. Her voice cracks, lacking the self-assurance I'm used to hearing from her.

"You think he's running an operation from within his home?" I shake my head. "I can't believe it. We were right there. We incapacitated his security team. We could've saved…" My voice trails off.

Sam turns to Mitzy. "Did your drones find any evidence of such a thing?"

"They weren't looking for that, but I can go back over the video and see if there's anything we missed. Anything that suggests there are girls…" Mitzy places a hand over her stomach. Like the rest of us, she's having a visceral reaction to this news. Mitzy, however, works with the facts. It's my belief it's an escape mechanism she employs to distance herself. "Off the top of my head, we didn't find any evidence of prisoners. Not that we were looking, and not that I would expect to find them in the living areas of the residence. He would've kept them below, and we didn't look down there."

"Below?" Brady clears his throat.

"Men like him tend to keep shit like that buried." Forest answers Brady's question for Mitzy. "Mitz, I need you to pull up the construction schematics. There's got to be a level below the house proper. Look for any evidence of vehicular traffic coming and going, any *events* where Maximus Angelo may have entertained clients."

"I will, but events are a regular occurrence. The man must throw a party a week. I assumed it was for political purposes." Mitzy's mouth twists on the word *assume*. She's a stickler about not letting predisposed thoughts and opinions blind us from the truth. Like us, however, she's human and makes mistakes.

"You know the drill, Mitzy." Forest takes command. "Assume nothing. Find the guest lists. Search for irregularities. Frequent fliers. Arrest reports. Anything and everything. Until further notice, this is our top priority."

"The parties he held could very well be covers for *things* below." I'm not squeamish when it comes to the world of human trafficking, but for some weird reason, my gut twists into a mess of knots.

My need to check in on Carmen becomes a visceral urge. I hope she's not involved in any of it. The thing is—my gut says otherwise.

"No doubt most were." Skye looks up at the ceiling and takes in a deep breath. "That's how things worked when Forest and I…" She pinches the bridge of her nose. "If he paid any attention to how Clark Preston ran his events…" Another look gets exchanged between Forest and Doc Summers. "Sam, CJ—Mitzy, you too…" Soft, but getting stronger, Doc Summers finds her voice. "Dig as deep as you must. In the meantime, let's figure out how Carmen Angelo fits into all of this. We're running out of time."

"How's that?" That twisting sensation in my gut intensifies.

"Maximus Angelo sent Matias after Carmen." Mitzy pipes up from the end of the table.

"How do you know?"

"I never stopped tracking his cellphone. He got on a plane for Los Angeles a couple of hours ago."

I forgot about the phone.

That's how Mitzy's tech team tracked Izzy in the first place. Matias forced her father to fly them across the Texas-Mexico border. From there, Matias forced Izzy to drive south, toward Nicaragua.

We followed Izzy's phone, tracking it, until it died. Then, Mitzy's team did the impossible. Using cellular data from cell phones in proximity to Izzy's cell phone, they were able to tease out and identify Matias's device. It never occurred to me they may still be tracking it.

"Then it's settled." Instead of Izzy, I glance at Booker. He's not happy, but knows this needs to be done. "You ready?"

"Yeah." Booker pushes away from the table and holds his hand out to help Izzy out of her chair. When she stands, he folds her into his embrace and kisses the top of her head. "You've got this. Rafe will be right by your side."

"I wish you were coming. Can't you…"

"No, luv. My presence would be distracting. Besides…" Booker grins at me. "Rafe's little cling-on is comfortable around him."

"Stop calling her a cling-on." My fingers curl into fists.

"Or what?" Booker eggs me on, knowing full well I won't start anything in front of the brass.

"Don't push me."

"Boys…" Mitzy's high-pitched voice breaks in. "You can do all that macho bullshit later. Right now, we've got a *guest* to interrogate."

With that settled, the meeting comes to an end. Booker, Izzy, and I head out first. The remainder of Bravo team follows. The brass, Doc Summers, Forest, Sam, CJ, and Mitzy, stay behind. Without a doubt, they're talking about Maximus Angelo.

What are the odds one of their abusers from childhood is someone they'd run into now?

In this business, I suppose it's not that odd. How much of Maximus Angelo's past is Carmen aware of? She's too smart not to know.

NINETEEN

Carmen

———————

About an hour after Rafe leaves me, another knock snaps my head up my pillow. Softer, and more hesitant than the pounding Rafe inflicts on the poor door, it can be only one person.

Isabelle LaCroix.

Despite my gut telling me it is her, I clear my throat and smooth out the trembling in my voice.

"W-who… Who is it?" Brushing my hair with shaky fingers, I close it and rise from bed with a nervous fluttering in my belly.

On the way to the door, a soft, feminine voice halts me in my tracks.

"It's Izzy." The woman clears her throat. "Isabelle LaCroix. You wanted to speak to me?" Failing miserably to conceal her nervousness, I pull up short.

Why is she nervous?

Why do you think?

Because I demanded it?

Rafe made this happen.

That voice in my head won't let me take credit for bringing Isabelle LaCroix to my doorstep. She's here *because* Rafe made it happen. Unsure what I think about that, my hand shakes as I reach for the doorknob.

Either way, this is no ordinary social call. Memories of the day we met, and the dinner that followed, pull me up short. I'd be nervous if I was forced to talk to the woman who treated me with such derisive disrespect.

I have to apologize for that.

"Are you alone?" I hesitate with my hand hovering over the doorknob.

"No." Isabelle LaCroix hesitates. "Rafe is with me."

"Don't turn her away, Carmen. This is your only opportunity to speak with her." That sexy baritone never fails to unsettle me.

"I want to speak to her alone." My fingers flutter as I imagine touching him.

"You know we can't allow that." The sound of him placing his palm against the door gives me pause. I can almost see him leaning forward, pressing his forehead against the wood, just like me. "Open the door."

Before he can tell me they're going to leave, I twist the knob and open the door.

Rafe stands on a powerful base; two massive legs of testosterone-infused power. Behind him, Isabelle LaCroix stands with tight lips and stormy eyes.

Rafe takes one step in, then stops. Standing head and shoulders above me, I crane my neck to look at him. When I do, his dark eyes pin me in place. The very air vibrates between us, lifting the fine hairs on my arms and anchoring a shiver at the back of my neck.

When he reaches out, I don't move. I'm transfixed. He lifts my chin using the gentle pressure of his thumb. The roughness of his skin sends tiny pulses of electricity skating down my spine.

"No need for introductions, but we should go over a few ground rules." Rafe releases my chin but doesn't move out of my personal space.

It's an intentional intrusion, and while I should take a step back, I don't.

"Excuse me?" Impossible to turn away from the hold he has on me, my lashes flutter as my mouth dries up from all my mouth-breathing.

"Command has agreed to a meeting with the caveat I stay." Rafe releases me, then steps to the side.

"That's not what I…"

"It's the best you're going to get."

Pulling away from him isn't easy, but I force myself to take a step back and turn my attention toward Isabelle LaCroix. "I just wanted… I need to speak with you—alone." My gaze bounces past Rafe's towering presence to land on Isabelle LaCroix.

"I'm sorry, but this is the best I could do," he says. "Take the win, Carmen, and imagine for a moment I'm not your enemy. Whatever is said, I'll keep in confidence."

"I never said you were my enemy. I wouldn't have…" At a loss for words, I struggle to regroup. This isn't what I wanted. I can't say what I want, ask what I need to know, or determine if these people can help me if he's here.

"Carmen…" Isabelle clears her throat. "Rafe's right about having to be here. Honestly, I'm not comfortable speaking to you without him, but if you want a little privacy…" She gestures toward the bedroom. "We could talk in there and leave the door open a crack. That might give you the privacy you want for our chat." Isabelle LaCroix spins around and places her hand on Rafe's arm. "If I need you, I promise to let you know."

My heart bangs away like a kettle drum and I shake like a leaf. While I've been asking—demanding this—for days, now that it's happening, I'm at a loss for what I'm going to say.

Rafe's bad enough when he comes to visit, making the room seem ten sizes too small, but Isabelle LaCroix is downright intimidating.

She makes *me* feel small.

"The door stays open." Rafe's attention fixes on me. "I wish you felt comfortable talking to me. This opportunity won't happen again." He points to Isabelle, letting me know this is the only time I'll get this chance.

With a gulp, it occurs to me he's upset. It takes a moment for that to sink in, and another moment to convince myself diving down the rabbit hole of why he might be upset isn't wise.

An awkward moment passes where no one moves. When Rafe coughs, I lurch into motion and retreat to the bedroom. I wasn't expecting to speak with Isabelle LaCroix in here, and I'm glad Lucinda trained me to make my bed each and every day.

She said, *Make your bed each morning and you will have accomplished your first task of the day. Do that and the second task, and the third, and all those that follow will be that much easier.*

The pain that always hits me when I think about Lucinda is as sharp today as it was years ago. I rub my knuckles against my breastbone, but it doesn't help.

It never helps.

Isabelle LaCroix follows on my heels. She stops to close the door, leaving a tiny gap. On the other side of that door, Rafe takes a seat on the couch. There's something odd about his ankle. About the way his foot inserts into his shoe.

"Well…" Isabelle LaCroix spreads out her arms. "You have me."

She pulls me from my thoughts and I sit awkwardly on the bed. There are no chairs in the room, which makes things a bit awkward.

"Um…" More nervous than I thought possible, I rub my palms against my jeans. They're suddenly a bit sweaty. "Do you want to sit?"

"No." Her arms cross over her chest and her shoulders roll back. "I'm here, and I'm listening. What I'm not doing is sitting down for a chat. Say what you want to say, and let's be done with this." Sharp and cutting, her tone makes me flinch.

"I don't know where to begin, except to say I'm sorry."

"Excuse me?" Clearly, that's not what she expects.

"I was cold and dismissive when I came across you in the hall with Matias, and downright cruel at dinner. I'm sorry about that."

"You certainly weren't warm and fuzzy. Prickly comes to mind. I don't know what's going on in that head of yours, or how you intend to manipulate the Guardians, but you're barking up the wrong tree." Her anger isn't a surprise. The biting sting of her words is expected. How much it hurts, however, catches me completely off guard.

"That's not… That's not what I'm doing."

"Why?" Isabelle sniffs. Her gaze catches on the corner of the bed as she shifts from foot to foot.

"Why, what?"

"Why didn't you do anything to help me? Did you know they kidnapped me? That they tried to kill my family? Did it ever cross your self-indulgent mind to do something?"

"You don't understand…" I press my lips together, at a loss to explain. I'm not what she thinks of me, but there's no way to deny I treated her horribly.

My throat constricts as I glance down at the bed. I place my palm against the soft linen. The texture soothes me. It also gets rid of the nervous sweat coating my palms. Not only am I out of my element, I'm in way over my head. My fate is sealed, but I can still save my friend before heading home like the submissive and obedient daughter I'm supposed to be.

Before I do that, I need to act fast.

Once I leave this place, and there's no doubt these people will kick me out sooner than I would like—probably right after this conversation—but once I leave, the clock starts ticking.

I'll have hours, at most, before my father's men track me down.

"Did you know what they were going to do to me?" Isabelle's tone turns harsh. Accusatory. "Did you?" She presses me to answer.

"Despite what I said, Father would never let Matias touch you."

"I remember exactly what you said, and that's not true." She takes a step back and leans against the door, closing it. "Not that it matters. What your father planned was egregious enough." Her voice rises and peaks on a harsh cry of frustration and anger.

"Izzy, are you alright?" The leather on the couch squeaks as Rafe stands and comes to the door.

I'm strangely offended he's not asking about me. The direction of my thoughts doesn't make sense. There's no reason for Rafe to give a rat's ass about me.

None of this makes sense.

"Oh, for the love of…" Isabelle's eyes pinch and her nose crinkles with disgust. "You knew, but you couldn't be bothered to break a nail helping another human being. I find everything about you reprehensible."

Rafe pushes the door open. "Are you okay?" He's imposing, intimidating, and very protective—of Isabelle. Not me.

A spike of jealousy jabs through me, but I bury that oddly inconvenient emotion as deep as I can before it has a chance to take root and grab hold.

Rafe is not mine. He's not here to protect me. He's here to defend Isabelle LaCroix and make sure I'm not a threat to her. I'd be lucky to have a man who loves me with a tenth of the protectiveness Rafe shows this woman.

Sadly, that's not my fate—to be loved.

I'll be lucky to convince my father Artemus is a poor match and our union won't result in the payout my father expects. If I'm extraordinarily lucky, I'll convince him to marry me off to a less reprehensible man.

As for who's next in line? I have no idea, but it won't be a man of *my* choosing. It won't be a union forged by the bonds of love. My worth is tied up in what advantage my father may secure to further his aspirations for more power.

Perhaps this, my inability to determine my own path, is the penance I pay for doing nothing to help those who suffered under my father's roof. Isabelle isn't wrong. I enjoyed the riches the suffering of others brought me.

"I'm fine." Isabelle LaCroix cranes her neck to speak to Rafe. "But this is useless." She turns toward me. "Unless you have something important to tell me, this is a waste of my time."

"Please…" I reach out, grasping the air. "Please, don't go."

It would be easier if Rafe wasn't here. Those incredibly deep eyes of his take their time checking on Isabelle. He doesn't even glance in my direction.

"Then start talking." She tries to push Rafe back, but the man is a mountain. I get the feeling he won't budge until he chooses to do so.

"Stop wasting Izzy's time." His words are more of a growl than anything else, reminding me I'm not among friends.

The look he gives me is sharp enough to cleave me in half, but what's worse… What's worse is the disapproval in his tone. I hold my hand over my chest and struggle to contain the beating of my heart. Rafe retreats and Isabelle LaCroix shuts the door. When she spins around, the expression on her face is far from friendly.

"What do you want to say to me and me alone? You have no idea who I am, but I can tell you I don't care who you are. Or who your father is. Not to mention, I'm in no position to do anything for you. I can't promise you anything. I can't negotiate anything for you. Hell, I'm not even equipped to interrogate you, and boy, are there a lot of Guardians chomping at the bit for a go at you."

Her words make me suck in a breath. Things are far more serious than I thought, not that it should be a surprise. I crashed their rescue party, and they deserve to know why. I haven't been forthcoming with an answer, but I can't risk a decade of planning. All I can do is try to get Isabelle LaCroix to sympathize with my plight.

There are three things I need. First, I have to take care of Rosalie. If I do nothing but that, I'll be happy. Her safety is my number one priority. Once I'm married and leave my childhood home, I'll be subject to my husband's rule. Any protection Rosalie has from Matias touching her will disappear.

"I'm not asking for something you can't give."

"I see. You don't want to talk to me. You want me to do something for you. Fat chance of that happening." She's angry, and I get it.

I would be, too, if our roles were reversed. While I deserve every angry dig, I won't let her anger keep me from securing Rosalie's freedom.

"How well do you know my father?"

"He's the Minister of the Interior for Nicaragua. He's rich. He controls directly, or indirectly, two of Nicaragua's most powerful cartels. He has men he can call upon to wage war on my family, abduct me, and do whatever the hell that whole charade was in your home. I'd say your father is a despicable man with the morals of the devil." Her voice rises until she's practically shouting.

I'm certain Rafe hears every word. I suppose that's okay. If I'm to ask them to trust me, I need to give them a reason to extend that trust.

"It's worse than that." My head hangs as shame overcomes me. I pause to allow Isabelle LaCroix a moment to process my words.

"Excuse me?"

"My father called me home after *allowing me the privilege of obtaining a college education.*" I use air quotes to emphasize my point. "It's an education I'll never have an opportunity to use."

At least, it won't if I can't reestablish communication with my contact in the CIA. As far as I know, the whole deal may be off. Everything depends on me living at home for at least another year, or two. My father took that timetable, stood it on its ears, and nullified everything with his arrangement with Artemus.

"Am I supposed to feel sorry for you?" Isabelle props her hands on her hips and stares down her nose at me.

"He forced me to come home and arranged a meeting with my future husband to plan the wedding. Instead of welcoming me home with a lavish party, he's forcing me into a loveless marriage to a man twice my age." My anger rises, meeting hers and surpassing it.

"You want sympathy?" Isabelle arches a brow. "Because you didn't get the welcome home party you deserved?" Her eyes roll in time to her snort of disdain. "You're shallower than I thought."

"It's not about the party." Dear Lord, this conversation is going downhill fast. Closing my eyes, I say a quick prayer for guidance.

"Seems like it is. The princess comes home to find out dear old dad no longer wants her mooching off his riches. That whole drama at dinner makes more sense now."

"What do you mean?"

"You were throwing a temper tantrum." Isabelle laughs. "You're one self-absorbed, self-entitled pathetic excuse of a human being."

"My father is more than just a powerful man." I cut her off, needing to get this conversation back to what matters. "I knew you weren't there willingly, but there was nothing I could do about it. I had to play along."

"Play along? You knew what he was doing was wrong and you *played along?*" Isabelle shakes her head, dismissing me. "I'm sorry, but this conversation, whatever you want to get out of it, is over." Her arms remain tightly crossed over her chest. "We're done here."

Anger rises within me; a molten rush of indignation mixed with over a decade's worth of helplessness. That rage burns in the back of my throat. The need to avenge my mother's death isn't an idle thought. It's the first vow I ever made, and I will fulfill the promise I made on my mother's grave.

Well aware that if I don't do something drastic, this opportunity will pass me by, I take in a deep breath and blurt out one of my deepest, darkest secrets. If my father ever discovers I know the truth, my life is over. Fingers curling, hands clenched, I suck in a breath and enunciate each and every word. I want there to be zero possibility of Isabelle LaCroix not hearing what I have to say.

"I asked if you knew my father. You said he has the morals of the devil."

"I stand by that statement."

"As do I." I lean in toward her. "There's a reason they say never to judge a book by its cover. You have no idea what's written between the pages. You've misjudged me."

"How so?"

"When I was ten, I watched my father kill my mother."

"That doesn't excuse… What?" Her lids draw back in surprise.

"He bludgeoned her. I saw the whole thing from the shadows, forced to say nothing, do nothing, and pretend for ten long years that I didn't know how my mother died. You don't get to judge me. You haven't lived my life. Every day since that night, I've worked toward one, and only one, goal. I vowed to make him pay. I've never been closer than I am now, but I came home to find out my father arranged this marriage. I have to get Rosalie out of that house before it's too late. She's my greatest weakness, and I can't afford for him to use her against me. I need the Guardians to rescue Rosalie like they rescued you."

TWENTY

Carmen

My words come out in a rush. It's a make it or break it moment for me. If I can't secure Rosalie's freedom, I'm not sure what to do next.

"Wait a minute." Isabelle takes a step back, then leans against the wall. "I'm going to need you to repeat that."

"I'd rather not."

"Humor me."

"Fine. Can the Guardians rescue my friend?" I'm not happy, but I need this woman's help.

"Not that part. The other part." Some of the stiffness in her body eases.

My nostrils flare as I suck in a deep breath. "Those are painful memories I'd rather not relive."

"I'm sorry for your loss, but if you want my help, I'm going to need you to repeat it."

"You mean the part when I was ten and watched my father beat my mother to death? Or the part about the girls trafficked through the place I grew up in?"

"How… Wait a minute. What girls?" The angry fire in Isabelle's eyes returns, burning brighter than before. She gives a shake of her head. "What girls?"

I close my eyes and realize my slip.

There's a lump in my throat that never goes away when I think of the atrocities committed in my home. Hot tears prick behind my eyelids, threatening to spill all over the place. I clamp my lids tight to stem a flow of tears I can't afford.

Weakness is a sin and it has no place in my life.

Tears are for the weak. Lucinda told me, taught me, and beat into me the importance of this one small thing.

I need to be strong and prepared for anything, but most of all, I must never, ever allow weakness, or fear, to guide my actions. I must remain focused and stalwart.

Never waiver.

Never lose faith.

Never give up.

Always—she emphasized this over and over—I must always keep the end goal in mind. A tiny win here or there could make the difference between defeat and revenge.

These are not the weighty issues a ten-year-old should bear, but it is my burden.

And I've carried it long enough.

This is why I had to wait. Lucinda told me I could do nothing but make things worse if I acted impulsively, or wasn't fully prepared. I needed to grow up, mature, and come at my father only after developing a solid plan.

This is my excuse when Isabelle LaCroix asks me the one question I can't answer.

Why did you wait?

My silence stretches.

Isabelle cocks her head and seems to come to some decision that makes sense to her.

"There's a lot to unpack here. Tell me what happened to your mother." She places a hand on my arm.

I flinch, but it doesn't faze her.

"And I'm sorry."

"Excuse me?"

"About your mother. I'm sorry."

Those hot pinpricks turn to stabbing daggers. I blink, squeezing my eyes shut, trying to keep my tears at bay, but her question demands an answer.

I draw in a deep, stabilizing breath and blow it out nice and slow. It helps to push the tears back. It helps to shove the pain back where it belongs. It does absolutely nothing, however, to ease my pain.

"It hurts as much now as it did then, but I think you'll understand me better. Before I say anything, though, I need your promise no one else will know."

"I can't make that promise." Her hand lifts, reaching for me again. Not to grab, but to console.

I draw back and Isabelle takes a step back.

I don't need anyone to feel sorry for me. I've lived with my pain for over a decade, and I will bear it to the end.

Isabelle's expression changes; turns softer. "I'm in a difficult position. Whatever we talk about, I'm obligated to report, but I'll try as much as I can to keep your secrets. Although, I hope to convince you to share with the others."

"I suppose that's the best I can ask for." Swallowing past that lump in my throat brings pain, but that sharp reminder steels me for the memories I must relive. Clearing my throat, I begin.

"I snuck out of bed to play spy with Lucinda."

"Who's Lucinda?"

"My governess. She humored me as much as she dared. I climbed out of my window and down to the top of the outer wall. I walked across it like a balance beam, then climbed up to the balcony outside my parents' room. I wanted to scare them, but when I peeked in, they weren't there. I thought to hide in their closet and jump out at them. When I climbed over the balustrade, the door to their room banged open. I scooted back to hide in the shadows."

"Wow, you were quite the tomboy."

"Even now, that feeling of glee and excitement returns to me. I was going to have so much fun surprising them. Little did I know that's what saved my life."

"What do you mean?" Isabelle twines her fingers together, twisting them this way and that.

She's nervous. For some reason that makes it easier to tell her more. I feel safe confiding in her, even knowing she's under orders to report back to her bosses.

"My father stormed in, dragging mother by her hair."

Images of that night fill my mind. The fragrant aroma of the garden. The humid air. The birds in the cages with their mournful song. Nighttime was always loud and full of life; the howling of monkeys, the buzzing of cicadas, and chirping of tree frogs.

I miss the jungle. I miss being surrounded by—life.

My mouth's dry, too dry to continue, but I muster enough spit to continue.

"My father flung my mother on the bed. She begged for mercy. I don't know what she did, but her fear filled that room. Father drew out his belt. He grasped the buckle and wrapped the leather around his wrist. His arm lifted and..." It's difficult to go on.

I pause for a moment, noticing my breathing is faster than before. My pulse pounds louder as blood courses past my ears. I look at Isabelle, needing her to feel the visceral pain I still live with to this day.

"Her screams echo in my dreams..."

Silence fills the space between us. Isabelle LaCroix glances down at her fingers, then blows out a breath.

"No child should ever have to live through that. I can't imagine how traumatizing that had to have been."

"I had help." If not for Lucinda, there's no way I would've survived.

"How is it that he never found out?" Her brows draw together in confusion. "I can't imagine, at ten, what I would've done, but I'm pretty certain I would've said something."

"Lucinda helped me. Spy was a game we played. We made up secret codes and kept silly secrets from my parents. She climbed up on the balcony after me, saw the whole thing, clamped a hand over my mouth, so I couldn't scream, then dragged me into the shadows where we hid until…"

"Until, what?"

"Until it was over."

My shoulders lift. How many times have I asked myself why I didn't do something to make it stop? If I'd run in there, he would've stopped.

But he wouldn't have. Lucinda's words echo in my mind.

I begged and pleaded with her to let me do something. At ten, there was nothing I could do, but I didn't understand how much danger we were in.

"How long Lucinda held me, I don't remember, but I'll never forget my mother's screams, or the terrifying moment when they stopped. That's when I knew my father was evil."

"Dear God…" Isabelle takes half a step toward me before coming to a stop.

"Lucinda taught me a difficult lesson no ten-year-old should ever learn, but offered hope as well. If I stayed silent… If I could keep the secret… If I could pretend the lie my father would tell me was true… If I trained my body and honed my mind… She told me those were my weapons and she promised, one day, my father would pay, but only if I did as she said."

"Oh, Carmen. I'm so… I don't know what to say."

"There's nothing to say. It happened and I had to live with what came next. Each day since that terrible night, I kept silent. I buried that secret. I did exactly as Lucinda said. She saved my life that night and every night that followed. I've been living a lie my entire life."

My arms cross in front of me. I call it the hug. It's the way I learned to comfort myself when I was only ten.

"What happened to you is reprehensible."

"Lucinda promised that we would avenge my mother. She said God would show us the path. In the years that followed, I kept my eyes open. Hardened my heart. I went to my knees every night, praying for God to lend me the strength I needed to live through the horrors my young eyes saw. She promised we'd have our revenge, like spies would, but I had to train and prepare. I had to wait until I was ready. She taught me everything I know, but mostly she schooled me in patience. We were going to wait for the night of my *Quinceañera*, when I could legally leave my father's home. That night, however, was the last night I saw her alive."

"Alive?" Isabelle's hand flies to cover her mouth. "Did he kill her too?"

"I wasn't sure at first." I give a half shrug and continue. "Father told me I no longer needed a governess since I was officially a woman. He told me Lucinda left to be a governess for children who needed her more than I did, now that I was a woman. She didn't want to say goodbye and wanted to spare me the tears of her leaving. I had to play along, but I knew that wasn't true and feared the worst. Years later, I found out what really happened."

"Is that when you found out about the girls being trafficked by your father."

"No." I hang my head in shame. "Rosalie told me when we were twelve."

"Twelve? And you're just now…"

"I'll be twenty-two in a month, and before you say anything, I know how long it's been."

Reaching for my hair, I pull the long tresses over my shoulder and use my fingers to comb through them. As I talk, I split the hair into three equal parts and absently form a braid. Keeping my fingers busy makes it easier to get the words out.

"I stood by and did nothing. I'm everything you say I am and more; probably worse, but I'm not ten anymore. I'm not twelve. And I'm not fifteen. I'm a grown woman, and this needs to stop." Finishing the braid, I release my hair as anger flares within me.

"I spent the last four years planning. I followed Lucinda's instructions to the letter. Everything was set, but my father ordered me home minutes after graduation. I had no time to finish…" I lace my fingers together and place them at the back of my neck. The braid slowly unravels. Tipping my head back, I stare at the ceiling and curse my fate.

"Why?"

"Why, what?"

"Why did he call you back?"

"An arranged marriage to a man who controls mineral rights to vast swaths of the jungle." I shrug, as if what that means is self-evident. When she doesn't look like she understands, I elaborate. "Marrying me off takes me out of his house. I'm no longer his responsibility. In return, Artemus..." I can't speak his name without a sneer curling my lip. "Artemus greases the wheels which allow my father to rape the land, enslave my people, and grow rich off their labor. Soon, he'll have enough power to challenge the president and run uncontested. Nicaragua will become a dictatorship, and all the people will be nothing but slaves. Not to mention, it puts all my planning to waste."

It's both funny and sad that avenging my mother's death is diminished by the horror my father intends to inflict upon the people and the land.

"I have to act while I still live under my father's roof."

"You mentioned girls." Isabelle leans against the wall. "What do you know about girls? You said you were twelve?"

"After my mother died, Lucinda brought Rosalie to be my playmate and maid. We clicked immediately and became the best of friends, but she was a worker, a different class than me. It didn't matter to us, but it did to my father. Being my playmate wasn't enough. She had to earn her keep, and she did that as a maid. One night, she confided in me. She'd been sworn to secrecy. Forbidden by my father to say a word about what happened beneath the house. She saw something terrible."

"What?"

"I remember how terrified she was. How her voice shook. How her hands trembled. She told me about girls who were regularly brought into my home, bought and sold like chattel during my father's infamous galas. Those girls were the same age as we were. I don't know what happened that night that forced her to confide in me. I've been too frightened to ask, and she's never..." That's not my story to tell. "But, I knew." I clear my throat. "I knew, and I did nothing. May God forgive me, but I did nothing."

"Why did she wait so long to tell you?" Isabelle's lids pull back in shock.

"Matias took an interest in her. I've often suspected…" I shake my head, refusing to head down that path. "I told my father I didn't like the way Matias looked at Rosalie. That it was *sinful* and I was going to tell the priests."

I stretch my neck, trying to relieve the tension coiling at the base of my skull. "Papa didn't want me saying anything to the priests. He said he would take care of it."

"Take care of it?"

"Matias never touched Rosalie again, but his hunger for her grows. As long as my father believes I'm loyal, Rosalie is safe, but if he ever suspects…" I can't finish the sentence. It's too painful. "You see why I need the Guardians?"

"I can't promise…" Isabelle shudders. "How could you know all of that and not do anything about it?"

"Because I don't have that kind of power." I brush back the hair that falls into my face as I stare at the floor. This is harder than I thought, but it feels good to finally speak the truth, as if speaking the truth imbues it with power. "You want to know why I jumped on Rafe?"

"That *is* the question of the hour. It makes no sense to anyone. We figured you were trying to escape."

"I didn't do it to escape." Swallowing against that hard lump in my throat, horrific images of what will happen to Rosalie flood my mind. "As long as I do as I'm told, my father keeps Matias away from Rosalie. No one touches her. Not Matias. Not the guards. Not even my father. I did what I did because I saw an opportunity to get her out of there. If I hadn't…" I run my fingers through my hair, frustrated and certain I'm messing this up. With a sigh, I puff out my cheeks and close my eyes. It's easier to say what follows if I don't have to see the disapproval on Isabelle's face.

"After that raid by the Guardians, my father would've locked down the estate. No one in. No one out. The militia is probably there right now, fortifying the place. I would've been locked in my rooms. *'For my own safety.'* You think I'm a horrible, wretched, good-for-nothing, self-absorbed pathetic excuse for a human being. I don't disagree. I left my best friend behind, but I had no choice. I had to get out of there. If I stayed, my father would've married me off before I could blink. The only thing that was keeping Rosalie safe was me. Now, she's in terrible danger."

"You think an awful lot about yourself."

"I'm not asking you to forgive, or even understand. I'm smart enough to know what it means that those men rescued you. They did what no one else was brave enough to do. What I need to know is if they can rescue Rosalie? Can I hire them without my father figuring out it's me?"

"You tell a good story, but it looks more like you didn't like the idea of dear daddy marrying you off and saw an opportunity to get your sweet ass out of there."

"That's not what happened."

"You sure about that?"

"I'm sure."

"How?"

"Because I contacted the CIA. They're supposed to be helping me, but I lost my contact info when my father forced me to go home."

"Lost?"

"Yes. It's back in the townhouse I share with my friend. That's why I had to come back, even if it meant leaving Rosalie behind. I'm the only one who knows about the girls who'll do anything about it. I'm trying to help them."

Isabelle's eyes flare.

"I told my father that I was going to find out who attacked him. It was the only way I could buy Rosalie time. If I was convincing enough, he won't believe that I ran away."

"And what if he doesn't believe you?"

"Then Rosalie is in danger. I need the Guardians to help."

"Why not ask them from the very beginning? Why wait to talk to me?"

"Because I don't know who they are. I don't trust them, but you do." I try to make sense of my actions. "They saved you.

They rescued you. I needed to speak to you to decide whether I could trust them too." I very well might be completely out of my mind.

"Why lie to him? Won't he think you ran away?"

"He knows I'd never leave Rosalie behind. As long as he thinks I'm spying on this organization for him, he won't do anything to Rosalie. He'll wait for me to contact him. I need the Guardians to rescue her before…" Frustration builds within me. "If they don't, then I have no choice but to go back and prove my loyalty to him. I'll just have to find another way to save my friend and save the girls he…" My stomach twists at the thought what is being done to those girls. "You think I'm a horrible person, but I'll happily trade my freedom for Rosalie's safety and theirs."

"You're kidding me?" The look on Isabelle's face is no longer irate, or disgusted. She listens to every word I say.

"Just like when I grabbed a hold of Rafe and held on for dear life, I'm taking a leap of faith that the Guardians will help me." It's risky and I'm asking a lot of an organization I don't know. "My top priority is to rescue Rosalie and the girls. After that, I will do whatever it takes to destroy everything my father's built."

"Let me get this straight…" Isabelle pushes off the wall and paces the length of the room. She ticks off each point on her fingers. "You told your father you would spy on us, but only to buy your friend time for the Guardians to rescue her?"

"Her and the girls."

"And if they don't…" Pivoting smartly, she does a precise about face and makes another lap of the room.

"If they don't, I have no choice, but to return and tell my father what I've learned about the Guardians, and pray he believes me. I live every day, every hour, every minute, and every second knowing what's happening beneath my feet. I can't do anything to save them on my own. I thought the CIA could help, but they're not convinced. At least, they haven't committed to saving the girls. I saw what the Guardians can do."

Unfortunately, Isabelle LaCroix isn't convinced. I see it in her eyes.

"You could've called the police." Isabelle dismisses me with a shrug.

"I was ten when my father murdered my mother. Twelve when I found out about the girls. You think I didn't consider telling the police? Who do you think disappeared during the parties and took what was offered for looking the other way? I thought about the priests, but they're as corrupt as the police. I hoped the CIA would help, but they haven't. There is no one I can tell."

"I'm not insensitive to what you're saying, but it's a lot to take in, and there's no way to verify any of what you're saying. I can't take that to the Guardians. I won't ask them to risk their lives for someone who may very well be leading them into a trap."

"There's no trap." My brows tug together, incredulous.

"I don't know the details, but your father was *very* interested in the Guardians after they pulled me and my friend out of the jungle."

"I don't know anything about that, but you're judging me from the comfort of a country where corruption isn't a fact of daily life. You have no idea what it was like growing up in that house. Every day was a battle not to say the wrong thing and ruin everything."

"Ladies…" Rafe knocks softly on the door. "It's been a while. Everything okay?"

Pushing the door open, he glances at Isabelle first. They exchange an unreadable look before he turns his attention to me.

"So far, Carmen's admitted she's here to spy for dear old dad."

"That's not what I said."

"But you did. That's exactly what you said." Isabelle LaCroix turns to Rafe. "And if that isn't the cherry on top of the cake, she wants the Guardians to rescue her maid and supposedly a stable of human trafficking victims."

"What?" Rafe turns his fierce gaze on me, making me cringe.

"The thing about my father is what I need him to think as to why I'm here, but that's a lie I told him. Not you. I'm not here to spy for him. Far from it. I want to tear down everything he's built. I want to free Rosalie and the others. That's what I care about. That's why I did what I did. But I don't know anything about the

Guardians. I couldn't trust them. That's why I had to speak to you first." My entire body vibrates with rage. "Whatever the price, I'll pay it." I can't do this alone. I need the Guardians to help.

Rafe's dark brows tug together and practically touch. His confusion is scrawled all over his face.

Tears prick in my eyes. It's a battle to keep them from spilling over onto my cheeks. "If you can't help me, then I'm wasting my time. I have to go home and salvage what I can." When I move toward the door, Rafe blocks my exit.

I try to shove past him, but he grabs my arms and shifts us both to the side. Turning toward Isabelle LaCroix, he issues orders. "Go to the conference room. Get Sam and CJ to come here." Rafe's voice softens. "We're going to figure this out."

"You believe her?" Isabelle looks at me.

"I have no reason not to. The only question is what do we do now?"

Isabelle rushes out of the room, which leaves me terribly alone with Rafe.

He's too close. Too tall. Too much of everything. His eyes are too kind, trusting where Isabelle LaCroix's were not. He makes me believe he's on my side.

"Hey? It's going to be okay." Rafe gives me a little shake until I look up at him. His warm, dark eyes pull me in, wanting something I can't express. "Is it the truth?"

"You think I made it up?"

"I think you're in way over your head. Why didn't you say something sooner?"

"Are you asking why I didn't tell complete strangers that my father killed my mother when I was ten. How I've been planning for a decade to bring him down? That not only does he traffic women and girls through my home, but I've known about it all this time and did nothing to stop it?" I prop my hands on my hips. "Would you tell that to people you don't know?"

"I probably wouldn't."

TWENTY-ONE

Rafe

—

It's impossible not to overhear Carmen's conversation with Izzy. The dormitories on Guardian HQ proper aren't meant for long-term occupancy. They're temporary lodging given to new hires until they arrange permanent living quarters. In this, we mirror military operations.

While most military families get a month of temporary lodging on base when they move to a new duty station, we're a bit more lenient with the time limit. In addition to new hires, the quarters operate much like a hotel for contractors working at Guardian HQ on a temporary basis. All that's to say, the quarters are sufficient, but limited in space, and the walls are thin.

I give Carmen the privacy she needs, but there's no way not to overhear every horrible word. My heart breaks knowing she grew up bearing such an incredible burden.

Revenge a decade in the making?

Inconceivable.

When Izzy leaves us to find the others and bring them here, I hold a very frantic Carmen in my arms. Her flight or fight instincts kick in, and my girl is choosing flight.

That's not happening.

Up close, her light fragrance floods my senses and penetrates deep into my mind—the primitive part of my brain. Ignoring that rush of sensation isn't easy.

It's downright impossible.

"I never should've left. I've made a mess of things." Carmen stops resisting and places her palm flat against my midsection. She leans in, laying the side of her face against my chest.

Her entire body shakes, which makes me want to wrap my arms around her even more, as if my embrace can protect her from the pain of her past, not to mention the ongoing nightmare she lives with daily.

She leans into me, fingers clutching the fabric of my shirt, as she repeats that phrase over and over, slipping in and out of Spanish with each breath.

"Shh…" I wrap an arm around her, tugging her close. She smells amazing and fits perfectly in my arms. "We're going to figure this out."

"How?" She tips her head back to look at me. "You don't understand."

"I know more than you realize."

"The last thing Lucinda said to me was to tell no one about our plan because there was no one I could trust."

"You can trust me. You can trust everyone here."

"I've made a horrible mistake." She pushes against me, and while I don't want her out of my arms, against my better judgment, I release her.

"You haven't made a mistake." The need to touch her overcomes me. "Do you believe in fate?"

"I don't know what I believe anymore."

"You were put here for a reason. Have faith this is where you're meant to be. I can help you."

She doesn't resist my touch. Doesn't yank out of my grip. If anything, Carmen folds into me, seeking solace. Taking a deep breath in, she tries not to cry, but when her eyes close, tears fall.

"You smell good." With her hand against my chest, her fingers slowly brush against the soft cotton of my shirt.

"You smell even better." My eyes close as I breathe her in, letting her light scent infuse every pore and sink into every cell of my body. It's as if she's part of me.

"I doubt that." She burrows a little deeper into my embrace.

Silence passes between us. It's one of those elongated pauses in conversation that normally feels awkward, but for us, it feels just right.

"I couldn't help overhear your conversation with Izzy." I thread my fingers through the length of her hair. Silky smooth, the strands slip through my rough and calloused fingers. I pause, uncertain how to express what I feel.

"You must think me a monster." She gives a little sniff and pulls away.

This time, I don't release her. Instead, I pull her closer, unwilling to let her out of my arms.

"Not at all…"

"After what I said? About doing nothing while…"

"To me, it sounds as if your father is the monster. Not you. Your childhood was horrible." Once again lost for words, it's hard to articulate what I feel. "It was much different than mine."

"Tell me about your childhood." Her palm presses against my chest, right over the pounding of my heart.

"My childhood?"

"Yes?"

"Now?"

"Please."

An odd request, but I sense this is her way of taking a step back. "It was carefree." Does it mean something that she wants to know more about me? "Two loving parents. Lots of friends."

"I bet you were a wild child." Her gaze lifts to linger on my face, then dips to my muscular build.

"I could be insufferable, but mostly I was a good kid." I can't help but laugh. The change in conversation feels good, like we need a bit of levity to wash away the horrors of her past. I keep my tone light. "When I was ten, I was in Little League, proving to the world I was the hottest thing since sliced bread."

"I bet the girls liked you."

"Girls were a nuisance. They barely deserved to be noticed and were kind of gross."

"Gross?" A tiny bit of laughter escapes her.

"Back then, I was small for my age. As for keeping secrets, at ten, I couldn't keep one if my life depended on it. I made so many mistakes."

A shadow passes over her delicate features when I mention keeping secrets at ten. I should know better and grimace with the poor choice of words.

"I don't believe you." She presses a lacquered nail in the middle of my chest, poking me. There's a lilt in her voice, but I sense the desperation in her tone to keep this upbeat. Because of that, I play along.

"Oh, it was *baaad*."

"How bad could it have been?" Lighter in tone, her expression lifts. Some of the shadow recedes.

"I blabbed to get attention, lost friends in the process. Spilled their secrets to gain myself new friends. I didn't care about the ones I lost. I hurt the new friends too, with stupid lies meant to lift me up and push them down. I repeated the whole cycle far too many times. I'm not proud of that. It took me a long time to grow up and see how hurtful I was to others."

"I don't believe it. I imagine you differently."

"Believe it. I blabbed my way through childhood and the majority of my awkward preteen years. Not my best decade. I'm much better at keeping secrets now."

"I would hope so." She lifts her hand to my face, and I lean in toward her touch. Her delicate fingers trace the hard line of my jaw. "I see you protecting the other kids and making the girls giggle."

"At ten, my biggest concern was what to put on top of my pizza after a game. It sure as shit wasn't keeping a secret like you did, protecting anyone, or having anything to do with girls. They were Girl-gross."

"That's funny." Her smile returns, lifted up by the story of my youth. "We were dealing with very different things when we were ten."

"I hate that for you. I didn't have to worry about my father killing my mother." My words make her flinch. "I'm sorry. I didn't mean to say it like that. That was incredibly insensitive."

And dumb.

I want to smack myself in the head for being such an insensitive prick. Not the best way to make an impression.

"No need to be sorry. We grew up in very different worlds."

It boggles the mind. For all her privilege, Carmen's life has not been easy. She kept a life and death secret at ten while I was busy being a Grade-A jerk.

"Our worlds were very different." I take her hand in mine and run the thick pad of my thumb over her knuckles. "Sadly, I didn't get any better as I got older. I was a gangly and awkward preteen, with arms and legs growing faster than the rest of my body. My brain struggled to keep up with the changes in my body. Seventh grade, I was just starting to take note of girls my age, but I was still a total jerk."

"Did the girls start noticing you? How old were you in seventh grade?"

"Twelve."

It doesn't escape my notice that when Carmen was twelve, she learned what men did to little girls; how they bought and sold them at will.

"I'm trying to imagine you as a kid, but all I see is the man you are today." She pulls back for a minute. Her gaze takes me in and there's genuine appreciation in her expression. Perhaps, dare I hope, interest? "I wonder what those girls would say about you now. I bet they didn't think you were a jerk."

"Trust me, they did. When I turned thirteen, my life reached a major turning point. Sadly, it wasn't an improvement."

"How so?"

"I suddenly realized those bothersome girls weren't as annoying as I once thought. They smelled good. Looked pretty. Their eyes sparkled. The new curves on their bodies brought my dick to life and put wild fantasies and *other* things in my head."

"Oh my Lord, you were precocious—and direct."

My dick comment definitely stirs a reaction. I take a mental note to tone down my language. There's no reason to scare her off.

"More like a precocious prick. The most important thing in my life at thirteen was how to get close to the girls so I could feel their boobs and brag about it to my friends. All I cared about was figuring out how to kiss a girl."

"I wish I had known you as a boy."

"If you had, there's no way you'd let me touch you now." It's not escaped my notice how she snuggles into my embrace. Nor does she pull away when I point it out.

Carmen's light touch makes the hairs on the back of my neck stand on end and wakes up other parts of my body. My dick twitches, stirring for the first time in far too long.

"You give good hugs." She lays her cheek against my chest. "I know I don't know you very well, but I feel safe when you hold me. I feel like I've somehow known you my entire life." She looks up at me. "Is that weird?"

"I don't think so." Truthfully, I feel the same, and I'm not sure what to make of it.

I'm deeply religious, more so than I let the other guys see. My relationship with God is between me and the Almighty. With that said, I know what people say about soulmates. Not that Carmen is mine, or that I'm hers, but it feels like I've known her longer than the span of a few days.

"I was never around boys growing up." Her voice turns wistful. "Never had the youthful experience of getting fondled like that."

"I hope not. Otherwise, I'd have to track down the losers who groped you and…"

"No need to hunt anyone down. I lived a very sheltered life."

"I bet you were breaking hearts left and right. You're absolutely stunning."

"To break hearts, I would've needed to be around boys."

"How is it possible you weren't?"

"It was simply the way it was. I knew boys existed, but none ever came to the house. My interactions were confined to seeing boys at Mass on Saturdays. That environment didn't encourage things like groping and kissing. Although, when I turned fifteen, it was abundantly clear the boys were interested in me. If it wasn't my father scaring them away, Lucinda kept the boys away from me. I was excited for my *Quinceañera*. That's when a girl becomes a woman and can start to date. Unfortunately, there wasn't a single boy who asked me out. Lucinda disappeared and my father actively discouraged boys from approaching his daughter." When she says *disappeared* there's a hitch in her voice. "I bet all the girls flocked to you when you were fifteen." The quick shift in topic back to me is telling.

"Guilty as charged. My voice deepened. My body shot up in height. Testosterone kicked in. My muscles bulked up and those spindly arms and legs turned strong and powerful. I went from being small for my age to freakishly huge. The chicks definitely noticed when I grew hair on my face and pubes popped up in my groin. My dick grew and had a mind of its own."

"I can't imagine you ever having spindly arms, and how did the girls know about hair on your *pubes*? Did you flash them?"

She draws a laugh from me with the way she pronounces *pubes*. It's obviously not a familiar word.

"Naw, but word got around. It took several years for me to grow into my body, but I did."

"I still would've liked to have known you then."

"Lord no! I was such a mess. Testosterone raged through my body and only two things mattered: the next girl I was going to fuck and which asshole needed to be taught a lesson. I kissed all the girls and told everyone how far they went. I definitely brought tears to pretty faces. Too self-absorbed to realize why such a thing might hurt, I didn't care about anyone but me. I went from jerk to a self-absorbed prick."

"You're too hard on yourself." Her head cants to the side.

"There's no excuse for the way I acted. I have a lot to make up for."

"Why were you teaching assholes lessons?" She's absolutely

adorable, savagely beautiful, and for now, wrapped securely in my arms. It's nice holding her close.

Feels right.

"If I wasn't kissing a girl, I was out during lunch period meting out justice to whatever random bully decided to pick on my friends. I was always the biggest kid in class and made it my personal mission to protect those weaker than myself. I'm also a bit of a closet nerd, which meant all my classes were with the nerdy kids. They got me on a level the jocks never understood, but as nerds, they attracted the attention of the bullies."

"You're a born protector. Despite the rest, you had a kind heart."

"Don't know if it was kindness, but it pissed me off when bullies abused my friends because they were nerdy, or geeky. And you're right, although I didn't see it at the time. I wasn't a total ass. I stood up for those who couldn't stand up for themselves. Inserted myself right into that conversation with my fists. Didn't matter if it was wrong or right."

"If they were hurting others, and none of the adults were stepping in, you probably made a huge difference in the lives of those kids. I couldn't imagine how horrible it must be to feel unsafe at school."

I blink, not sure I hear her right. She can't imagine feeling unsafe?

From the time she was ten, her every breath was unsafe. Instead of pointing that out, I continue telling her about my childhood. She seems to enjoy listening to me. Not to mention, it feels good to share bits and pieces of my past.

"I don't know about protecting others, but it made me feel good; like I was doing right in the world. I was bigger, badder, and scrappier than my peers, and I wasn't afraid to take a hit. Detention meant nothing other than a spike in my reputation. That came with a whole new host of sexy girls to kiss, fondle, and fuck."

"Sounds like your extracurricular activities were *extensive*." The way she emphasizes the last word brings a grin to my face.

"I was just trying to figure out life and have fun. I kissed all the girls, fucked those who would let me, defended my nerdy friends when needed, and taught the bullies a lesson about picking on my friends." I suck in a breath with the memories flooding my mind.

"Go on." She gently encourages me to continue.

"I was nothing like you."

"How's that?"

"I wasn't mature enough to bury the deepest secret of my life and pretend like it never happened. I didn't have to live knowing atrocities were being committed within my own home. I can't even wrap my head around the personal strength that had to take. You astound me."

"Me?" Her resilience, perseverance, and faith shake me to the core. "I'm barely holding it together. I'm a mess."

"You're a beautiful mess."

"You're just saying that to get in my pants."

I huff a laugh, not sure why it's funny when she uses colloquialisms in her speech.

"Not touching that comment with a ten-foot pole." No way in hell am I telling her exactly how much I want to *get in her pants*.

"You have a filthy mind."

"You have no idea, but you astound me." My awe of Carmen Angelo grows each day.

"Flattery?" That comment brings laughter to her lips. What a pretty and delicate sound. I could listen to her laugh all day long.

"You don't see what I see." And that's the honest truth. "I hate that you grew up in such a horrible place and that you witnessed such horrible things."

Despite my natural inclination to protect, I can't go back in time to save the little girl she once was. The helplessness she endured guts me. It kills me that men will kidnap and enslave those weaker than themselves, abusing and using them for *pleasure*. The inhumanity of it never fails to leave me enraged.

If I could, I'd kill every one of the bastards. The problem is finding the dark places where the fuckers hide.

TWENTY-TWO

Rafe

___

"I've never been as scared as I am now." Carmen takes in a deep breath. "I had a split second to react. I pray my father believes I'm spying for him. I fear what's happening to Rosalie in my absence." She clings to me, trembling as the words spill into the space between us.

"We'll do what we can to help you."

I know one asshole whose time has come, and I hope Guardian HRS doesn't stop with Maximus Angelo. I pray we get a list of every bastard who ruined a girl's childhood, forcing her to grow up much too fast, or never having the chance to grow up at all.

It's in our motto to help those who can't help themselves.

We can't *not* take this job.

Whether we can do it within the timeframe Carmen needs, however, is up for discussion. Talk about the million-dollar question.

"I didn't know what to do, and Lucinda…" Extremely faint, I almost miss her words. She chokes back a sob. My heart breaks for the loneliness expressed in so few words.

"You and Lucinda were very close."

"I owe her everything."

"If I may, I'm curious about what the plan was? How were you going to get revenge?"

"We couldn't trust anyone in Nicaragua. Everyone who matters is controlled by my father. Lucinda told me to trust no one, and I already mentioned the police. The only way to do anything was to reach out to the CIA and establish contact. She said they dealt with human trafficking and could help. The plan was for me to go to college in America. Once I got here, I was to reach out to the CIA and establish contact. They would take things from there."

"How far did you get with them?"

"Not far. Before I could convince anyone at the CIA to take me seriously, graduation came and went. My father ordered me home minutes after graduation. He sent his men to escort me home. I met Isabelle LaCroix the following day, and you know what happened after that."

"I do." A low chuckle rumbles in my chest. "You definitely took me by surprise. Tops my list of unusual introductions of all times."

"I didn't know what to do. I saw one of your teammates with Isabelle LaCroix, and it seemed like that wasn't the first time you'd done something like that. I made a split-second decision and acted."

"Your leap of faith."

"Yeah."

"Fortunately, we're exceptionally proficient with infil and exfil via helicopter."

"What does that mean? Infil and exfil?"

"Infil, short for infiltration. Exfil is short for exfiltration. Point being, we train for that kind of shit, but Izzy was put in a harness and clipped to Booker for the lift. You missed that essential safety step."

"I had no idea. I just thought—and you're so big..." A flush colors her honeyed skin the prettiest shade of pink I've ever seen. "I didn't realize..."

Her fingers lightly tap over my shirt. Each time they move, tiny ripples of sensation light up my nerves and awaken parts of my anatomy that need to behave. Fat chance of that. My dick's eating up the hero worship and getting ready to put on a show.

"Well, I wasn't going to let you fall."

"You saved my life."

"I don't know if I'd say that. I merely held you in my arms and kept you from falling."

"I never thanked you." She looks up at me again with an unreadable expression.

I don't dare attempt to decipher that look. Talk about treacherous waters. My dick likes it. It's eager as shit to receive those thank yous from Carmen.

Shifting a bit to the side, I keep our hips from touching. No need for Carmen to know about the filthy thoughts taking over my brain and manifesting in my dick. Best to focus on the mystery that is Carmen Angelo.

"I'm sorry about the CIA. They may work at the speed of glaciers melting, but Guardian HRS moves at lightspeed. You're in for a shock."

"How is that?"

"Sam and CJ. Sam's in command of Guardian HRS. CJ leads the Guardian teams. You need to tell them what you told Izzy." I reach up and gently run my knuckles along her jawline.

Everything about her fascinates me. From her sculpted cheekbones to those long, fluttering eyelashes sweeping across high-arched cheekbones. She definitely put a spell on me. The urge to lean down and kiss her puts a hitch in my breath. It would be so easy to…

Instead of kissing her, I drag my knuckles over her lips and trace along the gentle sweep of her jaw. Her mouth parts on a sigh while my toes curl and my dick jerks.

This close, it's hard not to push things further. With great difficulty, I force myself to remain professional. Well, as professional as possible considering my dick is practically drilling a hole in my jeans.

"And you feel I can trust them?"

Them? It's almost as if she separates me from the rest of Guardian HRS.

"With your life. As far as next steps, that's not for me to decide. Sam and CJ, among others, make those decisions."

"Do you think I'm a horrible person?" Her eyes shimmer with tears.

"I think you're incredibly brave, but you're no longer alone. You don't have to bear this burden by yourself anymore."

"It's my penance." She hangs her head in shame. "I ruined everything. I wasn't supposed to tell anyone. Lucinda was very clear about…"

Not caring what Lucinda was and wasn't clear about, my next move is inevitable. I need to silence the destructive thoughts in her head. I do the one thing guaranteed to shut her up.

Grasping her nape to control her head, I lean down and press my lips against hers. Expecting resistance, my senses swim and my breathing turns ragged as she melts into me and her lips gently part.

I take what I can, before she comes to her senses and pulls away from the unwanted advance, but Carmen doesn't pull away.

Her breathy moan signals all kinds of *Yes* and *More*. My fingers curl in her hair and tug on the strands. The pressure I apply increases as my mouth grinds against hers.

Desire and need for a whole hell of a lot more fills me.

Half expecting a slap to my face, I'm stunned when she gives me everything. She lifts on her toes and drapes her arms over my shoulders, meeting my kiss with a fiery passion of her own.

Maybe I shouldn't be surprised? All the signs are here. The smoldering attraction? The tentative touches? The way we gravitate toward each other?

It's been a year since my injury. A year since I held a woman in my arms. My technique is raw and forced.

Ravenous.

The longer the kiss stretches, the more I take.

Soft and delicate, she's intensely feminine with sinful curves, pillowy lips, and breathy moans that drive me wild. I lay claim to her mouth with unrelenting hunger.

The urge to shove my dick deep inside of her builds as I imagine plunging mercilessly into her wet heat, fucking her without restraint, penetrating her, fueling her desire, and pushing her to the brink and beyond where she can fly.

She meets my heat and passion with sublime feminine surrender. The kiss deepens, turning raw and carnal. Her hand slips from my shoulder, gliding down my hardened physique. Heat blazes beneath her tentative touch, lighting up nerves that sizzle and spark. There's nothing shy about her intent when her palm travels below my waist to cup my very hard and aching dick.

It's a shock, actually, and I jump.

"Oh…" She pauses as if stung. There's the tiniest flinch as she realizes how much of me there is beneath the zipper. "It's…"

A groan rumbles in the back of my throat, full of desire and scorching heat.

"Don't…" I cover her hand with mine, intending to pull her away from my dick, but my hips have a mind of their own, grinding against her palm in desperation.

Our mouths part for a breath while she gazes up at me with beautiful chocolate-brown eyes blown out by passion and lust.

Could it be? Is she as interested in me as I am in her?

It's been too long. I'm too excited. Too eager. Too out of control. I'll take her savagely if I'm not careful. Fuck her until her soul shakes. I'll rut, completely out of control, until I damn us both to eternal hell where the fire of our passion will consume and devour us.

Bending my neck, I take her mouth once again, plundering and claiming every nook and crevice as mine. Every flick of my tongue brings a whimper of desire from her incredible lips. Every nip and teasing bite lift her to her toes. Pleasure sparks between us as my moans, and her precious gasps, fill the air.

I pull at her, intending to remove her hand from my cock, but she resists with the tiniest pressure until I relent. Rocking forward and back, I allow her to explore as she desires.

My fingers curl in her hair, pulling more aggressively as her breathy moans intensify.

There's simply too much to take in. My restraint stretches and pulls, until it finally snaps. Needing to take her now, I lift her off her feet, wrapping her legs around my waist. With her lips glued to mine, the heat of her pussy pressed against my groin, and the confining clothing separating us, there's only one way this ends.

The two of us naked.

On her bed.

In each other's arms.

I carry her toward the bedroom as her fingers claw at my hair. She crosses her ankles at my back and squirms over the prominent bulge behind my zipper, but halfway to the bedroom, a twinge of sensation grinds me to a dead stop.

The stump.

What will Carmen do when she sees the disfiguring, amputated stump of a leg?

I should've fucked her against the wall like Piper suggested.

"What's wrong?" Carmen pulls back. Her fingers send sparks of pleasure shooting down my nape as her fingers curl in my hair.

"Nothing." I lift her up and off my hips, then settle her on her feet. "We're moving too fast."

Combining the first kiss and first fuck might be fine for a nameless chick in a bar, but I won't cheapen Carmen like that. Not to mention, the stump and my insecurities aren't ready for prime time. The revulsion in her face when she sees I'm one leg less of a man will wound me far deeper than I can handle.

"It's okay." Still a bit breathless, the naturally crisp cadence of her voice turns sinful and sultry. "I'm okay if you want to…" Her lashes flutter as she timidly gestures toward the bed. Her lower lip curls in, and I bite back a groan.

My cock jerks with desire to claim this beautiful woman, but I grab hold of my senses and take back control.

"We barely know each other." My dick might be eager, starved in fact, but something tells me we need to slow this down.

"But…"

"I'm not saying this isn't going to happen, but I'm not going to rush." My knuckles slowly glide along her jawline. Yeah, she deserves to be worshipped slowly. Not to mention, I need to figure out how to fuck her without revealing one bloody hell of a flaw. Chicks dig scars, but they run when they see the stump.

Thick and swollen from my kisses, her lips beg to be taken. Not sure how, or even why, but I manage to put on the brakes and bring us to an unsatisfying halt.

"You're nothing like I thought," she says.

"Is that a good thing, or a bad thing?"

"I don't know. Good, I think."

"What were you expecting?"

"Something rough and savage." A dusting of pink colors her cheeks. Those fluttering lashes are going to be the end of me. Her gaze dips down, as if she can't meet my eye.

"I'm all up for rough and savage, but..." I tip her chin up, forcing her to look at me.

"But, what?"

"Maybe we should walk before we run? Slow things down before we get ahead of ourselves." *Let me figure out something with the stump.*

"You want to go slow? But..."

"Not slow, just with a little more thought behind what happens afterward. I don't want you to regret anything."

"Considering where I'm headed, I'll regret *not* doing anything more."

And there's the truth staring us in the face. Carmen is headed home. Unless we find another way, her path takes her back to her father and an arranged marriage that will slowly snuff out the light in her eyes.

With no future between us, why am I waiting? Maybe she's eager enough to overlook the disfiguring stump. The thing's healing well, but it's still ugly as sin.

Grotesque.

"We don't know that you must return."

"I don't see any other way." She lifts her chin out of my gentle grasp and turns away.

"The Guardians will help you."

"I hope so, but I need to be prepared if they don't. When I go back, I don't want to leave with regrets." She places a hand on my arm. "Don't send me back without giving me this."

"I don't want to cheapen..."

"You're a natural protector, but sex with you won't be something I regret. Even if it happens just one time." Carmen lifts on tiptoe until our lips are a breath apart.

"Kiss me…" Her breathy words demand only one response. I close the distance between us, but a loud pounding rattles the door on its hinges.

"Hello?" The deepest voice I've ever heard makes me groan.

"Shit, it's Forest." Talk about a cockblock.

TWENTY-THREE

Carmen

THE POUNDING ON THE DOOR SENDS ME ONE DIRECTION AND RAFE the other. He makes a strategic wardrobe adjustment while I press on my cheeks and pray my face isn't as beet red as it feels, or that my lips aren't as swollen as I think they are.

Dear Lord, what a kiss. Swoon-worthy comes to mind, and with a man who literally can sweep me off my feet.

That kiss. Those lips. His erection?

Not going to lie, I'm just as eager to see it as I'm worried as to whether it'll fit. A tingle of anticipation at the juncture of my legs makes me press my thighs together to ease the ache. I try not to squirm as the door to my very small apartment bangs open.

A giant of a man pokes his head in. His expression transforms into one of the most genuine smiles I've ever seen. "You must be Carmen Angelo. We met on the plane." His brows tug together, thinking. "Or maybe we didn't? I think Sam and CJ already had you squirreled away by then. Anyway, my name's Forest. Izzy said we needed to get here STAT."

Shock-white hair. Ice-blue eyes. His head brushes the top of the doorway and the low ceiling isn't that far away. I thought Rafe was a big man. Whoever this is, he's a giant. Makes me think about Vikings and Ragnarök.

"That's not what Izzy said, beanpole." A woman's voice calls out from the hall. "Will you either go in, or get out of my way?"

"Haven't been invited in and I'm pretty sure Izzy said we needed to get here ASAP." He grumps to someone behind him.

"She didn't say ASAP either, and with your head poking in, I'm not sure why you're waiting for an invitation." A pretty woman in her mid-thirties pokes her head under Forest's arm. She squeezes through the small space between the massive man and the door-jamb. "Carmen, I'm Skye and you've already met my obnoxious brother, Forest. Izzy didn't tell us what was going on, only that Rafe said we needed to get here fast." The woman tugs on Forest's shirt-sleeve. "Come on. Move out of the way. You're scaring the poor thing."

"Who are these people?" I turn toward Rafe, looking for reassurance. He's the only person I know and might trust.

"These are the people who are going to help Rosalie." Rafe closes the distance between us and takes my hand in his. I've never felt anything as perfect as my hand being held in his sturdy grip. He makes me feel—safe.

It's like a dream, but I remind myself not to get carried away by worthless fantasies. Rafe is simply doing his job and that's it.

Except for that kiss! Pretty sure that's not allowed. The tiny voice in my head gets in a quip.

"I have a feeling it's going to get crowded fast." Rafe tugs me to the corner while Forest and Skye settle in on the couch.

"What do you mean?" It's as if my brain's a beat or two too slow.

As soon as I ask the question, the men from the plane who tried to question me, Sam and CJ, file inside and pull out chairs from the four-person table that makes up the tiny dining nook I never use.

My mouth gapes with the intrusion, but that's nothing compared to the way my eyes practically bug out of my head when a vivacious woman waltzes into my quarters as if this is some weird party on a Friday night and all are welcome.

A foot or two shorter than the men, and an inch or two shorter than me, her hair is dyed every color of the rainbow, and if I'm not mistaken, it sparkles as if sprayed with glitter. Her short pixie haircut pokes out in every direction, and there's a bounce to her step that compliments the contagious smile on her face.

"Hey, Carmen…" She gives a friendly flap of her hand in greeting. "We haven't officially met, although I know *tons* about you. My name's Mitzy. All these scary men are just putting on an act to keep you on your toes, but if you know how to handle them, they're all teddy bears at heart." She glances at Rafe. "Well, all but Rafe. What do ya say, Forest? Another one bites the dust?"

Forest glances over at Rafe—I think I imagine it—but his pale-blue gaze dips down to Rafe's crotch then over to my face. The corner of his mouth tips up in a grin.

"We'll see." Forest's voice is so deep, I lean forward, trying to separate the vowels and consonants from the background rumbling in his throat. "Too early to call."

"If you say so." Mitzy keeps looking from me to Rafe and back again. Her gaze lands on our hands. "But I'm calling it." She pulls something out from her pocket and tosses it in the air.

It looks like a—button?

I shake my head. I'm tired. So tired that I'm seeing things.

I yank my hand free from Rafe's and rub my palm on my pants leg.

"What's going on?" Taking a step back, my instinct is to flee. Only, there's no place to run. I'm cornered and growing more and more concerned by the second.

"That's what we're wondering." Sam leans back in his chair. He examines his cuticles, then fixes me with his penetrating gaze. "All we know is Izzy came back, tight-lipped, except to say we all needed to come talk to the one person who's refused to speak to any of us immediately. If you could shed a little light on that, it might help."

I clasp my hands in front of me and take a step back. Well, half a step. The back of my shoulders slam against the wall, making me jump in surprise.

"Sam, you're scaring the poor thing." Mitzy shoves Forest's arm off the armrest of the couch then perches where his arm was a moment before. Even sitting on the armrest, her head is still a few inches below his.

I've never met a man as big as Forest.

"Carmen?" Rafe gives my hand a light but reassuring squeeze. "You're in the company of friends. I know it doesn't feel that way, and this crowd can be a bit overwhelming, but if you want to help Rosalie, these are the people who can make that happen."

"I don't know where to start." Glancing around the room, those butterflies in my belly return with a vengeance.

This time, it's from unease and fear, rather than an excitement and thrills when Rafe looks at me with those bedroom eyes of his. Thinking about his eyes makes me curious about what we could've been doing in the bedroom if he hadn't put a stop to things.

Holy cow! If he hadn't, all these people would've walked in, not on a heated kiss, but something far worse. I'd never be able to look any of them in their faces again. Talk about mortifying.

"Honey," Mitzy says, "my suggestion is to start at the beginning and keep on going until you reach the end. Most of us have formed opinions based on a boatload of assumptions, but this is where you set the record straight and we figure out how we can help you."

"Help me?" I point to my chest. "You'd be willing to help me?"

Sam clears his throat. "What Mitzy means to say is we've been at this a long time. We know things you may not realize and are more—*familiar* with your father than we'd like." His gaze cuts to Forest and the diminutive woman who claims to be his sister.

I say claim because they look nothing alike.

"Those assumptions," Sam continues, "are more likely fact than fiction, but we're depending on you to set us straight. Following that, we'll decide on our next best course of action." He leans back. "Now, would you prefer to stand? Or sit?" He gestures to the two empty chairs at the table. "I have a feeling we'll be here for a bit."

"Stand." The shakiness in my voice is no surprise. My nerves are a jangled mess.

What does come as a surprise is that I tell them everything, starting at the beginning like Mitzy suggested, until I finish with the reasons why I clung desperately to Rafe during the *exfil* of Isabelle LaCroix. That moment seems lifetimes ago.

I still can't believe I did that.

Through the retelling, Rafe stands by my side. He takes my hand in his when my voice catches, or breaks altogether. He doesn't speak for me, although he heard every word I told Isabelle LaCroix.

When I finally come to the end, deafening silence greets my last words. That's when I realize Rafe's arm drapes over my shoulder. He pulls me in for a hug and kisses the crown of my head.

A side-hug.

But a hug, nonetheless. It's the first affection I've experienced since the last time Lucinda held me in her arms and told me to be strong.

Those tears I've been holding back? Rafe's stalwart support weakens my defenses. It's as if a damn releases. Tears pour down my face and I choke back a sob.

Rafe pulls me fully into his arms, spinning me around until I face him. Burying my face against his chest, he holds me while I cry.

TWENTY-FOUR

Rafe

"Carmen..." Forest's deep rumble rolls through the room. "Thank you for trusting us. I'm aware of the tremendous risk you take and humbled by your unwavering faith. Our paths were destined to cross, and I promise we will not let you down." He shifts his attention to Sam and CJ. "There's a lot to unpack. Thoughts?"

"Off the cuff, we're looking at one mission with two distinct objectives: Rosalie, then the girls." Sam jumps right in. "That's the biggest issue up front. Mitzy will get eyes in the air, but safe to say it's not going to be a walk in the park like it was extracting Izzy."

"Agree." CJ pulls at his chin. "He's a political powerhouse, which means he'll have augmented his forces with the military after our last op. We're going with our asses exposed. I'm not sure Guardian HRS wants to risk that much exposure."

"Agreed." Forest nods but doesn't add anything further.

"We'll need more than Bravo team." Sam turns to CJ and lifts one finger. "I say put Bravo and Charlie on the mission. Hold Alpha in reserve. Delta's busy on assignment, but we might be able to pull a few off that operation. It all depends on what Mitzy's intel says. We'll need official CIA cover."

Sam looks to Forest again. "Whatever we do, it has to be off the books, but with the full support of the United States. Blacker than black, or it's a no-go."

"The CIA?" Carmen shifts beside me. "Do you work for the CIA?" There's excitement in her voice that wasn't there moments before.

"No, luv," Sam says. "We don't *work for* the CIA. Although, we've been known to provide them an assist from time to time. In return, they help us as needed." He levels a finger at her, emphasizing a point. "Now, I just shared highly classified information with you. As you trusted us, I'm trusting you. Your father can never know what's discussed in this room."

"About her father…" Mitzy pipes in with her squeaky voice. "We need to feed him something about the Guardians to keep up her end of the story and buy us time to plan. Something she can call him about. It needs to be important enough to justify her staying here while we plan the op, without raising suspicion she's not spying for him." Mitzy taps her chin. "I'll think of something creative." Her gaze flits over to land on me, which draws me up short. "In fact —I may have the perfect idea. Welcome to the team, *Señorita Angelo;* you are our newest, and deepest, undercover operative."

"Me?" Carmen's eyes round and she points to herself.

Mitzy shifts her attention to Sam, ignoring me. "I'll have my team put together some kind of intel she can feed her father. Then we'll brainstorm infil and exfil. I've got some ideas. We can all agree it's going to be a shitshow. He's got the military on his side, tripling his numbers. We have to level the playing field."

"How do we do that?" CJ lifts his hands over his head, stretching. "You think it'll only be triple?" He exchanges a look with Sam. "We're going to need more Guardians."

"Not necessarily." When Mitzy shakes her head, the glitter in her hair flickers in the light. "I'm thinking a tech blackout followed by an invasion."

"How does that help?" Sam props his elbows on the table and rests his chin on clasped hands.

"We take tech out of the equation. It won't be easy, but our Guardians are easily worth ten of their men."

"What's going on?" Carmen's whisper barely penetrates the threshold of my hearing. "What are they talking about?"

I spin her around until she stands facing the room. Wrapping a hand around her waist, I obliterate any space between us. Her shoulders and back press against my chest. Leaning down, I whisper in her ear.

"Welcome to a Guardian HRS planning session."

"I don't understand." The poor thing shakes like a leaf. She's overwhelmed, but anyone would be.

"They accepted your offer."

"But we never discussed price. How am I to pay…"

"This isn't something you pay for. This is personal."

"Personal?" Like me, she keeps her voice low while those around us lob ideas back and forth like we're at a damn volleyball game. A person could get whiplash with how fast the ideas fly.

"I'll explain later." Still not clear myself, there's history between Skye, Forest, and her father. Not wanting to misspeak, I'll wait and get the details from Brady later.

It amazes me how good Carmen feels in my arms, as if she belongs with me. When I shift my weight, however, a twinge in my stump draws me up short. Normally, I forget the prosthetic, but this is an in-your-face reminder.

Fuck me.

Well, that's a lie. There's no way to forget the loss of a limb, but my body's adjusting to the new normal. Piper said this would happen. I didn't believe her, but here's the proof. Unfortunately, after days of not thinking about the damn leg, the sudden reminder is unwelcome. I release Carmen, as if stung, and cover up the weird reaction by pulling out a chair from the table for her to sit in.

Why does my body choose this moment to remind me I'm not whole?

Because you dared to dream while holding Carmen in your arms.

She's alone in the company of strangers, scared to death, and completely out of her depth. I've tried to be a friendly face among strangers—visiting her when I could, surprising her with chocolate cake, checking in to be sure she had whatever she needed. It feels right to look after her, but she continually catches me off guard.

I expect her to fall apart and lose her shit, but she holds herself together like a pro. She's on a mission of vengeance. That's the beginning and end of it. That kind of singular purpose is rare in an individual. With the strength of her faith bolstering her convictions, I can't help but wonder if divine intervention isn't at work.

Some force put her right where she needed to be. Her literal *leap of faith*, clinging to me, brought her to the only people in the world with the capability to deliver that justice. My faith in the almighty is strengthened after meeting this woman. As for my growing attraction for her, I can table that for another day.

Or try.

"It's settled then." Forest claps, signaling an end to this conversation. It yanks my thoughts from Carmen back to the room as a whole.

Mitzy points to Carmen. "You're with me." A woman on a mission, Mitzy crosses the room and takes Carmen's hand in hers. She tugs Carmen out of my grip. Once separated, she wraps her arms around Carmen. "Welcome to the Guardians. It's time you and I had a much longer chat." When Mitzy pulls a gaping Carmen toward the door, I can't help but step in behind them. No way in hell are they separating us.

"Hold up." CJ lifts his hand. "You're following me to the bullpen."

"Why?"

Carmen's nearly at the door. In another second, she'll be gone. My insides twist with indecision. Do I ignore CJ and follow Carmen? Or do I do my damn job?

There's only one answer to that question. I'm a Guardian. Saving others is what I signed up for. Falling for one of our clients—and I'm certain Carmen is officially a client—isn't in the job description.

"Bloody hell." I run a hand through my hair, trying to hide my frustration.

"She bit you good, Loverboy," Forest says.

"That's not…"

"Look, you can fight it or embrace it. Either way, there will be bumps along the way." Forest points at his watch. "We're working on borrowed time. I'd say we can stretch things a week at most and buy Carmen's friend as much time as we can. As long as her father sees the obedient daughter he expects, we should be good."

"How are we going to set off the EMP?" CJ asks Sam.

"I may have spaced out there for a bit, but what EMP?" That voice in my head has a good ole' laugh at my expense. I missed a lot.

An electromagnetic pulse, or EMP, is the death nail when it comes to the kind of operations we run—or rather the tech we use. An EMP takes anything electronic and renders it inactive. There are no HUDs, no laser targeting, no swarm of Mitzy's drones. None of the Rufuses. Rufi?

What the hell is plural for a robotic dog? Do they run in packs?

A pack of Rufuses…A Ruf-pack?

No, sounds like shit. Fuck it. This is not where my brain needs to waste energy.

Sam and CJ exchange glances, but Forest flat-out laughs. "Thinking about your woman?"

"Huh?" I shift on my feet.

"Carmen's bit you bad. The EMP, Loverboy, is Mitzy's idea." Forest tries to laugh, but winds up coughing instead. I'm not around the creator of Guardian HRS much, but he looks—off. Tired and dimmer than I remember. "It'll wipe out their security systems."

No tech means we lose communications with command. That means no dragonfly drones finding our targets for us. No Rufi—Rufuses—augmenting our forces.

"Maximus Angelo will be operating blind." CJ places his hands on the small of his back and stretches. "None of his men are prepared for that. The Guardians are."

This is true. We're Guardians. We train for every battlefield contingency.

Mitzy mentioned *dark*.

My ears heard it, but my brain failed to connect the dots. Inactivating our tech takes her entire team out of the equation. It's the equivalent of taking two major steps back several decades, but we have other ways to communicate.

Or does it?

Light and sound come to mind. We're proficient in MORSE code, as well as the Prisoner's Code developed by POWs during the Vietnam war. We can talk over great distances with nothing but a flame if the need arises. In close quarters, we use clickers developed for dog training.

Going dark isn't a concern. Something else, far worse, is worrisome.

My interest in Carmen grows by the day. There's no way to say where that attraction will lead, but attraction creates distraction. Distraction leads to mistakes. Mistakes turn deadly for me and my team. But I'm a goddamn professional and know how to keep that shit locked down tight.

Time to focus and put any thoughts of Carmen firmly out of my mind.

Good luck.

That little voice in my head can go fuck itself.

CJ heads toward the door leading out to the hall. "We've got shit to plan. Is your head in the game?"

"It is." *Message received.*

I fall in line behind Sam and CJ as they march toward the Guardian building where our team bullpens sit; one bullpen for each team. Inside, individual lockers hold all our specialized gear. In the center of the building is the briefing room where mission planning —the boots-on-the-ground tactical portions of our missions —occurs.

But damn if I don't wish I'd followed Carmen out instead of CJ and Sam.

TWENTY-FIVE

Rafe

By the time we stroll into the briefing room, the rest of Bravo team is already gathered.

No surprise, Izzy is here as well.

A nervous expression fills her face and she keeps nibbling on her lower lip. From the look on Booker's face, it's easy to connect the dots. He's pissed because she didn't tell him what happened. I wondered if she would slip and tell Booker what Carmen said, but from the anxious wringing of her hands, and the scowl on Booker's face, it's clear she kept her mouth shut.

Izzy, along with Angie, joined the medical branch of Guardian HRS not too long ago. That makes them a part of the Guardian family at large, but Angie belongs to Brady, and Izzy belongs to Booker, which makes them more than Guardian HRS family. They're honorary Bravo team members; our little sisters. That makes them closer than family. Unlike Bravo team, however, they're not trained warriors. Fortunately, every employee of Guardian HRS undergoes basic self-defense during orientation.

With her recent kidnapping and rescue, Izzy's yet to progress through the various onboarding courses standard for all new hires. We teach everyone basic self-defense, safety protocols, plus tips and tricks to keep our secrets secret. Which gives me an idea. That's something Carmen could definitely benefit from and may make her feel less isolated if she meets some of the other women.

"Booker…" CJ breezes past Booker, invading his personal space. Booker takes a step back before realizing CJ did it intentionally. "From the look on your face, looks like Izzy didn't share."

"You told me not to." Izzy crosses her arms in front of herself and blows out a puff of air.

"And we had every reason to trust you, but now we can tell everyone what happened."

"About time." Booker's scowl deepens when he looks at Izzy, but it's all for show. They're in love and there's nothing that can possibly cast a shadow on them.

As for the briefing, I hang out at the back of the room while Izzy and CJ trade off, explaining what we learned about Carmen.

When Izzy mentions Carmen watching her father kill her mother, Alec glances toward me. His bushy brows practically climb off his forehead. When Izzy mentions the girls, Alec slams his palm down on the table.

"No fucking way!" Alec turns to me, anger boiling in his eyes. "They were there? When we rescued Izzy? In the fucking basement?" A litany of curse words spills from his mouth.

"We'll mockup the grounds in VR. I'd rather set up the physical town, but VR is easier with the video the drones took. We'll find our way in." CJ continues on about the plans to go in tech-free.

That brings another string of colorful expressions from the group, but the guys swallow down their surprise easily enough. We've executed all manner of operations. I wish something like this comes as a shock. Unfortunately, it's another day in the office.

"What's Bravo's objective?" Brady asks for clarification.

"Come again?" CJ asks.

"There's Carmen's maid and an unknown number of girls, who may or may not be in the house when we arrive. Not *assuming* anything, but I expect the girls don't typically stay there long?"

"Unknown," CJ admits.

"Rosalie would know." Zeb digs dirt out from under his nails. "I mean…" He looks around the table. "If she's been sent down there to clean up, I assume she has knowledge of what, where, who, and when. She should be our first target."

"Agreed." Brady claps his hands together. "We get the maid, exploit her knowledge, then rescue the other girls."

"My thoughts were two missions in parallel." CJ pulls at his chin. "Rescue Rosalie and the girls simultaneously."

"Sounds like that'll make a lot of noise. Noise, we don't need to be making." Alec laces his fingers together and holds them behind his head. He swivels back and forth in his chair.

"So, which one are we doing? Rosalie first? Or both together?" Booker tugs Izzy tight to his chest. One broad arm wraps around her belly, holding her against his broad chest.

"I say we bring this to Mitzy and see what her team thinks," CJ says. "I'm for simultaneous extraction. Bravo can take Rosalie. Charlie team will go down for the girls."

"If there are girls when we hit the place." I rub at the back of my neck. "You know, if they're not there, we're sending one hell of a signal to Maximus Angelo to move his operations. We could lose them before we have a chance to save them."

"Obviously, there's still a lot to parse." CJ pulls back a seat and settles in. "Let's spitball this. No idea is too out there. Get comfortable." He makes a sweeping gesture and we all take our seats. "We're digging in."

For the next two hours, we think of every possibility. By the end, our ideas are more fantastical than realistic, but this is how we plan.

Build the perfect mission.

Poke holes until it sinks.

Build on failure

Ensure success.

All the while, I can't wait to feel Carmen in my arms again. Unfortunately, now that she's no longer refusing to talk to anyone, everyone wants time with her.

I want to be the one to show her around Guardian HQ, but I have to wait.

For Mitzy.

For Forest.

For Skye.

For Sam.

And CJ too.

When it comes to Carmen, I'm last in line. That's okay. It's bloody fine by me. I held Carmen in my arms. I felt her sweet surrender when our lips touched that first time. Her future belongs with me. I just hate that others need her now.

Call me love-struck; I don't give a damn. No doubt the guys will give me grief later, but I watched Brady go after Angie. Booker went ballistic when we chased down the bastard, Matias, who took Izzy. Just like I stood beside them, they'll do the same for me. It's what we do and who we are, and I don't give one damn if the guys know how much Carmen means to me.

It may not make sense. It may be way too bloody fast. Doesn't matter, and I don't care. Carmen is mine, and I'm hers until the end.

Meanwhile, I plan with my team. We build out several rescue scenarios. Poke holes. Plan some more. In the back of my mind, every way this mission can go wrong fills me with dread. Can I afford to lose Carmen before I make her mine? Before we get the chance to explore the crazy chemistry flowing between us?

My greatest fear is that the answer to that question is not one I want to hear.

TWENTY-SIX

Carmen

"EXPLAIN YOUR INVOLVEMENT WITH THE CIA SO FAR." THERE'S A bounce to Mitzy's step as she leads me out of the building that's been my temporary home these past few days. She's a bundle of energy that talks fast and thinks faster. There's also absolute assurance I'll answer her question.

And why shouldn't I? They've been excellent hosts to an inhospitable guest. My cooperation is long overdue, but I'm not sure how to answer.

"There's not much to say. I used a library computer to reach out. Months went by. I reached out a few more times. They were excessively cautious. Months would go between communication. Toward the end of my last year, they finally agreed to arrange a meeting. But that never happened."

A light breeze blows in from the ocean, carrying the faintest scent of brine in the swirling currents and whipping my hair into a frenzy. I swipe a few flyaway strands out of my mouth and tuck them behind my ear. Gathering my hair into a low ponytail, I pull it over my shoulder and grip the strands to keep the wind from snapping them in my face. Although shorter than me by a few inches, Mitzy challenges me to keep up with her energetic stride.

"Well, fortunately for us, the CIA takes our calls. We trade favors from time to time." She speaks as if it's no big deal.

"Favors?" Seriously, I'm not this dense, but I need to know how involved these people are with the organization I depend on to bring an end to my father's crimes.

"Forest called on his CIA buddies to assist with Izzy's rescue. They helped us set up that rescue." She glances over her shoulder, letting me know I'm slowing her down. I pick up the pace and trot to her side.

"How'd they do that?"

I should be concerned about the CIA interfering in my country, but that train left the station decades before I was born. The United States is acutely interested in stabilizing Central America no matter the cost, or the morals, of those involved. That, however, is not my fight.

"They provided intel." Mitzy continues without taking a breath.

Falling behind, I rush to keep up.

"Oh." I rub my bare arms, feeling chilled despite the warm breeze off the ocean.

Dusk is falling, which means the steady breeze brings a cold air in off the ocean, taking the heat of the day with it.

Despite my self-imposed isolation, I know approximately where I am. The faintest scent of salt and brine lingers in the air and that comes from only one source. Add in the gulls soaring far overhead and it doesn't take a rocket scientist to figure out I'm on a coast.

The West Coast.

No stranger to the California coastline, it's warmer here than in San Francisco. Whether fog rolling in off the Bay, or weird inversion layers forming at odd times of day, after spending four years at UCSF, I developed a healthy respect for the old saying, *The coldest winter in California is a summer spent in San Francisco.* I also took several weekend trips up and down the coast with my friends.

Not exactly sure where I am along the California coast, my guess is we're a bit south of the Bay, below Monterey and possibly Saint Luis Obispo, but north of the beach town of Santa Barbara.

"We're headed to my *lair*." Mitzy points to a massive building directly in front of us. She makes air quotes and grins like I should get the joke.

I don't and nibble at my lower lip, not sure if I'm supposed to laugh, smile, or ignore it.

"It's a joke between me and Forest." Mitzy doesn't seem to notice my confusion and gives a little flap of her hand. "He's got a *lair* somewhere in the mountains of Colorado. Built his own super-computer in a clean room. Mine is here. His supercomputer is newer than mine, but *Jacen's* better. If you haven't noticed, he's not like the rest of us."

"Jason?" My brows pinch together, confused.

"Not Jason. It's J.C.N., but it's easier to say *Jacen*. You'll hear people talking about it, but I meant Forest. Forest isn't like the rest of us."

"Supercomputer? He's got a private supercomputer?" Who are these people? "He's freakishly huge." I blurt out the first thing that comes to mind.

My comment makes Mitzy laugh.

"Forest is a giant, but that's nothing compared to his brain." She taps her forefinger against her temple. "The man is *freakishly* smart, and on the spectrum—if you hadn't noticed."

"I didn't."

"He's mellowing with age. When we met, he was totally weird to be around. Awkward is putting it lightly. That man's brain operates on a different plane than the rest of us mere mortals." Mitzy comes to a sudden halt and lifts her arms out to the side. "He created all of this. Him and his sister Skye."

"Why, if I may ask?"

Spinning in a slow circle, she seems to include all the buildings around us. "It's their mission in life to save as many unfortunates as they can. What you see here is their rescue operations—the Guardians and Protectors—but they also rescue kids in the foster system who've run afoul of foster parents abusing the system and abusing the kids." Mitzy points south. "They established a group home for their foster rescues and for those the Guardians rescue. We call it The Facility, and if you have time, I highly recommend checking it out."

"I'm not sure I understand what all of this is." While Mitzy props her hands on her hips, I scan the multitude of buildings, not sure what I'm looking at. For the most part, it feels like a college campus, but that can't be right.

"Don't worry. You'll figure it out. Let's pick up the pace." Mitzy heads off nearly twice as fast as before. "I'm sure Rafe will give you a tour later."

Mention of Rafe brings back the memory of that kiss and heat to my cheeks, making me glad Mitzy's a step ahead where she can't see me blush. When I press my hands to my cheeks, the wind grabs hold of my hair, turning the strands into stinging whips that assault my eyes. I wish I had a hairband to tie my long hair back and keep it under control.

"I'd like that." I finger comb my hair, then gather it all together again in my hand. "I never left the apartment. I didn't know if I could." Pulling an errant strand of hair out of my mouth, I press my lips together feeling guilty about how I've treated these people.

"You were under surveillance, but not under guard." She winks at me. "But I think you knew that. We've been watching. Wondering what your story was going to be." The way she says it sounds like they expected me to make something up.

"Do you believe me?"

"Shouldn't I?"

"Everything I said is true."

"Then I believe you."

"I didn't know who to trust. The way I got here…" I curl my lower lip between my teeth, unsure what to say.

"The way you came to us was unusual. Raised a lot of questions."

"I haven't been the best guest, and I'm sorry for that. The only one I felt halfway comfortable with trusting was…"

"Rafe?" Mitzy tugs at her ear.

"I trust him, but it's actually Isabelle LaCroix. I figured she'd understand, but once I jumped on that line, it felt like I made a huge mistake. Sometimes, I wish I hadn't..." I give a sharp yank on my hair. "I didn't think things through, and now that I'm here, I'm terrified about what might be happening back home."

"To Rosalie?"

"Yes."

"I guess that depends on whether your father believes the lie you told him and the truths we're going to share. Tell me again what you said to him."

Truths we're going to share? I don't understand what she's talking about, but if I wait her out, I have a feeling she'll explain. That's the one thing I'm most worried about. My father needs to believe I'll do anything to avenge him.

We're off again, closing in on the building in front of us. While I explain what I said to my father, my thought process when I chased after Bravo team, and the decision which launched me into Rafe's arms, Mitzy appears to take mental notes, ticking off salient points with a nod each.

My cheeks heat with the memory of clinging to Rafe and Mitzy notices.

"Rafe's certainly taken an interest in you." She slows her pace and glances at me. "Definitely protective."

Protective?

Curious to explore that further, it's too much to unpack, so I leave it for later.

"He's been exceptional." I twist my hair and think back to how he checks in with me each morning and night, brings me gifts like that chocolate cake, and never pushes me to answer any questions.

"Exceptional?" Mitzy's left eyebrow wings up and there's a smirk on her face. "Exceptional as in...?"

She's curious, although I have a feeling very little of what I've done has gone unnoticed. There's something about Mitzy that makes me feel like we're long-lost friends. It's a struggle to remember that we're strangers.

These people, at best, may or may not be able to help me. At worst, they can destroy everything I care about. That leaves a lot between the two extremes. I haven't come this far to mess things up by trusting too easily, or revealing everything I know.

It's a sobering thought, and I remind myself to be vigilant.

"A word of caution when it comes to Rafe." Mitzy pulls up short and I almost run into her.

"Oh, is he married?" A married man wouldn't have kissed me.

"No. Definitely not. I was just going to warn you that when our Guardians fall, they fall hard, and they fall fast. They're overprotective to a fault, but when it comes to their women, overprotective becomes downright fierce."

"We're not…" I get where she's going, but it's way too soon to be saying such things. We've only had the one kiss, but Mitzy speaks as if we're already a couple.

"From the way he looks at you, you already are, but don't worry. That possessive-protective vibe isn't their fault. It's wired into their DNA. In my opinion, the world could use more men who aren't afraid to act like men." She winks at me. "If that makes any sense."

I try parsing out what she says, but keep getting twisted around.

Mitzy laughs and taps me gently on the arm. It's more than a casual touch. It's the kind of friendly tap Kaye or Barbi would give. It's the touch of friends, but I don't know Mitzy.

"Um…"

"There's serious chemistry between you two. It thickens the air, but don't worry. When he claims you, you'll know."

"Claims me?" I tug on my hair again, not sure if I like how that sounds. "No man is going to *claim* me." That sounds like something Artemus would do.

"It's not as bad as it sounds." Her smile lights up her face. "Men like him can't help it. They're alpha to the core." Mitzy gives me a look I'm afraid to decipher. There's a short pause, then she laughs. "Honey, all the men here are alpha males. Ex-SEALs…" She lifts a finger. "Sorry, they would tan my hide if they heard me say that."

"Say what?"

"The ex-SEAL bit. According to them, once a SEAL, always a SEAL. There are no ex-SEALs as they're a SEAL for life. We're supposed to call them former SEALs. Point being…" Mitzy punctuates her comment with a jab of her finger in the air. "All the Guardians are either former SEALs or former Special Ops. Think Green Berets, Air Force Para Jumpers, Delta Force—you name it, we hire only the best of the best of the best. Which means the average daily dose of testosterone floating in the air is a million times higher than any other place on earth. It's amazing any of the women are allowed outside unsupervised. We've got Guardians and Guardian Protectors, and they live to save a damsel in distress, but don't let that scare you. As fierce as they look on the outside, in my experience, they're a gooey mess of emotions on the inside." Her wink makes me blink and nearly trip over my own feet.

Too stunned to speak, I keep my mouth shut as Mitzy takes off again.

"I don't know about the being *claimed* bit." If I had hackles, they'd stand on end.

The words are meant to come out strong and sure, but there's weakness in my voice, highlighted by a little bit of a warble.

"There's a huge difference between being a possessive and protective alpha male and a domineering asshole. Our guys respect their women and put them first in all things. When I say possessive and protective, I don't mean controlling. Wait until you meet some of the women our Guardians have fallen for and you'll understand."

"Unfortunately, nothing can happen between me and Rafe."

"Why do you say that?"

"My father…"

"If Rafe's claimed you, and I'm pretty sure he has, he'll move heaven and earth to keep you safe. Your father won't have a choice. One thing I've learned is never tell a Guardian he can't do something. He'll take the challenge just to prove you're wrong. I know what you're thinking, and yes, there are major obstacles, but you've barely seen what the Guardians can do."

"If you say so." I take a pause and gather my thoughts. "There's no place on earth where I'll be safe. My father will find me, and if he discovers I'm working against him, I don't know what he'll do to me."

Or to Rosalie.

TWENTY-SEVEN

Carmen

Mitzy continues toward the building that contains her *lair* and the supercomputer *Jacen.* I trot a step behind her, trying to keep up. She's a tireless bundle of energy I find exhausting.

"Your father will be taken care of. I've got something in mind. As for you, Rafe won't allow anything to happen to you." When I don't respond, she places her hand on my shoulder. It's another touch, the kind a friend would make. "Call it an inconvenient side-effect of the job," Mitzy says. "I notice things I never would've noticed before. Between you and me, I love watching a Guardian fall. You know, now that you're out of your self-imposed isolation, you should get Rafe to take you down to our private beach."

"What private beach?"

"*Insanity* perches on the cliffs overlooking a private beach." She says *Insanity* as if I should be familiar with the place. "Anyone who's associated with the band, or an employee of Guardian HRS, is welcome to take advantage of the beach."

"Band? What band?"

"Oh, sorry. I just assume everyone knows. Angel Fire. We live at *Insanity.*"

We? She includes herself with the mega rock band Angel Fire? My brows pinch with confusion, but I'm too self-conscious to ask.

"The beach isn't your typical beach, meaning there's no sand. It's rocky, but the tidepools more than make up for it. There's a fire pit and comfy chairs." She cups her hand over her mouth and drops her voice to a whisper. "It's great date night material. Get Rafe to take you down there at sunset. Light a bonfire. Snuggle in a lounge chair. Chances are you'll be the only ones there, and I won the bet by the way."

"The bet?" I shake my head, confused.

"Forest and I made a bet." She waits for me to catch up, but I have no idea what she's talking about. "He likes to think he can call it when a Guardian falls. He did it for the band and thinks he's got a monopoly on it."

"I don't know about Rafe." Secretly, a tiny thrill runs through me. I'd love for that to be the case. "And if I have to go back…"

"You're not going back, but now that you brought it up, let's get cracking. You've been incommunicado for too many days. Time to start feeding your father information and buy you extra time."

Something about the way Mitzy speaks—her unflappable confidence—makes me want to believe there's a chance for me to escape my fate. Whether that's with, or without, Rafe, I can't say, but Mitzy makes me believe in the Guardians and a future out from beneath my father's iron-fisted rule.

As far as my father goes, I can't imagine what she has in mind.

"Come on." She grabs my hand and tugs me forward. "We've got tons to do. Let me show you what I do for a living."

With that, she pulls me inside a modern masterpiece of a building. All clean lines and swooping curves, it's minimalistic while being spectacular. Once inside, she proceeds to blow my mind with everything that Guardian HRS can do.

Spoiler alert. It's nothing like what I imagined.

It's both more, and less, than I thought. One thing is certain, given a choice, I know where I'd like my future to be.

After an hour-long tour, Mitzy finally pulls me into her office. From her effusive personality and extraordinary intellect, I expect something haphazard and chaotic. What I find instead is an impeccably clean and ordered office. Like freakishly ordered. Nothing's out of place and everything's aligned to produce the perfect esthetic. Mitzy flounces down in her chair and gestures for me to do the same.

"What we need to do is figure out what truths we're going to tell your father and the falsities we're going to weave in between."

"Falsities?" It's a weird word.

"I prefer that to *lies*. Lies makes it seem like we're doing something wrong." She pulls out a pad of paper, legal-sized, and grabs a pen. Clicking the pen three times, she taps the paper with her finger. "The best lie, as you probably know, is one that's as close to the truth as possible."

"Um—okay?"

She draws a large circle on the pad of paper. "This is where the truth lies." Tapping outside the circle, she looks up at me. "And these are the lies."

"I'm not sure I get it." Indeed, none of this makes sense.

"Bear with me." She nibbles on the end of the pen while thinking, then begins to write several things down inside the circle. "You were terrified jumping on Rafe. That's a truth, so we put it here."

"Okay?" I still don't get what she's doing.

"You told your father you were going to spy for him."

"I did."

"So that's a truth."

"That was, most definitely, a lie."

"Your intent is the lie, but the *truth* is that's what you said to him."

"I guess?" Still not sure what we're doing.

"Why did you do it?" With this, she taps the end of the pen against her temple. "Didn't you have security guards?"

"Yeah, but your men took them out."

"They did, but how did you know that? Here's my question. Why did Maximus Angelo's daughter jump to his rescue? Why didn't you curl into a ball and cower? Not to be offensive, but that's what most people would've done?"

"Not me."

"That's what I want to work out. What reason does he have to believe you'd do anything at all?"

"I suppose because Rafe and the others came into the room. Our security should've been alerted. They should've come straight to my father and taken us to the saferoom."

"You have a saferoom?"

"Of course."

"Good to know." She writes a note in small print in the bottom corner. "CJ's going to want to know about that."

"Okay."

"So, security should've been there. They weren't—so why did you chase after Bravo team?"

"They hurt my father."

"Did they?"

"He was closest to the blast from whatever it was they threw at us."

"The flashbang."

"Right. He was knocked out of his chair and curled up on the floor."

Mitzy grills me about everything that happened in the dining room, questioning every thought and every action until my frustration builds and I finally lose it.

"What is it you want me to say?"

She cocks her head and puts the pen down. "What I want is for you to tell me what you did and why?"

"That's what I'm doing." I blow out a puff of air in frustration.

"No. You're telling me what you want to believe. What you're not doing is telling me the truth."

"But…"

"Trust the process. What we're trying to do is keep to the truth as much as possible. I want you to know it so well that your answers never change. If I'm wondering why you did what you did, he is too. If you can't convince me, then how are you going to convince him?"

"I can't tell him the truth."

"And what is the truth?"

"I told you." I told all of them, and Mitzy's pissing me off with her incessant badgering.

"I don't think you have."

"I was trying to save Rosalie."

"That's what you want to believe. It lends a sense of heroism to your actions, but you weren't acting like a hero."

"Saving Rosalie is the truth. That's why I did what I did."

"That's not the reason you jumped on that line and risked your life."

"Then please educate me." I lean back with a huff and cross my arms in front of me.

"The truth is uncomfortable, especially when we've told ourselves a lie to hide it."

"I'm not hiding anything."

"You didn't jump on that line to spy on your father. He knows this. And you didn't jump on that line to save Rosalie."

"Yes, I did."

"That's one hell of a risk to take for someone else, no matter how close the two of you may be, especially when you had no idea what the outcome would be."

"I don't know what you want me to say."

"I want the truth we're going to tell your father, because if I was him, I wouldn't believe a word you said to me." She leans forward, pressing the tip of her finger against the tabletop. "You were arguing with your father over the engagement."

"I argue with him all the time."

"Precisely, but this was different."

"I don't get it."

"You're not the kind of daughter who would risk your life to save his."

"I might."

"Why did you jump on the line?"

"Because why? What were you running from?"

"I was running from getting trapped in a loveless marriage to Artemus." My words rush out in a shout, full of frustration and anger.

"Bingo!" Mitzy leans back in victory and claps her hands. "Finally."

"Finally, what?"

"That's the truth we're going to tell your father."

My mouth gapes as Mitzy leans forward and writes in the middle of the circle. Using all caps, her precise and perfect penmanship scribes: *I wanted to run away.* With a final flourish, Mitzy looks up at me with a smile on her face.

"But if I say that, Rosalie…"

"Will be safe. When you call him, you're going to be scared, and you're going to regret what you did. You'll be properly remorseful, but since you're here, you're going to spy. It's all in how we work in the lies."

TWENTY-EIGHT

Rafe

T‍HE MOMENT WE LEARNED OF THE GIRLS AND YOUNG WOMEN trafficked through the hellhole that is Maximus Angelo's villa, there was no question as to our next move. Carmen, or no Carmen, we're on task. There's a mission to plan and lives to save. My only fear is Carmen will get lost in the shuffle.

"Explain how this EMP Mitzy's dreamed up lands us in a tech blackout." Hayes runs his hand down his face and pinches his eyes.

We've been at this most of the night and my focus is shot wondering what Carmen's doing. At least, I hope, she's getting a good night's rest. I scrub at my eyes, trying to dislodge the sleep crusting them. They burn from the all-night planning session. That itchy burn feels as if someone went crazy with sandpaper, leaving behind grit I can't seem to shake.

Overly dramatic, but I've spent the last twelve hours trying to focus on mission planning while Carmen is God knows where, with God knows who, doing God knows what. Granted, the list of subjects is exceptionally short—Mitzy—but anyone who's not me, doesn't deserve time with Carmen. She's mine. That's the beginning and end of it.

As far as mission planning goes, Forest wants to execute within the week. I scrub at my hair, trying to think through a fog of exhaustion.

Honestly, my participation in the all-night planning session has been less than my usual, but that's only because I'm trying to figure out the best way to help Carmen.

"Call me crazy…" Hayes holds out his hand, palms up, "but I don't get the need for a tech blackout."

"What's not to understand?" CJ runs his hand down his face and pulls at his jaw. He's as tired as the rest of us. Not because we're pulling an all-nighter. It's because all the plans we've come up with so far make no bloody sense. We're going to get our asses handed to us if we don't figure something out.

"I get the EMP." Hayes leans against the wall. He got out of his seat hours ago, choosing to stand rather than sit as the night wore on. "And I'm definitely not claiming to be an expert, but doesn't that shit have a range? Why can't we use Mitzy's drones or the Rufi?"

Looks like we've settled on *Rufi* as the plural form of RUFUS for the robotic dogs. He's right about the Rufi and drones. We could use one of Mitzy's dragonfly drones or one of the Rufi. The EMP would take it out, but we could recover the tech, which solves the problem of leaving them behind.

"It needs to be strategically inserted…" CJ pulls at his jaw, biting back whatever it is he wants to say. He's frustrated that none of us are on board with this part of the plan.

Hayes glances my way once again. "Why not drop it ourselves?" Hayes is on a roll and I love every word he says. "If we infil by air, we're right on top of them. Set Charlie team outside the walls, provide a distraction while Bravo swoops in from the sky. As we close in, we release the EMP. Our gear will get fried, but we're not planning on bringing any electronics, so it doesn't matter to us. Charlie team isn't either, but they can. How far is the EMPs effective range?"

Hayes is pretty fucking phenomenal. An off-the-grid kind of guy, his outlook on humanity is rather doom and gloom, but it makes him unstoppable on the ground. He doesn't look at shit the way the rest of us do. He's training for the ultimate test of humankind, preparing for the zombie apocalypse during his spare time, while the rest of us are trying to figure out what fast food crap we want to feed our bodies.

"Anyone know how fast the *Rufi* run?" Hayes glances around the room.

Part of our job as Guardians is to test out the tech Mitzy's team develops. From getting our asses handed to us by the robots while trying to extract prisoners, we've been involved in all phases of research and development.

"Fucking fast." Zeb, the quiet one of the bunch, sits, leaning far back in his chair, heels propped on the conference table. "Mitzy's little pets run circles around us. I'd say they can run at least fifty miles an hour. Probably faster. So, twenty minutes, plus or minus?"

"We don't need them on the ground when we arrive." I glance at my team. "Don't you see?"

Brady pushes back from the table. "All I want to see are the insides of my eyelids. You got something to say, get to it quickly. Don't got all fucking day with twenty questions."

"All I'm saying is Bravo infils from the sky. At some predetermined altitude, whatever Mitzy and her team decides, we set off the EMP and knock out their systems. Bravo lands on their bloody rooftop. Charlie team stays outside, providing cover. Let them draw the army out. Once we're inside, Mitzy releases the Rufi. Heck, she can send in her *dragonflies*. We can have an entire pack of the robotic menaces charging into position."

"How do we protect them from the EMP." CJ rubs at his eyes.

"That's the beauty of EMP." I glance around the table.

"Okay, Encyclopedia, care to share?" Brady calls me out, but for good reason.

I'm an encyclopedia of useless facts.

"EMPs destroy unprotected data, which is basically every computer system on earth. A nuclear blast over Europe will create an EMP field over all of Western Europe, including London. That blast basically wipes clean all unprotected data on all electronic devices rendering them useless. Our vulnerability is growing when it comes to EMP. We're talking data storage, virtual reality, driverless cars, electrical power grids, watches, cell phones, facial recognition, wireless devices—everything we take for granted. One EMP basically wipes the slate clean."

I glance around the conference room, looking to see if they get it.

"That's just for nuclear blasts. It's undifferentiated, but there is also intentional EMI, or IEMI."

"Wait." Zeb lifts a finger. "I thought we were talking EMP? What the fuck is IEMI?"

"Intentional Electromagnetic Interference. It's basically tactical EMP. Just what Mitzy's looking to employ. We're talking about a portable, battery-powered EMP burst that takes out all servers and electronics within a designated radius. Position the Rufi outside that barrier, shield them with a Faraday cage for good measure, set off the EMP, then deploy the Rufi. We get the best of both worlds."

"Rafe, I think you're onto something." CJ seems to perk up, energized by a new set of data. "I need Mitzy." He snaps his fingers and points to Hayes.

Hayes jumps and heads to the phone hanging on the wall. It's not a typical phone; more of a Guardian HQ walkie-talkie, but it does the job.

"Let's look at this again." CJ draws the rest of us in while Hayes talks on the phone. "We need projections. How long? How far? And if this goes for the Rufi, what about Mitzy's dragonflies? If we can arm them with tranqs…" CJ continues on, talking about arming not only the Rufi, but Mitzy's dragonflies.

The autonomous AI embedded in their programming is scary tech, but as long as they're on our side, I'm all for exploiting technology. Especially since we're going to be parachuting into what's essentially an active zone where we're outnumbered twenty to one.

The only easy day was yesterday. That saying remains as solid today as it did back in my Navy days with the teams. The briefing wears on until Brady finally calls it.

"Time to wrap things up." Brady places his hands on his lower back and stretches.

"Good session. Still lots to chew on, but making progress." CJ pushes back his seat and raps his knuckles on the table. "Take a break. Get some food. You've got until 1300hrs to take care of whatever it is you need to take care of."

Call me crazy, but CJ looks directly at me when he says that.

TWENTY-NINE

Rafe

RUBBING AT THE BACK OF MY NECK, SLEEP PULLS AT ME. MORNING comes far too soon after an all-night strategy session. With a yawn, I stretch my arms overhead and wonder where Carmen is and whether she's thinking of me.

My stump complains, sending ghost pains shooting through a limb that's no longer there.

Piper tells me good stump care is the key to full recovery, but I think someone failed to mention to my overly perky and positive physical therapist that until humans figure out how to regrow limbs, full recovery isn't possible.

Regardless, the stump's not happy. It's been shoved into the prosthetic sleeve for too many hours. It's red, itchy, and firing off nerves that haven't been there for over a year.

This is what worries me when it comes to operational readiness and my performance on the team.

How can I perform as a full member if I have to stop mid-mission to let my stump of a leg take a break from the prosthetic it's shoved inside?

So far, Piper's been silent on this issue. Not that my stump's an angry beast because of overuse. For the majority of the night, I sat on my ass inside the briefing room as Bravo team picked apart scores of mission scenarios in preparation for moving in on Maximus Angelo's estate.

Maybe I need to return in a better frame of mind?

Or, I can find out where Mitzy dragged Carmen.

"You going to grab some chow?" Hayes places his hand on my shoulder and gives a hard squeeze. "Are you going to go looking for her?"

No need to specify who that might be.

"Not sure." I shrug.

"You've got it bad." Hayes gives me a look. "Never figured you to fall for someone who's just as likely to be your enemy as your friend."

"Carmen's not our enemy."

"Right, but she's the daughter of our enemy. Blood ties are stronger than you think."

"I don't know about that. Her father's done pretty much everything in the book to destroy his relationship with his daughter. Do you think she's lying?"

Hayes is freakishly good at reading people. It usually takes me a few weeks, sometimes much longer, before I have a sense about who a person is. He reads people in milliseconds, and I've never seen him call it wrong.

"Nah. Carmen's on task. Just checking in."

"Appreciate it." He releases me, then thumps me on the back.

Without another word, he joins Zeb and Alec, who follow behind Brady and Booker. I'm the only one of the team not headed to chow, but I've got more pressing needs. Trying not to appear too desperate, I head outside and make the quick hike to Carmen's building. With a solid rap to her door, I rock back on my heels and wait for her to answer.

But there is no answer.

After three solid knocks without a response, I pound on the door, rattling it on its hinges. If Carmen's asleep, that surely will get her out of bed. Only, there is no Carmen, and putting an ear to the door, there's no activity inside. Nothing to indicate another human wandering around.

One of the doors down the hall opens. It's Reid Sawyer, one of our new Protectors. We seem to be making a thing of meeting up in the hall.

"Don't think she's in there." He jabs a thumb toward the door.

"How so?"

"She and Mitzy came back a couple of hours ago, then left. Haven't been back."

"You know where they went?"

"Sorry."

"Thanks." I try to hide my disappointment, but fail.

"I suggest calling Mitzy." Reid punches me in the arm as he wanders past.

"You headed out?"

"To get breakfast. Lyra's a bit worn out, so I figure I'll stretch my legs and grab a bite to eat while I'm at it. Care to join?"

"Nah, I'm good." My attention shifts to the door that remains frustratingly shut. "Besides, I guess I'm headed to the tech building."

Reid doesn't hide his shudder. "Good luck with that."

It's a joke Guardians and Protectors have when it comes to the *techies*. We stay out of their shit and they stay out of ours. The truth is we're all on the same team, working toward the same goals, but where's the fun in that? A little rivalry never hurt anyone.

"Thanks." I pivot and walk beside him toward the exit. "How's it going with Lyra?"

"She's a handful." With the grin on Reid's face, I can guess there's more going on beyond a client-Protector professional relationship.

Although, who am I to judge, considering I'm looking for Carmen?

We walk outside for a bit, shooting the shit, before he peels off to head for chow. I continue on toward the largest, and most stunning, building on Guardian HQ grounds. As Guardians, our building and training facilities are utilitarian.

Utilitarian, in this case, means no frills. The same can't be said for the Tech facilities. A marvel of glass, steel, and some of the best tech on the planet, it's by far the most secure building on campus. It's also where Mitzy rules her kingdom of geeks and nerds.

Sliding glass doors part before me as I enter the atrium. All sleek lines, swooping curves, and a blend of steel, glass, and white marble, the place looks pretty cool. I give a half salute, half wave, to the receptionist at the massive desk forming an entire wall of the lobby and angle toward the stairs leading up.

The young woman smiles and her cheeks turn pink. Her gaze dips, which is a turn-off for me—too submissive. I prefer a woman who's not afraid to look me in the eye.

Taking the stairs two at a time, I climb three flights up the curved staircase to a suite of rooms. As far as ruling over her kingdom, that's where things stop with Mitzy. She doesn't sit in a corner office with windows looking out at the world. There's no imposing desk to make her subject's knees wobble.

Nope. There's none of that.

I wind my way through a maze of desks, computer terminals, work benches, and stuff I can't name until I come to a rather nondescript office with a simple sign on the door that says, "Chief of Cyber Security."

Mitzy is far more than the Chief of Cyber Security, but it's enough. With a smart rap on the door, I wait for a response, knowing full well who I'll find inside.

But there's no response to my knocking.

No response to banging on the door.

No response when I grasp the doorknob and force my way in.

There's no response because no one's there.

"You looking for Mitzy?" A kid barely out of high school, wearing a white lab coat two sizes too big for his gangly form, pokes his head in Mitzy's office.

"That would be me." Rocking back on my heels, or rather one heel and the base of my prosthetic, I shove my hands deep into my pockets. "Any idea where your boss might be?"

"Yeah, she took the pretty *Latina* with her less than twenty minutes ago."

"Any idea where they went?" Not a fan of this young kid ogling what's mine, it's a struggle to keep the possessive, want-to-rip-your-head-off tone from my voice.

"She mentioned something about heading to *Insanity* to use one of the sound booths."

"The, what?"

"The sound booths." The kid looks at me like I'm an idiot, which I take particular offense to considering he's barely out of high school. Mitzy loves to recruit young. Says something about young brains aren't burdened with bad habits she has to break.

"Why would she…" I hold up a hand, palm out. "Forget it. I'll just give her a call."

"Cool." Without a by-your-leave, the techie kid ambles out of sight, leaving me to curse under my breath.

An interesting kid. Scrawny, like they all are, he isn't intimidated by my brawn, and like all of Mitzy's people, a fierce intelligence shines in his eyes. I take note of the way he holds my gaze. There's no sign I intimidate him at all, which is as it should be.

"*Insanity*, huh?" Talking to myself, I pull at my jaw while wondering why on earth Mitzy and Carmen need a sound booth.

A yawn slips out and I decide I'm not about to find them anytime soon, and since there's no way in hell I'm crashing Angel Fire's group home, *Insanity*, without an invite, I need to do something about that.

With Carmen safely in Mitzy's hands, I head to the chow hall for a bite to eat. None of Bravo team are there, but Charlie team gathers around a table in the back corner. I angle over to my fellow brothers in arms to grab a bite while catching up with the guys.

"What's up?" I swing a leg up and over a chair and take a seat.

"Hear Bravo's spinning up a mission and needs an assist." Tex, Charlie-One, scrapes his fork across his plate, scooping up the last of his eggs.

"Has CJ briefed you yet?" I glance around the table, where blank stares are returned.

"Not yet, but he told us to meet in the bullpen at 1300hrs."

"Sounds about right. Bravo will be there."

"Any idea what the mission is?"

"Nicaraguan Minister of the Interior has a gig on the side trafficking girls." There's no need to say anything more than that.

"Fuckers are like cockroaches." Tex curses under his breath. "Kill one and ten more scurry for cover."

"It's going to be a shitshow." I explain about the previous raid, Izzy's rescue, Carmen's unorthodox extraction, and concerns over going up against Nicaraguan military.

"Shitshow sounds about right. Love the idea with the EMP and agree about the Rufi." He glances at his teammates. "Looks like we've finally figured out the plural for Rufus. We're lucky to have them on our side, although the day will come when we face off against one of them in the field."

"Yeah." I rub the back of my neck. "Not looking forward to that."

We spend the next hour discussing the pros and cons of tech on the battlefield, but eventually it's time for Charlie team to head to the mats for a bit of one-on-one combat sparring.

With a few hours to kill before the meeting with CJ, Bravo, and Charlie, I head to the one person I don't want to see but for whom I have questions needing answers.

Fortunately, Piper answers on the first knock.

"What did I do to deserve such a treat? You coming to me without an appointment? Has the sky fallen?" She looks up as a joke.

"Laugh it up, fuzzball. I've got questions."

Once Piper realizes I'm here with real questions, the teasing stops, and she gets down to business.

"What are you worried about?"

"Who says I'm worried?"

"You showing up at my office without an appointment says so."

"I had time to kill."

"And this is where your feet brought you? To my doorstep?"

"Technically, I only have one foot."

"*Touché*, but how about you get to the point? What can I do for you?"

"Isn't that what I'm doing?"

"What's that?"

"Getting to the point."

"No. What you're doing is an exemplary job of beating around the bush."

"Fine." I glance down the hall, toward the physical therapy gym. "Mind if we head back?"

"Be my guest." She sweeps her arm, gesturing for me to go ahead of her.

It's weird because I'm used to opening doors for women and letting them go first, but it is what it is.

"You're not staring at my ass again, are you?" I look over my shoulder and catch her doing just that.

"I'm assessing your *gait*." Her nose crinkles with feigned irritation.

"If you say so." I wiggle my ass, seeing if I can get a rise out of her.

"I do say so, and stop that. I'm taken."

The urge to reply with *So am I* nearly slips out of my mouth. Fortunately, I clamp my mouth shut and manage not to embarrass myself.

Our little back and forth lasts long enough for the short walk down the hall. The physical therapy gym is a mishmash of treadmills, stationary bikes, exercise balls, bands, free weights, traction devices, and regular exercise machines. I head over to one of the therapy tables and jump up on the padded surface.

"What's on your mind?" Piper props her hands on her hips and glances at my leg.

I pull up my pants leg and pop the seal between the prosthetic and my stump. Kept on through a combination of suction and straps, the prosthetic pops free with a sucking sound I hate.

My stump immediately gives a sigh of relief. Not that it actually *sighs*, but the relief is real.

Best part of my day is taking the fake leg off and climbing into bed. It still feels weird, not having the weight of the leg on that side of my body, but it's better than the foreign sensation the composite creates under the sheets.

Automatically, my hands go to the stump. My fingers massage what's left of the muscles, bringing circulation back to the skin. After a quick rub, I peel back the compression sleeve and reveal the ugly mess.

Through the whole thing, Piper says nothing, but she watches me like a hawk. Trained as a physical therapist, she's taken on the role of personal therapist/psychologist for those of us with injuries severe enough to demand her unique skillset.

"It hurts."

"Gonna need you to be more specific." Without pausing, she pulls up a stool and rolls in front of me.

My good foot dangles over the edge of the table, swinging back and forth in a mockery of the injured leg. There's not much of the amputated leg to dangle over the edge of the table, and there's nothing left to swing. A few inches below my knee, the leg simply stops.

Never to be whole again.

"That's the thing. All I did last night was sit around a conference table. I didn't get in my usual run because I was taking care of…"

"Carmen?" Piper rubs her hands briskly together to warm her palms. It took a long time before I realized she did that for me; to make her chilly touch less shocking to the injured leg.

"Seems like everyone knows about Carmen." A grimace fills my face before I realize it's there.

"Word gets around." Piper says nothing about my response. "What did you do after sitting all night?"

"Went to chow. Hung out with Charlie team. They had questions about the mission as they're being brought on board."

"I bet they did, but tell me about your leg?"

"Why does it hurt when I've done nothing to stress it? And if I can't get through a night of sitting, how am I going to perform if I'm out in the field for days on end?"

Truth be told, most of our missions are quick in-and-out rescue operations. We're seldom in the field for any duration of time, but that doesn't mean shit doesn't happen. Max, Alpha-One, found himself running for his life in the jungles of Columbia when shit went south during a mission. With our upcoming op, I worry about the same happening to me.

Piper's got a gift, because while I say none of that, she reads it all in my body language.

"You want me to tell you that you're back at 100% operational readiness, but the truth is you'll never be the same. It's only been a year. You've made remarkable progress, and while the majority of healing and remodeling is finished within the first year, there's always going to be something. If you find yourself someplace unexpected, for longer than you intend, you're going to need to know how to deal with your leg and the prosthetic. If your prosthetic is damaged or lost, you're going to have to deal with that as well."

"Damn, you're not sugarcoating anything."

"I respect you too much to lie to you or to downplay very real considerations. So far, we've focused on healing and getting you back on the team, but we've done nothing to prepare you for every contingency, and you know what that means…" She gives me a long hard look.

"It means I'm not going to like what's going to come out of your mouth next."

"Pretty much." She cocks her head to the side. "Do you want it hard and fast, or easy and slow?"

"Isn't that supposed to be the dude's line?" I can't help but crack a grin.

Piper's super cool. She's also super taken by Bent, bassist for Angel Fire, which reminds me…

"Hey, how do I go about getting an invitation to *Insanity?*"

"Excuse me?"

"Didn't think I stuttered."

"I heard you, but that's kind of an odd ask. Why do you want to go there?"

Like most everyone else at Guardian HQ, I've been down to the private beach sitting below the cliffs *Insanity* overlooks, but I've never been inside. Specifically, I've never been inside where the sound booths are located, and I'm acutely interested in those. I'm also not worried about Piper blabbing about my personal shit. She's a direct kind of gal, so I give it to her straight.

"One of the techies told me Mitzy took Carmen to one of the sound booths at *Insanity*."

"And you want to look in on your girl?"

"Pretty much."

"And you don't trust Mitzy to keep her safe?"

"I don't trust anyone to keep *my woman* safe."

"Gotcha. Received and understood." Piper rolls the stool back and gestures to my stump. "Put your leg on. Fortunately for you, Bent and I have a lunch date at *Insanity*. You can ride with me, and we can check in on your girl."

"Much appreciated."

"I got your back." Piper leaves me to reattach my prosthetic. Only after I put it on do I realize she never answered my questions. Or rather, she gave me the honest truth. By the time I hop down from the table, Piper's back with her backpack slung over one shoulder.

"You ready?"

"Yeah." Only I'm not ready at all.

What kind of white lie can I tell Mitzy and Carmen to explain why I'm at *Insanity* rather than a mission briefing with Bravo and Charlie teams?

During the walk to her car, a quick text to Brady explains my absence for the 1300hrs meeting. He doesn't reprimand me, or force me to attend the briefing, but sends a thumbs-up emoji for encouragement.

A little before noon, Piper drives into *Insanity*'s massive underground garage packed with more supercars than I've ever seen in one place. It's a struggle to keep my mouth from gaping as Piper leads me toward a nondescript door.

"You're lucky," she says.

"How so?"

"The sound studios are right here." She taps a code into the keypad by the door, then pushes the door open.

I press my hand against the door, over her head, holding it open. Piper breezes into a long hall stretching out in front of us. Extending down the hall, doors alternate with floor-to-ceiling smoked-out windows.

"I bet that's them." She points down the hall where a red light blinks high up on the wall next to one of the doors. "Want me to hang around, or are you good?"

"As long as no one's going to kick me out thinking I'm trespassing…"

"Silly Guardian. No one is going to kick out one of Forest's heroes."

"If you say so."

Piper walks with me up to the window set into the wall. It's one-way glass, allowing us to look in without distracting whoever's inside.

No surprise, Mitzy sits in the mixing boot while Carmen perches on a stool in the adjoining room wearing headphones. The women appear to be engrossed in conversation, chatting back and forth, but Carmen appears to be anything but comfortable. When I reach for the door handle, Piper places her hand over my wrist.

"You can't go in while the red light's flashing."

"Then how do I…"

"Here." She presses a tiny button I didn't notice. "That alerts the sound technician someone's waiting to come in. Once Mitzy sees you, and they finish whatever it is they're doing, she'll buzz you in." Sure enough, there's a buzz and the latch disengages. "See?"

"Hey, thanks for bringing me."

"Good luck, Loverboy." Piper giggles, a sound that takes me by surprise. I've never heard Piper giggle. She lifts on tiptoe and gives me a quick peck on the cheek. "We're all rooting for you." With that she spins around and heads down the long hall while I stand with my hand on the door latch wondering what the hell I'm going to say.

THIRTY

Carmen

"I'm never going to get this right." Frustration rises within me as my words trip me up.

This sense of impending doom feels like it's ready to crash down on me. Mitzy and I have been practicing since early morning and I still stutter and stumble, mixing up my words.

I never stutter. I rarely stumble. If there's one thing Lucinda taught me, it was how to enunciate like a lady. *At all times, you must embody dignity and grace. You come from a powerful family, poised to capture great power and status. Either you will choose your path, or your father will choose it for you. Decide now, which fate you mean to be yours.*

The memory of her words steals my breath and leaves me gasping. After all these years, she's still in my heart, reminding me the fury and rage boiling up inside me can be a weapon or a curse. I am the master of my fate. Which means, if I stumble or fall when I speak to my father, he's going to know something's up.

I'll have to dig deep and draw on a font of strength that's yet to be tested in real life. I don't know if I'm up for the task, but I do know there is no other path. I have to convince my father of the lies I twist around the truth.

"Don't worry about it." Mitzy's a good coach. Her enthusiasm is contagious, and she makes me believe I can do this.

"I'm nervous." I pick at the fabric of my pants.

"That's why we're practicing. We're going to go over it again and again until you're completely comfortable with it. Then we'll bring in one of the guys and run through it all over again."

This is Mitzy's plan.

Practice until perfect.

Most of the morning, we put together a loose script I'm supposed to follow. Mitzy asks me the same questions over and over, with the hope I'll fall into a rhythm that sounds natural.

"Remember, a little bit of stuttering is okay. We want him to feel your unease. You jumped on the end of that rope because you couldn't think of another way out. It was impulsive, and you regret it. You want him to believe you did it for him, but the truth is you were running from the engagement with Artemus. Once the Guardians brought you here, you realized you made a huge mistake, but you also realized you could be of great use to him."

"I've got all of that. It's the other stuff I'm tripping over."

"Which is why we're practicing all kinds of variations. I want your brain to be un-muddled and clear. We're mixing truths and lies until you believe. It's the only thing that will keep you safe."

"Believe the lies?"

Her method kind of makes sense, but it's crazy and insane. Perhaps that's how it will work? Lord, if I know. Who am I kidding? It makes zero sense, and I'm terrified.

"That's the goal."

"Okay." I take in a deep breath, ready to start again. "Let's do this."

Since we're practicing a phone call, Mitzy says the studio is the best way to mimic such a thing. I talk into the microphone while she speaks into the headphones from the mixing booth. It's kind of how a phone call would be. If I close my eyes, it feels as if I'm speaking on a phone. At least, this part of her plan makes sense.

And I am getting my lines down. They're not real lines. I haven't memorized anything. We came up with canned responses I can twist on the fly to follow the course of the conversation.

Practice, as Mitzy says, makes perfect.

And I don't want to mess this up. I get ready to call my *father*, but Mitzy's voice cuts in through my headphones.

"Hang on."

"What's wrong?"

"We have a visitor."

"A visitor?"

"A Guardian who, from the scowl on his face, is not happy I've taken you from him."

"Rafe?" I can't see through the one-way glass separating me from the mixing booth where Mitzy sits, but is it weird I feel him looking at me? Butterflies unfurl their wings and flit about in my belly, turning excitement into fluttering joy.

I stand, intending to go to him, but take one step and get yanked back by the headset still attached to my head. Feeling like an idiot, I remove the headphones and rush to the door.

Rafe's there before I cross the distance, arms held out to his side and a smile on his face.

I don't think twice when I dive into his embrace, wrapping my arms around his midsection. I lay my cheek against his powerful chest and do nothing more than breathe him in. When his arms wrap around me, it feels as if I'm exactly where I belong.

This is crazy, isn't it? To feel such powerful emotions for a man I barely know?

"Hey there." He lifts a hand to the back of my head, threading his fingers through my hair. "What are you up to?" Gently, he kisses the crown of my head, then pulls back, tipping my head back until he can stare down at me.

"We're practicing." My fingers clench the fabric of his shirt, seeking out the hard planes of muscle the thin fabric conceals from my greedy fingers.

"Practicing, what?" The low rumble in his throat brings a thrill of anticipation rippling through me.

"What I'm going to say to my father." I snuggle once again into Rafe's embrace.

His warm scent floods my senses, and I close my eyes. I could live the rest of my life in this moment and be happy. In the space between breaths, I allow myself the fantasy of what a future with such a man might bring.

Joy and love.

Family and friends.

A life with purpose.

A future with Rafe would be wealth without measure; such a stark contrast to what awaits me if I'm forced home. That's nothing but a deserted wasteland where hopes, dreams, and love go to die.

"Really?" He gives a tight squeeze.

If it weren't for Mitzy in the mixing booth, I'd lift on tiptoe and steal a kiss. My plan is to claim as many as possible before I leave so that I have a stash of stolen kisses to last me a lifetime.

"Actually…" Mitzy's high-pitched voice calls out from behind Rafe. "You're just in time."

"In time for what?" Rafe pulls me toward him and tucks my head beneath his chin. We stand there for what seems like forever but is really only a few beats of our hearts.

"In time for our final practice. Forest wants Carmen to contact her father before the end of the day."

"You're shitting me." Rafe releases me, but it's only to spin around and take my hand in his. "Today?"

"No later than tonight." Concern rims Mitzy's eyes. She's worried about my ability to pull this off. "Which is why Rafe's timing is impeccable." Mitzy jumps in and explains what we've been working on to Rafe. "So, you can see, you're perfect to make our little simulation here that much better, and since you don't know what we've worked on, you'll give Carmen the perfect opportunity to practice on the fly."

"Okay?" He scratches behind his ear and looks at me. "Are you going to be okay if I pretend I'm your father?"

"It makes sense." There's no other answer. Not if I'm going to save Rosalie, or the other girls. I have to convince my father I'm still devoted to him.

"I won't be easy on you."

"I know."

"You'll be okay if I yell at you?"

My flinch is purely unconscious. I get what he hints at and understand why he might be uncomfortable. The last thing I want is for Rafe to remind me of my father, but there is no one else.

"I'll be okay if you're okay making me cry."

"I won't be okay with that, but I'll do whatever it takes to help you prepare." The corners of his lips twist into a distasteful grin. He's not happy, but Rafe will do what he can to help.

Behind us, Mitzy claps.

"Perfect. It's settled then." She looks between me and Rafe. "Carmen, back on the stool. I'll take Rafe and prep him."

"Don't prep me." Rafe holds up a hand. "Might be best all-around if we dive right in." His eyes soften as he looks at me. "If I make you cry, I promise to make up for it later."

A tingle of anticipation shoots through me, thinking of all the ways he can *make up for it later.*

"Thanks." It's hard to look in his eyes.

I swallow the lump in my throat that wasn't there moments before and return to my seat. Mitzy and Rafe disappear behind the door to the mixing booth while I settle in on the stool and adjust the headphones for comfort.

Then I wait.

Rafe says he wants to jump in, but I find myself squirming, wanting to delay as much as possible.

"*Go ahead.*" Mitzy's voice speaks to me through the headphones.

I'm not ready.

"Carmen?" Mitzy prompts me a second time.

There's no way to delay the inevitable. I suck in a breath and begin.

"Papa..." There's no need to fake the tremors in my voice. They're there and they're definitely real.

"*Carmen?*" Mitzy's done something to Rafe's voice, because he sounds different. His voice is sharp and grating like my father's voice.

I close my eyes and try to picture my father's face. Rafe barely gives me time to think, firing off a rapid succession of questions.

"Where are you? Are you safe? Has anyone hurt you?"

"I'm fine, Papa, but I'm scared." There's a tremor in my voice that wasn't there when I practiced with Mitzy.

"What were you thinking? Of all the reckless things…" Rafe's supposed to be my father, but all I hear is the voice of the man I'm slowly falling head over heels for in body, mind, heart, and more.

"I'm sorry."

"Sorry means nothing. We'll speak of this when you're home. Where you belong." The timbre of Rafe's voice changes, becomes sharper, harder, and more like my father's.

"Yes, Papa." I suck in a breath. "Please don't be angry. I'm scared, Papa. I'm so scared." Mitzy tells me to stick to the truth as much as possible.

It will bury the lies.

The sharpness in Rafe's tone softens, but the longer this goes, the more I hear my father rather than Rafe. *"Are you in danger?"*

"No. I'm safe."

"Are you their prisoner?"

"I'm not sure. They let me wander about."

"I'm getting you out of there."

"Papa?"

"Yes?"

"I'm so sorry. I wasn't thinking. All I saw was the smoke. You were curled into a ball. I didn't know if you were alive or dead. None of our security—none of them were there, and I just—I felt such rage. All I could think of was revenge."

"You shouldn't have run off. How many times do I have to tell you that you must think first? The men who took you are evil. Don't trust their lies."

"I don't trust them, but I had to do something. I had to know who they were. Who they worked for… All I could think about was you."

"Don't lie to me." Power reverberates in Rafe's voice as he chastises the choices I made.

"Papa?" I grab my belly. My fingers dig in. "I'm not lying." The conviction in my voice is long gone.

"You insult me."

"But, Papa…"

"The reason you ran isn't because you were worried about me. You ran from your obligations, casting shame on our family."

"No, Papa! That's not what happened. I didn't run. I tried to save you."

"Don't waste my time with your lies."

"But…"

"Enough. Tell me where you are. Matias will bring you home."

"I'm in some sort of compound. I'm not exactly sure where. I'm not allowed outside without a guard."

With the way Rafe alters his voice, I've forgotten it's him on the other end of the call. All I see is my father's face filled with righteous rage. Not toward me, but rather the men who took his greatest prize —me—away from him.

"I'm sorry, Papa." My voice drops to a whisper.

"Carmen…" His tone softens.

"Yes, Papa?"

"We will talk of punishments when you're home."

Punishments?

"All I thought about was finding out who did this to you."

"All you've done is complicate things. Sending you to the US was a mistake. I see it now. It filled your head with wild thoughts and made you forget your place."

"But…"

"Tell me why you ran."

My response is complete silence. Mitzy's tried to coach me through this, but I can't work my way around the lies.

"You're angry."

"Tell me the truth. Why?"

I sniff and rub at my nose. My entire body shakes and my fingers tremble.

"Artemus. You can't make me marry him. His other wives... I know what people say. They whisper bad things. You can't want that kind of life for your only daughter. Please, don't make me go through with it."

"This is why you ran? To shame me? Defy my wishes?"

"No." I let the fear within me pour out in a flood of emotion. "These people... I thought they could help me, but when I realized what they planned for you..."

"Who are they?"

"They call themselves Guardians, and Papa..." Cue the waterworks. Real emotion shakes my voice and allows tears to fall.

"Yes?"

"They're coming for you." That hitch in my breathing feels real. It is real.

I hate my father, but he's still my father, and I'm still the little girl who wishes for nothing more than her father's love. Loss and grief fill me, overflowing in my tears. My father may be beyond redemption, but his fate is in God's hands now. Nevertheless, it still hurts to lose him.

As for me, I'm not sure if I have any forgiveness to give. Which leaves me to mourn, not my father, but the father I wish I had. The Guardians exist to bring down men like him, and that means this terrible story ends only one way. It's a truth I need to face.

The door to the mixing booth opens. Rafe comes to me. He lifts me in his arms and simply holds me while a lifetime of suppressed emotion runs through me. He holds me until my tears run dry.

"Carmen..." The sultry tones of his voice are hypnotic. "I'm so sorry."

I respond by clinging to him harder than before.

After some time, I'm not really sure how long we stand there, there's a shift in the air.

"Hey, guys, sorry to interrupt." Mitzy keeps her voice low and her tone soft. "We should take a break."

"A break sounds perfect." Rafe speaks for us both, which works well for me, considering the lump in my throat is three sizes too big.

After swallowing my pain, I swipe at my eyes and pray I don't look a complete mess.

"That was harder than I thought it would be." The words slip out between sniffles.

Mitzy was right. A male voice on the other end of the line made the whole thing feel real. For most of it, I thought I was really speaking to my father.

Whether true or not, I'm ready for a break.

Rafe takes my hand in his and pivots to face Mitzy. "Should we order in? Or head out for lunch?"

I haven't eaten all day and my stomach rumbles in protest. Mitzy grabbed me early and we skipped breakfast. We've been working on this nonstop since the sun first peeked above the horizon.

"No need to order in." Mitzy's voice rises back to her normal pitch. "There's always something in the fridge. Come on. Let's see who else is up and about."

It takes a minute for that to sink in. The 'who else' Mitzy refers to can only mean the members of Angel Fire. Now I have a whole other reason to feel queasy. She doesn't wait. She spins around and practically bounces out of the room. Rafe takes my hand and pulls me down the hall after Mitzy, trying to keep up.

We're somewhere in what feels like a basement. It's a maze of corridors and random rooms. She leads us up a sloping ramp, rather than stairs, where we emerge outside on a patio overlooking the Pacific Ocean.

"Wow!" I can't help it. The word slips out all by itself.

Overhead, wispy clouds stream past a faded blue sky, pushed eastward by a steady breeze blowing off the ocean. The salty tang is stronger here than back at the Guardian headquarters, but it's not until I cross the sandstone patio that I realize how close we are to the ocean—or how high above it.

A sheer cliff drops easily a hundred feet to a rocky beach far below. Treacherous surf pounds the shoreline. Swells crest into waves and crash on the rocks. Beyond that, the ocean extends all the way to the horizon.

"Oh my, this is beautiful." I tug Rafe to the railing.

Protective glass panels form a security fence chest high, keeping the view clear and little ones safe. One look in the massive pool to our left speaks of kids at play with pool noodles, swim wings, and inflatable swans bobbing in the sparkling water.

"It sure is." Rafe drapes an arm over my shoulder and pulls me in for a squeeze.

It feels natural touching him, being in his arms, feeling his protectiveness as he watches over me.

These are the things I'm going to miss. Wanting to store as many memories as possible, I fill my lungs with the crispness of the breeze. My eyes mist with tears, and I tilt my face to the sun, loving the interplay of the heat on my face and the cool breeze fluttering along my skin.

"This is the most amazing view." I glance out toward the horizon where the union between the sky and water is an indistinct, hazy blur. Below us, waves churn the water to froth and pound against the rocks with a deep booming that's felt more than heard. Overhead, seabirds circle on thermal currents of air, taking advantage of the lift to soar high above us.

"Look out there." I point at the ocean. "Do you think they're hunting?"

Several birds circle high above the water. As I watch, one of them tucks its wings and drops like a rock. It disappears into the grayish-blue water.

"Did you see that?" I peer where the bird disappeared, thinking it should pop up any second. A few heart-stopping moments later, the bird emerges, bobbing in the sea foam churned up from the waves.

"It caught a fish." Rafe's rumbling voice only adds to the melody of the ocean, the rhythm of the wind, and the life I wish was mine to have. "Look." He points to where the bird bobs on the water.

With a flick of its beak, there's the tiniest flash of silver as a fish twists in the air, struggling to get free. The bird's long neck bounces as the poor fish disappears inside its gullet.

Another bird dives into the water, disappearing like the one before.

"This place is amazing." Mitzy joins us and props her arms on the metal banister capping the glass. "I love it."

"I can't believe you live here." To be honest, I'm jealous. Not only does she have this view, but she's married to a rock star, and she's doing a job she loves.

"Sometimes I have to pinch myself," she says. "I don't believe it either. Do you see those rocks jutting out from the rest?"

I glance where she points at a formation of rocks. Waves beat at the rocks, throwing sprays of water high into the air.

"Looks scary."

"It definitely is." Mitzy pushes off from the railing. "That's where I fell in. Noodles was out there surfing and rescued me. Which sounds just as scary as it was."

"Wait. What?" I spin around, certain I heard her wrong.

"Yeah, that's how Noodles and I met. He was my hero, saved me from getting pummeled against the rocks, and that's when I met Old Joe for the first and what I hope is the last time."

"Old Joe?" My brows pinch, certain there's a story there.

"A great white Noodles is convinced is his soul animal. Come on." Mitzy picks up the pace, marching back toward *Insanity.* "Lunch doesn't make itself."

Rafe and I exchange a look. He shakes his head as I gape. She couldn't possibly mean great white as in a great white shark. I must've misunderstood something.

THIRTY-ONE

Rafe

"Whatcha hungry for?" Mitzy glances over her shoulder, looking not at me, but at the way Carmen and I hold hands. "How does peanut butter and jelly sound?"

"PB&J?" I make a retching sound. "You've got to be kidding. I'd rather go out than eat that crap."

"Well, what do you want?" Mitzy's flippant reply comes with a dramatic rolling of her eyes.

She guides me inside to a massive kitchen with the largest center island I've ever seen. Ten stools sit on this side while a wall of cabinets, two double-sided refrigerators, an assortment of coffee makers and other countertop devices dot the marble counters. Smack dab in the middle is an eight-burner cooktop with two flat iron grills on either side.

"Since you're the finicky one…" Mitzy makes a sweeping gesture toward what's essentially a chef's wet-dream of a kitchen. "You figure out what we eat."

"Um…" A quick glance makes me reconsider PB&J's.

"Don't 'Um' me." Mitzy's psychedelic pixie hair shimmers as she flips it around. "Anything, and everything you might need, is here. Don't be shy." She flicks her fingers at me. "Go on. Be a snoop. Carmen and I will sit right here and have a chat."

A chat?

Only one thing for them to chat about.

"I never volunteered to cook." My words may sound grumpy, but I'm secretly thrilled. What are the chances I'll ever get to cook here again?

"That's right. You didn't. But complainers get what they deserve."

"I'd hardly count not wanting PB&J a complaint."

"If you're going to be picky, this is what happens. You're wasting time. Just whip up something interesting while I talk with your girl."

From Mitzy's tone, I shut up. Not that she says it out loud, but it's clear she's eager to debrief Carmen after our simulated conversation. There's still work to be done before it flows like it needs to—effortless and convincing.

That should be me debriefing Carmen. I held back when I pretended to be her father. If she were anyone else, I would've been fearless and ripped into her, but I couldn't do that to Carmen.

I can't be *that guy*.

Regardless, the simulated call leaves my girl reeling. I see it in the way she casts her gaze down whenever I try to catch her eye. Carmen knows her performance won't stand up to her father's interrogation. Hoping Mitzy can turn those emotions into something positive, I focus my energies on figuring out what to eat.

That begins with a short tour of the kitchen. Starting with the cupboards to the far left, opening each cabinet reveals the precision of a highly ordered mind. Not knowing who organized the kitchen, I appreciate their obsessive nature. In a few minutes, I know where to find every plate, cup, glass, pot, pan, and all the rest.

Arranged alphabetically, I take a moment to admire an extensive, and eclectic, collection of spices. That same dedication to order and function continues in the walk-in pantry.

With a good idea of what's available, it's time to peek inside the fridge. I do that with a smirk plastered on my face and an ear tuned in on Mitzy's debrief with Carmen. Never in a million years would I have thought I'd be in the gourmet kitchen of the mega rock band Angel Fire, standing in front of a fridge, trying to figure out what to make for lunch.

Which is totally my fault. Not that I'm picky. Far from it. I simply dislike peanut butter. Mitzy's trying to teach me a lesson, and make me feel uncomfortable, but I'm up for this challenge.

Born ready to delight and entertain.

A little-known secret is I'm a professionally trained chef, once removed. My parents met in the kitchen of a fancy restaurant. They married, then attended the Culinary Institute of America in Napa Valley together. After that, they opened the first of many successful restaurants.

I was groomed from birth to take over the family business but joined the Navy instead. There's still friction between me and my parents over that impulsive choice. They don't understand why I do what I do, and I've never been able to explain the calling.

That's how I see it.

I was born to protect. Endowed with the physical strength, and mental fortitude, to do whatever it took to save those who aren't able to save themselves, but I grew up learning how to create culinary masterpieces, absorbing my parents' knowledge by osmosis. I love cooking, but I always knew my destiny lay elsewhere.

As a result of my extensive training in the kitchen, I don't need a recipe to make something phenomenal. My parents taught me the fine art of creation through the melding of flavors rather than how to follow a rigid set of instructions.

I find pay dirt in the fridge.

Loading up with what I need, I work in silence as Mitzy goes over that phone call line by line. Either the woman has perfect recall, or she recorded the conversation and refers to it during the debrief.

"Hey, what's with all the noise?" Piper strolls into the kitchen with a huge bear of a man trailing behind her. "Rafe? What are you doing?"

"What's it look like?" I point at the array of ingredients in front of me. "Making lunch."

"You're going to need a lot more than that," she says.

The man behind her tucks the top of her head beneath his chin and grins at me as he wraps his arms around her. No guessing needed for who that is and I kind of suck in a breath, realizing I'm in the company of a rock legend. That's none other than Bent, Angel Fire's infamous bass guitarist.

"Come again?" It takes a moment for her words to sink in.

"There should be ten for lunch." Piper's mouth moves, counting silently. "I'm guessing no PB&J?"

"Excuse me? Ten?"

From the way Mitzy refuses to meet my eye, that sinking sensation that I've been conned grabs hold with a vengeance.

"The three of you, me and Bent, Forest and Skye… Ash is in his studio working on a new song. Bash and Holly are out with their youth band. They won't be here. Spike and Angel are busy as well. So that's…" Piper counts on her fingers, then looks to Mitzy. "What about Noodles? Is he here?"

"He's out surfing."

"Surfing as in conversing with Old Joe? Or down in Santa Monica with the locals?" Bent's voice is deeply resonant and powerful. He's also about my size, except for the barrel chest.

I snap my mouth shut when I realize it's gaping.

"Santa Monica." Mitzy catches me staring at Bent. "Introductions are in order. Bent, this is Rafe. He's one of the Guardians on Bravo team, and this lovely lady is Carmen."

"Cool." Bent comes around the kitchen island to shake my hand. His grip is firm—solid—but without the need for bravado. "Always an honor to meet one of Forest's Guardians. Respect, man, for the job you do." He thumps his chest with his fist. "Total respect. The world needs more men like you—heroes to protect the fallen." When Piper snorts, he laughs. "And feisty women. I know there are female Guardians, but you're not gonna be one of them."

"I can if that's what I want." Piper's face turns a pretty pink.

"Maybe we should go back to our room where we can discuss it?" Despite how the words sound, Piper's little squeak says there's far more going on under the surface. He cups his hand over his mouth and leans toward me, whispering. "Not that I can stop her."

I decide to reserve judgment and keep my nose out of matters that aren't mine. Instead, I deflect. "Love your music." I take note of how Mitzy mentions what I do, but doesn't explain why Carmen's here.

"Thanks, but that's nothing compared to what you do." Bent turns his attention to Carmen. "Nice to meet you, pretty lady."

"Nice to meet you too." Carmen's voice is soft and timid. "And I love your music."

"Thanks." Bent turns his attention to the food I pulled from the fridge. "Whatcha making?"

"I'm rethinking. How many am I cooking for?" Damn, Mitzy could've warned me. From the smirk on her face, she knew this would happen.

"Stop fussing. I'm fine." The deep, booming voice of Forest Summers echoes down one of the halls and he doesn't sound happy.

"You look horrible. If you would just…" Skye Summers, lead doc for the Guardian Medical team sounds frustrated.

"I'm not coming in for you to poke and prod. Lay off. I'm fine."

"Don't tell me to lay off, and you're not fine. Have you looked in a mirror lately? All I want is for you to…" Whatever Skye's about to say is suddenly cut off when they turn the corner and realize they're not alone. Skye comes to a sudden halt. Behind her, Forest nearly runs her down before coming to a stop himself.

"What's going on here?" He glances around the kitchen, taking in Carmen and then me. His gaze dips to the countertop, then shifts to Mitzy. "I thought it was PB&J day? What's this?"

"That's what I tried to tell your Guardian, but he decided to whip up something fabulous."

"Sad to miss PB&J day, but this should be good." Forest rubs his palms together. He sidesteps Skye, sticks his tongue out at his sister, and sits on the stool beside Carmen. "Nice to see you out and about."

Carmen doesn't say a word. Her shoulders roll in as if she wants to disappear.

Skye props her hands on her hips, gives Forest a withering glare he ignores, then joins the growing crowd on the stools opposite me. Rather than sit next to Forest, she perches beside Mitzy. "Can he cook?"

"Can I cook?" I roll my eyes and snap a towel over my shoulder. Rolling up my sleeves, I prepare to wash my hands. "Buckle up. You're in for one hell of a ride."

When Carmen's eyes round in surprise, I can't help the thrill running through me. I do this for her, partly to show off, partly to make her feel better about her performance during the call, but mostly to show off.

It's a little before noon. There's no way I'm making CJ's briefing at one, but I figure I get a pass since I'm with Carmen and Forest. Also, I already told Brady I wouldn't be there. He understands needing to keep an eye on Carmen.

"Move over." Piper shoves Forest, forcing him to shift one seat over. She takes his place, then reaches out a hand to Carmen. "Hi, I'm Piper, one of the physical therapists for the Guardians. Are you new? I haven't seen you around." Piper glances at Mitzy, who gives a sharp shake of her head.

Piper's eyes widen, but she seems to receive the message. Not a new hire, but a client.

"Nice to meet you." Carmen looks trapped between Piper and Mitzy but looks far more comfortable than she did a moment ago with Forest breathing down her neck. He spins on his stool, going round and round like a kid as Bent takes a look at what I put on the countertop.

"Looks like you've done this before, but we are going to need more than this to feed all of that." He gestures to our audience on the other side of the kitchen island.

"You know your way around a kitchen?" I doubt it. Bent doesn't look like the kind of guy who spends time in a kitchen.

"Not really, but I know how to slice and dice. Give me a bowl and a spoon and I can mix shit too."

"Sounds good to me." Now that I'm feeding a small army, I head back to the pantry, grab a few things, and take another dive into the fridge. When I come up for air, I practically drop the carton of eggs when none other than Blaze, my rock idol and lead singer for Angel Fire, stares at me with glowing, green eyes. His iconic neck tattoo, a spiderweb dripping blood with a dragon on it, is absolutely insane and incredible this close.

"Hey there." He lifts a hand and waves. "Name's Ash. Need any help?"

"Um…" I try not to stutter, and do a somewhat fair impersonation of being cool. "Sure."

Bloody hell! I can't believe I'm in Angel Fire's kitchen putting Ash and Bent to work as my sous-chefs. *This is insane!*

Because I'm not totally lame, I get my shit together and figure out what to feed all these people. It needs to be better than good. Not just great. It needs to leave an impression, but not take too long to prep and cook. Fortunately, I have an idea.

"What can I do?" Ash wanders around the kitchen island to wash his hands. He looks to me for direction.

"Wash up, grab a knife, and start chopping." I point to a stack of veggies I rescued from the fridge. Handing the carton of eggs to Bent, I point to a large bowl. "Get cracking."

Bent laughs and takes the carton from me. "All of them?"

"Yup, and there's another dozen in the fridge. Use them all."

"You want them mixed, separated…"

"You know how?"

"Learned this nifty trick with an empty water bottle." He opens the carton of eggs and starts cracking. I cringe when a piece of eggshell goes in the mix.

Note to self. Check their work.

"Hey, how long is this going to take?" Mitzy calls out over the noise.

When did it get so noisy in here?

Sure as shit, the volume jumped several notches.

"Forty minutes, give or take."

"Great. I'm taking Forest and Carmen back to the sound booth for another go. You good?"

Not good if she's going to separate me from Carmen. Not that there's anything I can do about it. Mitzy's question is rhetorical because she's already up and on the go with Forest and Carmen in tow. Piper and Skye close the gap, sliding over the stools until they're seated beside each other.

"He still won't come in?" Piper keeps her voice low, but my hearing is acute, and I know how to read lips.

"He's being an ass about it." Skye pulls at her sleeve. "I'm not wrong, am I? Overly protective?"

"Maybe it's nothing. He's got a lot going on, what with the tour for the band on the horizon, and the expansion of Guardian HRS with the Protectors and Angels. It could just be a lack of sleep."

"Maybe." Skye shakes her head. "It's probably nothing. He says I'm acting like a mother hen, but I'm worried. His trigger's coming back."

"Have you talked to Paul about it? Or Sara?"

"Not yet. I don't want to make waves."

Piper glances up, notices me watching, then tugs on Skye's sleeve. "Let's leave the men to the cooking."

Piper and Skye move to a seating area off the kitchen, leaving me to get back to the making of a culinary masterpiece with two of the worst sous-chefs in the history of cooking. Bent's already broken three yokes, and I count no less than five pieces of eggshell in the bowl. Ash is savage with the knife, brutally maiming, then murdering, defenseless vegetables.

One deep breath and I dive in.

Despite the vigorous assistance of my helpers, I manage to pull off a miracle, changing *what's for lunch* no less than three times before we're done. With Bent destroying the eggs and Ash mangling the veggies, I put their eager assistance to much better use after I discover the pasta maker.

After that, it's as simple as making the toppings and sauces for the pasta and coming up with a salad that will *Wow!* the most discerning palate. As for that miracle, from pasta to sauce, toppings to salad, I finish a starter plate of firm mozzarella wrapped with crisp prosciutto, drizzled in a balsamic vinegar reduction as two new people wander into the kitchen.

"What happened to PB&J day?" A man nearly as tall as Forest takes in the decadent aromas percolating in the air, but his tone conveys disappointment.

What's with these peoples' fascination with peanut butter?

Not to brag, but I'm an excellent chef. I'm beginning to wonder whether the palettes of these people are discerning enough to notice the difference between PB&J and what I'm creating.

"Evidently, we're having a treat." A pretty brunette places her hand on the man's arm. "Ash, are we trying out a new cook? At the last house meeting, I thought we decided not to…"

"Oh, no. Rafe's one of Forest's Guardians." Ash stops bruising the salad with his vigorous mixing long enough to make introductions. "Rafe, this is Sara, Forest's wife, and Paul, Piper's brother and Forest's…" His voice trails off.

"Still can't say it." Paul laughs. "We get that a lot. Sara is the best of our throuple. I'm second best, and Forest is…"

"Forest is our foundation." Sara gathers her long hair over her shoulder. "I'd ask if we could help, but it looks like a disaster zone over there. So I'm going to suggest we set the table?" She looks to Paul when she mentions *we*.

"Yeah, how many?" Quick to jump in, Paul glances around, counting people.

Ash yells out a number I don't try to remember. Lunch for three has turned into quite the interesting feast. Fortunately, I tend to overcook. There will be more than enough for two extra mouths.

While Sara and Paul go about setting the table, I corral Bent to mix a mint vinaigrette for one of the salads and set Ash to slicing fresh mushrooms, cherry tomatoes, onions, and eggs destined for the second salad.

While they work, I finish off a lemon, butter, and wine reduction, add seasoning to a red sauce simmering on the stove, and gently stir the Alfredo sauce to keep it from clumping. Shrimp cooks in a lemon and garlic wine sauce, and I've got chicken sizzling on the grill. There's something for everyone.

The kitchen smells amazing and everything is going to come off perfectly. While Sara and Paul set the table, Ash and Bent complete their designated tasks. To my surprise, they do a great job straining the pasta. They manage to stir in the three different sauces, in three different serving dishes, without messing it up.

Not knowing people's preferences, I made three pasta dishes: a lemon butter sauce, classic Alfredo, and a delicious red sauce complemented by red wine. There's shrimp scampi and grilled chicken on the side for those who want to add protein to their meals. Then, of course, there are two salads to choose from. The oven dings and I pull out parmesan cheese bread. The garlic bread needs a bit more time to brown around the edges and I slide it back under the broiler.

"You want this on the table?" Ash lifts one of the pasta dishes.

"How do you normally serve meals? On the table or spread out on the island?"

"We're not nearly that organized." Bent's got the other two pasta dishes cradled in his massive arms. "I say we put it all on the table and just go for it."

"Sounds good to me." Ash heads to the table, deposits his dish, then returns for the salad.

Sara takes a look at all the dishes, then pulls out a drawer filled with all manner of serving forks and spoons. Before I know it, lunch is served.

It's more of a heavy lunch, or early dinner. When I look at the homemade pasta and the salad, a feeling of contentment comes over me. There's nothing more satisfying than creating something with your hands that makes other people feel good.

Piper and Skye join us, but three people are missing.

I worry about how Forest is treating Carmen. He's not known for taking the easy road, but it's probably best for Carmen. If she can convince Forest, she'll have no problem when it comes to speaking to her father.

Everyone takes a seat and looks at me, waiting.

"Go ahead and dive in. I don't believe in waiting for others. It's best to eat the food when it's piping hot and at its best." With a look down the hall where Carmen disappeared nearly an hour ago, I take my place with a very unique, but tight, group of friends.

Not friends. These people have created an amazing family. It reminds me of my team.

The ties I share with my Bravo team brothers are thicker than blood. I rub at my chest, missing my team. These people are amazing. They're warm and welcoming. I don't feel like a guest, but I'm definitely not one of them.

My family is elsewhere, planning a mission that will free Carmen from her father's iron-fisted rule and free young girls from a fate worse than death.

I should be with them, but the moment Mitzy and Forest return with Carmen in tow, all I can think about is the woman standing before me. Somehow, she's managed to work her way into my heart like no other woman who's come before her.

Carmen's face brightens when she sees me. She glides across the room, making a beeline straight for me. My chest swells with pride and my grin widens.

"I don't know what you came up with, but it smells wonderful." Carmen lifts on tiptoe and brushes her lips over mine.

It's a light kiss. A soft kiss. It's the kind of kiss that rocks the very foundations of my world.

It changes everything.

We're no longer strangers.

We're a couple.

"Hey, Forest," Ash calls out to the group. "I know we said no to hiring a cook at the last house meeting, but how mad would you be if we tried to lure Rafe away from the Guardians?"

"I guess that would be up to him." Forest turns his ice-blue eyes on me.

"It's just lunch. I'm happy if you enjoy it, but I've already got the best job on the planet." I feel a need to say the right thing, especially since I'm sitting down at a family meal with the co-creators of Guardian HRS.

Something small and round flies through the air.

Forest grabs a mangy button out of the air and looks at Mitzy. "Why are you giving me the button back? You called it and won."

"Because you don't realize the power of what you've created. I told you that's exactly what Rafe would say." Mitzy leans back, arms folded over her chest in victory. "Rafe, this is way better than PB&J. If you weren't already taken, I'd hire you on the spot, but since you are, I consider myself honored to work for you, and speaking of…" Mitzy folds up her napkin and places it on the plate she scraped clean. "Carmen's ready."

"You are?" I turn toward Carmen and grasp her hand in mine under the table. "You don't have to… Not until you're sure."

"It's time." Carmen nods and squeezes my hand, letting me know it's the truth.

"Okay, then. Let's clear the dishes and…" I scoot back from the table.

"Uh-uh." Forest wipes the corner of his mouth. "In this house, he who cooks does not clean. He points at the rest of those gathered. "You know what to do." Tossing his napkin on the table, he looks to Mitzy, then glares at Skye. Brother and sister exchange something in that gaze. She's not happy with him, and he's not happy with her.

Not my business.

I hold Carmen's hand as she takes to her feet and clasp it tightly in mine as we work our way back to the sound booth. It's time for Carmen to face her father.

"Okay, we're all set up. You ready?" Mitzy looks to Carmen, concern etched on her pretty face in the form of harsh lines.

"As ready as I'll ever be." Carmen still holds my hand. She has since we entered.

"Maybe one more run thru?" Mitzy's gaze shifts to me.

"What do you think?" I turn my attention to Carmen. "We can run through it a few more times."

"Honestly, I just want to get this over." She gives my hand a reassuring squeeze. "More practice isn't going to help. I know my father, what he'll say, and what he'll think. I'm as ready as it's going to get."

"Okay." I spin around to Mitzy. "I guess we're doing this."

"Looks like." Some of the concern eases in Mitzy's expression, but remnants linger.

That same doubt gnaws at my gut, but I trust Carmen knows what she's doing.

"Come on…" Mitzy gestures for me to head to the mixing booth.

"Can't you stay?" Carmen grabs at my arm. "I'd feel better if you did."

"Rafe can't." Mitzy shakes her head.

"Why not?" Carmen pushes out her lower lip in a perfectly kiss-able pout.

"The sound booth is designed to record what's inside with crystal clear clarity. Your father will pick up that there's another person in the room. It's simply how it works." Mitzy steps around me to grab Carmen's arms. "You've got this."

With that, I join Mitzy in the mixing booth while Carmen settles in on the stool. She looks small and fragile sitting in the room all by herself.

"She does—you know." Mitzy flicks a few switches. "Forest put her through the wringer and she was amazing."

"I know." I rub my hand over my bicep. "I can't imagine what she's going through." Truly, I have no reference.

"You ready?" Mitzy taps on the microphone and leans forward.

"I am." Carmen bows her head. Praying?

"Okay. I'm dialing."

I grip the armrests of my chair and brace as the phone rings.

"Hello?" A cultured voice sounds on the other end.

Carmen sits a bit straighter in her seat and takes in a deep breath.

"Papa, it's me."

THIRTY-TWO

Carmen

"Carmen, where are you, my love? I've feared for your safety." Where is my father's anger? *"Where are you? Are you safe? Did those men…"*

"I'm safe." I take in a deep breath. "Papa, I miss you."

What did Mitzy say? Believe the lies? I can do that and more.

"Those men…"

"Believe they're helping me."

"Helping you?"

"They think I ran to them for help, not realizing…"

"But you did run to them. You tried to escape me."

"No, Papa. I didn't…"

"I know you too well, my darling. You want me to believe you did this for me, but you were trying to escape Artemus and run from your family obligations."

"He's a monster, Papa. Please don't make me marry him. Find some excuse. Tell…t-tell him I'm not pure. I may have convinced his mother I might be pregnant. Surely she won't …"

"Carmen…"

"If Artemus wants a virgin bride, it's not me."

"We will discuss that later. Tell me where you are and who the men are that took you?"

Mitzy's prepped me to spin a version of the truth and I do that feeling far more sure of myself than I thought possible.

"They're called Guardians."

"Tell me about their founder."

"Their founder?" He skipped over a lot to ask that. Something about this doesn't make sense, but Mitzy anticipated this question. I know what I can and cannot say. "Forest Summers?"

"What is his intent toward me?"

"I don't know. Why would he—"

"Find out!"

"I haven't been able to figure much of anything out so far. They keep me in a dorm and I don't go out."

"How are you calling me now?"

"I lifted the cell phone of one of the janitors." I make my voice appropriately scared. "I don't know what to do."

"Find out what Forest wants with me."

"But, Papa…"

"No excuses. You ran, dishonoring me and your family. Do this and restore my faith in you. Do not, and you know what happens."

"But, Papa—I don't know if I can."

"Find a way. Where are they keeping you?"

"I'm not sure. California, I think. Somewhere near L.A.?" This is Mitzy's idea, telling my father where I am without telling him *where I am.* I think it's dangerous. She believes it's necessary; part of the truth and lies twisted together.

"Find out and call me. Matias will bring you home. As for the Guardians, gain their trust. Tell them what they need to hear and find out what they want with me."

"Papa, I can try, but…"

"You either will, or you won't. If you don't find out, don't bother coming home. There will be nothing and nobody left for you here." Buried in the subtexts of his words is a very real threat against Rosalie. There's no need to voice it. *"Do you understand?"*

"Yes, I understand." I swallow the lump in my throat. "But it will take time." This is the one thing Mitzy said we needed to get.

Time.

She needs time to organize a rescue operation.

"You have five days."

"That's not enough…" My voice breaks. "Papa, it could take weeks."

"Make it work. I expect to hear from you within five days." My father won't stoop to threatening Rosalie outright, but he doesn't have to say the words to make the threat stick.

I know exactly what he means, and he knows there's no confusion on my end. Unlike him, however, I will address it directly. I need to know.

"Don't hurt Rosalie. Please, Papa…" My voice shakes with real fear. "Don't give her to Matias."

"Get my answers and come home. Your playmate is safe until then."

Playmate.

My father belittles Rosalie constantly. To him, she's nothing but property. A tool to keep me in line.

"Please…"

"You know what you have to do." With those final words, he ends the call.

Eerie silence fills the sound booth as what just happened sinks in. The door to the mixing booth opens and Rafe bounds to my side. He scoops me into his arms, lifting me off my feet, and spins me in a circle.

"You were incredible." Rafe's praise brings a smile to my face and erases the tension in my body. After a brisk rubbing of my palms together, the stress after talking to my father eases somewhat.

"I can't believe it's over." Fine tremors shoot through me, fear over what my father may be doing to Rosalie.

"Yet you were amazing. You're not giving yourself enough credit for what you pulled off." He folds me into his embrace and I snuggle in, loving the feeling of his strong arms wrapping around me. "You bought us time."

Five days.

"I wish it were more." My gaze casts down.

I wish it was a week, or a month, or the rest of my life, but that is not happening. My father is curious about the men who took me.

Or rather, he's curious about one man in particular; it's personal to him. Why is he so interested in Forest Summers?

"What you did was fabulous." Mitzy pulls off her headset and sets it on a stand. She glances up at the mountain of a man standing behind her. "Wasn't it, Forest?"

"If that's what you want to call it." His eyes pinch with distant pain and there's a message in his stony gaze. What that message may be is beyond me, but I swear it's almost as if Forest's seen a ghost.

Placing my hand on Rafe's chest, the steady beat of his heart soothes me. He strokes my cheek with the pad of his thumb, wiping away the dampness that remains from my tears.

"Um…" Mitzy pauses for a second, looking at me clinging to Rafe. "Forest and I have things to discuss. Guardian high-level stuff that would bore you. Rafe?"

"Yeah?" He runs his thumb gently over my skin, brushing my cheek, moving around the shell of my ear, and returning back again. It's as if he can't stop touching me. As if, like me, he's searing this moment into his mind.

"Since you're here, why don't you take Carmen down to the beach? It's awesome weather and might be good for her to get out a bit."

"Thanks." Rafe's sultry scent does strange things to my body. "How does that sound? Interested in a walk on the beach?"

I'm both incredibly relaxed and exceptionally keyed up after speaking to my father. Now that the conversation is over, tension flows out my body, leaving me feeling drained.

"Yeah, that sounds like fun." I'd like to see the ocean before I leave.

"We'll see you later." Mitzy and Forest leave us, which makes me acutely aware of Rafe and his determined touch.

My skin tingles with the deftness of Rafe's fingers dancing over my skin, wanting more, but too afraid to ask for what I really need. He brushes a strand of hair back from my face.

"I won't let him hurt you. The Guardians will put an end to what he does to those girls, and we'll rescue Rosalie. Have faith."

"I won't be able to live with myself knowing something I did made her life worse."

"She's lucky to have a friend like you." Rafe wraps an arm around my waist, pulling me in tight.

"I'm lucky to have her." I place my hand on his chest and smooth out a wrinkle in the fabric of his shirt. "Promise me you'll do whatever you can to make sure she's safe and that'll be enough."

"It'll never be enough." His heated look says so much more, and I have to agree. "But I promise."

I'll never get enough of him. I want tomorrows without end; a forever he can't secure.

Lazy and hooded, desire smolders in his eyes. Like a drug, his desire reaches out to me, drawing me in, making me crave more. If I don't watch out, Rafe will become an addiction I'll never recover from. I lift my hand to trace the line of his brow. Stubble over his jaw tickles the pads of my fingers as I explore his face.

"You're so bloody gorgeous. When I look at you, I can't help but want all of you."

"You can have me." My breathy sigh says it all.

He can have all of me.

Here.

Now.

However he likes.

"I want more than you're willing to give." A frown tugs at the corners of his mouth.

"Rafe…" I suck in a breath and try to calm the fine tremors in my hands. "What if that's what I want?" My heart leaps at the words we exchange, at the things I admit, and what we don't say. Too scared to ask for what I want, I bite my lower lip and close my eyes.

His fingers feather along the angle of my jaw, then sweep down my neck where they flutter along my collarbone. I should run away, but that's not what I want.

"In so many ways, you amaze me." His eyes smolder with desire.

Obscenely attractive, he's handsome, sexy, strong, powerful, and knows what he wants. His restraint makes my knees weak and my legs shake. A heady warmth gathers between my legs, building into an agonizing ache.

"Ask me." Warmth rushes through me, exploding outward in a flash of need I barely comprehend.

"Ask you, what?" His deep voice is like a warm caress, something I want to melt into.

I lift on tiptoe and set my mouth upon his lips; soft, tentative, I know what I want, even if I'm afraid to ask for it outright. It may be a mistake to bring sex into a doomed relationship, but it'll be far worse wondering what I could've had.

"Ask me to give you what you want…"

THIRTY-THREE

Carmen

I KISS RAFE, FLUTTERING BUTTERFLY KISSES ALONG HIS JAWLINE, following a similar path his fingers traced on me moments before. When I nibble on the shell of his ear, Rafe's body shudders. When I place a line of kisses down his powerful neck, his breathing hitches.

My hands move, running down the hard ridges of his biceps, sweeping around to his washboard abs. Rafe sucks in another breath when my hand moves below his belt to cup the hard length of a very engorged and erect cock.

His throaty moans wrap around me like a warm blanket on a chilly night. Deliciously cozy, any shyness melts away. I know what I want. I want it now. For the first time with a man, I'm not ashamed to ask. There's not enough time left for us, and I don't want to live my life regretting *not* giving myself to this incredible man.

"Carmen…" His voice sounds different; throatier and carnal. "Don't…"

"What if this is what I want?" I look up at him as my fingers curl around the prominent ridge of his cock, then drag my nails along either side of the bulge, eliciting a needy moan from him. "Will you honestly stand there and deny me? When I know this is what you want as well?"

"I don't want to take advantage of you." A hungry growl rumbles in the back of his throat. Rafe hangs on by a thread. I feel it in the way his muscles clench and the way his cock twitches beneath my palm.

I've never instigated sex. Always following the lead of the boy to make the first move; I waited for him to cajole and convince me to do what he wanted.

I'm not going to waste time being shy or coy. I know what I want and that's to feel the man standing in front of me come unglued as he claims me. Heat radiates between my thighs; a steady throbbing, needy sensation grows by the second. It turns into a delicious ache that makes me squirm.

"I want this." My fingers curl around the fly of his jeans, stroking the too thick fabric. "Are you saying no?"

"I don't want you to regret…"

"For the love of all that's holy, if you want to make me beg, I'll get on my knees and beg. Tell me you want this as much as I do? Don't lie and tell me you're not going to have sex with me because you want to save me from regrets later on. I already regret wasting the time we've had so far." I reach up to cup the side of his face. "Give me this."

"*Fuuuuck!*" The desire simmering in his voice crashes into me with the power of a tsunami sweeping me away.

Rafe palms my cheeks and kisses me with primal rage and fury as he demolishes my mouth, my eyelids, and my neck. The fury of his kisses is incredible. He touches me everywhere at once. When he comes up for air, his chest heaves and his pupils dilate; blown black with lust. "Bloody promise you won't regret this."

"I promise." Glancing around the sound studio, I'm pretty sure Mitzy and Forest are gone.

Regardless, while I may not be able to see outside the one-way glass looking into the hall, I'm not eager to be the star player of a strip show, but I'm less eager to lose this moment.

The yearning Rafe stirs within me frightens me with the power it contains. I want him, but his need for me is a carnal imperative.

"Where should we..." I nibble at my lower lip, suddenly unsure and shy.

Rafe releases me, marches to the one-way glass. There, he presses a lever. A screen lowers down from the ceiling, blocking the view from the hall. With one eye on me and the other on the door leading to the mixing booth, he disappears inside for barely a breath. Something large crashes to the ground, then Rafe is back.

From the heated look in his face, I know better than to ask. He prowls toward me, taking each step with great deliberation.

"You have until I get to you to back out. If you don't, I'm taking what's mine."

Taking what's mine? Take me. Take everything.

A thrill of anticipation rushes through me.

My spine straightens with bravado I don't feel. Rafe is a menacing creature when driven by lust. He's terrifying but in a holy-wow-sexy kind of way. My heart leaps inside my chest. My breaths turn to eager little pants. I'm turned on and curious about the man transforming before my eyes into a feral creature fueled by lust.

No longer Rafe, he's a man driven by one, and only one, need. The desire to rut and fuck fuels every step, and it does something strange to me. Instead of confident and sure, I find myself willing to submit to the dominance he displays.

There's no need for me to be strong when he can be fierce enough for us both. A tiny tingle of anticipation rises within me, curious and heady with what's about to happen.

Halfway across the room, he suddenly stops. "Last chance, because I won't stop once I reach you."

I love how he gives me an out, but I'm committed to see this through. Terrified comes to mind, but it's not the terror of fear, but rather what we'll become when we join as one.

Everything about him fascinates me.

"Don't stop." My voice shakes, not out of fear, but with anticipation.

Something shifts in the air or shifts between us. Everything is different now or will soon be vastly different than what we were before.

I both love and hate that.

I love how he's totally unashamed of the change overcoming him. I adore his glorious smile and the smirk I find, more often than not, on his face, but this masculine prowess and determination is something I'll never forget.

One look around the studio brings several questions to mind. Most importantly, *how* this is going to work. The floor is hard, most likely cold, and unforgiving.

There's no couch.

No chair.

There's only the one stool I've been perched on for most of the day. Other than that, there's a keyboard, a drumkit, a smattering of guitars. Wires are everywhere, strewn across the floor and draped over the instrument stands. Mics stands litter the space.

I don't see where we'll…

Rafe's on me before I complete that thought, scrambling my consciousness the moment he places his mouth over mine. His hands wrap around my waist and slide down to cup my ass.

We've been here before. His hands on my ass, lifting me into the air. All we're missing is the helicopter overhead and the jungle far below. I loop my arms around his neck and lift on tiptoe to even out the difference in our heights. Only as I rise up, my body continues into the air, leaving my toes dangling in space.

Yeah, we've definitely been here before.

He lifts me off my feet, guides my legs around his hips, then walks forward until my back presses against the far wall.

"Last warning." The words rumble in the back of his throat, nearly unintelligible. "I'm not a gentle lover."

I shake with what that might mean, but I don't want to water any of it down with pleas to go slow. I'm no virgin, and I don't need to be warmed up. I'm burning as it is. There's no reason to go slow, because I ache to feel him inside of me.

"There's no need for kid gloves." How else do I express my need, other than to give him the green light he desperately needs?

"You sure about that?" He nips at my neck, pinching the skin to emphasize what might come next.

"Don't hold back." I need this memory to last me through what will soon be the darkest time of my life.

"Carmen…" He pauses, perhaps because of the tear I shed.

"Rafe, if you care about me at all, don't…" My throat closes up on me, too ashamed to speak the truth. I need this more than I can say in words.

"Don't what, luv?"

"Don't stop. Whatever you do, please don't stop. I need this." I curl my fingers into a fist and bang my chest.

Rafe presses me against the wall, scraping my shoulder blades and spine against the flat surface. He kisses the tip of my shoulder and moves to the sweeping curve of my neck. He nuzzles that spot right behind my ear making my toes curl, my lashes flutter, and my eyes roll back.

It feels so good. His hands cup my ass, holding me, but there's no need with the way his body pins me against the wall. The yearning he stirs within me is as frightening as it is liberating, and I ache for him.

With the boys I've been with before—and I do mean boys—we turned out the lights as if what we were doing was dirty. In that darkness, we fumbled. What Rafe does right now is positively filthy, but there's no fumbling in the dark. He doesn't make me feel like I'm committing a carnal sin.

This feels right.

"I've wanted you from the first moment I held you in my arms." His admission stirs a thrill in my heart. He shoves his groin against my pelvis, letting me know he's hard and aching. I already know that. I felt his girth in the palm of my hand.

Do I tell him about the fantasies I've had from day one?

Not now.

That voice in my head reminds me to take note of every sensation, every touch, kiss, and caress. I'll need this in the days, years, and decades to come.

I'll need to be able to look back at the one time a Guardian held me in his arms and fucked me like a man on the verge of losing control.

My eyes close as he moves a hand from my ass to my breast. Deft fingers curl around my soft curves, gently at first, then with conviction and something more. Rafe takes control of my body with his mouth, his talented tongue, and the skill of fingers created to make women scream.

His thumb rolls over my nipple, turning it into a tight-peaked nub. One moment, I'm covered by my shirt. The next, I'm bared to Rafe's hungry gaze. A single flick of his finger at my back releases the loop and hook closure of my bra. He works with me, stripping me until I'm bared to him from the waist up.

Then the heat of his mouth covers my nipple and the first of many screams fill the room.

I don't know how Rafe manages it, but my clothes seem to peel off my body like they're nothing. As he sets me down on the floor, his hooded gaze peers up at me. Helping me out of my pants, he goes to his knees to divest me of my clothes.

With my pants on the floor, he lifts up on his knees until his face is even with my crotch. I squirm, feeling self-conscious, as he presses his face against the juncture of my thighs.

"You smell like heaven."

I've never smelled myself, but I've read all the books. I'm here to say I don't believe a single one of them, but seeing Rafe on his knees, the blissful expression on his face as he floods his lungs with my scent? It makes me reconsider.

"Rafe..." My voice shakes. I shift foot to foot, feeling overly exposed and self-conscious.

He slaps the side of my leg. It's harsh enough to sting but doesn't hurt in the slightest. If anything, it breathes life into the fire raging within me. I squirm as Rafe's nostrils flare and I wait.

His fingers hook around the fabric of my panties. Not one who's ever worn a thong, I wish I wore one now. Instead of sexy and sensuous lace, Rafe peels down uninspiring, white cotton bikini briefs. He lifts one foot, and then the next, as I step out of my panties, and to my chagrin, he wads them in his hand and brings them to his nose.

A deep inhale and I'm just about dead, mortified by what's

happening, but too damn turned on to want to make any of it stop. I figure he's in control and I'm just along for the ride. Never felt that way with a boy before, but Rafe's no boy. He's a man who knows what he wants and knows exactly how to go after it until I belong solely to him.

Which is what will happen here. I'll leave a part of my heart behind when I leave this place. There's no way I'll ever forget Rafe, but I will always have this to hold me through the worst of the worst to come.

Is it bad I use him this way?

Are you? Using him?

To that question, I have no answer. The moment Rafe puts his mouth on me—down there—I don't have a single conscious thought left in my body.

THIRTY-FOUR

Carmen

Rafe turns me into a ball of sensation as his fingers, tongue, and mouth send pleasure coursing through my veins. With a lick of his talented tongue, I fly into a realm of ecstasy where I exist as a being of sensation only.

When I finally come down, Rafe holds me in his arms.

"Wow." I push back the hair in my face and glance around the empty room. Can't help it, but a girlish giggle escapes me.

"What's so funny?" Rafe runs his thumb down my forehead, pushing hair from my face. His gentle touch continues along my jaw.

"I never pictured our first time would be in a place like this."

"You pictured our first time together?" Amusement fills his throaty rumble.

"Yes."

"You naughty girl." He grins down at me. "What did you imagine?"

His question brings an immediate flushing to my face. I glance down, too self-conscious to answer.

"Hey…" He presses his thumb under my chin and forces me to look at him. "I've imagined it too. Don't feel ashamed about wanting this, and now that I know you *have* thought about it, I want you to tell me so I can fulfill all your filthy fantasies." While his pupils remain blown black by lust, his gaze softens.

"My fantasies aren't all that filthy." It's a sad truth. Adventurous isn't something I've ever been accused of. Is it weird I'm eager to *broaden* my horizons with Rafe?

"Tell me." There's a command in his voice that brings a fluttering sensation to my belly and a tingle between my legs.

"My fantasies are lame. Tell me one of yours."

"Okay, I'll go first, but you're not getting off the hook." He moves his thumb from under my chin and presses it over my lips. "This is one. Definitely high on my list."

"What's that…" Then it hits me, and that flushing in my cheeks turns into a raging fire. "Oh!"

I can count on my hand the number of times I've done that. Adventurous is definitely not a good word to describe my sexual experiences. Truthfully, taking a guy in my mouth never really turned me on. Not the way I feel staring into Rafe's eyes as he tells me what he wants.

"Yeah, definitely top on my list." There's that roguish smirk.

Realizing he made me come, and I've yet to return the favor, I slip a hand between us and wrap it around his turgid length hidden behind that zipper.

"Mmm… That too." Rafe closes his eyes. "Your hands on me. Stroking me. Definitely that."

"Is that all?" Feeling somewhat emboldened by his reaction, I debate going to my knees.

"Oh, that's just the tip of the iceberg, luv. I want you in every way a man can have a woman. I want you spread out before me, on your knees as I fuck you from behind, bent over the couch. In the shower." He winks. "I can't wait to sink deep inside your wet heat."

He reaches down to cup my mound and a moan slips out of me when his thumb rubs across my clit. "Very responsive. I like that. Ready for round two?" There's a wicked gleam in his eyes as he looks down at me.

With our eyes locked together, he strokes me with talented

fingers that scramble my brain. I'm panting before I know it. When he slides two fingers inside of me, I lift up on tiptoe and tip my head back, exposing my throat. He takes advantage and nuzzles my neck while those fingers of his send me over the edge a second time.

I cry out as I come. Rafe holds me through the aftershocks of the powerful orgasm and nibbles at my ear.

"You're incredible." His heated breath makes my skin tingle.

Once I get my breathing back under control, I lean my cheek against his chest. Tiny sparks of electricity continue to shoot along my nerves—aftershocks of pleasure I've never known until now.

"You're still dressed." I look up at him and pout.

"I am."

"Don't you want to..." My shyness wins out because I can't say what I want without turning fifty shades of red.

"Do I want to fuck you?"

"Yes." I nibble at my lower lip and look up at him.

"More than anything in the world." He cups my cheek and kisses me softly. "You're incredible, absolutely incredible."

"Should we go back to your place? Or mine?" Mine? Like that dorm is *my place?*

"You think I can wait that long?"

"I just thought there's no bed here."

"Sweetie, I don't need a bed to fuck you."

"Then how?" Brows tugged tight; I'm genuinely confused.

"Shh..." He presses his finger over my mouth and reaches for his back pocket. "Here."

Handing me a foil pouch, he reaches between us again. Undoing the button of his fly, he lowers the zipper of his pants, then pushes the fabric down to his thighs.

"Touch me." Rafe takes my free hand, grabs my wrist, and places my hand over his swollen shaft. This close, I can't see him, but I definitely feel—everything.

"You're so..."

"Yes?"

"Big." I roll my lower lip in. "Is it going to..."

"Fit?" His head tips back and laughter pours from his throat.

"Yeah, it'll fit. But first, I want to feel your hand on me." He curls his hand over mine, then shows me how to touch him.

From root to tip, my hand glides over his velvety shaft, feeling the hard steel beneath. As my hand glides down, his hips jerk forward.

"That feels amazing." Rafe leans down and claims my lips as his own.

His mouth grinds over mine, hard and determined, rough and maddening, delicious and terrifying. He engages with his whole body, taking everything I thought I knew about sex and throwing it out the window.

His tongue jabs in. Ravenous. Fucking my mouth with brutal hunger. His fingers curl in my hair, balling into a fist as he tugs sharply at the roots.

"Harder. Grip me harder." His pelvis thrusts forward and a groan escapes him as I tighten my grip and slide up and down his shaft. "Condom." Breathless, there's strain to his voice.

Knowing we're about to have sex for real, my hand shakes as I tear the foil and sheathe his turgid length. Pleasure sparks within, growing with the anticipation swirling within me. I've never had sex anywhere but a bed, and I have a feeling Rafe's about to open up a whole new world of experiences.

With that thought in my head, he releases my hair and grips my ass. Lifting up, he settles my legs around his hips. His cock stands straight and tall, and I worry about the fit. If there will be pain. If…

With a sudden thrust, Rafe breaches my opening. Slick with arousal, I slide down his shaft. My inner walls stretch to accommodate his girth, and the delicious sensation of fullness fills me. Pleasure sparks in my body as his hips rock back and plunge forward again. He seats himself fully inside of me and pauses.

Not sure what I'm supposed to do, a whimper escapes my lips as his hips roll in a sinuous dance.

"You feel like heaven." Panting against me, Rafe takes away any questions I may have as to how this works. The pleasure sparking within me curls my toes, almost making them cramp. Before I process the feeling of him slowly pulling out, Rafe surges forward, slamming me down on his shaft as his hips rock up.

He plunges in and out, without mercy, as I hang on for the ride. I've never come from this part of sex—penetration—but my body seems to wake and stir. As he claims me, every thrust, every agonizing glide out, ignites an enthusiastic response. My body heats. My blood boils.

As Rafe increases the pace, every touch feeds the fire flowing in my veins. My insides spark and ignite. My nerves sizzle from the sensations licking their way to my core.

Rafe turns desire into a palpable force; a craving so intense it shakes me to my core. As my insides tighten and burn, he moves faster and faster. His guttural gasps mingle with my whimpering cries until they unite into a frisson of pleasure coursing through us both.

Another scream erupts from my throat as a powerful wave of pleasure rushes through me. My muscles pulse, milking his cock as his powerful thrusts falter, but he recovers enough to rock slowly in and out, barely moving as we recover together.

"Rafe…" I can barely join one thought to the next. "That was…" Screw it. There are no words.

"Yeah." Rafe's body stills. He kisses the tip of my shoulder with reverence. "I don't want to lose you. Not when we've just found our way to each other."

I comb back unruly strands of his hair from his eyes and press the back of my head against the wall. Tomorrow, there will be bruises along my spine, and I don't care. He warned me he wasn't a gentle lover. Now, I have the proof.

His hips rock forward, a slower cadence than before. This time, it's not for pleasure, but rather a melding of our souls as our bodies entwine.

"You're not going to lose me." I throw my arms around his neck and hold on tight. "You're not going to lose me." Maybe if I say it enough times, with enough conviction, it will come true. But the truth is I feel as if our time together is numbered.

You're not going to lose me, but I'm going to lose you.

Rafe

WITH THE WAY MY LEGS TREMBLE, IT'S A WONDER I DON'T DROP Carmen on her ass. I manage to settle her on her feet before that happens. So far, so good.

"We should probably get dressed." Quickly disposing of the condom, I yank on my jeans, pulling them up with a grimace. She doesn't notice the prosthetic, but how long will that last?

You can always fuck a girl against the wall. Piper's comment intrudes where it's not wanted, reminding me of my disability in a moment where I felt whole for the very first time in over a year. I manage to spin around before Carmen can see the grimace on my face and hate myself for doing so.

Behind me, Carmen dresses in silence. The entire room reeks of sex. With a long, slow inhale, I fill my lungs with Carmen's essence and make a solemn vow to protect her no matter the cost. When I turn around, it's with a smile and adoration shining from my eyes. No way in bloody hell am I ruining this moment for Carmen because of my insecurities.

"How do I look?" She comes her fingers through her hair.

"Radiant. Gorgeous."

"Freshly fucked?" She's pretty when she jokes.

"Such language from a lady. *Tsk, tsk, tsk…*" I tease. "You look radiant because you're freshly fucked." Already, I want more. "And you're all mine." That last part comes out in a growl I didn't necessarily intend.

Down boy.

"Is it that obvious?" The flush in her face spreads to her neck and chest.

"Somewhat. We can hang here for a bit longer, if you like, but I don't think we're fooling anyone. I'm sure we can sneak out of here, head to the garage, and slip outside without being seen. I'd love to take you to the beach for a bit. Unless you have something else to do?"

We need to get out of this room and find our way to a more private place. In this case, I want to take her down to the beach.

The rocky beach below the cliffs of *Insanity* is amazing for many reasons. Near the water, the smooth stones turn to gravel and sand, but the rocky formations dotting the beach are filled with hundreds and hundreds of tide pools. If we're lucky, we're near a low tide and can scramble over the rocks.

I want to take her there because there's no other place for her to go that's safe, except back to Guardian HQ. Once there, she's not leaving The Facility until our last day.

"Don't we need to get back to Guardian HQ?"

"We do, but I'm pretty sure Mitzy is busy with Command and Control."

"They don't waste any time, do they?"

"They don't."

"Then beach it is?" She cups her face, patting lightly at her skin. "How bad is it?"

"Still looking freshly fucked."

"You love that, don't you?"

"I love knowing I'm the one who fucked you."

"I bet you do, and for the record, I enjoyed it very much." The wink she gives me is devastating in its intensity.

"Come here." I pull her to me, cup her face, and kiss her smack dab on the lips. "Then I will ensure you enjoy it many, many more times. For now, how about we skip this place and grab some fresh air? Have you been to a California beach?"

"I was here four years and the closest I got to the ocean was Pier 41."

"Then you're in for a treat." I take her hand in mine and drag her toward the door. "Hang on." I stop at the door leading out and remove the chair I shoved under the doorknob.

"You didn't…"

"I most definitely did. No one was going to accidentally walk in on you while we were…"

She comes to me and gives me one of her featherlight kisses. "Who knew there was a gentleman buried under the beast?"

"I'm an officer and a gentleman, always, but a beast only when I'm with you. Unless, of course, that's not what you prefer?"

"I kind of enjoyed the beast." She peeks back to the sound booth and lays her hand on my bicep. "I'd like more of that."

"Nice." With a jiggle and a yank, I free the chair. Then hold the door open for Carmen. "That way." I point down the hall toward the garage and wonder how we're going to get back to Guardian HQ considering Carmen came with Mitzy and I came with Piper.

With a shrug, I decide we'll sort that out later. This may be my only opportunity to show Carmen the beach. We slip out of *Insanity* without being seen by anyone except the multitude of security cameras monitoring the place.

"You're going to love this. It's a short walk to the gondola we ride down to the beach."

"Gondola?"

"With the steep cliffs and hundred-foot drop, it's the only way down."

"Cool. This is definitely going on record as best day ever."

"Because you got to have lunch with Angel Fire and hang out on their beach?"

"Because I never knew you were a gourmet cook. Lunch was fabulous. I got to hang out with a rock band. And…" I count off each one.

"Yes?"

"I got my brains fucked out by you."

"Mouth, fingers, and cock. A triple hitter, if I do say so myself."

"Oh my Lord, that's not sexy."

"Maybe not, but it's true."

"True." The brightness of her smile is like a window into her soul. I'll never get enough of this woman.

"I'll work on my dirty talk." Eager to get to the beach, I pick up the pace.

Fortunately, the residents of *Insanity* spent time and money setting up the beach below. In addition to the station house, where the gondola rides down on its tracks, there are restrooms for those who need them, a fire pit for those chilly winter days, chairs to lounge in and admire the waves, and a host of flashlights for those interested in combing the beach at night.

"This thing is safe?" Carmen eyes the gondola with concern.

"Do you think Forest would build anything that's not safe? Or fail to maintain it at peak efficiency?"

"I am putting my life in your hands." She gives the gondola another wary eye before stepping foot inside.

Made for a handful of people at most, we get to enjoy a ride down in complete privacy. Carmen stares out at the ocean, pointing excitedly at the birds soaring overhead, seals lounging far down the beach, and at the surging ocean.

I kiss the tip of her shoulder and nuzzle her neck on the way down. The gondola comes to a stop with a lurch, throwing me against Carmen. I steady myself and pull back on the sliding door.

"We're in luck," I say.

"How's that?"

"It's low tide, which means the tidepools are exposed, and it looks like it's just us on the beach.

"Just us?"

"Just us."

"I like the sound of that."

As do I, and I've already decided a future without Carmen isn't one I want to live in. Which means, I'm going to have to come clean about my leg—or lack thereof.

But, I'll save that conversation for another day.

Hand in hand, we set off down the rocky beach. I take her north, toward the seal colony, but we're not getting anywhere near the seals. There's a cave I want to show her, exposed only when the tide is low. We have just enough time to get there and work our way back before the tide shifts.

And I plan to ravish my woman inside that cave and show her exactly how beastly I can be.

THIRTY-SIX

Carmen

THE DAYS SEEM TO PASS IN THE BLINK OF AN EYE. RAFE AND I CAN'T keep our hands off each other, trying to compress a lifetime of intimacy into the few days left to us. We had sex early this morning, and before he disappeared for a planning session with the rest of the Guardians, he whispered *I love you* while nuzzling my neck.

I don't know if he meant it.

Maybe, it slipped out accidentally?

Best not to dwell on it. The clock is ticking.

The Guardians plan their extraction for the fourth night. One day before my time is up. That's the day my father expects me to return home. I won't. I never want to be there again unless it's to burn that place to the ground.

With extensive coaching by Forest and Mitzy, I continued to feed information to my father over these past few days. Nothing sensitive, but enough to placate him.

I hope.

We also trickled out the tiniest bit of information about Forest. Like my father's interest in him, Forest's keen to know more about my father. While curious as to what shared history exists between the two of them, I know better than to ask.

It can't be good.

A loud knock on my door pulls me from my thoughts.

"Coming!" I grab a small gym bag and leap to my feet. Rafe, and the rest of Bravo team, might be busy, but there are four ladies who are not.

I open the door to Isabelle LaCroix, or just plain Izzy now. It's weird how familiarity breeds friendship. For the longest time, she was this unknown force, a foe, I had to unravel. *Isabelle LaCroix,* that name, its formality, kept her at a distance. Now, I see her truth. She's brave and ferocious when she needs to be, but welcoming and friendly now that we're on the same side.

"You ready?" The brightness of her smile brings an answering grin to my face.

"As I'll ever be."

Joining Izzy in the hall is Angie. During the past few days, I've learned all about their harrowing escape through the rainforest where Izzy was rescued, but Angie was retaken.

It was during the mission to rescue Angie that my cousin lost his life. Which is justice served, as far as I'm concerned. He tried to rape Angie, which is why Brady placed a bullet in the back of his head. The bastard deserved it.

Lord knows, he's guilty of far worse.

I don't lose sleep over it.

Angie and Izzy are engaged to Brady and Booker, two of Rafe's Bravo team members. For some reason, that makes me feel connected to them. There's a kinship there I wish to pursue, but I keep them at a distance. Because of my father, I don't feel worthy of their friendship. Not with his evil hanging over my head, and to be completely honest, I'm afraid.

I'm afraid something's going to happen to Rafe, to Rosalie, to one of the members of Bravo team. Those men are putting their lives at risk because I inserted myself into their lives. Because I dragged them into this mess.

On the walk over to the gym, Izzy and Angie keep up a nonstop conversation about settling in at Guardian HQ. It seems I'm not the only one who is new around here. Which is one of the reasons the three of us have been practicing every day.

With Bravo team planning the mission, I have plenty of time on my hands. Rafe suggested I train with Angie and Izzy. I think he's worried about my state of mind if I have nothing to keep me occupied. I also think he's trying to foster a friendship between me, Angie, and Izzy. In addition, since he doesn't have the time to train me himself, he turns that task over to Jinx and Lily, two more amazing women who happen to be Guardians themselves.

Like Izzy and Angie, they work for Guardian HRS. In their former lives, they were both DEA agents—Lily worked in the field while Jinx worked in cryptology—and they appear to have made the transition to Guardian HRS without a hitch.

I tie up my long hair, learning not to leave it down where it can be used against me while we spar. Lily and Jinx pull no punches when it comes to basic self-defense.

It's early. The sun is barely over the horizon, yet the people of Guardian HRS have already been up for hours. This means the gym is relatively empty for our training.

The *gym* at Guardian HQ is more than a simple gym. In fact, it's nothing like any gym I've ever known. An area the size of a football field has been enclosed to form the floor of the gym. Along one wall, a full three hundred feet in length, an elaborate rock wall challenges newbie and expert alike. A track runs around the outside of the main field. That field is divided into several subsections. Part obstacle course, ropes course, free weight gym, state-of-the-art workout equipment, the place boggles my mind.

We head to the very center of the gym where the sparring mats sit and Lily and Jinx wait for us. Today, we're learning how to escape various restraints. While Lily and Jinx wait, they spar with each other.

On first glance, it's clear Jinx is the master at whatever martial art that is. Jinx dances around Lily, flowing with grace and pinpoint precision. It's a dance that packs a punch, with fists, feet, and sweeping kicks meant to take down an opponent.

They both wear black workout pants and black tank tops. Jinx's golden skin and flowing, dark hair is in stark contrast to the white-blonde hair and fair skin Lily claims. An unusual color: there's only one other person in the world I've ever seen with the same shock-white hair.

Forest Summers

I asked if they were related, but that answer is 'No,' although I don't know if I believe it.

"She's amazing." Izzy slows her step and grabs Angie's arm. "I wish I could move like that."

"Same." Not sure if Izzy means Lily or Jinx, but I agree.

Each of them flows together through space, almost as if they're one creature. Their fluid dance oftentimes has them stopping midair to pivot in an entirely different direction as arms and legs sweep through the air. I find it mesmerizing, but that's not what we're here to learn.

"No kidding." Angie glances over her shoulder, noticing that I trail behind.

Which I do.

They're the best of friends and I'm the awkward third wheel. I should consider myself lucky they include me at all, but it's my understanding the basic escape techniques are a mandatory part of Guardian HRS onboarding for new employees.

"Come on, Carmen, don't leave us to face them alone. We need you." Angie takes my hand and draws me close.

"Me? I barely know what I'm doing." I've had three days of practice.

"You're a natural." Izzy reaches out to play with my ponytail. "You've got this."

In addition to the daily practice sessions with Lily and Jinx, Rafe and I spend most of our evenings going over what I learned that day. I've got a handful of moves down solid, but it doesn't come naturally. My shadow could probably kick my ass. Angie and Izzy are just being nice.

"Hey, ladies!" Lily sees us and waves us over. She and Jinx break apart, sweat drips down their faces, and while they breathe deeply, I wouldn't say they were out of breath, but it's clear they exerted themselves.

"It's amazing watching the two of you fight." Angie looks on with admiration. "Any chance I'll ever be able to do any of that?" She directs her question to Jinx, the master of the flowing Brazilian martial art.

"Once you're signed off on the starter stuff, I'm more than happy to teach you." By *starter stuff*, Jinx refers to Krav Maga.

A military self-defense and fighting system, it's derived from a combination of techniques taken from several martial arts disciplines. Things like aikido, boxing, judo, wrestling, and karate. Rafe mentioned it's what they teach all their rescues and all Guardian HRS hires, regardless of position, precisely because of its superiority in real-world situations and extreme efficiency.

I've received a crash course over the past few days, but that's not what we're practicing today. Lily and Jinx have been selective in what to teach. Basic self-defense comes first, to instill confidence, and I admit I feel a little bit more of a badass after learning what I have so far. This next bit, I'm not sure about.

"Have a seat on the mat." Lily gestures for us to join them on the mat while Jinx goes off to the side, returning with a small duffle bag. "Today, we're going to teach you how to get out of restraints. Duct tape. Zip ties. Cuffs. Rope." As she says each thing, Jinx pulls the item out of the duffel bag and tosses it on the mat in front of us.

"First, Zip ties." Jinx holds up a bundle of Zip ties. "Behind your back. Wrists in front. Around your ankles. And finally, the beauty of shoestrings. We're doing the same for Duct tape. "Carmen?" Jinx gestures for me to go first.

This is the one thing I dislike about their particular teaching style. Before showing us how to escape a situation, in this case, restraints, they put us in it to see what we'll do.

I hate it.

Absolutely hate it.

With a sinking feeling in my belly, I know I'm going to make a fool of myself as Jinx cinches my wrists together with Zip ties. Once finished with me, she points to Izzy. With a groan, Izzy joins me and presents her wrists.

When she gives me a look, followed by a dramatic eye roll, I can't help but laugh. My laughter spills over to Angie. Soon the three of us are laughing our asses off.

"You guys are supposed to be taking this seriously." Lily blows out a puff of air.

"If you can't laugh at yourself, who can you laugh at?" Angie's quick to reply, which just makes us laugh even harder.

"I can't wait to see what Booker thinks when I escape his cuffs." Izzy's comment definitely catches our attention.

"You're joking!" Angie tries to stand, but falls back on her ass with her hands Zip tied together.

"Not joking." The smile on Izzy's face grows. "You should try it. Although—it may not be as much fun when you know you can free yourself." Izzy turns to look up at Jinx and Lily. "When are you gonna show us?"

"I think we should leave them here, grab some coffee, go for a walk—maybe then they'll be ready to learn?" Lily glances at Jinx.

"No!" Half panicked, I'm not a fan of that plan. "We'll be good." I elbow Angie in the ribs and give Izzy my most lethal stare.

"Fine." Izzy scoots around to her butt and crosses her legs. "How do we get out of this?"

"There are three ways to get out of Zip ties. You can use something around you to disrupt the mechanism. You're trying to break the locking mechanism." Lily shows us the tiny ridge we need to break inside the locking box. Only Angie figures that out. Lily doesn't let that get us down, but moves right into the next thing.

"Before your captor first engages the Zip tie, you're going to help him out."

"Why would I do that? Doesn't make sense to me."

"Listen and follow along, grasshopper." Jinx reminds me to pay attention to Lily.

"Place your hands together palms down, knuckles of your forefingers and thumbs pressed together." Lily shows us what she means.

"Form a tight fist. Maintain this position and keep tension in your fists as the Zip tie is tightened."

Jinx acts the part of the captor, locking Lily in. Dubious, I follow along.

"Now, relax your fist and turn your hands until your palms face each other. See the gap?"

Wow. Stunned speechless, I watch with avid interest.

"Now, all you need to do is shimmy your hands back and forth, working your way out."

To my amazement, it works. Jinx moves around the three of us, locking Zip ties around our wrists. Together, we follow Lily's instructions step by step and free ourselves.

"Here's something else to try. You're going to break the Zip tie this time."

I look at Lily dubiously, but the first technique worked. No reason this one won't as well.

"First, you want to tighten the Zip tie."

"Tighten? That doesn't make sense." I glance down with concern.

"Just watch." Lily places the end of the Zip tie between her teeth and tightens it.

Not ready to do the same, I watch.

Beside me, Angie and Izzy follow along.

"The tighter the better." Lily glances at her handiwork. "All right. This is where you commit. What you're going to do is bring your hands above your head. Spread your elbows out as wide as you can. You want them to move past your hips, so focus on keeping them as far apart as you can." She shows us what she means. With her arms over her head, Lily continues.

"Next, forcibly thrust your arms down and back. Think of squeezing your shoulder blades together as if you're trying to make them touch. You've gotta commit with this one." Lily takes in a breath, the slams her arms down with intent and purpose. The Zip tie snaps, releasing her. "*Voila!*"

"Wow."

"Go ahead and try it." Lily walks to me while Jinx goes to Angie and Izzy.

Angie attempts twice before getting hers to snap. Izzy gets it on the first try. Not to be the loser of the group, I tighten the Zip tie with my teeth, raise my hands overhead, spread my elbows wide and—big breath—I snap that sucker clean off my wrists.

"I did it!" Jumping up and down, I can't believe it was that easy. "What's next?"

For the next few hours, I'm the perfect student. Lily and Jinx show us how to get free of duct tape and some tricks with ropes. By the time lunch rolls around, I feel pretty good, like a badass, but then Bravo team arrives.

Won't deny it, but seeing those six men swagger toward us is beyond sexy. They're downright terrifying, but gorgeous as well. Rafe's brooding gaze takes in the scene. Instead of the signature smirk I expect on his lips, Rafe's brows tug together. Tension vibrates in his powerful frame, and I know why.

Tonight, they leave on their mission to rescue Rosalie.

"Hey…" I close the distance between us, and immediately, Rafe's arm wraps around me.

"Learning anything fun?" He plants the perfect kiss on my lips and sweeps me off my feet.

"We were thinking…" Brady grabs Angie and pulls her in close.

"What were you thinking?" Angie walks her fingers down Brady's chest, derailing his thoughts, but he recovers quickly enough.

"He was thinking it would be fun to grab a bite to eat." Booker slings his arm around Izzy's shoulder. "We're not due to fly out until this afternoon and figured we could try out that new burger joint that opened up."

"What do you think?" Rafe looks to me.

"Is it safe?"

"What do you mean?" Izzy asks. "Why wouldn't it be safe?"

"I don't know. I was just thinking I should stay here. At least until—you know."

"Carmen," Brady says, "you couldn't be safer with six Guardians watching out for you."

"That's the truth." Angie playfully punches Brady in the gut. "No one is going to bother you with these six brutes protecting you."

I nibble on my lower lip, wanting to go. Not for the burgers. I'm not much of a burger fan, but I am interested in being included in their plans.

"I'd love to go." I turn to Rafe. "As long as you think it's okay?"

"Luv, I'll be right by your side."

THIRTY-SEVEN

Carmen

Rafe and I sit in the back seat of a white SUV, while Hayes drives and Alec takes shotgun. My knee bounces with nervous energy as we drive down to this new burger joint the guys are eager to try. All of Bravo team is with us. Brady, Booker, and Zeb ride in a nearly identical SUV ahead of us. Angie and Izzy join them.

I stare out of the window, quiet and pensive, except for my knee-bouncing display of the nerves twisting in my guts.

"Don't be nervous." Rafe reaches over and places his hand on my knee.

When he does that, I shift that nervous energy to my hands, bringing my fingers to my mouth, where I nibble on the cuticles.

"This is the first time I've been out from behind the safety of Guardian HQ and I'm nervous about tonight."

"It's going to be okay." He gives another squeeze of my knee, then loops his arm over my shoulder. His solid presence is exactly what I need. "I'll be back before you know it. I'm not going anywhere. It's just another mission."

"I know." Injecting as much confidence into my voice as I can, I try to believe what he says, but I need to prepare myself in case something happens to him.

This is why I need Angie and Izzy. How do they handle it when their men go on missions? It's not like they're at a day job. No one's pushing paper, flipping burgers, or driving a delivery truck around. Rafe, and the rest of his team, are going out with bulletproof vests to protect themselves if they get shot.

If they get shot.

Their jobs are dangerous enough that they wear protective gear. What about the parts of their bodies that aren't protected? Brady didn't get those scars from a walk in the park. I haven't been brave enough to ask, but I'm fairly certain *that* injury happened on the job.

What Rafe does—being a Guardian—doesn't come without exceptional risk. Thinking about it makes my anxiety shoot through the roof. I'm not going to be able to sleep tonight. I'll be up the whole night pacing until I know Rafe's safe.

We hold hands the entire drive. Too soon, we arrive at a quaint oceanside hamburger joint. Nothing fancy, except that it's on the beach. We head into the restaurant, grab a table for nine, and order food. It's a boisterous group, firing jokes rapidly back and forth. Even Angie and Izzy join in. I'm the quiet one; trying to figure out what's an inside joke, a regular joke, or just a random funny comment. I feel like an outsider, not that they don't include me in the conversation, but there's precious little common ground between us. I've lived a very different life.

As far as the food goes, my burger is easily the best burger I've ever had. Rafe steals half my fries. Zeb asks if I'm going to eat the other half of my burger, eyes lighting up when I offer it to him. They order a pitcher of beer, swallow that down, then order more pitchers for the table. Angie and Izzy excuse themselves to use the ladies' room. For half a second, I consider joining them, but I don't want to look like I'm the lost puppy dog following them, too desperate to break into their little group. Instead, I wait until they return.

As soon as the check comes, I tap Rafe on the shoulder.

"I'm going to use the ladies' room."

"Don't be gone too long." Rafe kept a hand on me through most of lunch. Either on my leg, squeezing my knee, holding my hand, or brushing his knuckles down my arm. He loves to touch me.

I excuse myself from the table and head to the ladies' room. Located down a long hall, I work my way toward the back of the restaurant, where there's a line outside the door to the women's restroom.

Typical.

I get in line and look down at my feet. It's crazy how much has changed in less than a week. It feels like years have passed since graduation, but it's been only a few days. In that time, I jumped on a stranger, dangled on the end of a rope, rode in a helicopter, found myself in the company of strangers, and found those strangers to be not only heroic men but open, warm, and friendly.

And then there's Rafe.

The door to the bathroom opens and the woman standing in front of me goes in, leaving me alone with my thoughts. I've heard about love at first sight and soulmates, but those are stories for other people. Fairy tales. Never in a million years would I have thought such a thing could happen to me. Dare I believe it has?

Or will that jinx it?

My eyes close and I repeat a prayer of thanks. My life hasn't been easy, but I count the blessings I've been given. I make the sign of the cross and bring my hand to my mouth.

"Amen."

"*Señorita…*" That abrasive voice sends a chill slithering down my spine.

I know that voice. Panic surges within me and I try to rush past him.

Matias grabs my arm, tight enough to leave a bruise. "I found you." Blunt, and to the point, Matias doesn't mince words, but his eyes gleam in victory.

I take a step back as terror stabs at my heart. I tremble, fighting a rising tide of panic.

"What are you doing here?" Raw panic fills my voice. *How did he find me?*

I glance down the hall, but I'm too far from the seating area.

When I try to rip my arm out of Matias's grip, he whips me around, twisting my arm painfully behind my back.

Trying not to let fear paralyze me, my mind works furiously to figure out a course of action, but panic clouds my thoughts.

"I'm taking you home." He covers my mouth with his hand and pushes me ahead of himself.

Fear paralyzes me. Not my body, but my mind. My entire body shakes and terror mounts with each step taking me away from Rafe and the safety of the others.

When Matias walks me through the kitchen, I think someone will help me. The kitchen staff must see the terror rimming my eyes, but other than strange looks, they don't try to help. Maybe this is a common occurrence for them?

More likely, Matias paid them for their silence.

My heart hammers inside my chest as Matias leads me out the back door. I'm running out of time and options. Despite the heat, I suppress a shiver as fear spikes in my veins. In near-total panic, blind terror makes me stumble, but Matias is behind me, holding me up. Pushing me forward.

I want to scream and resist, but that's exactly what Matias expects. Which means, it's exactly the wrong thing to do. My legs wobble and I break out in a cold sweat as dread twists in my gut. That twisting sensation sends a wave of nausea threatening to overcome me, but I swallow down my fear.

Or try to.

Fear claws up my throat and catches in my jaws. I thought I knew what real terror was, but it's nothing like this. Numb and in shock, my voice fails me.

Blinking against the harsh glare of the sun, it takes a moment for my eyes to adjust to the harsh light. A car peals out from a nearby parking spot and races toward us. Skidding to a stop. The tires screech, and smoke billows from the exhaust.

The hairs on the back of my neck stand up. If I get in that car…

Every instinct tells me to run, but that would only prove to my father that my loyalties no longer lie with him, and that would be signing Rosalie's death warrant.

I jerk my head side to side, dislodging Matias's hand from my mouth.

"Let me go." Panic fuels my voice and I try to modulate my tone.

Matias only tightens his grip.

"Get in." Matias scowls at me.

"Why are you treating me like this?" I crane my neck to look at him, but Matias doesn't answer. "My father would be furious if he knew you were manhandling me."

"I very much doubt that." Matias releases me, but blocks off any escape. His words make me cringe and I shrink back in fear.

"What are you doing?" I try to sound as indignant as possible. "You think I'm going to run?" I flinch when he raises a hand, but Matias draws his hand back as if stung.

"I think you were looking very cozy with those brutes in there." His gaze darkens and his words fill with menace.

"I look cozy because my father told me to get close to them. How else am I to get the information he wants?" I stomp my foot and make a move to get around Matias. He crosses his arms and points to the car.

"Your father says playtime is over, *Señorita.*" Coarse and grating, his voice sends a chill slithering down my spine. "Get in."

A bolt of panic hits when I realize I'm trapped. I try to hide my fear from Matias, but he's the kind of man who feeds on fear.

"Of all the stupidest things…" I pretend to be indignant and pissed off.

Matias has been chewed out by me more times than I can count. My sharp tongue is legendary in the house, but I have a sinking suspicion that no longer holds true.

I try to act tough on the outside, but inside I'm screaming. Fear creeps up my spine and licks along my nerves. Panic seizes my brain, making it difficult, if not impossible, to think.

What's worse is there's no way to tell Rafe what's happening.

Believe the lies. Mitzy's words come back to me.

I can still salvage this. The Guardians are prepped and ready. When I don't return to the table, it won't take them long to know what's happened. I have to believe they will save me. Until then, I'll turn the lies into my version of the truth. Convince my father I'm still his dutiful daughter.

What hurts the most is there is no final goodbye with Rafe. We spent the morning in bed, making love. He promised to move heaven and earth to protect me.

I must have faith in him, but that doesn't mean I won't prepare for the worst.

Without hesitation—because going home is presumably what my father wants—I get into the car. Before I can buckle in, we race out of the parking lot. I close my eyes and tip my head back. A few deep breaths will help calm my nerves. I take these moments to prepare myself for the battle to come.

There's no love lost between me and Matias. He works for my father, which means he tolerates my presence. That's as far as things go. Which is why I don't engage him in conversation. I literally have nothing to say to the man.

After an hour of driving, Matias and I have yet to speak. Another hour through congested traffic and we've yet to utter a word to each other.

Unlike Juan, who picked me up after graduation, Matias doesn't force me through the civilian airport. Which is wise considering I have no form of identification. Or maybe that's the weird part. Why wouldn't Matias have brought that with him?

This time, instead of flying commercial, we head to the private terminals. I open the door myself, climb out of the car and pause on the tarmac to take in the plane. The flight's seven hours long. Two hours to drive to the estate brings me to nine hours.

The Guardians will be three to four hours behind me. Their mission—the extraction—will take advantage of the cover of darkness. That means my father will have several hours to question me and decide whether I'm telling him the truth or not. No, not several. Two at most. I forgot about the drive from the restaurant to here.

Two hours.

That's how much time I'll have to play the game and convince Father I'm still on his side.

Without a look toward Matias, I take the air steps into the jet, select my usual seat in the middle, and strap myself in.

I play the irritated, but dutiful, daughter perfectly. With the exception of the pilots, no one joins us. Deciding silence is the best policy, I turn away from Matias to stare out the window.

Before too long, we roll back from the parking space and taxi toward the runway. Matias climbs out of his seat to crack open the bar. He pulls out a beer and tosses a water bottle in my lap.

"Hydrate."

"Thank you." I don't care to speak to Matias, but it would be improper not to say anything. Those, however, are the last words out of my mouth during the seven-hour flight to Nicaragua.

Once on the ground, we're met by a single SUV. I keep my head up, chin level, and march to the vehicle. Each step brings me closer to my father. Each step may be my last.

The ride to the villa takes a couple of hours, but soon the imposing walls come into view. My fear intensifies the closer we get. Adrenaline spikes, coursing through my veins, and I feel the color draining from my face.

Funny how growing up here, these walls formed the basis for the endless fantasies of a child. With no fear, I braved these walls, balancing on top of them, walking on the narrow ledges all the way around. I climbed the trellises in the courtyards to reach the parapets of whatever imaginary castle played center stage in my imagination that day.

I fought off dragons and hordes of horrific beasts. I was saved by brave princes and valorous knights in shining armor. Not once did I see those walls for what they were—a prison to keep those inside from escaping.

I lived my entire life inside a prison, never seeing it for what it was.

Rocks crunch beneath the tires as we drive into the gated motor courtyard. Once through the entrance, the iron gates close, sealing me in with real monsters.

I suppress a shudder as the car comes to a stop. Matias exits. This time, I wait for him to come around to open my door. It's what I would normally do, and I must believe the lie that I am the doting daughter returning home after making a foolish decision to run away.

I'm properly penitent and keep my head bowed. Matias heads inside, not once looking back to see if I follow.

"Where is my father?" This is my lie. It's the core foundation of the truths I need to twist.

"He's in the library."

"Good." I slow my step and take the first turn that will take me to my father.

"*Señorita…*" Matias pauses. "His instructions are to take you directly to your room. Dinner will be brought to you, and he will see you later."

"Later?" I shake my head, knowing that is definitely out of character. My hand presses against my belly as a feeling of unease overcomes me.

So far, Matias is acting like his normal, brooding self. There's nothing about him stirring up an alarm. Most likely, he speaks the truth. My father probably does have business contacts in the library and he won't want me barging in on that.

"He doesn't want me to join him for dinner?"

"His instructions are quite specific." Matias rolls his wrist and tries to hide a triumphant grin.

"Of course." I pivot sharply and head toward my rooms. When Matias follows on my heels, I spin around to confront him. "What are you doing?"

"Seeing you to your room."

"I don't need to be '*seen to my room.*' I know exactly where it is and prefer not to have you breathing down my neck. If you want to do something, send Rosalie to draw a bath for me. I'm anxious to get this Guardian filth off of me."

"If you say so."

"I do." Flicking my fingers at him and ignoring his scowl, I head toward my rooms before I say, or do, the wrong thing.

Already my scalp tingles, as if there's something terribly wrong. However, if there is something amiss, Matias would never leave me to my own devices.

No one approaches me on my way to my room. There are no guards stationed outside my door. There aren't even guards at the crossing corridors on either side. Everything appears to be as normal as it ever was. Even my room looks the same as it's always been.

The door shuts behind me. So far, so good. I may actually be able to pull this off. Exhausted, I go to my bed. Turning around, I fall backward until I bounce on the expensive mattress. Profound fatigue pulls at me, and I let my eyes close for just a second.

I'm home.

I lift up a prayer to the Almighty asking for him to watch over Rosalie and the poor women and girls locked up somewhere below. I pray for forgiveness that I waited so long before seeking help. I send up prayers for the men of Bravo and Charlie teams that their mission is a success.

In that sea of nothingness, I allow myself to drift and find a place of peace and serenity where I can prepare for the battle of my life.

THIRTY-EIGHT

Carmen

"Carmen." Someone shouts my name. "Carmen, wake up!" That feathery voice… It's achingly familiar and terrified. "Carmen, you have to wake up."

"Rosalie?" Sleep crusts my eyes, but I recognize my best friend's gentle voice.

"You have to wake up." She shakes me awake.

When I rub the sleep from my eyes, her blurry features come into view. Overwhelming joy fills me as I leap out of bed and wrap my arms around Rosalie.

Seeing Rosalie safe and sound is like a heavy weight lifting from my soul. Joy bubbles up from inside of me and happiness washes away my fear.

"I've missed you so much." I hug her tight, but she hugs me tighter.

"I've missed you, too, my sweet friend." Angelic and soft, her light and airy voice is the best welcome home.

"I missed you more." We stand there for a second, holding each other, then laughter fills the room.

I squeeze her a few more times.

She squeezes me more.

I could weep for joy if not for all the rest. I'm truly happy to see my friend, but I fear for us both.

"I can't tell you how good it is to see you. How have you been? How have things been since…" Finally, we sit on the bed. Scooting back, I draw up my legs, hugging my knees, and look at Rosalie. My heart feels whole and I dare to hope. My mood lifts seeing Rosalie.

"Since you jumped on a rope?" Rosalie arches a brow. "What were you thinking?"

"I don't even know where to begin." I glance up toward the corner of the room.

There aren't any cameras in my room. Or, at least, there's not supposed to be, but Rosalie gets the message. More likely than not, the room is bugged.

"It was total chaos that night." Rosalie shifts on the bed, crossing her legs and resting her wrists on her knees. "I didn't know you were gone until the next morning. I've been so worried."

"It was—something." I tuck my hair behind an ear.

Rosalie's smart enough to know when to ask questions and when not to. It's the unfortunate reality of our existence.

"Matias told me to draw you a bath. When I got here…" She gestures toward the bed. "I figured it was best to let you sleep. But the bath is steaming, and you've got less than an hour to get ready."

"Ready?"

"Your father's summoned you."

I don't care to see my father, but it's inevitable. He's a black mark on this world. Any happiness I feel seeing Rosalie disappears with his summons. The need to tell Rosalie about everything I've been through rises within me, but it's too dangerous, and that makes this all the harder as a result.

"Well, I don't want to keep him waiting." I scoot off the bed and head to the bathroom.

Peeling off my clothes, I test the waters of the bath. There's no need. Rosalie draws the perfect bath. I hate that about our friendship. Because of our circumstances, she's forced to serve me. I feel guilty as a result, but that won't last forever. A quick glance at the clock confirms we're little more than a few hours from freedom.

"How is my father?" I slip into the tub with a sigh.

Rosalie moves behind me to wash my hair. I prefer a shower, but if anyone's watching us, this is what they would expect.

"It took a day, or two, after the raid for his hearing to return. The doctor said he suffered a concussion, but he appears to have recovered."

"How mad was he?"

"About what?" She leans forward to scoop water into a cup. My eyes close as she pours the water over my hair.

"What I did?"

"I wouldn't know. They don't tell me such things, but he seemed more concerned than angry."

"I lied to him." This part of the conversation is for any silent listeners out there.

"You would never lie to your father."

"I thought if I could find out who invaded our home then I could do something about it, but that's not the truth."

"Your father is your world." Rosalie knows how I feel about my father, and she knows we're putting on a show for our silent watchers. "He knows you would do anything for him."

"But I didn't." I hang my head as Rosalie wets my hair. "I don't want to marry Artemus. When those men attacked, I saw an out. I did it to escape and brought shame to my family's name."

"God forgives all." Rosalie pauses for a moment to make the sign of the cross. Like me, she's deeply religious. "The important thing is you're here now. All will be forgiven."

"Perhaps, but I don't know about Father. He may not be as forgiving."

"How did you get here? Did you escape?"

"I wasn't a prisoner. They were more concerned about rescuing me. I stole a phone and called home. Papa sent Matias, and here I am."

"Where you belong."

"Yes. Right where I belong."

"I'm sure your father will forgive you. In that chaos, who knows what choices a person might make?"

"I hope so."

Rosalie and I go through the motions of getting ready. She washes my hair while I soak in the tub, then holds a towel for me as I climb out of the warm water. I wrap myself in a fluffy robe while she gets out the tools of her trade. All I do is sit in front of the mirror while she styles my hair and puts on my makeup for me.

It's weird falling into these roles.

For four years at UCSF, I did all of this myself and I hate having to play this game with Rosalie. I hate that her worth is deemed less than mine purely by the circumstances of our births.

In less than the allotted time, my hair looks amazing. My makeup is flawless. Rosalie helps me into a loose-fitting cotton dress and I slip on casual sandals with the slightest lift in the heel. Prepped and ready, there's only one thing left.

It's time to face my father.

Leaning in, I hug Rosalie and whisper in her ear. "Don't leave the room." I don't dare say more, but Rosalie is smart enough to figure out the message.

She knows help is coming and where she needs to be. Most importantly, she knows I've made a plan that includes her. Her grip on me tightens and her eyes shimmer with tears. I leave her to clean and straighten my room and make my way down to see my father. My feet drag and my heart hurts.

The urge to run overwhelms me, but I'll never leave Rosalie behind again. The closer I get to the dining room, the more daunting everything seems.

None of this works if I don't do my part. I've got a role to play. As I approach my destination, my stride lengthens. My steps become more determined. A single tug on my hair is the only thing that belies my unease. I roll my shoulders back and clasp my hands behind my back. The moment I turn the corner, however, my steps falter.

To my left is the courtyard with the iron cage. The raucous calls of terrified birds fill the air. Sitting in the middle of the courtyard is a table set for four.

Three of those seats are taken by men. One is my father. One is

Father Manuel Ortiz, the priest from our local church. The third is none other than Artemus himself.

I come to a screeching halt and spin around. Only Matias is there with a sneer stretched across his ferocious face. I never heard him coming.

"Wh-what is this." I whirl around, feeling trapped. My gaze bounces to the birds locked in the cage, to my father, the priest, and then to Artemus Gonzales.

Matias closes the distance, stepping close until the fetid heat of his breath rushes across my skin.

Trapped.

I'm trapped.

The men stand. My father's eyes narrow as he approaches with sure-footed steps. I brace for whatever this is, but tears threaten. I push those back, unwilling to display any weakness, and focus on the anger rising within me.

When my father locks gazes with me, darkness swirls in his dangerous gaze. Evil incarnate, there's no love in those eyes for me. There never was. Instead, there is something far worse.

Victory.

"You look surprised, my dear." His smooth, cultured voice belies the evil infesting his soul.

"What's going on?" I rub at my arm as terror washes through me.

"Business." My father watches as my attention shifts to the cage. "Isn't that right, Artemus?"

"Business. Family. Pleasure." There's an evil gleam in Artemus's eyes. "It is nice to see you again, my love. We have business to conclude." His gravelly voice grates on me.

"You and I have nothing to conclude. What's the meaning of this?" I sweep my hand toward the wrought iron cage and the terrified birds locked inside. Wide straps hold the cage securely to a sturdy pallet for moving someplace else.

The bottom drops out of my world as the pieces fall into place. Around me, the world spins, and I'm surprised I don't collapse as a result.

"My love, it's a wedding gift." Artemus rakes his callous gaze down my body, focusing on my breasts until a sublime smile fills his ugly face.

"What?"

"Your father told me how much you enjoyed the birds. How you kept them as pets and would listen to their song for hours. What better gift for my new bride than a remembrance of her childhood?" The harshness of his voice says exactly the opposite.

"That's not what that is." My gut churns with fear. My attention shifts to my father. "What's the meaning of this?" I clutch my belly and scan the area, desperate for escape.

"As Artemus says, this is business."

"Business? After I risked my life to save you? This is how you reward me?" My voice rises until I'm nearly screaming. I point at Artemus while my voice shakes with rage. "Have I not made myself clear? I will not marry this man."

I desperately cling to the script Mitzy and I developed, but it unravels before my eyes. We planned for every contingency, several variations of this theme, but not what's happening now.

"Silence!" My father's roar sends the birds into a panic. Their terrified calls fill the air. "You are marrying Artemus. It's been arranged."

"Never."

"Today." He speaks with finality.

"Today?" My voice shakes and fear gnaws at my insides.

Father Ortiz's presence makes a little more sense, but I'm not done.

"I will never marry this man." My defiant words mask the fear coursing through me, but I'm not fooling either of them.

"You will, and it will be today." My father reaches over his head, snapping his fingers. Then he gestures for Father Ortiz to join us.

Father Ortiz shuffles to my father's side with the bible reverently held in his hand.

"No…" My voice is numb with shock as I stagger back and run into the solid wall of muscle that is Matias.

Movement in the periphery catches my eye. I scream when my

father's zealot, Juan, drags Rosalie by the hair toward us. She stumbles, nearly tripping, and grabs at the hand fisted in her hair. She cries out when Juan gives a harsh yank. Tears run down her face as her terrified gaze meets mine.

"Papa—please." I revert to begging. "Please, whatever this is, don't do it." My scalp prickles and the hairs on the back of my neck stand on end. I don't dare move, but I have to do something.

My father's hand shoots out, too fast for me to react. His long fingers curl around my throat, closing off my windpipe. Pulling me to him. His jaw snaps, as if biting me.

"I indulged you too long, thinking you served me, but that isn't the truth, is it?"

I claw at his fingers as he lifts me to my toes. Gulping for air, my lungs burn as my father's terrible visage fills my face. "You belonged to me long enough, but now you will serve your purpose as Artemus's dutiful wife."

"I won't..." Deprived of oxygen, darkness encroaches on my vision. I desperately gulp for air, finding none in my father's deadly grip.

"You will marry him and serve him. You'll be an obedient wife. If I learn you are not fulfilling your marital obligations, or causing issues in your new home, your dear friend will..."

"Maximus, if I may." Artemus moves into view as my vision dims.

He places his hand over my father's arm. My father forcibly releases me, which sends me crashing to the floor.

Artemus bends a knee and places his thumb under my chin and his forefinger over it. Gripping harshly, he forces me to meet his watery gaze.

"Your father told me about the birds, my love. About how you couldn't bear to see such beautiful creatures caged. About how you set them free. This will serve as a reminder. You are the bird, and I hold the key to your cage."

I jerk out of his grip and clutch at my neck. "I will never marry you."

Artemus grabs me by the shoulders. Shakes me until I see stars.

"You already belong to me, my love. As for your friend, your father tells me the two of you are close. That you will do anything for Rosalie."

Juan yanks Rosalie into the courtyard and holds her in front of him. Scraped and bruised, her knees bleed. Her left eye is red and swollen, and there's a cut over her cheek. Even now, she fights, but we're outnumbered and outmatched.

Artemus flicks his fingers. Above me, a terrifying grin fills Matias's face as he whips out a switchblade. With a flick of his wrist, the terrifying weapon opens. He closes the distance to Rosalie and presses the sharp edge against her neck.

Her ear-piercing scream brings me to my feet. I reach for her as Matias draws the blade against her skin, but Artemus yanks me back.

"No!"

Matias stops. The cut is superficial but deep enough to draw blood.

"My love, do you see now that you belong to me?" Artemus preens like a rooster strutting his stuff.

If I thought my father was an evil man, it's nothing compared to the ruthless killer prowling behind Artemus's dark gaze. A demon lurks within him, a miasma of immoral and wicked intentions defiling the air.

"Go fuck yourself." Not the best thing to say to the man who holds my fate, and that of my friend, in his hands, but I've had enough.

He slaps me across the side of my face, dropping me to the hard floor. When I look up at him, our gazes lock. My entire body clenches as his jaw works side to side. Then, a smile fills his face.

He enjoyed hitting me.

My stomach clenches and I swallow the bile rising in the back of my throat.

My father stands over me, his gaze dark and simmering with fury. I misjudged him and turn my attention to Artemus. Only now do I realize where the balance of power lies.

Everything about Artemus screams power, and if he were the

lesser of the two men, he never would've laid hands on me.

Not in my father's house.

That's when I see the truth.

Artemus has every intention of claiming me as his. He intends great harm, but not until he slakes his lust and breaks me first. Not until I give him what he wants.

But all is not lost.

I refuse to surrender hope.

Rafe is out there. He loves me with the entirety of his soul and is backed by the power and might of the Guardians. They are avenging angels, warriors with the will to fight, and saviors who save those who cannot save themselves. They are blessed by God.

I may not be able to save myself, but I can forestall the inevitable. If Rosalie and I are to survive, I need to buy the Guardians time.

With Artemus watching, I force myself to my feet. Chin level, fingers clenched, I face him down with the will of God raging in my blood. I believe in the Almighty, and he will not fail me. He will lend me the strength I need to survive. With a breath in, I face evil and pray.

"If what you want is me, then hear this." I make sure there's no doubt this is a demand and fill my words with fury.

"That is not how this works." Artemus leers at me, undressing me with his lusty gaze.

"You want a wife. A woman to bear the son you failed to conceive despite the two wives who came before me." I know what Artemus wants. He yearns to create a legacy.

He comes from a family with no name, no standing. I provide that name. I give him legitimacy and status. Our children will not be the sons and daughters of farmers, but a part of the ruling elite. I make what I can of that and run with it.

"If you wanted a slave, you wouldn't waste your time with me. You'd be downstairs at the cages picking out your choice for the night."

My father's lids pull back, although he shouldn't be surprised. I may have been silent all these years, but I'm not an idiot.

"Yes, Papa, I know about the cages and the women you keep down there." Rolling my shoulders back, I purchase the time I need with the only thing I have of value.

My body and my name.

"If you wish for me to be an obedient wife and submit to a union sanctioned under the eyes of the Lord, our Father, we marry in a Catholic church. Not this courtyard. I won't marry you here, and I won't marry you now." I turn my attention to Father Ortiz. "Explain why that is."

I hate to put the Father on the spot, but there's got to be some bit of good inside of him. His soul is likely as dark as the robes he wears, but he still wears the cloth.

"No," Artemus says as if laying down the law. "She will marry me here and now." He isn't willing to give this up, but I desperately need to buy time.

"Father…" I beseech Father Ortiz.

Father Ortiz clears his throat and shuffles his feet. "She is correct. The diocese requires a marriage to take place within the church as it is a setting intended for worship and prayer. It ensures the presence of Jesus Christ blesses the union."

"Fine." My father's molars grind as he relents. "Artemus, we move this to the church."

"Now," Artemus growls.

"Tomorrow." I cross my arms and stand firm.

"I will not wait…" Artemus's face turns red with indignation.

"Tradition demands those who-are-to-be-wed spend the evening before their wedding apart and in prayer. That they refrain from seeing each other until the ceremony. To do otherwise is to invite failure into the union. Perhaps that's what happened with your previous wives?"

Artemus exchanges a look with my father, but I'm not done with my demands.

"As I don't have a bridal party, Rosalie will be my Maid of Honor. She will watch over me the night before my wedding, praying with me, and bear witness to the union. To do otherwise is to invite bad luck to the marriage."

My father and Artemus turn to Father Ortiz.

"Is this true?" Artemus's fingers curl into fists.

Father Ortiz clears his throat before answering. "She speaks the truth."

"Finally…" My gaze locks with Rosalie's. There's no way to explain, but I pray her faith in me is strong enough.

"Another demand?" Artemus shakes his head. Everything about him screams power. Why did I never notice before? He holds himself with absolute assurance, and I know I've pushed things too far.

"I was going to say—give me this and I will walk down that aisle. I will speak my vows and marry you, but only if you honor God, tradition, and my place in society. Give me these simple things…" I can't finish that sentence. If I do, I'll retch.

Artemus's brows pinch. Gray dusts his clipped, dark hair, and deep lines furrow his bushy brow. If I'm lucky, my soon-to-be husband will die before the sun rises.

If not…

"Maximus, confine your daughter to her rooms for the remainder of the night. No one in. No one out." He turns to me. "Your maid may stay with you to prepare for our nuptials. Tomorrow, you submit to me."

Pressing my lips closed is the only way to keep myself from saying something that will destroy this win. Although, I think it's going to be a very long night.

"Matias," my father says, "escort my daughter to her rooms and place a guard at her door."

"*Sí, Señor.*"

Matias grabs my upper arm and yanks me off my feet. He drags me back to my rooms. Behind us, Juan does the same with Rosalie. At my door, they toss us unceremoniously inside.

Once alone, Rosalie and I turn to each other. We hold each other and cry for what seems like hours, but I can't help but rejoice. All is not lost.

Bravo team is on the way, and hopefully, I've bought the time they need.

Rafe

Darkness takes forever to fall over our staging area in Nicaragua. Still dusk, it's too early to load up and head out. I feel *off*. Divested of all our electronics, my gear is several kilos lighter than normal, but that's not what's wrong.

I've never been on a mission where the stakes are personal. It clouds my judgment, and that worries me.

I stop myself when I reach up to check the optics on my helmet for the third time. It's a practiced response, automatic before every mission, drilled into me from my team days in the Navy, but the optics have been removed.

In addition to the optics, our radios and targeting scopes are gone. Won't lie, I feel a bit naked without the fancy tech, but we train for these scenarios. Instead, I stretch my neck, working out the kinks, and bounce on my heels to dissipate an excess of nervous energy.

"How're you holding up?" Brady grabs the back of my neck and gives a firm squeeze. It's his way of checking in on me.

"Ready to get going." I glance toward the horizon where the last fading rays of the sun still light up the sky.

"You look distracted." That's Brady's not-so-subtle reminder to get my shit locked down tight.

"Sorry." I turn toward the rust bucket of a plane that's going to fly us to our infiltration point. "What a sorry-ass ride. There's more rust than metal on that thing."

"Ha, ain't that the truth. But it's airworthy and won't draw suspicion." Brady's right about that.

In this part of the world, there's a certain state of decay and disrepair inherent in all vehicles. The high heat and humidity do nothing but accelerate that process.

The rest of Bravo team loads their gear onto the decrepit plane. I stowed my weapons and parachute earlier, thinking I could rush the timeline. Unfortunately, the sun refuses to cooperate and takes its bloody sweet time disappearing below the horizon.

"CJ says another twenty minutes, then we can go." Brady gives a jerk of his chin toward the chicken bus appropriated for the second part of this mission. "Those things are hilarious."

Decommissioned school buses make their way down from the US, traveling to Central America, where new life is breathed into them by the locals. Repainted and refurbished, they form the backbone of public transportation for the locals. Part of that refurbishment is an insanely bright color scheme with tons of garish detail added in for good measure.

Charlie team loads onto that bus. Unlike Bravo team, they're fully kitted out in all of Mitzy's technical marvels. Ten Rufi—looks like the pack continues to grow—march themselves up and into the bus while Tex, Charlie-One, looks on.

He carries what appears to be fencing material but is, in reality, the bones of the Faraday cage they'll use to shield the Rufi, as well as their sensitive electronics, from the EMP burst Bravo team will set off on our way down to Maximus Angelo's estate.

After Carmen's abduction, we went through several iterations, settling on the simplest plan. Not wanting to sacrifice any of her tech to deliver the EMP, Brady's going to carry an EMP generator strapped to his chest as we parachute in. At a predetermined altitude, he'll set it off, which should plunge the entire estate into darkness and chaos.

Some of us worried what would happen to Brady when the EMP goes off. Strapping oneself to a bomb with the plan to set it off is crazy, but Mitzy assures us the EMP doesn't affect humans. There's no explosion, just a burst of energy.

"Any word from surveillance?" I scratch behind my ear and wait for an answer.

Mitzy and her team will provide oversite from inside the jet Guardian HRS flew down for the mission. That jet stays at the airport here in Managua. There's no need for them to be closer.

"About what we expected. They've improved their defenses, added scores of men to bolster forces. Mitzy counts about a hundred armed men on the ground."

"A hundred?" That's twice what we anticipated, but not a problem.

Bravo and Charlie together, twelve men, take that number down to ten-against-one odds. I round up because there's always something that messes with the best-laid plans. If we add in the Rufi, our ten-to-one ratio becomes more like five-to-one. Not to brag, but considering we're all former special ops soldiers, and Guardians to boot, we're looking at being outnumbered two-to-one. I'll take that any day.

"That's what she says."

"A walk in the park, then?" A smile fills my face.

"The only easy day was yesterday." Brady clamps his hand on my shoulder and gives a hard squeeze. "Come on, let's join the rest of Bravo and go through things once more.

"Yeah, let's do that."

It's been hours since Matias took Carmen from me. She's been in enemy hands far too long, and I struggle to control the intrusive thoughts assaulting my mind.

Until I know for certain, I imagine she's safe in her room, waiting for Bravo team to rescue her and her friend. Every time I imagine something else, it feels like someone's twisting my nuts hard enough to make me puke.

Granted, seven of those hours were eaten up by the long flight down here, for her and for us. When I told Carmen she would be surprised by how fast Guardian HRS can spin up a mission, I don't think she believed me.

Hell, I hardly believe we're only a couple of hours behind her. Fortunately, we spent the last few days working the mission, and we were already prepped. All we did was move up the timeline by a few hours.

But that's still too many hours of not knowing what's happening to my woman. Rage riots through me, demanding action, retribution, revenge, and worse. Fortunately, my teammates keep me focused on what's important.

Do the job. Work the mission.

The way I help Carmen is to do my bloody job the best way I know how, and that means I need to take my personal feelings out of the equation.

A wistful smile fills my face remembering how Carmen and I spent these past few days. We barely came up for air, spending most of that time wrapped in each other's arms, getting to know each other intimately.

We're ready to go, but the sun keeps us grounded. We have to jump in total darkness, which means we wait. The men guarding Maximus Angelo's estate expect a ground attack, and we won't disappoint them. Charlie team, the Rufi, and even a dozen or so of Mitzy's dragonfly drones, will attack from the ground.

What those men won't expect is Bravo team descending from above. We can't risk them catching us parachuting in. Therefore, we wait to infil under the cover of darkness.

The door to the chicken bus squeals as it draws closed. The suspension hisses as the refurbished diesel engine roars to life with a puff of black smoke and a throaty growl.

Brady and I wave to our fellow Guardians, sending Charlie team on their way. We'll see them soon enough. Once they pull out, Brady and I pivot sharply and march over to the rest of our team.

"Gather round," Brady calls out, and everyone stops what

they're doing for the last huddle before our mission begins. "Once in position over the landing zone, we'll drop in."

Over the next five minutes, Brady walks us through our mission objective, assault plan, and extraction points. Bravo's mission is to retrieve Carmen and liberate her best friend, Rosalie. Two of us will stay with the women until they're safe, while the others will assist Charlie team with the rescue of those captive below.

"This is our objective. Don't miss the landing. We'll ditch the chutes on the roof, then proceed. Booker pulls out the building schematics, where a red X marks the spot indicating where Carmen's room is located.

While most parachutes are white, ours are jet black to blend in with the night sky. If any of Angelo's men look up, we should be invisible in our black tactical gear and black parachutes against a black sky. Even the metal fixtures on the parachutes are matte black. We're fortunate there's a new moon; the less light, the better.

Our hope—an assumption we shouldn't make—is Carmen will be confined to her quarters. Before she left, she mentioned her father often restricted her to her room when punishing her, or when one of his notorious Galas was in full swing. If not, she knows to grab Rosalie and head to her room, where she's to wait for us.

To that end, we'll insert on the roof above her room, rappel down, and enter through an outside facing window. I'll grab Carmen, this time using a harness to secure her properly, while Hayes will do the same for Rosalie.

During our insertion, after the EMP, Charlie team moves in. Hayes and I will extract Carmen and Rosalie, exiting via the same window. This is my least favorite part of the plan. We'll rappel to the ground.

From there, we'll be on foot. All we need is to make it to the tree line and disappear into the jungle. A short hike will rendezvous us with our support team, and we're done. The rest of Bravo will stay behind to assist Charlie team in freeing the hostages held in the basement.

Nervous energy courses through me and it's a struggle to focus.

Distraction is the greatest enemy in our line of work, so I lock my shit down, take my seat, and go over the rescue in my head again.

And again.

Beyond hot, sweat beads on my forehead and drips into my eyes. I blink to clear my vision from the salty sting and swipe at my brow. It's not until we're in the air and gain a bit of altitude that the heat finally relents.

"Let's lock and load," Brady calls out to the team. We gather the last of our gear and load up into the rust-bucket of a plane.

A few minutes into our flight, Brady gives the hand signal to don parachutes. I partner with Hayes and perform our buddy checks, confirming everything checks out perfectly.

Gear checks are part and parcel of the job. They're so ingrained in what we do, they become routine. Which is why we always have a buddy check our work.

Hayes's gear checks out. I slap him on the back indicating he's good to go. Spinning around, he checks my gear, then thumps me on the back when everything checks out. We turn to Brady and return two thumbs up.

Alec and Zeb are moments behind us. Booker takes a bit longer with Brady's gear check. In addition to his weapon and parachute, Brady carries the EMP generator in a box strapped to his chest. Booker checks the generator with a keen eye.

It's not much more than a small box. Underwhelming, to be honest, and while Mitzy assures us EMPs have no known effects on living organisms, it's a bit off-putting strapping one to your chest.

This device is small, with limited range. Which is why Charlie team waits some distance away. The EMP generator will create a transient electromagnetic disturbance, permanently disabling any solid-state electrical device within its sphere of influence.

While there's no consensus on the radius of vulnerability, Mitzy says the EMP should take out anything within a half mile. In our case, that means we have to jump out of the aircraft and wait long enough for the plane to get out of range before setting off the EMP. Wouldn't make sense to bring the plane down on top of us.

Which means, Brady needs to activate the device less than a

hundred feet above the landing zone. That's barely enough time for the plane to climb to a higher altitude and get far enough away to be safe from the pulse, but it's perfect for creating chaos within the villa.

The flight to our insertion point doesn't last long. During that time, my thoughts go out to Carmen, and I say a little prayer she and her friend are all right.

"Five minutes!" Sam flies with us, taking over the role of jump-master. CJ stays behind with Mitzy to coordinate the activities of two Guardian teams. At Sam's call, Bravo team takes to our feet and gather in line. We secure our ripcord releases to a cable running down the center of the plane while the tail section opens to a pitch-black sky.

"Four minutes!" Sam calls out over the roar of the wind whipping around us. One last buddy check occurs as he counts down the remaining time.

Hayes and I, once again, check each other's gear and make sure everything's secure.

"One minute!" Turbulence tosses the aircraft.

Below us, faint lights dot a dark landscape. We're well outside the city limits of Managua. A patchwork of farms and the encroaching jungle, there are very few lights to brighten the night. Very few, except for Maximus Angelo's family villa, where flood lights turn night into day.

Hayes and I exchange a look. Maximus Angelo, for all his bravado, is scared of the dark. I only wish I could see the look on his face when we plunge him, his guards, and his house, into utter darkness.

"Ten! Nine!…" Sam counts while we shuffle down the tail section. "Three! Two! One!"

On one, Brady leaps out of the plane. Booker follows. Third in line, I join them in a freefall cut short by the deployment of my parachute. Fully steerable rigs, it's easy maneuvering toward the villa. The rooftop is flat and sparsely guarded. Eight men man each corner and focus outward from the walls.

Unlike the last time we were here to rescue Izzy, the No-Kill order has been rescinded. Nonetheless, stealth is our greatest ally. Unlike the men below us, who will only see a dark sky, I clearly make out Brady and Booker below me. The bright lights below cast their silhouettes in stark relief.

I keep an eye on two of the men on the southeast wall. Watching my altimeter, I pull out my tranq gun and wait. None of Bravo team, with the exception of Brady, carry any electronics. He has two; the EMP device and a red strobe light affixed to the top of his helmet. Only we can see it, and we wait for that light to go out.

A hundred feet from the roof, that red light blinks for the last time, then goes out. It's the only sign the EMP went off.

Less than half a second later, the entire landscape below us plunges into total darkness as anything electronic on the ground dies.

I take out the two men at the southeast corner, then ready myself for landing. The area erupts with the shouting of men and random gunfire, but up on the rooftop, there's nothing but silence. Hayes, Zeb, and Alec take out the remaining men on the roof, leaving Bravo team in command of the high ground.

My touchdown is feather light as I flare the canopy at the last second. Once on the roof, I gather up my parachute, roll it into a ball, and disconnect it from my harness. Around me, my Bravo team brothers do the same.

Charlie is about two clicks out. Mitzy says the range of the EMP is half a mile in radius and she built in a margin of safety for Charlie team. They'll be coming in hot, riding in Jeeps appropriated for the mission. Beside them, the Rufi will keep pace, peeling off in a predetermined pattern on a mission all their own.

Behind the eyes of the robotic dogs, a human directs the robots. Their objective is to take out the militia without causing an international incident. Again, they use tranqs.

I'm done with nonlethal means. Locked and loaded, it's time to get my girl.

FORTY

Carmen

————————

After Matias locks us in the room, Rosalie and I spend a moment crying as terror runs through us, but I eventually pull away from my friend. Crying isn't productive.

"What's going on?" Rosalie's eyes are wide, frightened, and brimming with tears.

"I wish I knew." A glance around the room yields nothing. Not sure what I expect to find, I look for hidden cameras and microphones until giving up.

"I can't believe he's going to make you go through with it. Why is he doing that?" Rosalie wipes at her cheeks.

"It's simple." My search of the room continues. I check the desk and drawers, the couch and pillows. I look at the bookcase and peek inside the orchids Rosalie loves. "Artemus is signing over drilling rights to his land. My father will fund the mining operations and reap the profit. That profit will fund his bid for the presidency and pay for the bribes it'll take to get what he wants."

I stop to breathe in the light perfume of her favorite orchid sitting on the bookcase. She spends nearly as much time in my room as me. When I found out she loved orchids, but couldn't have any of her own, I suggested she keep them here where she could take care of them and enjoy them.

"And Artemus gets the social standing to legitimize his position. I don't know what agreement they came to, but some of those profits will line his pockets."

"We can't let this happen. His previous wives…"

"Failed to provide him with a male heir. I won't make that same mistake."

"Oh, Carmen, you can't…" She curls in on herself as that sinks in. "What are you looking for?"

I stop, realizing what I'm doing and how it might be perceived by the invisible watchers. Pressing my hands to my cheeks, I blow out a breath. "I was looking for my mother's broach."

"Why?" Rosalie cocks her head.

"Something old. Something new. Something borrowed…" I shrug and allow my shoulders to slump.

"You're not really going to keep with tradition, are you? After the way you were treated?"

"Papa wants me to marry Artemus, and that's going to happen, but at least it will be in the church and sanctioned by God. All I can do is be a pious bride and do what I can to honor God."

"Carmen…" Rosalie shouts and rises from the couch. "You can't…"

"What else can I do?"

"We can run away?" Rosalie's desperation is a palpable force.

I move to my friend and grasp her hands in mine. "We can't run away. The door is locked, and my father's men will track us down. If we run, it will only make things worse—for the both of us."

Rosalie collapses on the floor and sobs. I join her there, holding her in my arms. Rocking her.

"It's going to be okay."

"Matias… He's…" She sniffs and pulls away. "He's worse than ever. Once you're gone…" She doesn't have the courage to finish that sentence. I don't either.

"I'm going to do everything I can to make sure you stay with me." That begins with playing my part for those who watch and doing what I can for Rafe and his team when they finally arrive. "Come, let's enjoy the sunset, together." I pull her off the floor and draw her in for another hug. "Do you have anything I can borrow for tomorrow?"

"What about a dress?" Rosalie cups her cheeks. "We don't have a dress."

"I'm not worried about that. Come on…" I take her hand and pull her toward the window.

From what I know about the planning sessions, Rafe and his team plan to land on the roof and enter through the windows. Thick wooden shutters cover those windows and I want them open for the rescue.

Drawing back the thick curtains, I gasp in alarm. Freshly installed wrought iron bars cage me in. I stare at them in horror, then give them a shake. The bars don't move.

"What's this?" I glance at Rosalie, but she shakes her head.

"I don't know."

I stagger back with a hand over my belly to tamp down the sudden queasiness in my stomach. These are the windows Bravo team is supposed to use to rescue Rosalie.

"We're in trouble." I glance up at my dear friend and pray for strength. "We're in serious trouble."

Together, we take a seat on the couch, holding hands as the minutes tick by. I lean over to whisper in her ear, telling her about the rescue planned later tonight. Rosalie takes everything in stride, never betraying to our silent watchers any kind of surprise.

Or hope.

With the windows barred, there will be no rescue from that direction.

"So, what do we do now?"

"I don't know." I have no idea what comes next.

Which is precisely what we do. Rosalie and I hold hands, letting the minutes turn to hours. Outside, the sun sinks below the horizon. The Guardians will be here soon, but they're not going to be able to rescue us. I sink back in the couch. Rosalie does the same.

"I'm scared." She leans her head on my shoulder and I grip her hand a little tighter.

"So am I." Leaning my head back, I stare at the ceiling and think of another way.

What can I do to warn Rafe? But there's nothing. There's absolutely nothing. My eyes drift closed and I take in a series of deep breaths. Next thing I know, someone's in my room, shaking me awake.

Rosalie screams beside me as a man lifts her up and out of the couch. It's not a Guardian. It's Matias. I blink to clear my vision and recognize Juan roughly shaking me.

"What's going on?"

"Change in plans," Juan sets me on my feet. "I'm sorry, but you're coming with us." He glances over at Matias and the expression on his face catches me off guard. The man may be my father's zealot, but he's not a fan of Matias. "I'm sorry, *Señorita*. I truly am." He wraps a hand around my upper arm and pulls me toward the doorway.

"What's going on?"

"Precautions." His eyes pinch as he leads me out of my room.

Behind us, Matias bodily drags Rosalie by the hair. He yanks her to him, cops a feel, and grins like a madman.

"Juan, you don't have to do this." Maybe if I try reason, he'll listen. Clearly, he's not happy about whatever order he's been given.

"Please, don't struggle. I don't want to hurt you." Sadness fills his brown eyes and he refuses to look me in the eye.

"Where are you taking us?"

"I'm taking you to the safe room."

"Why?" Then his words sink in. "You're taking us both to the safe room." I clutch at his shirt. "You're taking us both?"

Again, Juan refuses to look me in the eye, but he mumbles something under his breath. *"May God forgive me."*

"No!" He asked me not to fight him, but I claw to get free. To get to Rosalie.

Juan shakes his head, clearly bothered, but easily subdues me. He stops, grabs a hold of me, and lifts me up and over his shoulder like a sack of potatoes.

Behind me, Matias's eyes gleam in victory. He sneers, sniffing in triumph. His hand forms a fist.

"Rosalie!" My shout is too late.

Matias clocks Rosalie in the head, dropping her to the floor where she doesn't move. He bends down, cradles her head, then presses his lips to hers. My insides writhe with the violation of my friend. Looking at me, he licks his lips, sending a message.

Matias lifts Rosalie over his shoulder and stands. Juan and Matias walk with purpose down the hall and head to the stairs, but where Juan takes a right toward the saferoom, Matias pivots to the left toward the kitchens and the back of the villa.

"Please, Juan. Don't do this. You don't have to do this." I continue to plead and cry as Rosalie disappears from sight, but Juan says nothing.

When we enter the library, my father and Artemus sit in plush leather chairs smoking cigars. Neither one of them rises. They don't say a word. It's as if I'm nothing to them.

Juan presses the electronic latch that opens the saferoom behind the bookcase. There's not much inside. A couple of chairs, a couch, a set of bunk beds, food, water, and guns locked behind a wire cage. He deposits me on the couch and spins around to look at my father, who stands on the threshold.

"Give me your hands." Juan pulls Zip ties from his back pocket.

"You can't..."

"*Señorita,* give me your hands." Juan stands firm under the steely glare of my father.

I hold my hands out, palms down, knuckles of my thumbs and forefingers touching. As Juan wraps the Zip tie around my wrists, I maintain tension as he pulls the nylon band tight. He steps back, to check his handiwork, then leaves.

"There's been a slight change of plans, my darling daughter. Your friends are going to enjoy the welcome we've prepared." My father closes the distance and yanks on the end of the Zip tie, tightening it painfully. When he leaves, he slams the door to the safe room closed. The lock turns from the outside, sealing me in.

The first thing I do once the door to the safe room shuts, is rid myself of the Zip ties. Lily's instructions return to me. *"First, you want to tighten the Zip tie."*

My hands turn a nasty shade of dark red and splotchy purple. Numbness fills my fingers, making them feel fat, like sausages.

My father is beyond cruel. He knew what he was doing when he tightened the ties. It's another lesson. He's not afraid to dispense pain. Lily's words return to me, as does my success at getting out of the Zip ties once before. I know I can do it. Now, it's a matter of repeating that success and breaking my way free.

I grab the end of the Zip tie with my teeth and tighten it down. It's already tight enough to cut off the circulation to my hands, but Lily said *the tighter the better*.

I bring my hands above my head and spread my elbows out as wide as I can. With my hands high over my head and my elbows spread, I commit and chop down.

The Zip ties hold.

"No." Up again, my hands go over my head.

A tremor of fear fills me as doubt creeps in. What if I can't snap the nylon? What if the circulation to my hands stops? Shaking my head free from damaging thoughts, I recommit and thrust down as hard as I can.

The Zip tie snaps, freeing my hands, but they cut deep into my wrists. Bruised and bleeding, I take a moment to see how worried I need to be. The cuts are significant, but not life threatening.

I head to the small lavatory, really more of a closet than a bathroom, and find the medical kit. My swollen fingers fumble at the latch and I drop the contents to the floor. Blood drips down my arms and falls to the floor. There's way more blood than I thought.

Sensation rushes back into my hands. A million pinpricks, tiny needles are everywhere, making me hiss. Gritting my teeth against the pain, I go to my knees and grab the supplies I need: gauze and a wrap.

My fingers don't work right. They fumble and I can't seem to grip anything. I try to work the scissors, needing to wrap both my wrists, when suddenly the lights go out, plunging me into darkness.

FORTY-ONE

Rafe

"Bravo Three, Bravo Four, are you ready?" Our anchors are set. The rope's threaded through the figure-eight attached to my harness, Hayes and I step to the edge of the ledge. Below us, men race around, all order and discipline are gone in the sudden darkness. In another few minutes, Charlie team will arrive with ten robotic dogs leading the charge, adding chaos to the confusion.

I glance over at Hayes. "You set?"

"Ready, Freddy." Hayes lifts his arm out to the side, thumb up. It's the Go sign.

Next in line, Zeb and Alec wait to rappel down after us. Hayes and I will enter first. Take out any guards inside. Zeb and Alec will join us, providing cover while we get the girls in their harnesses. Then it's a simple matter of rappelling down to the ground and getting them to cover.

"Bravo Three and Four, cleared to go." Brady gives us the go-ahead. Hayes and I don't waste any time. We brace our feet on the edge and lean out into empty space. With a bounce out, we drop down to Carmen's room and come face to face with iron bars.

"Abort!" Hayes calls out, warning Zeb and Alec.

A burst of light flashes from inside, and the whizzing of bullets follows.

"Abort!" Hayes looks to me as we spin away from the window. Two options present themselves. Down, the easy way, leads to confrontation with the guards running around like chickens with their heads cut off. Or up, a much harder climb out. Since we're former US Navy SEALs, we never take the easy way.

With a jerk of his chin, Hayes echoes my sentiment. We clip off our lines and climb. Overhead, the rest of our team provides cover, shooting at men below who notice us scaling the wall. Bullets ring out all around us, digging deep into the stucco and brick of the wall. We pull up over the edge at the same time and roll to our backs, breathing hard.

Alec and Zeb take a knee and shoot at the enemy forces gathering below while Brady checks on us. We both give the sign we're okay. No injuries. Then we roll over to join Alec and Zeb.

"What now?" Hayes calls over his shoulder.

"What the hell happened?" Brady lifts his voice to be heard over the gunfire.

"Iron bars over the window." My reply is clipped and short. I glance down below and take note of where the men are by the flashes of their weapons. Each of those flashes is a bullet aimed at me, but their aim is shit. Mine is spot on. I take out a dozen men in about as many breaths, while Brady and Booker put their heads together.

We've got backups to our backups, and they're deciding where best to engage. With Carmen not in her room, there's no saying where they may have taken her. Then one of her comments sounds in my ear.

"The safe room." I have to yell over the shouting below. My shots are nonlethal but pack a punch and incapacitate. Mostly, I blow out femurs and shins, trying to stay away from the torso where there may, or may not, be body armor. Regardless, the men who bite my bullets aren't going to get up and rejoin the fight.

"Do you know where?" Brady looks to me.

"In the library." I wish we had schematics. Normally, that information would be loaded into our HUDs. It was the last time we were here. Right now, we operate blind and deaf, with no way to contact Command and Control.

"Ground floor is most likely." Brady makes a decision. "We'll work our way down."

A high-pitched whine sounds in my ear. Down below, the men's screams suddenly turn from shouts to cries of terror. A quick glance down reveals why.

The Rufi are here. Bloody hell, those things are fast. Movement in my periphery makes me shake my head, but that's when I see a tiny dragonfly drone carrying a package the size of my fist beneath its belly.

"Brady…" I point toward the drone. He'll take care of that while I help out the cavalry.

The more men we incapacitate now, the fewer we have to fight later. A wicked grin fills my face when I look below. Three of the Rufi create chaos and confusion for the men on the ground. As they give chase, their targets fall to the ground, victims of Mitzy's highly effective tranquilizers.

"Here." Brady shoves an earpiece at me.

"Bloody hell." I take the tiny radio and twist it in my ear.

"*Bravo-One, comms check.*" A disembodied voice calls out.

"Bravo-One, reading loud and clear."

"*Bravo-Two…*" That voice checks each of us.

Brady taps my back. "Time to go."

"*Bravo-Three, comms check.*"

"Bravo-Three check." Can't help the grin on my face.

Now that we're hooked back in with Command and Control, we're able to report back. While Brady talks it out, Bravo team moves as a unit to a door leading down into the villa. By the time we breach the door, three of the tiny dragonflies join our unit. Their job is to guide us toward the safe room.

"*Bravo team, we've got eyes inside, but no sign of Carmen or Rosalie.*"

"Did you try the safe room?"

"*The drones can't see inside.*"

"Copy that."

"Charlie breached the south wall and is headed to the basement. We've got seventy percent containment of outside forces."

No need to ask how the outside forces are being *contained*. Those men are being picked off like flies, secondary to the assist by a pack of robotic dogs.

"Copy that," Brady responds in a clipped tone.

Alec breaches the roof door. Zeb taps his shoulder and moves to the lead. Brady and Booker follow. A dragonfly drone follows each pair inside. They hover at eye level, tracking us as we work our way down.

Tiny lights on their bodies are our guides. They flash on the left, right, front, or back and tell us which way to proceed. Mitzy's tech team also informs us of *un-friendlies* between us and our target.

Bravo team moves as one, slowly making our way down and toward where we believe Carmen and Rosalie have been taken. With the open courtyards, we can't depend solely on the dragonflies to be our eyes.

Men take shots at us from across the open-air courtyards. Each time they shoot, I fire at the flash from their gun. My nonlethal shots are now deadly. I go for the head; specifically, the eye trained down the barrel of the weapon turned on me.

We're death-walking and devasting as we cut a swath through the building. As far as how Charlie team fares with their mission, we have no updates. Until they need us, we are on task.

We enter one of the open halls bordering a courtyard. Zeb takes out a couple of guards and we continue on. Halfway past the court-yard, I glance at an iron cage inside filled with fanciful birds that fill the air with their terrified squawks.

Didn't Carmen mention something about birds in a cage?

An overturned table lies in the middle of the courtyard. Three chairs stand upright around where the table would've been. Movement catches my eye.

A woman screams as a man yanks her into the far corner of the courtyard. At first, I think it's Carmen, but I know Carmen on a visceral level.

"Rosalie?" I call out, and the terrified woman looks up.

The man grabs Rosalie and places a knife to her throat. He slowly backs away, dragging the terrified woman with him. Away from our objective.

"There's no sign of Carmen," Brady says.

"Affirmative." The disembodied voice answers. *"We read only the man and woman. No others."*

"Shit." I turn to Brady, waiting for him to make the call, while remembering the vow I made to Carmen. There's no way I can chose between saving her and saving her friend.

"Rafe, you're with Alec and Zeb. Get to the safe room. Confirm if Carmen is there. Booker. Hayes. You're with me."

"You know who that asshole is…" The growl coming from Booker is positively inhuman.

"I do." Brady nods, accepting what Booker's going to say next.

We all recognize the man holding a knife to Rosalie's throat. He's the man who kidnapped Izzy, forced her to drive from Mexico all the way to Nicaragua, where he shoved her in a box and delivered her here.

Booker swore to put a bullet in Matias's brain but didn't get the chance when we rescued Izzy. The three of them move off, advancing slowly on Matias. I give the man a 30/70 shot of making it through the night.

"He's mine." The look on Booker's face is murderous.

"Understood." Brady bows his head.

I tug Hayes, pulling him close. "I promised Carmen I would rescue Rosalie. Don't make me break my promise."

"I've got you, brother." Hayes places his hand over mine and gives a squeeze of assurance. He'll fulfill my vow or die trying.

Knowing he's got my back, I let him go.

Matias continues backing up until he's protected by shadow and darkness.

Brady gives a signal and Bravo team splits up.

FORTY-TWO

Carmen

Pitch black, I can't see my hand in front of my face. My wrists bleed, and I fumble around for something to wrap around them.

When the supplies fell on the floor, they scattered. At first, panic sets in. I make a mess frantically feeling for things and realize I'm not helping myself.

Sometimes, it's better to do nothing than jump in and do something that messes everything up. More words of wisdom from Lucinda.

I take her words to heart and close my eyes. Somehow, if I close them, it feels as if I chose the darkness rather than it controlling me.

I set a grid in my mind, then reach out methodically to find things on the floor. Each time my fingers feel something, I grip it tight and hold it against my chest. As time goes by, feeling returns to my hands and my fingers behave.

Discarding things that don't help, like the tin of bandages, I finally find a four-inch square of paper. A packet of sterile bandages. I rip the top and find a bandage inside.

Slowly, methodically, I set the package under my knee, then reach out once more. I need tape or the wrap I was going to use. It takes time, and the floor grows sticky with my blood as I continue to search, but I don't give in to panic. Instead, I push my fear away.

That's when my fingers feel the ribbed surface of the stretchy wrap. With a slow breath in, I feel around my knees for where I left the scissors. In total darkness, I manage to wrap first one wrist, and then the next. With that done, I keep my eyes closed and remember where I was when the lights went out.

The door is somewhere behind me to my left. I keep to my knees, it feels safer than getting to my feet, and crawl until I reach the wall.

Fumbling my way back, I find what I think is the door. My father locked me in, but with the power out, does the lock still work?

Knowing something about how our safe room was designed, that question is one I have an answer to. Mag locks are powerful magnets, which is why they make very effective locks—unless the power is cut.

Cut the power and the magnets fail.

Which is why the safe room has a separate power supply from the rest of the house. A safe room's not very safe if it unlocks when the power goes out. That generator should've kicked in, but for some reason, it failed.

Which brings me to the next question. Where am I safest? Here? Or outside?

Rafe and his team are supposed to rescue Rosalie. Not me. But Matias took me, adding me to the list of those needing rescue. Did Bravo team see the bars over my windows? What would they do next?

I wrack my brain, knowing I'm wasting precious time. If Rafe thinks to look for me in the safe room, I'm good to go.

If my father comes back…

Suddenly, I'm on my feet. My hands roam the wall, searching for the door and mechanical release.

I've been in this room a total of one time. During that orientation, I was taught two things. First, how to use the toilette. I know, not sexy. The second was how to lock the door from the inside.

"Ah…" I can't help but jump for joy when my hands find the mechanized lock.

Now, how does it work? It's been years since my one foray in here, but I don't remember it being difficult. Nevertheless, I can't afford to mess this up.

I pull on the door latch, but it doesn't budge. Then, I remember the lever I'm supposed to hit.

I press the lever and pull on the latch. A satisfying *snick* sounds as I lock myself in. Before I move, I unlock the door, just to make sure I can unlock it again. If I lock myself in, I'm the only one who can disengage this final fail-safe.

Once I assure myself I can unlock it again, I spin around and slide to the floor. With my back to the door, I pull my knees to my chest and try not to think about Rosalie.

Eyes opened or eyes closed, it's darker than dark. I keep trying to wave my hand in front of my face, but there's nothing to see. Head back, I close my eyes and find what comfort I can in prayer.

Moments later, a loud banging on the other side of the door makes me jump.

I can almost make out words. Placing my ear to the solid door, the sounds are too muffled to make out what's being said. I make a fist and bang on the door.

Bang. Bang. Bang.

Then, I stop to listen and jump when three loud bangs are returned.

What now? What am I supposed to do? In the short five days of training with the Guardians, I don't remember anyone mentioning a scenario like this. I mean, I'm sure it's in the training manual, just not the first days of mandatory training.

All I can think of is to return three more bangs on my end.

I place my ear to the wall and jump when I hear an oddly distorted, but achingly familiar voice.

"Carmen? Is that you?"

"Rafe!" My pulse accelerates as I shout his name. Twisting around, I bang three more times. Then, I press my ear to the door and listen. The voice is indistinct, and frustration rises within me, but it has to be Rafe.

It sounds like instructions. Or questions. It's hard to say. Not knowing what to do, I do the three-bang thing again, feeling foolish. I press my ear to the door and hold my breath.

"Carmen, we can't open the door." The voice trails off, but I know exactly what to do. I'm up on my feet to unlock the door. When I push, however, someone pushes against it. Confused, I lean into it, but that's when the popping sound of gunfire suddenly goes off.

Rafe, and his team, are taking fire.

FORTY-THREE

Rafe

"Bloody hell." Right after we find Carmen, a dozen men pin us down.

Alec takes cover behind a pillar. Zeb dodges behind a massive desk. I squeeze behind Alec. The men are idiots, blowing through their ammo like it's the bloody Fourth of July. We let them shoot and count their spent rounds.

"I'll take low and right." I tap Alec on the shoulder.

"Copy that," Alec agrees.

The moment the bastards pause to reload, I take a knee while Alec stands over me. Unlike the men, our shots are measured and strategic. Men on the right fall with each of my shots. I take out five. Alec claims three, leaving four. Zeb alternates with us. He takes down two more. Which leaves two for me.

After the barrage of bullets, an echoing silence descends on us. We don't have much time before reinforcements arrive. Two of the dragonfly drones came with us. The other followed the rest of Bravo team on a hunt for Matias.

I bang on the door to the safe room, letting Carmen know it's safe. The door opens too slow and I yank on it. Carmen stumbles into my arms, covered in blood.

"Are you hurt?" I imagined holding her in my arms, but all I can think of is whether that's her blood, and if so, how significant are her injuries?

"It's fine." She lifts her wrists. Blood streams down her arms to her elbows and over the backs of her hands. An elastic bandage wraps around each wrist, covering a sterile bandage underneath. "It was the Zip ties."

"We've got to move. Can you walk?"

"I can run. Matias took Rosalie…"

"We know. Brady, Booker, and Hayes are on it."

"Rafe…" She places a hand on my chest. With the bulletproof vest, I can't feel her touch.

"Hayes promised he'd get her, and Booker has a personal beef with Matias. They will rescue Rosalie."

"Time to go." Alec taps me on the back and urges me to get on with it.

"Hold on to my belt." I grab Carmen's injured wrist gently and place her hand over the belt loop in the middle of my back. "Don't let go. If you can't keep up, you let me know. I'll carry you out."

"It's just my wrists." She glances at the bloody bandages wrapped around her wrists. "I can run."

"Good. Don't let go." I check her grip and give a nod to Alec and Zeb.

Zeb moves first, going to the doorway. He glances down one hall and then the other. The dragonfly drone is with him, signaling our path out of this bloody hell hole with flashes of green.

"You ready?" Alec checks me.

"Copy that."

Alec and I move out as one, with him in the lead and me trailing. Once we get to the doorway, we wait for Zeb to wave us through. He'll guard our rear.

We move swiftly through the villa. Gunfire sounds all around us, but the dragonfly drone keeps us away from the action. This requires a bit of backtracking from time to time, but we make steady progress.

To my surprise, the drone leads us toward the stairs we took coming down. We pass the courtyard with the toppled table and the wrought iron cage.

Instead of the raucous noise earlier, the birds are relatively quiet. There's the occasional fluttering of wings and nervous chirp. That cage brings Carmen to a dead stop.

Before I know what she's doing, Carmen races out into the open, sprinting toward the cage.

"Carmen, no!" The moment she's in the middle of the open space, a gunshot rings out, missing her by mere inches. "Bloody hell."

Without thinking, Alec, Zeb, and I move into a protective formation. Once again, we communicate with a series of hand signals and affirmatives given by a firm shake of our head. I race after Carmen while Alec and Zeb step out and sweep their weapons in an upward arc.

A shot rings out overhead, hitting my prosthetic and knocking me down. Carmen screeches to a halt and screams. Mouth open. Eyes wide. Terror fills her breaths. But that bullet doesn't do shit to stop me. Tucking my body, I shift all my forward momentum into a roll and spring right back on my feet.

"Carmen—get back here."

Carmen glances back at me. She hears me, but turns to the cage. Her fingers fumble for a moment, then she lifts a large bar and swings the door to the cage wide open. Rushing inside, she flaps her arms, scaring the birds. Feathers go everywhere as dozens of tropical birds escape their cage. Squawking and screaming, they fly up and into the night sky.

Another shot fires from above. The wrought iron sings as the bullet strikes it. Bloody hell, that was far too close. I run into the cage, grab Carmen by the arm, and drag her out of there. My stride is off. Something's wrong with the prosthetic, but not bad enough to stop.

Once under cover, I yell at Carmen. "Hand on my belt loop. Do not let go. Is that clear?"

Her lids pull back in surprise, but she responds with a shaky nod.

"Move out." I glance at Zeb, unclear where the dragonfly drone is, or where it's leading us. Zeb points to the stairs, taking point this time while Alec brings up the rear.

We take the stairs two at a time. Carmen keeps up beautifully. Zeb stops to take a shot, then moves out.

"Where the bloody hell is this thing taking us?" We're nowhere near an exit.

"Up." Zeb's one-word reply is answer enough.

"The roof?"

"Looks like." He takes off down a hall, stopping at every door along the way to sweep the room before moving on. Before long, we're close to where we started. The door to the roof stands open. Zeb stops at the door and places a finger over his mouth. He taps his ear letting us know he's listening for movement overhead.

All around us, gunfire rings out into the night. Most of it seeming to come from outside the walls. The drone is gone. Presumably, to check out the roof. While I don't see it return, Zeb does. He taps me on the shoulder and moves up. I bring Carmen to the rooftop, followed by Alec on my heels.

"What now?" I glance around the roof. Our parachutes lie exactly where we left them, wrapped into small heaps of black on black. My gaze sweeps the roof until I see the ropes we left behind.

"Looks like we're back to the original plan." Alec gestures to the ropes. "You take Carmen. Zeb go with them. I'll cover you from above. Join you once you're off the rope."

"Sounds like a plan." I turn to Carmen. "We're going to rappel off the roof. Do you understand?"

"Y-yes." Poor thing trembles like a leaf. Hands clasped in front of her, she twists her fingers and seems to look everywhere at once.

Not wasting anytime, I pull out the harness I intended to use earlier. "Let's get you set."

Kneeling in front of her, I hold the harness. She places her hands on my shoulders and steps into the rigging. I shimmy it up her legs and guide the straps for the waist over her hips. With a snap of a carabiner, I secure the webbing and check my work. Zeb and Alec approach the edge of the roof.

"We're clear," Zeb calls out as he grabs both lengths of line. Walking far enough back from the edge to conceal our movements from those on the line, Zeb secures his weapon and attaches to the line.

I secure my weapon, then take a knee. "Carmen, hop on."

She's nervous, but complies. Alec comes to me, helping to secure Carmen to my back. It's awkward, but works.

"Good to go." He taps me on the shoulder once he's done.

When we practice this particular extraction, it's with each other. Carmen weighs less than half what my teammates weigh, which makes this a walk in the park.

I barely feel her, but then she wraps her hands around my neck, inadvertently choking me. With the tactical vest and bulletproof lining, I don't feel any other part of her, and while this may not be the same as holding her in my arms, I'll take it.

I'll take it because she's safe. I'll take that every day.

Zeb holds the line while I clip in. He heads to the edge first, after checking the ground to see if it's clear, then he leans out and drops down.

"I gotta breathe, babe." I pull Carmen's hands away from my throat, then wince when I forget about the bandages around her wrists. "You doing okay?"

"Scared. Terrified. Overwhelmed. But otherwise, peachy."

I huff a laugh at her attempt at humor.

"It kind of feels like we met this way. Only you were hugging me in front, and the heat of your pussy…"

"Oh my Lord, don't say it. You're joking right?"

"Close your eyes, luv, and hang on tight!" With her distracted, I back up to the edge.

Without pausing, I lean out, look down, and jump into the air. The rope hisses through the carabiner as we fall. We swing back in a gentle arc. My legs absorb the shock, and I kick out again.

There's something definitely wrong with the leg. A hitch or a twist. Something's not right.

We swing out again. There's no action on this side of the building. Distant gunshots report the same can't be said for other parts of the villa. This time, when we swing in, I land on the ground, favoring my good leg.

Carmen reaches between us and unclips herself from the harness. When she climbs off my back, I take a moment to check the prosthetic. No surprise, it's twisted and warped from that gunshot.

A wry grin escapes me. This is the first bullet I've taken that doesn't hurt. Grudgingly, I suppose the blasted prosthetic has its good points.

The rope hisses overhead and Alec joins us on the ground. Once he's off the rope, the three of us do a quick check and decide where to go next.

"Exfil is half a mile that direction." I point toward the jungle, where a dirt road sits half a click in. We make it to that road and we're out of this place. It's also where Charlie team will converge once they rescue whatever hostages they find. "Can you run?" My question is for Carmen. Her attention focuses in on my leg—the fake one—and it's clear she's confused. "Carmen?"

She shakes her head and looks at me. "Sorry. Yeah. I'm good."

One glance at her feet and I'm not happy. She wears sandals with straps. Not the best gear for tromping through the jungle in the middle of the night. It'll do, at least until we get to the tree line. Once in the jungle, there's no way I'm letting her walk in those shoes. That's only asking for trouble.

"Let's move out," I call it and we set out at a jog. There's no reason to sprint. Me and the guys could do it, but not Carmen. We keep to a pace she can maintain and manage to make it to the edge of the jungle unobserved.

Several yards in, I hold up my hand, calling us to a stop.

"I'm going to carry you from here." I hand my weapon to Alec. He attaches it to his vest without being asked.

"I can walk."

"Not in those shoes. Not in the jungle. And definitely not at night." I give her my back and gesture for her to hop on. "Trust me. We'll move faster if I carry you." When she hesitates, I tap my shoulder. "Come on." I give a sigh of relief when she grabs my shoulders and hops on my back. This isn't the time for arguments about whether or not she wants to be carried. It's about getting a job done.

Carmen gets it.

Or at least, I assume she does.

FORTY-FOUR

Carmen

I remember little of that mad dash through the jungle. Dark and spooky, it amazes me how loud the jungle is at night. All around us, it teams with life. Monkeys holler. Panthers roar. Insects chirp, and unknown things slither in the darkness.

Rafe runs with his teammates, moving at a pace I would never be able to match. Alec leads the way. Zeb guards the rear. And the men run, leaping over roots and trees, jumping over crevices and small streams. Their endurance is impressive.

It's dark. I'm scared. Vegetation keeps slapping me in the face. Fine wispy strands of *stuff* catch in my eyelashes, my eyebrows, my hair, and my mouth. I say *stuff* because if those are spider webs, I'm going to lose my shit.

My wrists burn from where the Zip ties cut into my skin. My knees throb from crawling on the floor. My arm aches from the abuse Matias inflicted, and that's made worse from clinging to Rafe's back, but finally we emerge from the forest and reach a deeply rutted road.

Lights flicker in the darkness.

"That's our ride." Rafe crouches and I climb down from his back. The four of us pack into a Jeep. Zeb takes shotgun. Alec sits in the back with Rafe. I sit on Rafe's lap. We speed over the rutted road, bouncing wildly over the ruts, until coming to a slightly better-maintained dirt road.

Slightly better.

Here, one of the brightly colored buses waits in the oppressive darkness. Rafe ushers me inside. We move all the way to the back, where I collapse on the back bench seat, thoroughly exhausted, although I exerted no effort during the run through the jungle. Alec and Zeb don't join us inside the bus. Instead, they climb onto the roof. I want to ask why, but figure it out. We're away from the villa, but far from safe.

Tense moments pass. When I try to speak, Rafe places a finger over my lips. I get the message and stay silent. We stare into each other's eyes for a millisecond before Rafe grabs my face in his massive hands. Squishing my cheeks and tilting my face, he kisses me with intense hunger, lustful obsession, and fiery passion. It's a recklessness I wholeheartedly return with passion of my own.

None of this seems real. It still feels as if we should be running. As if we're being chased. My heart is still firmly lodged in my throat and fear flows through me. With each passing second, however, some of the terror swirling in my veins slowly leaves my body.

I'm with Rafe, and I'm safe.

Movement at the front of the bus breaks us from our kiss. The bus rocks as others climb on board. Terrified, half-naked, half-starved, filthy women and young girls stagger onto the bus. They look at me with haunted eyes, moving like the dead.

More than half are walking skeletons. They shuffle to the back of the bus, terrified and unsure if this is a rescue, or something far worse.

I squeeze Rafe's hand and take to the aisle. Going to the first woman, I greet her with a smile and calm words. Speaking in our native language, I guide first one woman and then the next to a seat at the back of the bus. Rafe stands, moving with me. Unlike me, however, the women cower before him.

"Rafe, maybe you should take a seat?" He looks to me, then

gives a nod. It's not where he wants to be, but he understands. For these women, men are to be feared.

Woman by woman, I provide reassurance and comfort. What comfort I can. I encourage and congratulate them on finally being free. I offer up hope and prayers to the Almighty. I grasp their hands, give a reassuring squeeze, and settle them into a seat.

I cringe when a girl no older than ten or twelve is next in line. Leaning down, I give her a hug, but she's listless and doesn't respond. Her inner light is gone, snuffed out by monstrous men, and she moves robotically, if at all. There's no resistance when I guide her to her seat.

"You're safe. You're going to be all right." I raise my voice and speak to the women huddled in the bus. "You're all safe."

Most of the women say nothing. Some praise God. The little girl with dirty hair caked in mud says nothing at all. Her expression is vacant. Her eyes hollow. She's a ghost.

My heart breaks for the little girl. Fortunately, one of the women reaches out a hand. The girl takes it and crawls into the seat beside the woman. There she curls inward, trying to disappear.

In all, there are a little over a dozen women ranging in age from far too young to older than I would expect. Although, it's difficult to place an age on a woman who's been abused, tortured, and raped for who knows how long. Their gaunt faces and emaciated bodies make me cringe and rage at the injustice of life.

Not for the first time, I yearn to destroy everything my father's built.

My heart aches for these poor souls. I wish we'd saved more. I wish I'd had the courage to do it sooner.

Before I know it, I'm at the front of the bus. Looking outside, six men stand protectively in a semi-circle around the bus. These are men I don't know, but they're Guardians. The men of Charlie team.

I glance outside, looking for Rosalie, but there's no sign of my friend. If all of Charlie team is here, the raid on the villa must be over.

But where is Rosalie?

Someone gives a signal, because the six Guardians board the

bus. I walk backward, giving them room, until I find myself at the back with Rafe at the rear.

"Where's Rosalie? I don't see her." I keep my voice down, barely more than a whisper, but panic tugs at the edges of my mind.

The engine chugs to life with a cough and a sputter. The air brakes release, and the bus lumbers forward.

"I'll find out." Rafe gives my hand a squeeze and moves to the front of the bus. There, he leans down and speaks to one of the men. There's a bit of a discussion, then Rafe turns around to rejoin me.

"There's no word on the others."

"And we're going to leave them?"

No. No. No!

Panic grips me making my heart thunder. Fear for Rosalie makes my knees buckle.

"We have no choice." Rafe grabs me, preventing me from falling. "But there are contingency plans and contingencies to those. Don't worry about Brady and the others."

But how can I not? I don't ask that question, turning my attention to the women Charlie team rescued.

"What about the women? What happens to them?"

"We take them with us."

"Shouldn't we reunite them with their families? How can we not do that?" They're free and I can only imagine reuniting with their family is the most important thing on their minds.

"They won't be separated forever. Trust me, we've done this enough to know what works, what doesn't, and what's best. The first thing is to attend to their medical needs. Get them cleaned up. Do an initial assessment. Most of that will happen on the flight home. Then we'll find their families and give the women a choice."

"A choice? What does that mean?"

"The trauma they've endured takes a toll. Many are not the same person they were before. Some may never fully recover. For others, they're welcomed back into their families with open arms. For the rest, that reunion is tainted by the trauma and rape. They'll all be taken to The Facility, where they'll receive the medical, psychological, and trauma care they need. After that, they'll begin rebuilding their lives."

"Can I share that with them?" I have no idea how Guardian HRS works, and much less about what The Facility can do.

"Yes. They'll take comfort in hearing it from you."

With Rafe's support, I take to the aisle again. I stop at each row, ask the woman her name, and reassure her she's been rescued.

I recite each name in my head until I have all their names memorized. I hold hands. Give hugs. Answer what questions I can. Rafe supplies answers to the questions I can't answer, and I translate for the women.

At first, the women shy away from him, but by the time we reach the airport, the very beginnings of hesitant smiles and brighter eyes flit across their faces.

Excitement between the women grows as the reality of their rescue sets in. Some still can't believe it's true. Some are too trauma-tized to react. When we drive up to the plane, their excitement grows until it's a palpable thing.

"Carmen," Rafe tugs on my arm.

"Yes?"

"Tell the women what comes next." He briefs me on how they'll board the plane, the questions they'll be asked, and the brief medical exams they'll undergo—if willing.

Nothing is forced on any of them.

My heart swells with joy as I witness the transformation of the women from the empty husks that boarded the bus to joyous women who eagerly climb out of the bus and board the plane.

As we speak the same language, I become the de-facto inter-preter between the women and the Guardian medical team and guide each woman through the initial intake process.

But there's still no sign of Rosalie.

The women eye the first-class seats hesitantly, not sure if they're permitted such a luxury. The medical team takes over, relieving me of my assumed duties. I go to the front of the plane where Mitzy sits with CJ staring at a screen.

"Any word?" I've asked no less than a dozen times. Each time, Mitzy gives a sharp shake of her head.

"None." Mitzy glances at CJ. "We're going to have to call it soon. We can't sit on here with these women. All it takes is one phone call."

I lean against the bulkhead and scan the banks of computer screens. Numbers flash across one screen. A map fills another, dotted with several different colors. There are several other screens I give barely any attention to as I listen in on Mitzy and CJ's conversation. One catches my eye. Tucked in the far corner, it looks like there's a chess enthusiast on board. For some reason, that makes me smile.

Guardian HRS is a formidable organization, but seeing those series of chess moves reminds me these people are human. Not particularly good at chess from the string of moves on the screen, but an enthusiast of the game.

"What about your drones?" CJ scratches the back of his neck. His lips twist as if he doesn't like the sour taste in his mouth.

"Only one went with them. It's not reporting."

"Shit." CJ pulls at his chin. He turns to me and gestures for me to take a seat next to him. "Do you know what this is?"

I look at the screen and nod. "It's a map of the area around my home." I recognize the walled complex that's been my prison, as well as the surrounding jungle I used to play inside when I was just a kid.

"Brady, Booker, and Hayes went after Matias," CJ explains. "Last report, we have them here." He points at a white dot on the screen, but the way he looks at me says there's more buried in the subtext he doesn't say.

But I know.

"Matias has Rosalie."

CJ nods.

A wave of nausea comes over me. I grab the nearest chair for support as the floor drops out from beneath me.

"What are these?" My voice shakes, because I know. About twenty dots in red converge around the tiny white dot CJ pointed to.

"Those are your father's men."

I swallow past the lump in my throat and look at CJ. "What do we do?"

Three men against how many? A dozen? More? I don't dare count, but I can't help myself. A little over two dozen men pursue of the rest of Bravo team.

"We make a decision." CJ glances over his shoulder. "Your father and Artemus escaped. Matias as well, although he's not with your father."

"But Rosalie…"

"Carmen…" He places a hand over mine. "If we don't leave soon, your father will close this airport. We'll be grounded. We lose the advantage we've gained tonight." Again, he looks over his shoulder at the women who survived hell and are witnessing a miracle.

How can I take that from them?

How can I abandon Rosalie?

FORTY-FIVE

Carmen

How do I choose between the women we saved and Rosalie? It's impossible, and while I won't make the final choice, CJ wants to hear my thoughts.

A voice speaks in my head. A voice I haven't heard in a very long time. It's not Lucinda. For the first time since her death, my mother speaks to me.

May God's grace protect those in need.

My heart feels as if it's being ripped in two. I rub at my nose and swipe at my tears. I can't. It's impossible to choose, but a choice must be made.

I know this.

The needs of the many outweigh the needs of the few. With a heavy heart and tears welling in my eyes, I swallow the lump in my throat and speak.

"We have to go." My throat closes up on the words.

"Yes." CJ squeezes my hand. "Have faith in the Guardians. They will bring Rosalie home."

I stagger backward and find Rafe's arms folding around me. CJ looks to Rafe and they exchange words without speaking. A signal is given because the door to the jet closes, and the engines whine as they spin up.

People move up and down the aisles, checking that the women are strapped in. Rafe pulls me to the back of the plane, where I collapse in his arms.

"We saved everyone, but Rosalie." A blubbering mess, my words are nearly incoherent. Nevertheless, Rafe seems to understand. He holds me through takeoff while I weep in his arms.

Later, someone touches my arm.

"Carmen?" I blink and stare into the kindest face I've ever known. Doc Summers, Skye, looks down at me with a serene smile. "We could use some help, if you're feeling up for it."

"Help?"

"Yes. We've got fourteen women to process. You were so kind and comforting to them. I was wondering if you could help."

"What do you need?" Listlessness fills me, but I can help these women. It's a moral imperative that I do what I can for them.

"We have two full-sized lavatories in back," Skye says. "If you could take them back, two at a time, so they can get cleaned up?"

"What about clothes? And..." I glance around the cabin. "They need shampoo, combs, brushes, and..."

"All taken care of, and Carmen..." She places a hand on my shoulder.

"Yes?"

"You're going to be surprised by what happens. It's magical." Her words make no sense.

"I have no idea what that means."

"Take two of the women to the lavatories. Show them how to take a shower. You should probably limit their time. Mention that up front. What they need right now is to feel human again. It's amazing how powerful a hot shower and a bit of soap can be."

"Okay." At least taking care of the women will take my mind off Rosalie. I explain to the women what we're going to do and gesture to two of the women furthest back.

To my surprise, they refuse to be separated. The two of them head into the lavatory on the left, clinging to each other. After I show them how to adjust the water, use the soap provided, and show them the clothing we've provided, shock fills their faces, then joy pushes all evidence of their fear away. I leave the two women to help each another and head back to grab two more.

Ten minutes.

That's what I say, and they don't spend a single second past their allotted time. Once the first pair of women is done, they rush to grab the next two, crowding inside the lavatories, helping them through the process.

Eyes get brighter. Smiles push away listless expressions. The women begin to speak, talking softly to one another, helping one another. They comb each other's hair. Hug. Praise God. They absolutely adore the clothing Guardian HRS provides.

I stand back, amazed. This must be what Skye alluded to with her mysterious comment about magic happening. In tragedy, these women find fellowship and strength in each other.

Another tear slips free. I swipe it from my cheek and check in on Rafe. He's not in his seat. I wander to the front of the plane looking for him.

The Guardians divide the plane into three main sections. Four if you count the lavatories in the back and the gear lockers beyond. Up front is Command and Control. Immediately behind that are four medical tables, two to a side.

To my surprise, Rafe sits on one of the medical exam tables. The medical team gathers around him, blocking my view. Something's wrong and it takes a minute before what that might be kicks in.

I was certain Rafe took a hit to his leg back in the courtyard, but when he rolled on his shoulder and popped back to his feet, I thought I imagined it. Add to that how he ran through the jungle and scaled down the wall? I dismissed the whole thing and put it out of my mind.

But the medical team surrounds him. They wouldn't do that without reason. Curious, I peek between those gathered, trying to see.

Skye notices me and gestures to the man blocking my view. One of Charlie team, he turns toward me.

"Here." Stepping back, he makes a hole for me to see.

And what I see makes my heart stop.

Rafe's leg…

Is not a leg.

Where his leg is supposed to be, a piece of metal is there instead. That metal has a chunk missing out of it. I gape at the mangled metal, certain my eyes play tricks on me.

When I look at him, my brows practically touch with the confusion flooding my mind. I try to formulate a question but can't seem to string together the words. He tries to hide his reaction, but the pain of rejection is scrawled across his face.

Which is weird.

"I thought you were hit, but there was no blood." I look at the leg, look at Rafe, then look at the leg again. "You tucked, rolled, and popped to your…" My voice trails off.

How did I not know?

"I thought I imagined…" I turn to Skye Summers. "He ran with me clinging to his back and rappelled…" I shake my head, astounded.

"Fortunately, he took a bullet to the prosthetic rather than his other leg." Skye examines the metal. "It's a mangled mess, but still serviceable. We'll have a new one waiting once we're home." She glances up at Rafe. "I'd like to look at your…"

"Stump?" Rafe spits out the words and withdraws when I try to touch him.

"Yes, Rafe." Doc Summers doesn't take Rafe's lip. "I want to look at your stump. No need to be a grump about it, but we need to see if all that running hurt the…"

"Stump?" I think I hear wrong. Are they talking about his leg?

"Yeah. I've got a bloody stump." Rafe practically bites my head off.

"Why are you being mean to me? Why didn't you tell me? Why hide…" I don't finish that sentence. A feeling of betrayal overcomes me, making me question a lot of things.

"Don't you have something to do?" His upper lip curls.

"Check yourself, dude." Alec wanders past, stopping to listen to our very odd, and painful, exchange. "Your ass is showing. Apologize."

"Because I have a stump?"

"No, dickwad. Apologize for being a bloody ass for not telling her sooner. After all the fu…"

"You better watch what comes out of that mouth next." Rafe shifts his anger from me to Alec. "Or I'll beat you over the head with my mangled leg."

"I'd like to see you try, but seriously, dude? This is how she finds out? That's fucking harsh." Alec shakes his head and turns to me. "Give the fucker some grace. His ass is showing."

"Why you bloody…" Rafe makes a move to climb off the table, but without the prosthetic, he's not getting very far. Fortunately, he figures that out before he makes a fool of himself.

"Rafe." I place my hand on his arm again. As expected, he flinches at my touch.

I felt something was off when he never made love to me in bed. Or the shower. He slept on one side of the bed, never switching with me. I didn't think much of it, but it all kind of makes sense. Not that I understand why he never mentioned it.

I know why I never noticed. Rafe's quite talented when it comes to making love. Not to mention inventive. We've made love every-where but the bed and shower. Now, I know why. Not that it matters. It changes nothing.

"If Doc Summers needs to check the stump, then let her check the stump." I glance at the twisted metal of the prosthetic. "That had to hurt."

"Prosthetic limbs—they don't feel pain." He's being mean on purpose. Trying to push me away.

I don't have the energy to fight with him.

"I don't care if you've got one leg, two legs, or three legs, but I agree with Alec. You're being a major jerk about this." I point to the leg. "Do you think this makes a bit of difference? To me? You're practically bionic. If it wasn't for that prosthetic, that bullet would've shredded the lower half of your leg. Then I would've had to tie you to my back, rappel down that wall, and then carry your sorry ass on my back through the jungle. If you didn't bleed out, that is. Frankly, with the way you're acting right now, I probably would've left you behind."

My words bring stunned silence to all gathered. Alec's eyes practically bug out of his head. Rafe's jaw gapes like he doesn't believe what just came out of my mouth. From the way his gaze flicks from side to side checking out the reactions of the others, the gears in his head start to move.

Slowly.

But they're moving.

Skye simply leans back, arms crossed over her chest, with that serene, all-knowing smile fixed in place.

Mitzy gives one of those slow claps and shoulders her way to the side of the bed. "*Dayum*, Carmen dressed you down in *style*. Nice job, girl." Mitzy pats me on the back. "I'm totally going to enjoy welcoming her into the chick brigade."

"Chick brigade?" I glance at Mitzy, confused, but hopeful.

"Yeah," Mitzy gives a vigorous nod. "Us chicks gotta stick together. If we don't, these macho dudes won't know which way is up, or how to tie their shoes. Not to mention the stupid stuff that comes out of their mouths." With a snap of her finger, she points to Rafe's leg. "Why don't you show Skye that stump while I welcome Carmen officially into the Chick Brigade?"

Rafe snaps his jaw shut. Alec huffs a laugh. Skye doesn't move a muscle until Rafe finally leans forward and separates his prosthetic from his leg, muttering something about women under his breath.

Mitzy leans toward me and uses a whisper that everyone can clearly hear. "Let's give Rafe space to stew about what an ass he is for keeping this from you. Then he can *apologize* to you later." Mitzy uses finger quotes implying a particular type of apology. Pulling me away, she leans in and whispers for real. "Give him space to get his thoughts together."

Mitzy leads me away as Alec lets out a low whistle. "Fuck, they got you good. Looks like Stumpy bit the bullet. Zeb, you owe me a button."

"You bloody hell did *not* place a bet about me getting shot." Rafe glares at his teammate and takes a swing, but Alec dodges out of the way.

"Not about getting shot. That was over whether you told her or not." Zeb tosses a button at Alec with a grin plastered to his face. "You're in so much trouble, brother." He looks at me and shakes his head.

I don't know what it is, but that look makes me feel included. I'm a part of the gang rather than an outsider. A smile fills my face as my joy and warmth fill me up from the inside out.

The men's voices continue as Mitzy leads me to the front of the plane. I love Bravo's banter. I adore how they tease and support each other. What I don't know is what I think about Rafe keeping something like that from me.

When we get to the front of the plane and the bank of computer screens, one of the technicians turns toward Mitzy. "We've got contact," he says.

That can only mean one thing.

"Is it Rosalie?" My hands clasp in front of my chest as hope stirs within me.

"Let's find out." Mitzy gestures to a seat next to the bulkhead. I squeeze past her people and try to follow what they see.

"That's Brady and Booker." Mitzy points at the screen. "Why are we only seeing two of them?" A grainy black-and-white image fills the screen, slowly panning a full 360 degrees, but there are only the two men.

"Where's Rosalie?" My voice shakes and I press my hands together, getting ready to pray.

"Unclear." Mitzy's response is quick and dismissive, letting me know my questions are only slowing her down.

I resolve to be silent and try my best to follow along.

"Where's the audio?" Mitzy asks.

"It's cutting in and out, but I can confirm it's only Bravo-One and -Two. There's no sign of Bravo-Four or the girl."

In this case, that girl is Rosalie.

"They've got company." Mitzy points to a grouping of red dots.

"What do you make of that?"

"Looks like they split off. Brady and Booker are drawing the men after them. Which means Hayes is with Rosalie." Mitzy spares me a glance, but I press my lips tight together and keep silent.

Is it too much to hope Rosalie is safe?

"Wish we'd sent a second drone with them instead of the others." Mitzy leans back and pulls at her hair. "Oh well, can't cry over spilt milk."

"What do you want us to do?" The man asks for direction.

"Keep with Bravo One and Two. If they make secondary exfil, we'll find out. If they're captured…"

I lean close, needing to hear what happens if they get captured.

But really?

Do I need Mitzy and her team to tell me what I already know? My palms press tighter still, and I pray for Brady and Booker's safe return. I lift up another prayer for Hayes and Rosalie. If she's with a Guardian, I know she'll be safe.

Then I sit back and watch Mitzy and her team work.

After some time, I give up trying to follow along and stare at the small screen I noticed tucked into the corner earlier. It's definitely a game of chess. The algebraic notation, standard for recording and describing chess moves, is clear, but few of the moves make sense, and there are more than a couple errors.

My father taught me to play when I was four years old, and I had some aptitude for the game. He taught me the system of coordinates used to uniquely identify each square on the chessboard, how to name the pieces, and the notations for moves, captures, castling, and all the rest.

One of the things we did when I was much younger was play a game where we merged chess and hide-n-go-seek. We'd leave clues around the villa as to where we hid our next move. Follow the clue and we'd find each other's next move scribbled on a piece of paper.

I loved that game, but my father never let me win without earning it. I had to earn my **1-0**, the notation declaring White won. There were very few of those, but enough to keep me interested.

Our games of chess ended sometime after I turned twelve. After what happened to my mother, and what Rosalie told me about the girls, I distanced myself from my father. I don't think he noticed or cared.

"Whatcha doing?" Mitzy swaps seats with the techie sitting beside me.

"Just trying to make sense of this game." I gesture toward the screen.

"What game?" Mitzy glances at the computer screen, brows pinched in confusion.

"That game." I point to the series of algebraic notations. "Who's the chess player?"

"What do you mean?"

"Those are notations for chess, but it's really weird." I peer at some of the moves that make no sense.

"Chess? You're kidding me. Those are chess moves?" Mitzy waves to her team, getting them to gather around. "Carmen says these are chess moves. Why didn't we see that? Who plays chess?" She twists around, checking her team.

No one lifts a hand or says a word.

"I can't believe it's chess." She snaps her fingers. "Pull me up a chessboard."

Before I know what's happening, we sit in front of a virtual chessboard.

"Let's play," she says. "The rest of you know what to look for." Her team leans in with that comment.

"Um, I don't understand what's happening." With all eyes focused on me, it's hard not to feel a little uncomfortable.

"Just go with it for a second. I don't want to cloud your judgment. Who goes first? Black or White?"

"Traditionally, White goes first."

"Let's do this." She scrolls to the beginning of the list of chess moves.

It's an odd list; engraved on some kind of metal. For the life of me, I can't see why anyone would do that.

There are far too many lines for a single game of chess. I catch several **1-0** and **0-1.** Those indicate wins. There are a bunch of

1/2-1/2, which indicate draws, and far fewer **0-0** indicating forfeits. On quick glance, there's at least a dozen games on the list.

I glance at the screen and make the first move for White. Mitzy doesn't understand the notation, but after I explain how each square is identified by a unique letter and number, she starts to move Black's pieces.

We come to the end of the first game, with White winning. Mitzy moves us to the next game while her team takes notes. I soon get lost in the rhythm of chess, except when the moves don't make sense.

Those pull me out of the moment.

Before I know it, we've drawn a crowd. Looking over my shoulder, Rafe gives me a tentative smile. A flick of his eyes asks if I can join him. My nod is cautious.

Clearly, he wants to talk and apologize for earlier, but Mitzy's got me roped into this weird game.

Given time to think about why he never mentioned his leg, I've come to a decision. It changes nothing between us. It changes nothing about him or my feelings for him.

I want to make one thing clear, however. While I know there will be things he can't share with me—work things—I don't want secrets between us. An amputated limb is a huge secret. After all the time we've spent together, he actively concealed it from me. I love the fool, but he needs to know this is the last secret he keeps from me.

"Mind if I take a break?" I nudge Mitzy and point toward Rafe.

"Yeah. Sure." Distracted by the game, Mitzy barely notices me leaving. As soon as I vacate my seat, she pats the cushion and invites one of her teammates to sit down and take over White's moves.

When I make it to the aisle, Rafe takes my hand in his. A quick glance down reveals two legs planted firmly on the floor. Even knowing about the prosthetic, there's nothing when I look at him that speaks to the loss of a leg.

"What's all that about?" He points to the excited group of technicians.

"Chess."

"I got that, but why are you playing chess with Mitzy?"

"I'm not." I point toward the screen. "She showed me a picture of a piece of metal with chess moves engraved on it."

"A piece of metal?"

"Yeah. Isn't that weird?"

"Not really." There's a look in his eye I can't make out.

"It's not a very well-played game of chess. There are tons of mistakes littered throughout. Almost as if the movement of the pieces is random, and I do mean random. A novice would play better. For that matter, the way the games end makes even less sense."

"How's that?"

"There's no defense of the King."

"From the look in Mitzy's eye, and the attention her team's giving that game, I have a feeling you did something amazing."

"Me?" I glance back at Mitzy and her team gathered around the screens. "I don't get it." Truly, I'm confused.

"They've been trying to crack the cipher on that brad and keep coming up empty."

"I don't follow. What cipher?"

"That piece of metal is the brad of a rabbit's foot."

"Still not following."

"I don't blame you. It's pretty weird."

"Enlighten me?"

"When Angie and Izzy joined Doctor's Without Borders, they were each given a rabbit's foot for good luck from one of their team-mates. Turns out he was working for one of the cartels."

"Huh?"

"The rabbit's foot, both of them, were filled with diamonds. At first, we thought the diamonds were what was being transported, and they very well may have been, but Mitzy and her team found a coded message cut into the metal of the brad." Rafe points to the screen. "They haven't been able to crack it. You come along and break it in less than a second."

"It's not like it was hard. That's how my father taught me to play..." I cover my mouth with my hand. Eyes wide, I glance at the computer screens. "It's an accounting system."

"Accounting?" Mitzy hears our conversation and butts in. "Holy shit that makes sense. Like a ledger." She turns to her team. "Let's figure out what Maximus Angelo was keeping track of…" Her voice trails off, but we're all thinking the same thing.

That code is an accounting of those unfortunate souls my father bought and sold through the years. My stomach twists at the vileness of the man I call father and shame fills me that I took far too long to do something about it.

Rafe senses my unease and grabs my hand in his. Threading his fingers with mine, he pulls me down the aisle, toward the back of the plane. I leave Mitzy and her team to pursue the odd chess moves and follow Rafe.

"Mind if we talk?" His dark hair falls over his eyes and he gives a practiced flip of his head to flick it to the side.

"Not at all." I'm not mad at Rafe. Far from it, but I'm a little perturbed he didn't trust me with the truth.

"Privately?"

"We're in a jumbo jet, flying through the air; there is no privacy." My statement isn't exactly true. There's the conference room I found myself in when this whole adventure began, but that room's occupied by the medical team to conduct the private exams for the rescued women.

"There is the lavatory." He rubs at the back of his neck, something I've come to learn he does when nervous.

For some reason, the moment he says the word *lavatory*, all I can think about is what are my chances for joining the mile-high club. The corners of his mouth tilt up into a wicked grin.

"I love the way your mind works." Low and throaty, I know what that voice means.

"Huh?"

"You're an open book to me, luv, but before *that*, I wanted to talk about *this*." He points to his leg.

"I want to talk about it too." As Rafe pulls me toward the back of the plane, I ignore the looks Zeb and Alec give us. No doubt they'll be betting on the outcome of mine Rafe's *talk*.

FORTY-SIX

Carmen

Knowing this is a huge deal for Rafe, I brace for whatever he has to say. My stomach's a knotted mess, and I'm intensely curious.

What does a stump look like? What does it feel like? How much pain is he in on a daily basis? Tons of questions flood my mind.

Rafe holds my hand as we walk down the aisle. He hesitates at the door to the lavatory. I place a hand on his arm.

"It's just a leg."

He doesn't look like he believes me. He looks scared to death that I'll reject him.

"Do you think I'm so shallow that I'll abandon you over a leg?"

"No, but I'd be lying if I didn't think this changes things."

My brows knit together at the intensity of his fear and vulnerability. No need to dance around the subject. I figure the best way is to dive right in.

"When did it happen?"

"A year ago."

"How?"

"During a mission." He points back toward the front of the plane. "It's how Brady got his burns and Alec lost two of his fingers.

Hayes and Zeb were sprayed by shrapnel. Booker's the only one who didn't get injured, which is a good thing since he's our medic."

I cover my mouth in shock. Not with their injuries. The men appear to have healed, or are healing from those, but it's a stark reminder how dangerous the job of a Guardian can be.

"Did anyone…" Too choked up, it's hard to say the words.

"No one was killed. Just flesh wounds."

"You're saying the loss of your leg is a flesh wound?" My eyes pinch, and I cock my head, teasing.

"Yeah." He rubs at the back of his neck again.

"You lost more than a bit of flesh. Bone. Muscle…a leg!" I make a general gesture toward his leg.

"But I'm still here. Still kicking."

With one leg. I understand how self-conscious he is about the amputated limb.

"Why didn't you tell me?"

How did I not notice?

That's my biggest question, and I don't like the answer. It means I was too self-absorbed in chasing my pleasure that I never stopped to really look after Rafe. How can I have had sex with him and not know?

"I think that's obvious."

"It's not." I dig in. "Tell me."

"I don't know how to begin."

"Mitzy gave me some good advice once. She told me to start at the beginning and keep on until the end. Try that."

"Are you mad at me?"

"Initially?"

He nods.

"I was angry. Then embarrassed when I realized I was the only one who didn't know. But I'm not anymore."

"I never meant to hurt you. Eventually, I was going to tell you."

"Could've fooled me. Honestly, I'm okay with the stump." He needs to hear it means nothing, but I refuse to let him off the hook.

"How can you be?" It's a bigger deal to him than I realize, and I pay better attention to the words I use.

"Because it changes nothing." That's the truth, and I pray he hears the truth in my voice.

"It changed a lot of things for me." Rafe's head hangs, and he refuses to look at me.

"What things?"

"Hard to say without sounding conceited." He peeks at me, then looks away.

"It's better we talk this through."

"I know." He takes in a deep breath. "I know what I look like."

I miss the transition and what he's trying to say. He knows what?

"What's that supposed to mean?"

"I'm a chick magnet."

"A chick magnet?" I cover my mouth as laughter escapes me. "That's a bit narcissistic."

"Told you it would sound bad."

"Okay, sorry. I didn't mean to laugh." But I can't help the grin filling my face, or the laughter bubbling up inside of me. He waits until I get it together. Finally, I lift a hand, palm out.

"Okay, hit me. So, you're a chick magnet? How does that affect anything?"

"I'm a big guy, with a body in peak physical condition, with rugged good looks. I'm handsome and easygoing. A chick magnet."

"Yes, you said that. Twice, in fact. I think we've firmly established you're a chick magnet, but what does that have to do with the leg?"

"I'm getting to that."

"Then get to it."

"Recovery after the accident wasn't easy. In the first few months, there were several surgeries. The healing took time. I went through several iterations of prosthetics. Part of that recovery was talking to the shrinks about the loss of my limb and body dysphoria."

"Body what?"

"Basically, learning to accept, and live, with a body that's fundamentally different than before. But my point is, after the best of the best of the best help…"

"Three bests?" I try to lighten the mood.

"Yes." He shakes his head, but his entire demeanor feels lighter. Rafe looks at me and counts on his fingers. "Medically, psychologically, and excellent physical therapy. I had the best of all three, and I thought I was healed."

"That is the goal, right? Sorry, but I'm confused."

"I thought I was the same as before. That I was fixed, and it was nothing big."

"*It is* nothing big, but it's also *huge* when you hide it. Like I said…"

"Hold up. I'm not done. Once most of the healing was done, and I was feeling more like my old self, I went to the bar to do what single guys do."

"What's that?"

"Seriously?"

"Yes."

"I went to pick up chicks and get laid. That clear enough for you?"

"Loud and clear." A giggle escapes me. I'm doing the best I can to make him feel at ease talking to me about something that's a big deal for him. I don't know if I'm failing or succeeding. At least he's still talking.

"Look, I'm not a saint, but bragging about the girls I've slept with isn't exactly the kind of conversation I'm comfortable having with you."

"Why?"

"Because you're special."

"I am?"

"You know you are." His grin is back, and that tension from before isn't as evident.

My questions aren't meant to be stupid. They're designed to get him out of his head and relax. I really want this to be a good conversation, a productive conversation.

"Okay. We've agreed you're a chick magnet, and I'm special. What does any of this have to do with your leg?"

"The first time I went out after the accident, I was a bit wound up and needed to get laid. I went to the bar, picked up a chick, but when she saw the leg, she ran."

"She ran?"

"Right out the door."

"Oh…that must have hurt." I can't imagine how that rejection must have felt, but it had to be bad. Really bad. I understand a little better why he kept it from me. Rafe feared I'd run away.

"My ego's hard to bruise. I figured it was a one-off thing and the chick's problem. Only the next time, the same thing happened. And the next. And again. Finally, I had to accept the truth."

"And what's that?"

"I'm disgusting."

"Disgusting." I take note of his use of pronouns. Not the leg. The leg wasn't disgusting. Rafe internalized that reaction. He feels disgusting because of the injury. It's hard to hear, but exactly what I need to help him.

"That's what I said."

"Show me the stump, and I'll be the judge of that."

"Carmen…"

"I'm not kidding. I can't love you if you hide pieces of yourself from me. Show me the stump."

With those words, the tension bunching in his muscles melts away. Instead of trying to hide the disfiguring injury, Rafe nods, but he also braces for the worst.

"Not here." He pushes open the lavatory door. "In here."

He gestures for me to head inside the lavatory. Unlike typical lavatories on planes, this one is a spacious oasis and more than full-sized.

"You sure you want to see it?" His uncertainty returns.

"I do." He gives me an odd look when I say those words. By themselves, they mean nothing, but in another context, it confirms a lifetime vow. "I want to see it. Feel it. Kiss it…"

Without another word, Rafe kicks off his shoe and places his foot on the commode. Not a foot, but rather the flexed carbon and metal prosthetic.

He pulls up the leg of his pants and removes the prosthetic.

While I watch, he sets the leg to the side, then rolls down what looks to be a cotton sleeve that covers what's left of his lower leg. Scarred and puckered flesh reveals itself to my eyes, and Rafe refuses to look at me. Actually, he holds his breath, waiting for a reaction.

Transfixed by what's left of Rafe's leg. It simply—stops a few inches below his knee. I reach out, fluttering my fingers over the scarred and mangled flesh.

"I want to hear more about the explosion. How did you not…?"

"Die?"

"Yes. I can't imagine."

"That's a story for another time." Rafe grabs my fingers and lifts them to his lips. "Will you help me roll this all the way down?"

A thrill rushes through me. I know this is hard for him. The fact he tried to hide it from me speaks volumes, but I love that he doesn't shy away from including me now.

I want to spend the rest of my days learning everything I can about Rafe. Some of that begins now, with the most vulnerable piece of him. Together, we roll down the cotton sheath, exposing the stump. Under the cotton sleeve, the skin's angry and red, working toward a bruise.

"Does it hurt?"

"Not unless I'm running through the jungle with you on my back with a twisted prosthetic."

"What happens now?"

"What do you mean?"

"How long will it take to get another one made? Will you be on crutches? A wheelchair?"

He huffs a laugh and pulls me close. "I always carry a spare in my gear."

That's when I realize the prosthetic he pulled off isn't the same twisted metal I saw earlier.

"I wish you hadn't kept this from me."

"I couldn't bear losing you."

"I wouldn't have left."

"But you might have run off screaming from the mangled monster."

"I'm going to say this now, and as many times as you need to hear it, but you're no monster. Those other women have no idea what they missed when they ran. They, and their opinions, mean nothing."

"All I care about is what you think and how this changes things." There's that hesitancy again. For such a strong man, there's vulnerability beneath his steely exterior.

"I guess that depends on two things." I glance up at him with a smile.

"What?"

"Never hide something like this from me again. Don't lie to me. I deserve better."

"There will be some things…"

"I know." I hold up a hand, forestalling him. "I get there will be work things that you can't share, and I'm not talking about those. I'm talking about this." I point to the stump. "For better, or for worse, we can't hide the pieces of ourselves we're worried about because we fear how the other person will react. Promise me this will never happen again."

"I'm sorry, luv. I shouldn't have been afraid to tell you. I promise not to do it again."

"Then that's all I need."

"You said two things?" He's curious, and I love that about him. "What's the other?"

"I want you to make love to me without the prosthetic."

"But…" He glances around the lavatory, then his eyes widen. "Like now?" Some of that insecurity returns, but it quickly dies in the banked heat of his desire flaring to life.

"No time like the present."

"And how's that going to work? It's hard to hold you against the wall when I'm shy a leg."

"I thought we'd start with one of your fantasies and work from there." I lick my lips, sending a very specific message.

"Bloody hell…" Low and throaty, he's definitely on board.

"If you can't stand…" I move toward him and unfasten his pants. "Have a seat, and let's see what happens."

With all the sex we've had, I've yet to take him in my mouth. Truthfully, the fear of gagging holds me back, but this is one thing we can do that won't bring the lack of a leg into the mix.

Half expecting him to hesitate, Rafe yanks his pants down his thighs and sits on the closed toilette seat. I kneel in front of him, loving the way his breathing hitches, and help him out of his pants. Leaning down, I kiss first his good knee and then the one on the damaged side.

His entire body stills as I explore the scarred and puckered skin with my hands, learning to love his flaws and the things that make him great. Slowly, very slowly, Rafe relaxes to my touch. I start with a soft touch, then massage the angry tissue. It's abraded and raw, something I attribute to the mission because I can't bear to think he lives his life in such constant pain.

When Rafe tips his head back and sighs with my massage of the stump, I lift up and attend to another needy part of his anatomy. If I gag, I'll gag, and he'll have to love that about me. But I don't gag as I slowly take him in my mouth.

FORTY-SEVEN

Carmen

THE SEVEN-HOUR FLIGHT FROM NICARAGUA TO CALIFORNIA LASTS forever, but I keep busy between Rafe and his stump and the women we rescued. Officially a member of the Mile High Club, I don't even care about the stupid bet Zeb and Alec placed on what happened, or not, in that lavatory.

As for that magic Skye mentioned, the women Guardian HRS rescued pull together in an amazing show of survival and support. They cling to each other. Encourage each other. Some talk about their families. Most are eager to get home, but terrified of the reception they'll receive.

Every single one of them takes Guardian HRS up on their offer to take a pause on life and rest and recuperate at The Facility. Over the next week, I help them with that transition.

Somehow, I've become the spokesperson of the group. While plenty of staff at The Facility are fluent in Spanish, the women vote me as their unofficial go-between.

Rafe and his team do whatever it is Guardians do between missions, while I spend my days at The Facility helping the women navigate this next phase of their lives.

Rest. Recuperation. Recovery.

Those are the 3-Rs of the initial phase of their journey. Psychological help is part of that. Training in self-defense is another part, meant to instill confidence and restore their perceived sense of power over controlling what happens to them. They love that I train with them. Somehow, I've become their beacon of hope.

Those who want their families contacted give permission for The Facility to reach out. None of the women opt to go home. None of them want their families brought here to reunite. None take advantage of the video calls that are offered.

This is something I don't understand but is what The Facility personnel anticipate. The road to recovery is long and convoluted, with many setbacks as the women work through the trauma of what they endured. As for me, working at The Facility keeps my mind busy and helps me not to obsess over Rosalie.

Except times like now.

Toward the end of the day, when I wait for Rafe to pick me up and take me home, I come to the cliff's edge and stare out over the ocean. It's a quiet time of contemplative meditation, where my prayers turn to Rosalie.

It's another beautiful day, with another stunning sunset over the Pacific. A storm brews on the horizon. Dark, menacing clouds build, and lightning flashes offshore. That storm blows in toward the coast.

Toward me.

But there's still time to enjoy the sunset. For now, the blue sky overhead turns into vibrant swaths of crimson and ochre stretching overhead. A light breeze ruffles my hair. Gusts blow off the ocean. The waves surge back and forth, with the wind kicking up froth on the crests of waves.

The birds don't run from the impending storm. They soar overhead without a care in the world, diving into the gray waters in search of their evening meal.

The soft tread of footsteps sounds behind me. It's Rafe. Every day since we arrived, he drops me off at The Facility and picks me up at day's end. We spend each evening here, at this quiet place on the cliff's edge, staring out at the ocean as the sun slips beneath the waves.

"How was your day?" Rafe sits beside me, knocking my shoulder playfully.

"It was great. I can't believe what they do here."

"I'm glad you're volunteering. I hear rumors they may not want to let you go?"

"Those rumors are true. They offered me a job." I should be excited by the offer but find myself melancholic.

"That's great." Rafe wraps his arm around me and gives a squeeze for good measure. "Have you thought about whether you're interested?"

My response is an unenthusiastic shrug.

That question comes with a host of things we need to discuss

"Talk to me, babe. What's on your mind?"

"It feels wrong to think about my future when Rosalie…" My voice catches. "Until I know more about Rosalie, I don't feel like I can move forward." I don't think I *should*.

It feels like abandoning my friend.

Less than a day after we landed in California, Brady and Booker made their way out of Nicaragua without Hayes and Rosalie.

"It's been a week since the raid."

"Have faith." He holds me tight.

"I don't know if I have any faith left."

"Hayes is a survivalist. Like a mega-survivalist. If there's anyone who can keep Rosalie safe, it's Hayes." Rafe has said the same thing every evening since we left Nicaragua. "Brady and Booker were very clear in their report. They separated Matias from Rosalie and took off into the jungle. When your father's forces pursued, they drew off the men. Hayes and Rosalie are safe."

"How do you know?" I shake my head because if that was the case, wouldn't I know? Wouldn't I feel it?

Each night as I lay my head down to sleep, terror courses through my veins thinking about Rosalie. Where is she? Is she safe? Is she wounded? Or dead? Lost somewhere in the jungles of my home?

After we make love at night, Rafe holds me while I tremble and worry. I spend my nights drifting between wakefulness and sleep, with guilt gnawing at me.

"I can't think about what I'm going to do until I know whether they're alive, dead, safe, or captured."

"I understand, and that's why I love you as much as I do. Your compassion for others is a gift beyond measure. I consider myself incredibly lucky you chose to jump on me."

That's the joke. I jumped on him.

And it's a beautiful beginning to our story.

"I'm sorry," I say.

"About what?"

"Not being able to give you an answer."

He asks about my plans. What I want to do with my life, while obliquely wondering if he might be included in those plans. He never asks outright. Rafe would never demand such an answer.

But he asked me about moving out of the dormitory. About moving in with him.

The thing is, I'm not sure.

On one hand, I can't imagine living a life without him. He's the other half of my soul.

But do I give up on my dreams?

Do I give up on my passion for the environment?

Now that I'm not facing marriage to Artemus Gonzales, I'm free to consider graduate studies in environmental conservation.

I'm not sure if I want to give that up.

Also, as strong as my feelings are for Rafe, our relationship moved at the speed of light. There's no doubt I love him. I love him with the entirety of my soul.

When I see him across the distance, my heart leaps with joy, and a surge of happiness courses through me. He lifts my mood when it's down, filling me with an inner glow of contentment and joy. He's the light to my darkness, and when I'm with him, it barely feels as if my feet touch the ground.

I'm head over heels in love with the man beside me. Is it crazy that my heart dares to hope for endless days spent by his side? My love for him is so intense; it scares me and only grows deeper with each passing day.

Sometimes, you've just got to have faith. That's what Lucinda would say to me when I questioned why we had to wait for so long before moving against my father.

"A penny for your thoughts." Rafe sweeps a strand of hair off my face.

"I was just thinking about the future." I take his hand in mine, threading my fingers through his.

"I was thinking the same thing." He leans forward, pulling something out of his back pocket. "I had a friend make a few calls." He hands me an envelope.

"What's this?"

"Open it." His measured gaze turns a little bit goofy.

My hands shake as I open the envelope and pull out a nondescript folded piece of paper.

"Rafe?"

"Go ahead." He nudges me, encouraging me.

As soon as I open the top fold, the UCSF seal shines in the amber glow of the sunset. My hands shake as I unfold the paper and stare at the words congratulating me for being accepted into UCSF's Master's Program in Environmental Science.

"What is this?" My heart pounds with excitement.

"Looks like UCSF has a returning student."

"But how? I never applied."

"Friends in high places. I know a guy who knows a guy who…"

"Stop it." I turn to him, bursting with joy and feeling wonderfully alive again. "When did you do this?"

"When I decided I couldn't bear to see you leave." He gestures back toward The Facility. "These people want you. I've heard nothing but amazing and great and wonderful things about how you're helping the women we rescued, but I know your heart is here." He points at the acceptance letter. "I don't want you to settle on something because of me. I want you to be happy."

"But how would that work?"

"Easy."

"But I'd live up there, and you'd be down here."

"First off, *up there* is only a couple of hours away. Secondly, most of the classes are online these days, so you wouldn't have to be up there all the time. Thirdly, I called Kaye and Barbi. We extended the lease on your townhouse, so when you have to be there for in-person classes, you have a place to stay. And, I kicked Kaye out of the room with the king-sized bed. That's ours."

"Ours?"

Rafe doesn't realize it, but he's the source of a greater joy than any I've ever known before. That whisper of happiness turns to a flood of joy washing through me.

"If you'll have me." The tone of his voice deepens.

"What does that mean?"

"Hang on." He lifts a finger, telling me to wait. Getting up, Rafe stands over me and fishes something out of the front pocket of his jeans.

A small, black-velvet box appears in his hand.

My eyes widen and my mouth gapes as he goes to one knee.

"Carmen Angelo, I will not ask your father for his blessing, and hope you forgive that break in tradition, but I did ask Kaye and Barbi, and they said to tell you, *"We're cool if she's cool."* So, I hope this makes you happy, because if it doesn't, I'm going to feel all kinds of foolish. But I want you in my life. Today. Tomorrow. And all the days that follow. And as soon as Hayes brings Rosalie home to us, I'm going to ask for her blessing as well, but until then, how do you feel about getting hitched?"

"Hitched?" My cheeks hurt from the massive smile plastered all over my face. "That was the most beautiful proposal until you ruined it with *getting hitched.*"

"Aw, but did I really ruin it?" He holds up a beautiful diamond ring that reflects the amber glow of the blazing sunset overhead. "What do you say?"

"I say today is the best day of my life." I hold out my hand and wriggle my fingers. "Yes. Yes. And yes. A thousand times, yes."

"Thank you." He presses his palms together and looks to the sky. "I was a little worried for a second."

"Are you going to put that ring on my finger?" I keep wriggling my fingers, waiting for him to slip on the ring.

It fits perfectly, but not as perfectly as the feeling of Rafe stealing a kiss and lifting me into the air. He spins me in a circle as we laugh with joy filling both our hearts. When he sets me back on my feet, I'm breathless and overjoyed.

"I'm glad you said yes." He wraps an arm around my waist and tugs me tight. Together we stare out over the ocean.

"Were you worried?"

"Nah, but if I had to go back to the guys and tell them you said no, I'd never live it down."

"Do you think they took bets on it?"

"Nah, they know you love me and can't keep your hands off me." He curls his fingers, blows on them, then pretends to polish them on his shirt. "Remember…I'm a chick magnet." He winks as I laugh into the wind. Chick magnet, indeed.

"What about The Facility?" I glance over my shoulder. "I hate to leave them hanging."

"You can spend as much, or as little time, as you want. Instead of taking a full-time position, volunteer. They know you're splitting your time between here and UCSF."

"And that doesn't bother you? That I'll be here and there?"

"Not if it means you're doing what you want." He spins me around until we're face to face. "You've lived under the shadow of your father for your entire life. Living in fear. Living with guilt. It's time to spread your wings and live the life you've always wanted. I consider myself lucky to stand by your side."

"You're a little corny when you try to be all mushy." The wind kicks up, whipping my hair into my face.

"You love my mushy side." He grabs my face and plants a sloppy kiss on my lips for good measure.

Two can play at that game. I not so subtlety reach between us, arousing the man I love with a long stroke along his shaft.

"Bloody hell, woman." The sloppy kiss turns heated, then I find myself lifted off my feet and slung over his shoulder. The air temperature plummets as the storm kicks the wind into a frenzy. That storm's almost upon us.

"Hey, what are you doing?"

"Taking my woman home."

With that, Rafe marches back toward The Facility's parking lot, where he tosses me in the car and speeds back to his place. On the drive home, the sky opens up, dumping rain in a blinding deluge.

Behind us, the storm stirs up the ocean, turning the waves to froth as it makes landfall. The sky darkens. Lightning strikes. Thunder booms as the storm unleashes its fury on the California coast. Overhead, lightning splits the sky and thunder drowns out all noise. As Rafe and I rush inside and escape the rain, my mind drifts to my dearest friend, Rosalie.

Rafe and I escape the storm, finding shelter in each other's arms, where we make love late into the night. We talk about our hopes and dreams. We talk of our future, but sleep eventually drags us to bed. I wait for my fiancé, my very own Guardian, to fall asleep before crawling out of bed.

On my knees, I press my hands together and offer up a prayer of thanks. I can't escape the feeling something awful is about to happen. I can feel it down to my bones.

Rosalie's in grave danger.

My prayers end with giving thanks to God for granting me the courage to take that leap of faith. That day feels several lifetimes ago, but it was fate.

I found my soulmate, a man I love with the entirety of my heart, who I can't wait to spend the rest of my life loving.

That incredible man sleeps beside me, oblivious to the thunder and lightning rattling the windows and the wind howling outside.

Before I go to sleep, I kiss the diamond ring on my finger and lay back with joy filling my heart and worry gnawing at my gut for Rosalie.

But I know Rafe's teammate, Hayes, will keep her safe, and Bravo team will bring her home to me. They'll do whatever it takes to rescue Rosalie, because that's what Guardians do. They save those who can't save themselves, and one person at a time, they make the world a better place.

BRAVO TEAM; A WHOLE NEW SERIES OF PROTECTOR ROMANCES showcasing the Guardian Hostage Rescue Specialists. Rescuing Rosalie is the next book in the exhilarating new BRAVO TEAM series.

Read Hayes and Rosalie's story, grab your copy of Rescuing Rosalie Today.

HAVE YOU MET THE MEN OF ALPHA TEAM? THEIR SERIES IS complete; seven sexy, swoon-worthy books and all the gritty suspense you love.

If you haven't, check them out: Guardian HRS Alpha Team series.

THESE FORMER NAVY SEALs, DELTA OPERATIVES, AND SPECIAL Ops soldiers turned **Guardians & Protectors** are guaranteed to capture your heart and leave you breathless.

TURN THE PAGE FOR A SNEAK PEEK AT THE EXPLOSIVE COMBINATION of Hayes and Rosalie.

FORTY-EIGHT

Rescuing Rosalie

A SNEAK PEEK!

Matias presses the hardened steel of his blade against the delicate skin of my throat. Adrenaline courses through my body, seeking escape, but it finds none. With a soul blacker than black, he's my nightmare of all nightmares come to life.

The sharp steel brings a gasp to my lips and panic rushing through my body. My heart leaps into my throat, where it firmly lodges in place and silences my screams.

There's no voice.

No sound.

Nothing but terror flowing through me.

The villa is under attack. Gunfire sounds all around me. With the power out, Maximus Angelo's private estate, is plunged into darkness, turning the expansive grounds into complete chaos. The shouts of men sound in the distance. Those are cut off suddenly, only to be punctuated with gunfire and distant screams coming from a different direction.

The air seethes with violence as men assault Maximus Angelo's estate.

As Nicaragua's Minister of the Interior, Maximus Angelo's

estate is generally immune to violence, except tonight it's all around me.

I'm not the only one scared to death by the sounds, the smell of gunpowder, and the chaos. Terrified squawks puncture the night air, screams of captive birds trapped within a massive wrought iron cage standing in the far corner of the courtyard Matias drags me through.

Starlight shines down on us, providing minimal light, barely enough to make out shadows moving in the darkness.

But there are shadows.

And they are moving.

Silent shadows with lethal intent.

Those shadows advance into the courtyard where Matias drags me against my will. Six warriors cloaked in black separate from the shadows. They're a terrifying force, even if I know they're avenging angels sent to free me.

Matias sees the men and hauls me in front of himself, turning me into a living shield, as he faces off against this unexpected threat.

Unlike Matias, I don't fear these men. My best friend, Carmen, whispered their intent in my ear, confiding in me. These are the Guardians, sent to rescue her, those captive below, and me.

I know this because my best friend, my sister from another mother, told me Guardians were on their way to rescue me.

Now, I don't know what that means. I don't know what a Guardian is, but Carmen does. She told me they were on their way, and that they would rescue me.

I didn't believe her, but the proof is in the shadows advancing on Matias. They level their weapons on the man I can only describe as a demon cloaked in a man's body.

"Back off!" Matias roars at the shadows. "Back off, or I'll kill her." His grip tightens around my waist, nearly lifting me off my feet. He pulls me back a step.

"Let the girl go." The voice is deadly calm.

"Never!" Matias takes another step, dragging me with him.

The men might think we're cornered, but they're wrong. There's a reason Matias hauled me here, to this courtyard.

The men train deadly weapons on us, but other than that, none of them moves. They can't take a shot without killing me.

As for me, and the mounting terror inside of me, every step Matias takes brings us closer to a hidden door leading out of here. Those men are my salvation, but I fear they are destined to fail.

"Release her, or die." The man's voice is death walking. It's not a taunt, or a threat. It's a promise.

My fear multiplies with each step Matias takes to the far corner of the courtyard. It wraps icy fingers around my heart and squeezes until I can barely breathe.

"Lower your weapons, or I will kill her now." The steel of Matias' blade bites into my flesh as he shows these men, he too, doesn't bluff.

At first, there's nothing but heat, a tiny sting—barely a flash of sensation—but then warmth slides down my neck, cooling as it pools in the hollow of my throat.

The men advance, fanning into an arc around us, weapons level and trained on us.

My terrified fingers dig at Matias' wrist, knowing he holds my life in his hands. If the knife cuts any deeper, that trickle of blood will turn into a flood. I'll bleed out and my life will fade with each terrified beat of my heart.

To be honest, that would be a blessing. I'd rather die than live through what Matias intends. He's the devil, and if he takes me, I won't live through his twisted desires. Death now would be a mercy.

The men move, matching Matias' retreat.

Matias presses the flat of the blade against my skin, threatening, but he doesn't want me to die.

The man's soul is as black as his eyes. A vile creature, he's evil incarnate. A devil walking this earth. And he has me in his iron-fisted grip.

"P-please…let me go."

"Never." He yanks me back, taking two steps toward the hidden door.

My throat closes as fear takes over, paralyzing my body, as well as my mind. I gulp as my lungs seize and my heart stumbles.

I'm one step closer to death. Despite the distant sounds of gunfire, there's an odd stillness to the air. The birds in the cage flutter with unease, but their terrified squawks are silent for now.

It's as if time slows to a crawl.

A sudden burst of gunfire cracks through the air, much closer than before. I flinch at the flurry of wings beating from the birds trapped in the cage. Their terrified cries intensify and my heart pounds in response.

As for the Guardians, they barely move a muscle. Laser focused, they take another step.

Legs wobbly, knees knocking, my hands shake and my stomach churns. I hold my head steady as Matias takes another step toward his freedom and my misery.

He drags me back, moving inextricably toward the hidden door. A servant's entrance, that door hides a warren of passageways designed to keep servants out of sight as we perform our duties.

As a maid who's lived half of my life within these walls, I know this door well. I also know about the heavy lock on the other side.

Some may think it strange, to lock a servant's door from the inside, but Carmen's father doesn't like the esthetic of a lock on the outside. He says it *'offends his sensibility and that of his guests.'*

Its true purpose is far more nefarious. That lock prevents escape of the trafficked women and young girls trapped in the basement; not that any of those poor souls are capable of breaking free of their cages, or the irons that keep them chained in place.

But maybe tonight, justice will be served?

Maybe the Guardians will free them, if not me?

I pray for their rescue. Carmen said the Guardians would free us all, but I would be happy knowing they, at least, are freed from this terrible place.

With the Guardians training their weapons on us, he backs us up to the door. It takes a moment for my mind to swim clear of the fear flowing within me to figure out why we stop.

Matias can't hold both my waist, the knife to my throat, and open the door on his own. A tiny ray of hope flickers within me, only to be snuffed out a moment later.

"Open it." Callous and cold, there's no need to wonder what will happen if I refuse.

The cold steel of the knife presses against my throat. One slice and I can escape this nightmare. All it will take is a struggle, but I'm a believer in the Almighty. I *will not* take my own life. I may not hold the knife, but my actions would result in my death, and I refuse to give Matias that pleasure.

I reach awkwardly behind me, around Matias' bulk, to locate the latch I know all too well.

How many times have I opened this door? A thousand? Ten thousand?

It's been a little over a decade since I was brought to this place to serve as Carmen's playmate and maid. My fingers fumble over the stone and find the latch by touch alone. With a twist of my lips, my heart breaks as the men in black break their group in two. Three men disappear into the shadows, leaving only three behind.

They're giving up on me.

"Hurry girl!" Matias growls into my ear. "Or I will spill your blood and spit on your corpse."

I hurry, but only because the image of Matias' spittle on my dead body turns my stomach and brings bile rising in the back of my throat.

With a practiced flip, I open the door. Matias leans into it with his shoulder and drags me into the darkness behind. The three Guardians rush as one, but they're too late. Matias shoves me to the floor and spins to shut the door and slam the locking bolt in place.

My knees scrape on the uneven stone, drawing blood. I scuttle to the side, not to escape Matias—there is no escape from this man—I do it to avoid having him step on me when he spins around.

Normally illuminated by a string of dim light bulbs overhead, the servants' hall is pitch black. Nevertheless, Matias reaches down, grabs my arm and yanks me to my feet. He hauls me behind him, while I stare back the way we came.

In my mind's eye, I imagine those men breaking down the door to save me, but the farther we get from the door, fear creeps up my spine and grabs hold of my mind.

Tonight is not my night to be saved. As I stumble through the darkness, I lift up a prayer that my death comes swiftly.

READ HAYES AND ROSALIE'S STORY, GRAB YOUR COPY OF RESCUING Rosalie Today.

ELLZ BELLZ

ELLIE'S FACEBOOK READER GROUP

If you are interested in joining the ELLZ BELLZ, Ellie's Facebook reader group, we'd love to have you.

Join Ellie's ELLZ BELLZ.
The ELLZ BELLZ Facebook Reader Group

Sign up for Ellie's Newsletter.
Elliemasters.com/newslettersignup

Also by Ellie Masters

The LIGHTER SIDE

Ellie Masters is the lighter side of the Jet & Ellie Masters writing duo! You will find Contemporary Romance, Military Romance, Romantic Suspense, Billionaire Romance, and Rock Star Romance in Ellie's Works.

YOU CAN FIND ELLIE'S BOOKS HERE:

ELLIEMASTERS.COM/BOOKS

Military Romance

Guardian Hostage Rescue Specialists

Rescuing Melissa

(Get a FREE copy of Rescuing Melissa

when you join Ellie's Newsletter)

Alpha Team

Rescuing Zoe

Rescuing Moira

Rescuing Eve

Rescuing Lily

Rescuing Jinx

Rescuing Maria

Bravo Team

Rescuing Angie

Rescuing Isabelle

Rescuing Carmen

Rescuing Rosalie

Rescuing Kaye

Military Romance

Guardian Personal Protection Specialists

Sybil's Protector

Lyra's Protector

The One I Want Series

(Small Town, Military Heroes)

By Jet & Ellie Masters

EACH BOOK IN THIS SERIES CAN BE READ AS A STANDALONE AND IS ABOUT A DIFFERENT COUPLE WITH AN HEA.

Saving Abby

Saving Ariel

Saving Brie

Saving Cate

Saving Dani

Saving Jen

Rockstar Romance

The Angel Fire Rock Romance Series

EACH BOOK IN THIS SERIES CAN BE READ AS A STANDALONE AND IS ABOUT A DIFFERENT COUPLE WITH AN HEA. IT IS RECOMMENDED THEY ARE READ IN ORDER.

Ashes to New (prequel)

Heart's Insanity (book 1)

Heart's Desire (book 2)

Heart's Collide (book 3)

Hearts Divided (book 4)

Hearts Entwined (book5)

Forest's FALL (book 6)

Hearts The Last Beat (book7)

Contemporary Romance

Firestorm

(Kristy Bromberg's Everyday Heroes World)

Billionaire Romance

Billionaire Boys Club

Hawke

Richard

Brody

Contemporary Romance

Cocky Captain

(Vi Keeland & Penelope Ward's Cocky Hero World)

Romantic Suspense

EACH BOOK IS A STANDALONE NOVEL.

The Starling

~AND~

Science Fiction

Ellie Masters writing as L.A. Warren

Vendel Rising: a Science Fiction Serialized Novel

About the Author

Ellie Masters is a USA Today Bestselling author and Amazon Top 15 Author who writes Angsty, Steamy, Heart-Stopping, Pulse-Pounding, Can't-Stop-Reading Romantic Suspense. In addition, she's a wife, military mom, doctor, and retired Colonel. She writes romantic suspense filled with all your sexy, swoon-worthy alpha men. Her writing will tug at your heartstrings and leave your heart racing.

Born in the South, raised under the Hawaiian sun, Ellie has traveled the globe while in service to her country. The love of her life, her amazing husband, is her number one fan and biggest supporter. And yes! He's read every word she's written.

She has lived all over the United States—east, west, north, south and central—but grew up under the Hawaiian sun. She's also been privileged to have lived overseas, experiencing other cultures and making lifelong friends. Now, Ellie is proud to call herself a Southern transplant, learning to say y'all and "bless her heart" with the best of them. She lives with her beloved husband, two children who refuse to flee the nest, and four fur-babies; three cats who rule the household, and a dog who wants nothing other than for the cats to be his best friends. The cats have a different opinion regarding this matter.

Ellie's favorite way to spend an evening is curled up on a couch, laptop in place, watching a fire, drinking a good wine, and bringing forth all the characters from her mind to the page and hopefully into the hearts of her readers.

FOR MORE INFORMATION

elliemasters.com

facebook.com/elliemastersromance
twitter.com/Ellie__Masters
instagram.com/ellie_masters
bookbub.com/authors/ellie-masters
goodreads.com/Ellie_Masters

Connect with Ellie Masters

Website:
elliemasters.com
Amazon Author Page:
elliemasters.com/amazon
Facebook:
elliemasters.com/Facebook
Goodreads:
elliemasters.com/Goodreads
Instagram:
elliemasters.com/Instagram

Final Thoughts

I hope you enjoyed this book as much as I enjoyed writing it. If you enjoyed reading this story, please consider leaving a review on Amazon and Goodreads, and please let other people know. A sentence is all it takes. Friend recommendations are the strongest catalyst for readers' purchase decisions! And I'd love to be able to continue bringing the characters and stories from My-Mind-to-the-Page.

Second, call or e-mail a friend and tell them about this book. If you really want them to read it, gift it to them. If you prefer digital friends, please use the "Recommend" feature of Goodreads to spread the word.

Or visit my blog https://elliemasters.com, where you can find out more about my writing process and personal life.

Come visit The EDGE: Dark Discussions where we'll have a chance to talk about my works, their creation, and maybe what the future has in store for my writing.

Facebook Reader Group: Ellz Bellz

Thank you so much for your support!

Love,

Ellie

Dedication

This book is dedicated to you, my reader. Thank you for spending a few hours of your time with me. I wouldn't be able to write without you to cheer me on. Your wonderful words, your support, and your willingness to join me on this journey is a gift beyond measure.

Whether this is the first book of mine you've read, or if you've been with me since the very beginning, thank you for believing in me as I bring these characters 'from my mind to the page and into your hearts.'

Love,
Ellie

THE END